SILVER GAMES SERIES

REMNANTS

JESS STEVENS

Remnants (Silver Games Book 1) — 1st Ed.

Copyright © 2025 by Jess Stevens

Book cover and design by Mayhem Cover Creations

Editing Services by The Blue Couch Edits and Editing4Indies

Additional edits by Lauren Joskowitz

ISBN: 979-8-9922688-1-2

AUTHOR'S NOTE & CONTENT WARNINGS

Welcome to the Silver Games series, a dark fantasy romance I'm so excited to share with you. Imagine The Princess Bride set in a near-future, post-apocalypse Los Angeles with a love triangle, blood magic, and dark spice. In this story, Prince Humperdinck is an alpha possessive MMC who isn't willing to give up the FMC so easily.

Remnants is a work of tantalizing (I hope you agree) fiction and may contain trigger warnings for some. I am in no way condoning the actions and behaviors in this book. If dark romance isn't for you, that's okay! However, if you don't have any triggers and prefer to go in blind, please skip to Chapter One. If you do have triggers, please read below.

Content warnings for Remnants include: sexually explicit scenes, captive/captor, J/P (jealous/possessive) MMC, bondage, punishment, violence and descriptions of violence/murder, death, OTT (over-the-top) MMC, forced markings (he tattoos her without her consent), needles, drugging, addiction, profanity, war, and hostages.

Remnants is the first of three in the Silver Games series and will only get spicier from here. If you're still in, welcome to the game of gangs where Silvers are the ultimate prize. We're just getting started.

Xo,
Jess

CONTENTS

*For the girls who don't want to live
simply or play it safe.*

PART I

THE RULES

1

Lissa

Love in this ruin of a city was decidedly dead. But the people dancing in front of me did a good job pretending it was all fun and games. For a night, at least.

I watched the frenzy of the club from the shadows, hidden just behind the wall of an alcove next to the bar. A black velvet curtain hung across the small storage area lined with cleaning supplies, extra chairs, a filing cabinet, and even an unclothed mannequin.

It had become my second home these past few months since Tayna started working at the club. Staff rarely came in during work hours, making it an ideal hiding place. Plus, the curtain meant I could peek out from the darkness, a spectator watching the lives beyond. I could pretend I belonged among them when I decidedly did not.

On the dance floor before me, bodies writhed against the flashing electric blue lights that strobed across connected hips and hands trailing down curvy silhouettes. Some women who worked at the club were up on pedestals, clutching poles and wearing only scraps of lace. Some had their heads thrown back, their mouths open slightly as if the music alone had them on the edge of some primal pleasure.

It was something I'd never experienced—the pleasure or the display of it.

My best friend Tayna swore I would never be forced to.

"I'll always protect you, Lissa," he'd whisper against my ear on those nights when the gangs got just a little too close to the corner of the city where us street rats hid.

But women had few options. If they were wealthy enough, they were paired with the males of other rich families to form alliances in the gangs that ruled this city—the only city that remained for hundreds of miles. If they were poor, well, clubs like this were all too common. And this was one of the kinder establishments I'd seen. It was a high-end place owned by the Veiled, one of the most powerful gangs in the city. The women who worked here still had life in their eyes. They had some semblance of control. They could tell the men no. They were the lucky ones, gifted with enough beauty or skill on the dance floor to elevate their status, even in the slightest way.

A woman had a third option, but it was hardly a choice. The girls born with silver in their veins were taken from their families at a young age to serve whatever gang got their hands on them first.

The gangs ruled this ruined city. The Veiled in the desert to the East. The Slips in the industrial area of the South. The Tanks along the coast. Some smaller gangs took up the extra space. And then, there were the Cards on the cliffs to the North—the most powerful of them all. The Cards ruled this city after a bloody fight with the Veiled some years back. The relative peace that had followed between the gangs was tenuous at best.

To be a silvered person, but especially a girl, was to enter a kind of servitude at birth. All choices, all freedom were forfeit as soon as that metallic gleam was seen in an infant's eyes. There were no good options for a Silver. But being taken by the Cards was the worst of them all.

Gideon Valmontry led the Cards. He had since his father, Ishmael, was killed eight years ago in a rival shoot-out with the Veiled during the height of their fighting. And Gideon was ruthless. He had decimated the Veiled in return, ending the bloodbath by killing their leader and his son, along with dozens of other members. To this day, blood was spilled if the Veiled and the Cards were in a room together.

Unless it was a place like the club—the only neutral territory in this crumbling city. Here, with the dancing and the music and the lights, was the only time fucking and forgetting were the priorities rather than killing. Forget churches. God was dead in this city.

Beyond Gideon's ruthless mission for revenge, he expected total and complete loyalty within his ranks. He'd killed members of the Cards for as little as speaking to nonmembers without permission. His Silvers were kept on tight leashes. They were rarely seen outside their compound on the northern cliffs of the city. If they were allowed out, capes of black blanketed their bodies, covering everything but their mouths. Heavily armed guards surrounded them.

Silvers were protected above all else.

Because Silvers meant power.

They couldn't wield any on their own. Left alone, a Silver was like an electric current without a wire, but their blood was a powerful force that could be used to give abilities to tools, weapons, or even people. The Silvers' blood powered the entire city and beyond— though I'd never ventured outside this city, and it was rare that any survivors found their way here. If they were smart, they'd avoid this city. It most likely meant servitude or death, no matter which gang found them first.

And then there was me.

I didn't fall into any of the three categories for women.

When I was ten, the Cards killed my mother. She was a casualty in the war with the Veiled. As an unclaimed Silver, she'd chosen to fight rather than become one of Ishmael's slave Queens, and it had ended with her death. She was strangled, of course, so as not to waste any of her blood.

I'd barely survived, running from the house into the night as a newly minted orphan. I never knew my father. It had always just been my mom and me.

Until it was just me.

After a few months of dumpster diving and hiding in alleyways, I found Tayna doing the same. Together, we'd managed to remain hidden for the past eight years, staying in the small pockets of the city no one looked at too closely.

At eighteen, most orphan girls my age worked in places like the club. Or worse.

I saw them on the streets at night sometimes while Tayna was working. Their heels were too high. Their skirts too short. Their young faces painted with too much makeup. Their gazes too blank.

I would take an empty belly and hiding in an alcove closet every night over those vacant eyes.

Tayna, just a year older than me, had kept me safe, kept me in the shadows as I was now at the club.

It was an unusually busy night, and I anxiously waited for Tayna to get off from his shift bussing tables. It was always the most risky time for me when we were apart. He was my protector. But being my protector also meant making money in some way to buy food. So we'd designed a system. He worked in the club, and I hid in the shadows and alleyways nearby. While he worked, I would forage, which was just a nicer way to say I would dumpster dive for anything useful.

Tonight, I'd managed to find something that wasn't entirely useful. It wasn't food, as my cramping belly knew all too well, but it would be fun. I clutched it beneath my jacket, the weight making me anxious as I scanned the crowds, searching for Tayna.

It wasn't abnormal for members of the gangs to show up here, especially on the weekends. The club was the one place rival gangs could mingle without bloodshed. It was neutral territory. Guns were checked at the door. It was a truce, of sorts, that the gangs honored with their word.

For a night.

That didn't mean fights never broke out. But they were rare.

In the booths that lined the wall, I'd already clocked a group of Tanks in their army-green fatigues and a group from an up-and-coming gang, the Fortas, in another booth across the way, sporting leather jackets with crud patches on the sleeves and bandannas around their heads.

The Cards sat in the center of the house, their booth packed with tall, broad men in black and darkest red. Each had a suit of cards tattooed on his arm, denoting rank and status within their brotherhood. Their outfits were tailored to show off the markings. Their suit —hearts, diamonds, clubs, or spades—never changed, but they could signify status the more ink they added. Gideon, as the Ace, was the highest of them all, followed by his second, a brute King named Dia.

I watched as a guy with the six of clubs on his bulging biceps took a curvy blond woman by the waist and twisted her in his arms. He was so broad he practically cocooned the woman, and she snaked a willing hand across his neck, pulling him in for a deep kiss. Locks of his dark hair fell in his face as she ran her fingers over his scalp.

When they broke apart, he pulled her onto the dance floor, and she gracefully swayed her hips flush against him. Their foreheads connected as they moved. She reached her hands up, and as if they'd practiced this before, the man traced down her body until he reached the edges of her shirt. His fingers played over the taut muscles of the woman's abdomen before his hands started traveling up. This time, he caressed beneath the fabric.

They were kissing again, their hips keeping with that sensual rhythm.

I bit my bottom lip, knowing it was rude to watch such an intimate exchange, yet unable to look away. There was such freedom in the way they moved together, in the way she allowed their bodies to meld and his hands to roam.

He continued to trace his fingers up over her ribs until I could see the black lace of her bra peeking from under her arms. Still, he didn't stop.

My breath hitched as he cupped her breasts fully in his hands, kneading and massaging. His fingers worked their way beneath the lace until the woman broke the kiss to throw her head back and moan. He stroked her, watching her pleasure with a feral expression.

Something low in my belly clenched as he claimed the woman's mouth again and—

"Lissa," Tayna said loudly near my ear. "There you are."

I realized I had snaked a hand up to my chest, digging my fingers into the edge of my collarbone as I watched the couple.

I quickly straightened.

"Same place as always." I grinned, turning to him.

His mahogany hair was sweat-slicked and mussed from a night working, and he smelled a bit like a mildew-covered rag, but I hugged his lanky frame anyway, feeling such relief that we were back together. We had made it through one more night.

"Let's go home," I said, grabbing his hand before he could look too closely at the couple I'd been watching.

He slung his faded, dirt-stained backpack over his shoulder and followed me.

Tayna and I... we were, well, we were more than friends. He was my everything. And some nights, especially on those long winter nights, we'd cocoon against each other for warmth. I would feel his hot breath against my ear and his long body flush with mine, and I would want... more.

But we'd never taken that step together.

At times, our hugs would linger or our mouths would hover too close or he would grab my hand and my heart would squeeze, but taking that next step, as much as I wanted it, also felt dangerous. I couldn't lose Tayna. And what if we did that—more—and it ended badly? It felt like too much of a risk in a life where everything was already perilous enough.

And so I took comfort in the feel of his hand, fingers linked with mine, and let that be enough. Even if that couple in the club made me ache for more.

As we snaked silently out the side door of the club and into the dark alleyway, I pulled up the hood of my worn gray sweater with my free hand, keeping the fabric low over my forehead as we dodged the rubble of the eroded buildings around us. I remembered my mother telling me stories of this city. She'd said it used to be one of the most beautiful cities in the world. Seventy years ago, it was a destination for movies and festivals and music, all situated on the edge of the ocean. Less than half of the buildings that made up that once great city were still standing. And the dilapidated gray city was anything but grand.

Tayna released my hand, only so he could shove them into his pants pockets to keep them warm.

Spring was on the horizon, but this had been an especially brutal winter. At night, the bite of it still cut through our measly layers of clothing as we hurried along the darkened path to our home.

"I got us something that'll keep us warm tonight," I teased, glancing back over my shoulder at Tayna, who kept pace just a step behind me. I cut across the buildings until they opened onto a dirt path leading us south.

He lifted his eyebrows. "A successful night, then?"

I unzipped my jacket just enough that I could pull out the half-filled bottle of tequila I'd scavenged. It'd been sitting outside the door at one of the other clubs as if a bartender had started on it during their break and then forgotten about it. Or they'd intended to return to finish it. Either way, I didn't feel even a hint of guilt that I'd found it first. Survival, I'd learned, was often synonymous with stealing.

"You little thief." Tayna laughed, grabbing the bottle from me and studying the label. "This isn't entirely shitty, either!" He unscrewed the cap and took a swig, wiping his mouth as he swallowed. He had fine wisps of light-brown stubble dusting his chin in uneven patches that hinted at the man he was becoming.

I took the bottle from him and swigged just as deeply as he had.

Only for the contents to burn like a flame down my throat and into my chest.

I sputtered, choking and then heaving on a cough that had Tayna barreling over with laughter.

"This tastes terrible!" I gagged.

"You get used to it," he said, taking the bottle again for another deep pull before handing it back. "Maybe start with a smaller sip."

I hesitantly took the bottle, my gaze catching his and narrowing in a challenge. And then I took another large gulp. It still burned and made me stutter, but it was better that time, and the warmth that bloomed in my stomach despite the chill outside made me smile.

"I brought you something too," he said, dropping his backpack from his shoulder and unzipping the top pouch. He withdrew a crumpled brown paper bag, and I resisted the urge to snatch it from him. My hollow stomach tightened at the sight.

"Don't get too excited." He smiled at my ravenous gaze, and dimples pebbled each of his cheeks. "It's half an order of cold fries. A few pieces of bacon I swiped off a plate. Some orange slices from the bar. And..." He lifted his eyebrows, holding the bag just out of reach. "Two pickle spears."

I lifted my arms into the air as if I'd won a huge prize. Tayna knew pickles were my favorite.

I swiped the bag from him and dug into the food. We were in the open of the city, near the ocean boardwalk. Not the safest area to linger, but I couldn't be bothered to wait until we reached our home to eat.

"Slow down," Tayna said, swiping a fry from the box as I shoveled a handful into my mouth and began chewing the dry, soggy bits.

I didn't even notice the taste.

Starting with the fries was a strategic move on my part. Fill my belly with the crappy parts so I could savor the pickles at the end.

I licked the salt from the paper box once I'd finished the small portion of fries.

God, I wished there were more.

"Come on, Lissa." Tayna took my hand before I started on the bacon. He led me to a rusted park bench beneath the dead remnants of a once-large tree. It was late into the night, and this part of the city was quiet except for the ocean waves in the distance. I didn't see anyone else around.

White streaks of ocean salt stained the buildings in front of us. Where the paint wasn't peeling and worn, graffiti covered the walls as high as a person could reach. The gangs had taken to tagging any available surface they could find throughout the years, and the city was dotted with neon lettering and block print.

A half-crumbled apartment complex sat to my right, and on the only remaining cinder block wall, a large ace of hearts had been painted across the entire space in Gideon's honor.

The stark reminder of the haves versus the have-nots made me slow in chewing my bacon as I stared at it.

"We'll get out of here," Tayna said, stretching out next to me, stealing a bite of my bacon before handing it back to me.

He was usually able to find scraps for himself during his shift at the restaurant, but that didn't mean either of us got the amount of food we needed. It showed in our gangly bodies and hollowed faces, but Tayna especially. He seemed to just keep growing inches without any nutrients to fill in the rest of his frame. When we first found one another as children, he'd only been a hint taller than me. Now, he stood at least a head and a shoulder above me, all limbs and arms and not enough food.

"Where will we go?" I asked, leaning into the bench with him as I took the last bite of bacon and started on the oranges.

"We'll get out of this city. That's for damn sure. We can find an old farmhouse, maybe some wild horses we can tame. We could plant a garden like the one your mom had. I think we could probably catch some chickens, too. And maybe we could find some puppies and raise them so they love us."

"Ack," I groaned, scrunching my nose. The only dogs we ever saw were the ones who snarled and gave chase if we got too close. They were feral beasts.

He laughed. "No, not like the ones here," he said, following my thoughts. "Like the ones in that book we found."

"*Where the Red Fern Grows.*" I smiled despite myself, biting into an orange slice and sucking to make sure none of the juice dribbled down my chin.

"Yeah," he sighed. "Like from *Where the Red Fern Grows*. We'll name them Dan and Ann." Tayna took another swig from the tequila bottle and offered it to me, but I shook my head, already a little light-headed from the two gulps I'd had earlier.

Tayna's daydreams of our future life were often closely correlated with whatever books I'd managed to scrounge in my scavenging while he was working.

They were prized and rare things. I'd heard the gangs had full houses turned into libraries. In the city, though, books were more likely to be used as kindling. I was just lucky enough that my mother taught me to read. I'd taught Tayna in those quiet, scary times at night when we were young and alone.

"I think I'd like to live on a farm with you, Tayna." Although, I said that about all of his daydreams. It had been a tree house on an island, a boat traveling the ocean, a forest near a lake, a castle on a hill, even an old school where we could test things with something called a chemistry room. All of it sounded good to me as long as we were together.

I sighed, looking back at the sprawling graffiti card that was our reality instead.

And stilled.

Three men had emerged from the rubble, standing casually enough near the cinder block wall. They were watching Tayna and me. I couldn't tell from their clothes which gang they belonged to, but they were too well-dressed not to be in a gang. Their gazes were dark. Even at this distance, I could feel it.

"Tayna," I breathed, pulling my hood down farther to shield my eyes. My fingers tingled beneath my sweater.

He was already standing, taking my hand over the fabric, and glancing nervously over his shoulder.

We knew better than to play it cool, especially at night.

We ran, sprinting into the darkness and between the buildings like the clever street rats we had learned to be.

I didn't even realize I'd left my pickles behind.

2

Lissa

The men didn't give chase, but that didn't stop us from continuously glancing over our shoulders as we ran, just to be sure. We weaved through the streets, dodging bodies and avoiding eyes that watched us cautiously. No doubt most thought we were thieves, outpacing our latest target. But that was fine by me. No one would interfere. No one cared. Thieving was one of the most common occupations on the streets.

We didn't slow our steps until we reached the building we called home, and even then, we waited, hidden in the bushes, to be sure we weren't being watched.

We lived in an old factory warehouse once filled with pieces to make cars and trucks. Now only scraps of rusty metal remained. Tayna and I had long since swept the scraps to the side to avoid stepping on any of the sharp bits. But we'd strategically avoided changing anything too drastic to the base-level floor. If anyone were to stumble their way upon this place, they would see a lot of dirt and a lot of useless junk, old busted headlights and misshapen bumpers.

Only the richest gangs, like the Cards, had things like vehicles, and anything useful had long since been pilfered from this ware-house. People didn't even bother looking in this area of the city anymore, which made it the perfect location for Tayna and me.

Up two flights of stairs, there was a lofted room. It seemed like a space where someone once stood to look out over the work that happened below. There was a small single-stall bathroom and the room itself. Both were made of thick metal, with only one window carved into the far side of the larger room.

We kept it locked with a deadbolt and key Tayna had managed to steal from one of the restaurant lockers. He unlocked the door now, giving a final glance over his shoulder as we went inside.

I felt around blindly for the lamp and managed to flick it on. The dull light gave a soft glow to the loft, which was a small, haphazard space.

"I'll need to replenish the lamp soon," I murmured, almost to myself as much as to Tayna.

Tayna flopped on the sorry excuse for a bed we'd laid out on the floor, made from scraps of clothing we'd found and shoved into old pillowcases. He began unloading a handful of copper coins from his pocket and laying them across the plastic chair next to the bed.

"Not a bad night," I said, eyeing the money.

"We won't starve," Tayna agreed. "I'll head into the square tomorrow to make some trades."

The square was the weekly market where merchants gathered to sell what they had to offer. It had only started up a few years ago when Gideon had apparently realized that if everyone kept stealing from everyone else, the Cards and the Veiled wouldn't have a city left to fight over.

The square was a tenuous thing, but I loved it. It smelled like fresh-baked bread and fried fish, and it was the one time when there were enough people around that I could get lost in the crowd.

I turned from where I'd pulled out my two remaining clean syringes from the small corner shelves next to the minifridge to give Tayna a wide-eyed stare he knew well.

"You can't go." He sighed.

"Tay," I whined.

"Come on, Lissa. Don't make me say no to you. I hate saying no to you. Weren't those dudes looking at us tonight enough of a scare for one week?"

"I know, I know," I said, twisting a thick rubber band around my forearm and dragging my ponytail over my shoulder so it was out of the way. "But I haven't talked to anyone besides you in over a month. And it'll be daytime so I can wear my sunglasses."

Tayna groaned out my name and fell back on the bed, shoving aside the stuffed turtle I'd found a few weeks back.

"Don't hurt him!" I glared, which made Tayna smile and pull the turtle into his chest in a way I wished he'd hold me.

I averted my attention back to the supplies in front of me on the small plastic table. Tayna watched me as I opened one of the syringes from the sterile packet. Could he see the turn my thoughts had taken?

After the silence had lingered for a few more moments, I cleared my throat. "So is that a yes, then?" I added more quickly, "We could even take some of the silver to Madame Cartenoth's shop to see what she has to trade."

That had him perking up from the bed. "Don't you dare take too much from yourself."

I poked around on my arm for the vein I liked to use while holding the end of the uncapped needle between my teeth. "I won't. The oranges you got me tonight will help for sure."

It was only two vials. I would need to find more syringes soon, but clean needles were hard to come by. Between the gangs using them for their Silvers and the more desperate people in this city using them for any kind of escape they could find, I'd gotten lucky that I'd managed to swipe a full packet of them from a traveling nurse who'd set up a short-term clinic near the club.

That was nearly six months ago.

Coins couldn't buy us syringes, either. We'd need real money for that. Or an entire month's supply of silver. And we couldn't buy them anyway as two teen kids. Not without creating suspicion we couldn't afford.

If we couldn't find more needles, I'd have to resort to slicing myself with knives, which I hated. It was so much worse than the needles. But I would do it if that's what it came to. It was the only way Tayna and I survived.

I held the needle to my skin and froze. Something always made me hesitate. It never got any easier. I took a deep breath. I could take my time. There was no rush other than my stuttering heartbeat telling me to do it and just get it over with.

My mother used to hold ice against her arm. She told me it helped. But I was a far cry from the luxury of having ice now. I was lucky to have a clean syringe.

My hand shook.

And then Tayna was in front of me, crouching at my feet with a hand on my knee as he said, "I can do it."

But I shook my head. "I have it."

I'd done this dozens of times before, so with him bent in front of me watching, I slid the needle under my skin, sighing as the vial began to fill with dark silver blood. It shimmered faintly against the soft lamplight.

Under my skin, the blood looked just like everyone else's. I had blue veins, and my mother told me that while it coursed through my body, my blood looked normal. It was red. But the second it was oxidized, whatever power lingered there caused it to glow with that telltale silver gleam. My eyes also shone with a ring of silver around the center of the otherwise green pupils, like a cat's at night that denoted my kind.

My kind.

The Silvers.

Government experiments that went horribly wrong. It started over a century ago as a mission to save the world. As Earth's dwindling natural resources became more and more scarce and the sun grew hotter and hotter, the Silvers had been the answer. They seemed to be the miracle humanity had waited for. If coal and wind and oil could fuel technology, why not human blood, too? Why not a resource that was close to home and could be produced en masse?

What was meant to be a forced mechanism of human evolution to save our species ended up being the downfall of us all.

Violence broke out as countries jockeyed for control.

Silvers were drained in the street, the shells of their bodies left to rot. Some fought back, trying to use their abilities on spelled weapons to gain some semblance of control.

But then the bombs came. Silvered bombs.

And the world crumbled into rubble.

Now, seventy years later, it was left to the gangs to vie for the remaining measly scraps. I would not be part of that tug-a-war. Just like my mother, I would rather die than be forced to power their guns and their knives and, worse, their leaders. Because, yes, the silver could be used to make weapons more deadly and cars more durable. Silver blood powered the lights in the town and the machines that cooked food and the compounds that protected the gangs. Much like batteries, the vials of silver were an energy source, *the* energy source that now sustained the remnants of humanity.

But another person could also consume it, giving them abnormal strength, heightened physical abilities, and an extended lifespan. A steady supply of silver blood meant a person could recover more quickly from sickness. Their cuts and bruises would heal at alarming rates. They could lift a car with ease, punch harder, and move fast.

"Next one," Tayna said, watching the now-full syringe in my arm.

With a deep breath, not giving myself too much time to think, I replaced it with the second. The silvery blood looked so dark against the dim light of our loft that it was like the chrome wheels I'd seen on the Cards' trucks.

Tayna refused to drink even a sip of my blood. He scoffed at the very idea, wrinkling his nose in disgust if I ever so much as suggested it.

I'd forced it on him once, mixing a small amount into his water when he'd come down with a bad cold. He hadn't spoken to me for two days as punishment.

I understood why he'd been mad. The choice to abstain from silvered blood was important to him. While small doses of silver had incredible benefits, taking too much too often caused addiction. His parents had been dependent on the silver, and it had not ended well for them. He didn't talk about it much. He'd only opened up about it briefly in those quiet moments between us on nights when we huddled together in the dark. But I knew what the silvered addiction looked like. It wasn't uncommon. The gangs were quick to exile the junkies, who had nowhere to go but the streets. With sunken black eyes, bulging muscles, and dark veins protruding over their skin, they muttered to themselves in rasping voices, slumping against the crumbling walls. They often didn't survive long like that.

They would see me as salvation. Nothing more than the silver blood in my veins. But Tayna protected me, and my blood was the only thing I could offer to protect him in return.

Because while the silver gave other objects and people power, it gave me nothing. In fact, it made me violently ill if I drank the blood myself. I'd done it once. Just to see. And I'd spent the day regretting it, clutching my stomach in bed and moaning while Tayna tried to feed me small sips of water.

So we used it in other ways.

My blood powered the small lantern that hung in the corner of the room. We used the silver for our flashlights, the small refrigerator in the corner, and the old toaster oven when we could afford bread slathered with melted butter. And we even used it sometimes to play games on an old console we'd found. The screen was cracked, but the car racing game that had been plugged in when we'd found it still loaded. The vials fit into the slots where the rotted batteries had lived. It used a lot of silver, but it was worth it.

I pulled the final syringe from my arm. "Done," I said triumphantly, and Tayna pressed a napkin to the puncture wound as my breath caught at the feel of his hands sandwiching my elbow. His fingers lingered gently over my skin.

"I hate that you have to do this." His brow furrowed as he watched the small bead of silver blood soak through the fine layers of the napkin.

"It's okay." I shrugged, swallowing against the flutter in my chest.

He shook his head. "It's not okay, Liss. It's..." He looked like he wanted to argue the point. His mouth parted slightly.

And I waited.

But then he swept his finger over the vein in my arm, and when he pulled back, the puncture wound was healed.

While I couldn't drink the silver myself, having it in my veins did afford me certain benefits. I'd always healed quickly, wounds stitched themselves closed in seconds, and I'd never gotten sick with a virus or infection.

The two vials of my blood would last a month if we were careful.

I forced out the breath I'd been holding and shook my head as if to clear it. After putting the caps back on the vials, I tucked them into the fridge next to the other near-empty vial we'd been using for the past couple of weeks.

Tayna was shrugging on his sleep sweater when I turned back to the room. I glimpsed the smooth contours of his stomach as he pulled the fabric down his frame. It made me bite my lip and think of that couple in the club tonight. My heartbeat ratcheted up once again. Silently, I tried to clear the tightness in my throat without any luck.

"What?" He caught me staring, his hair mussed from where he'd pulled the sweater on.

I shook my head and pulled my sleeves down around my hands.

So he flopped onto the bed and opened his arms to me. "Come here."

I crawled onto our pile of pillows and blankets, settling into his arms, my hand on his chest, the stuffed turtle pressed comfortably at my back, and our legs wrapped around each other.

We always got into bed like this. Our limbs naturally folded into each other, yet the embrace had my nerves spiking tonight. I was keenly aware of every inch of my skin pressing into Tayna's lanky frame. Each brush spiked with intimacy. His soft breaths fanned across my hair. My arm rested against his side. His fingers trailed across my shoulder blade. My toes hooked around his calf.

Tayna reached over his shoulder to grab our latest book from the open folding chair next to the makeshift bed. "Let's see." He brought his arm back around me so I was tucked up against his armpit, one hand holding me while the other held the book.

It was a story called *A Wrinkle in Time*. I'd found it while wandering through the old neighborhoods last week. It was under the bed of an abandoned house, open on a page, the text faded and lost to the years. It still felt like stumbling across a great treasure, and Tayna and I spent a night last week writing our own story to fill in the blanks.

Tayna pulled the piece of paper napkin we'd been using as a bookmark, and I tried to control my breathing.

He began to read, "*In the forest, evening was already beginning to fall, and they walked in silence...*" As he read, Tayna's free hand absently stroked my arm. I held myself tight against him so he wouldn't notice how shivery his touch made me feel. I suddenly understood why that woman had wanted to move her hips along the man like she had.

My body reacted to the feel of his fingers, warm and shivery with pleasure. I found myself responding, unable to help myself as my core clenched. This was new, this unshakable desire. My fingers traced up his shirt, grazing over the ridges of his abdomen. He was scrawny, to be sure, but there was also a strength to him. He was becoming a man, and I wanted to discover...

I pressed my hand against my mouth, biting my lip as I struggled to control my impulses. My body vibrated with this sudden urge to touch and be touched.

Tayna kept reading, but I was beyond comprehending the words. "*Charles and Fortinbras gamboled on ahead. Calvin walked with Meg, his fingers barely touching her arm in a protective gesture...*"

The smallest whimper escaped from between my lips as I tried to suppress the desire. Panic crashed over me, and I hurriedly unhooked my leg from where I had wedged it around Tayna's thigh.

"*This has been...* You okay?" he asked.

I nodded jerkily, forcing my hands to my sides, my fingers splaying in my attempt to control my limbs. "Just need to use the restroom."

I scrambled from the bed, wanting nothing more than to escape the space where Tayna felt too close, and my body felt too hot.

He nodded and set the bookmark back in place. "I'll wait for you."

And I marched from the room like it was a life-or-death mission.

God, he'll know something is wrong with me.

The bathroom was a small stall just outside our main room. I quickly locked myself inside and took a few steadying breaths.

It had never been like this with Tayna before. A thick tension clouded over the room. Well, maybe when I'd started my period. That had been awkward and filled with stuttering pauses while we figured out what to do. I'd ruined a pair of jeans. He'd thought I was dying. I'd had to choke out an explanation about women's bodies. But then we'd laughed. And the awkwardness had dissipated. Tayna spent his entire week's coins to get me some reusable cloths.

There had been moments, stolen seconds when I'd thought about him, thought about what we might do... what our bodies might do... but this feeling of wanting him so badly that it burned in my chest? That was definitely, unquestionably new.

It made me feel like I imagined people felt when they drank silver. And I understood the addiction.

I needed to make it stop.

I used a small amount of water from the bottle on the sink to wet my toothbrush. Or, well, what I used to brush my teeth. Apparently, it was designed for animals, back when people kept them in their homes. Some kind of thing you put on your finger and rubbed around their gums. But it made me feel clean, so I used it every night. Then I splashed some cool water on my face from the gallons by the sink.

Silver didn't work on plumbing. It was only compatible with things that needed electricity. So we were out of luck when it came to a working bathroom. But we managed well enough. We kept gallons of water on hand from the rivers running north into the ocean. We hiked up the hill once a week to pack down as much as we could carry. Tayna had managed to set up the toilet so it worked as long as we only flushed once or twice a day.

It suited us just fine now that he was working at the restaurant.

My routine calmed me, but my heart ratcheted right back up when I returned to our loft to find Tayna sitting up with the book beside him. He had his arms slung over his bent legs, and he looked up at me expectantly. He patted the scraps of fabric and blankets next to him, so I tentatively sat down. My limbs felt stiff, and I had no idea where to put my hands.

Could he hear my heart right now? Did he know my breathing was coming in and out in these short, stuttering bursts that made me feel like I might be having a heart attack? Maybe something was wrong with me. I'd never been truly sick before. Maybe this was what being sick felt like.

"Alright," he said, "out with it."

"I'm good." I couldn't meet his eyes. My voice felt strained and reedy. "Just wanted to brush my teeth."

"Did you take too much blood?"

I shook my head.

"Did something happen while I was at work?" he pressed.

Again, I shook my head. He wasn't going to let this go.

"Did the tequila upset your stomach?"

What were the right words to tell him?

"Are you worried about those guys we saw?"

"No, I—" My breath hitched. "Well, yes. But no. But it's just that... I—"

"Out with it, Lissa," he pressed, and I could feel him like a static charge as he leaned closer to me.

"At the club, I—"

I looked at the door.

Then I dared to look at Tayna and regretted it. His face was close.

Too close, but I couldn't move away.

He had an eyebrow quirked at me. "It's me, Liss," he said. "We tell each other everything."

We did. But I—Oh my god. I couldn't tell him *this*. I couldn't.

"Lissa." He strung out my name in that way that made me cave every time he wanted something.

I looked back down at my lap. "There was this couple at the club, and they were..." I threw out my hands as if he would fill in the blanks, but he stayed silent. "They—I saw—Well, they just looked..."

My stomach flopped in my belly, and I did feel lightheaded. Maybe I had taken too much silver, and it was making me do and say strange things.

Or maybe it was the tequila.

It was *so* not about the couple in the club. It had nothing to do with the couple in the club. It was about me. It was about what I was feeling, what I wanted, what I had realized but maybe wanted for a long, long time.

I love you.

The words were bright in my mind. On the tip of my tongue.

But then Tayna asked, "Was he hurting her?" And I could feel his warm breath as it brushed along the side of my cheek.

"No!" I said quickly, "No, he wasn't hurting her. Not at all! I was watching—Well, I saw them and I-I—"

Oh hell.

Before I could think about it anymore, I turned, grabbing Tayna's face in my hands and slamming my mouth on top of his. It was a clashing of lips and teeth, and I felt him tense beneath me. I had a wild moment of panic as he gripped the sides of my face like he might pry me from his mouth.

And part of me wished he would just put me out of my misery because I had no idea what I was doing.

But he held me steadily instead, his mouth beginning to move over mine.

I gasped, and when my mouth parted, his tongue slipped between my teeth.

Heat coiled low in my belly, deeper than what I'd felt before.

His chest was rising in heavy pants as though he was just as breathless as I felt, but still, he kissed me. He scooted closer to me, wrapping me in his arms as he guided our mouths together. My eyes fluttered shut as he once again parted my lips with his.

My hands fisted into his sweater. I wanted to trace my fingers beneath it to feel his skin.

He groaned into my mouth and then pulled away, just slightly, instead landing light, gentle kisses across my lips.

My lids fluttered open.

His golden eyes glowed brightly against the warm light of our room as he stared at me with such a pleased look that I smiled.

"Was that okay?" I asked tentatively.

His eyebrows shot up. "Okay!" He laughed, and I reveled in the dimples I was seeing up close for the first time. "Liss, I've wanted to do that for... I've thought about..." He shook his head. "It was really, really okay."

"Okay." I sighed, relief and satisfaction washing over me as Tayna pulled me into his arms.

This time, I snuggled into him, our bodies flush as he threw a few blankets on top of us.

My fingers traced my lips, still swollen from the kiss, and I swear I fell asleep wearing a grin. I wasn't thinking at all about the men we'd seen or why their eyes had been so focused on me.

3

Lissa

Tayna and I compromised the following morning.

He would go to the market, and I would be allowed to visit Madame Cartenoth's shop.

It was a fair deal. Madame Cartenoth didn't ask questions. She didn't even look too long at me as I kept my sunglasses on in her shop. Nosy shopkeepers didn't tend to last long in this city. And Madam Cartenoth was smart. She'd owned Tea and Trinkets now for well over a decade.

It was a strange space filled with baubles from another time. People would come to Madame Cartenoth to sell, hoping she would give them coin for their old knickknacks. And she did if she found them interesting enough.

Madam Cartenoth might as well have been a bauble in the shop herself. She must nearly be old enough. She always draped her short frame in colorful, patterned garments, even going as far as wrapping one around her head. She wore thick-framed glasses, and I'd always wondered if they even had lenses or if she simply liked the look. Not that I'd dare to ask.

Not that she gave me the time to ask.

She busied herself with making me a tea instead. The first time I'd stepped into her shop, she said she didn't much like the look of all the bones in my arms before shoving a warm mug into my hands. She'd made one for me every time I'd entered the shop since.

Between the selling and the rows of collectibles, Madame Cartenoth's real talent was for brewing tea. Not light brews, but cups filled with rich, medicinal concoctions that were a lifesaver when medicine or silver blood was nearly impossible to come by.

As I entered the shop, I slipped her a small silver-filled vial between my fingers. It was as much as I dared to spare, no more than a handful of drops, but it was something.

She took it as she passed by me, tucking the small vial of my blood into her robes. I knew she would use it wisely and only on those who needed it the most.

While she made the tea, I looked around the shop for anything new and interesting.

I picked up a rainbow-colored thing made of wood with large red slats that got progressively smaller until ending at the small purple tile. A wooden dowel was attached to the contraption with a string. Unsure of the purpose, I looked for a keyhole but came up short.

Madame Cartenoth came up behind me, grabbed the dowel from my hand, and struck it down the length of the contraption. Music. It made music! It was a small piano. Notes of hollow chimes filled the space, and I laughed, trying it for myself before she held up a finger to my face. "Strum it enough times, and I'll charge you a usage fee."

It only made me laugh and strum it again.

She knew I didn't have any coins. Tayna would spend the few he'd gotten during his shift last night on whatever food was cheapest at the market. And the blood I gave her was enough to buy the entire damn shop. But I didn't give it to her to make purchases. No, it was the only way I'd found to push back against the power in the city. It was my small defiance against the Tanks and the Veiled and the Cards most of all. They couldn't have all the power of this city.

They couldn't have me.

After a few more minutes, Madam Cartenoth returned, holding out a cup for me, but it was a paper cup today, not the usual thick ceramic mug she gave me during my perusals.

"Today isn't a day to linger," she explained. "The Cards are busy. They're out. I see them passing by the window. I can smell the trouble in the air."

"What are they doing?" I asked, taking the mug from her. Even the outside burned my fingers, biting into the cold of the damp ocean morning. I pulled my sweater over my hands to use as a shield, not daring to take a sip.

"Word has it, Gideon is recruiting," she crooned in her gravelly voice. "Apparently, their numbers are lower than usual after that bloody mess with the Veiled last month. But this..." She glanced over my shoulder and out the front windows that stretched floor to ceiling next to the door. "These stupid boys are going to get us all killed." She looked back at me. "Well," she said, raising a thin brow just over the rim of her glasses. "Go!" she shooed at me, and I did just that.

But as I stepped onto the market street, I froze, barely halting my instinct to run back inside.

In front of me, two Silver women were browsing between the stands. They wore night-black robes lined with lush fur. The hoods were pulled over their brows to shield their faces from view. On the sides of the cloaks, a large, blood-red Q was stitched into the fabric.

Card Silvers, then. Gideon called them his Queens, and if the rumors were to be believed, he treated them close to it. As long as they served his every whim, at least.

Four of Gideon's men walked beside the Queens. Each was marked with varying ranks of hearts on their sleeves. Hearts, in the Cards, denoted the most brutal of the members. They wouldn't hesitate to cut one out.

I shivered, slinking into the shadows but unable to draw my gaze from the women.

One had long blond hair that peeked out from beneath her robe. Her hands were decorated with silver jewelry, and her wrists clanked with bracelets as she pointed at a fruit pastry. The other was slightly shorter but no less graceful in her movements as the blonde purchased the pastry, and they continued on their way, gliding between the rows of goods for sale.

I tried to imagine owning a cloak like that. It looked so soft and warm, to be cocooned in such finery.

But I would never trade my life and my freedom for a cloak.

I clutched the paper cup of tea to my chest and dared a sip as I watched them pass. It was earthy, even a little bitter, but mellowed by floral hints of rose and lemon verbena. I sighed into the mug, letting the steam waft over my nose and cheeks, thawing them against the ocean chill in the air.

As soon as the women passed with their guards, I found myself walking to the pastry stand. An entire table was laden with fluffy baked goods. Some were so decadently covered in sugar they looked like they were sparkling beneath the haze of my sunglasses. Others were laden with fresh fruit like the one I'd seen the Queen purchase. They were berries of the richest reds and purples and blues.

I hadn't eaten anything since the pickles and fries Tayna had given me the night before.

"How much are they?" I asked the mustached man who stood behind the table.

"For which one?" He looked down at me with skeptical eyes as if he half expected me to snatch one from the table and run with it.

I wasn't going to say the thought didn't cross my mind, but, well, I just wanted to see them, to imagine what it would be like to purchase one without a second thought. They looked crumbly and gooey and sweet.

I clutched my little cup of tea closer to my chest, knowing he must see in me the opposite of what he saw in those Silver Queens. My frame was small from lack of consistent food, my hair was dull from being washed with bar soap we'd managed to purchase, and my clothes had small holes pocked throughout. The sunglasses always made people twitchy, too. Wary.

The mustached man said again, enunciating each word as if he thought I was stupid, "Which. One?"

"Um..." I pointed at one with almond slices on top.

A shoulder rammed into my back, and I gasped as my paper cup of tea was tossed onto the table, covering the front half of the pastries in hot liquid. The sugar, so beautiful and sparkling only a moment ago, now dribbled down the front of the table and onto the pavement.

I glanced over my shoulder. Whoever had hit me hadn't even realized it. Or they hadn't cared to stop.

"I'm sorry!" I blurted, looking back to the mustached man, whose lip curled in anger and disgust.

"Now you'll find out how much they are." The man's voice was dark. "Because you will pay for the ones you've ruined!"

I took a step back, shaking my head. "I don't have any money." Based on the man's reaction, that was the wrong answer. So I added quickly, "It was an accident."

"You worthless—"

Now, I did turn to run, but a hand closed around my upper arm before I'd even made it a step, yanking me backward.

My sunglasses went spiraling to the pavement.

"— little bitch." The man shook me.

Some people stopped to stare at the commotion, but no one intervened. These were the streets. And no one dared to bring attention to themselves.

No one dared.

Which was why I trembled as the man ripped me back.

I closed my eyes, both to shield them but also in anticipation of a blow.

Instead, I heard someone yell, "Hey!"

Tayna.

My uncovered eyes flew open toward the sound of his voice, and all it took was seeing his desperate, fear-stricken gaze for me to truly understand this was bad. So bad. He was pushing through people to get to me, but he was too far away.

And people around me were gasping.

My gaze whipped back to the mustached man, who had his hand

raised as if to slap me but was paused midair. He dropped his grip on me instead, and I stumbled back.

"Liss!" Tayna screamed, reaching my side and grabbing my hand. "Run!"

We made it all of three steps before two broad-chested Cards walked into our path.

Tayna yanked me behind him, turning so we could sprint back the way we'd come, but four more Cards filled in the space behind us.

Surrounded.

We were surrounded.

One of the Cards stepped forward, his eyes trained on me, locked in on the silver of my gaze. He was massive; even his head was meaty from muscle. As he crossed his arms over his chest, the Eight of Hearts strained across his left bicep.

I shrank behind Tayna, and the corner of the man's mouth twisted up in amusement.

"Well, well, well..." His voice was gravelly, no doubt from indulging in those cigarettes the Cards loved so much. "We'd heard rumors a little Silver mouse was hiding in the alleys. No one said she had the rat king with her." He laughed and then leaned in, his eyes going wide as he said, "Boo!"

Tayna's grip on me tightened as the man's putrid breath wafted across my face.

Too close.

They were too close.

I glanced over my shoulder only to see the other men closing in on us.

"Lissa," Tayna hissed. "You need to run."

But there was nowhere to go.

The Eight of Hearts guy grabbed Tayna's arm just as one of the men behind me pounced, wrapping me in a bear hug and hauling me backward.

I began flailing, kicking my legs and screaming but connecting only with air.

When I opened my eyes, Tayna was on the ground, the Eight of Hearts kicking him repeatedly in the stomach as he curled over on himself in the fetal position.

"Tayna!" My voice was raw as I screamed his name over and over and over again.

No part of me would let them take me, but more than that, no part of me wanted to continue watching them hurt the only person I loved in this crumbling world.

My protector.

He was my protector.

And they were hurting him.

And just like that, I felt something within my chest snap. Some thread unraveled, pooling into my veins.

My screams turned to something else. Something deep within my core, down to my very bones, came alive. When I opened my eyes, all I saw was silver electricity streaming from my fingers. My skin lit with hot-white light.

And then I really screamed as electric fire erupted from my skin.

The hands around me dropped, and I fell to the dirty pavement. My hip hit the muddy streets, and wetness coated my cheek as my head followed, smacking the ground.

The electricity fizzled from my skin.

Everything spun around me.

I pressed myself up to my hands, gasping for air.

My lungs burned. My ears rang. My arms were bruised. My vision swam.

But still, I scrambled to stand.

I had to keep moving. I had to get to Tayna.

A charged, burnt smell surrounded me, but my skin was no longer glowing.

So I crawled to Tayna's curled form on the ground as I rasped his name. A sob choked me.

His body was limp and covered in mud from the street. His thin arm was thrown behind him, the jacket burned from his body, leaving only scraps of fabric behind to cover him from the cold.

There was a burn across the corner of one eye that was so deep, I could see the bone of his brow beneath.

Around me, the Cards were lying prone in the streets. So were some of the shoppers for that matter. The chest of the Eight of Hearts guy was smoking.

Pastries, now soggy and caked in dirt, were tossed around me.

I pressed my eyes shut, trying to clear the haze from my vision as I reached for Tayna and shook him. "Tayna," I choked out.

He didn't move.

"Tayna!" I shook his cold, limp body, but he didn't open his eyes.

His face was slack, his mouth hanging slightly limp.

"No." I grabbed his face, feeling how cold it was. And then moaned, "Nooooo." I scrambled to pick him up; I tried to pull him to sit up. He just needed to wake up. He needed to wake up.

The lips that had kissed me just last night and made me feel so many new things were gray and dull.

I began yanking my sweater over my head. I needed to warm him up.

Maybe Madame Cartenoth could make him a tea.

We could—

My blood. He needed my blood.

I could heal him.

I could save him.

"What," a low, cold voice said just above me, "is happening here?"

Shining black boots stopped just before where I was crouched in front of Tayna, and my tearstained eyes tracked up the length of dark jeans to a crisp leather jacket and a cruel face that stared down at me without the hint of emotion on his carved features.

I was hauled up, hands gripping my arms as the cruel man in front of me toed at Tayna, his expression lighting at whatever he saw in the lanky, limp form.

"He's gone."

"Please," I said, begging this man but also begging any gods who would deign to listen to a forgotten little mouse. "Please, I can help him. Please let me help him."

"Clean up this mess," the man snapped. He turned, and I saw the Ace of Hearts stitched into his jacket. It only confirmed what I already knew. This man was Gideon Valmontry. "And take her back to the compound."

"P-please," I sputtered.

I didn't know how all of this had happened, but I knew it was my fault Tayna was now lying hurt in the street. This had all, somehow, been my doing. That electricity had come from *my* fingers.

The man's midnight-blue eyes met mine, and I glared at him, hating him with every fiber of my soul. He just stared right back, not breaking my gaze as he said, "This one is mine."

PART II

THE CARDS

4

Lissa

Five years later.

I stared out the window as Karadin, a young doctor only a few years older than me, straightened out my arm on the chair and tapped at the inside of my elbow, finding the vein.

"There she is," Karadin practically sang in that commanding voice of hers. We'd done this hundreds of times by now. A Silver's ability to heal quickly was the only reason I didn't have permanent bruises.

"Do you want to watch?" Karadin asked, the butterfly needle poised in her gloved hand.

I just shook my head.

She slid the needle into my vein without another word.

A blink held a second too long was my only reaction as I kept my gaze aimed outside. I could see the ocean from the clinic window. The waves crashed against the cliff face, and the mist reached so high, I could see the flecks of it shooting skyward in a lulling rhythm.

It was a beautiful day on the verge of spring, but I just wanted it to be over.

Endure.

Today was simply about surviving; every heartbeat was an effort to keep going and make it through.

"You're quiet today," Karadin said, connecting the first tube to the needle with deft fingers. She would take four total.

Tears pricked the back of my eyes. I nodded and opened my mouth to speak, to find the words, but they died on my lips.

Instead, Karadin picked up the empty space of silence as she switched to the second vial. "It's your five-year anniversary at the compound today, isn't it?"

My throat tightened, and I reminded myself to breathe. The last thing I needed was to pass out while Karadin was drawing blood. Those Queens who had a tendency to pass out during their draws were always relentlessly teased. I didn't need to hear the other Silvers snipping behind my back about how I couldn't hack it. The Queens already hated me enough.

I managed a tight, "Yes."

It was all I could muster. My chest felt like it was caving in on itself.

Karadin had the sixth sense of a healer, and she didn't press me. She was the only one I'd allow to do my draws, the only one I trusted in the clinic other than myself.

The memory of my first draw at the compound flashed in my mind. I'd screamed and fought until I was hoarse, and my starved body was drained. I was still covered in mud from the streets, but the Cards had brought me straight to the clinic for a draw. Silver electricity kept sputtering at my fingertips, and I'd burned the nurse enough times that they'd finally called for Gideon. He'd held me down with his bare hands until the draw was done, looming over me with a narrowed expression of... curiosity. Sure, he'd taken enough silver to heal from the burns I'd inflicted across his palms, but it must have hurt like a motherfucker to endure burn after silver burn from my skin. I hoped it hurt. I hoped it hurt so badly he was thinking about it today, too.

This goddamn day.

My five-year anniversary with the Cards.

Karadin switched to the third vial and rested a hand on my arm while keeping the vial steady with her other. Her brown eyes were too big for her face, too all-seeing and all-knowing, made even more striking by her severe ponytail. She looked like she was trying to transfer some of her strength to me.

She knew my history.

She was one of the few I'd told about Tayna, and the terrible day five years ago when I'd discovered my silver wasn't just in my blood like the others. My silver was a living, breathing power, just under the surface of my skin.

And it could kill.

Karadin switched to the fourth and final vial. When it was full, she went to pull the needle from my arm, but I stopped her. "One more."

She paused. "Lissa..."

"One more," I insisted.

"Do you really think today is a good day to—" Her gaze moved to the door. My guards stood just on the other side.

"One more," I said again. "Please, Karadin. On today of all days, just one more." I knew that using today as the final peg in my argument was cruel. It was a manipulation when she was aware of how much this day affected me. But I'd gotten particularly good at manipulation over the past five years.

Karadin scrunched her nose and pursed her lips, fighting her better sense. "You promise you'll eat a full meal?" She gave me a stern look.

I nodded.

"Not sugar, Lissa"—she held up a warning finger—"a full meal."

"A full meal," I promised.

This time, she nodded with thin lips, attaching another vial to the needle.

We watched as it filled with dark silver blood.

Karadin's nostrils flared delicately as she pulled the needle from my arm, slipping it inside another insulated tube to be sure it didn't open. She didn't bother bandaging the puncture hole on my arm. Not when it would be healed within minutes.

"Are you sure you know what you're doing?" she asked, passing the vial to me, where I folded it into the hidden pocket in my fur-lined black cloak. The silver felt warm even through the fabric pressed against my ribs.

"Of course," I said.

She peeled off her gloves and got me a cup of orange juice from the dispenser in the clinic lobby, chilled by a core of ice in the center. I chugged it and stood, ignoring the tinge of light-headedness that followed in the wake of the sudden motion.

I blinked it away. "Thank you, Karadin."

"See you next week." She sighed. The worry pinched between her eyes, causing deep creases in her forehead.

I took her hand quickly, giving it a squeeze, and forced the smallest of smiles for her. It was all I could offer.

"Don't get caught," she breathed, low and stern like an order.

"Only once," I said and left the room.

My guards waited for me outside. Kenji was slumped against the wall, picking at his nails. His short locks fell over his forehead into his eyes. He'd slung his leather jacket over his shoulder, and his Jack of Hearts tattoo was on full display on his umber arm.

Laykin was straight-backed, his tall frame rigid and his posture as perfect as the slicked-back blond hair he took so much pride in. He looked like a golden retriever who had just scented a squirrel.

"At ease, soldier," I told him dryly.

Kenji looked up. "Doesn't he just look like he has a stick rammed extremely far up his—"

"Finish that sentence, and I will show you how far a stick can go up your ass, Kenji," Laykin interjected. Smartly, Kenji didn't finish his sentence, letting out a low chuckle instead. Laykin might have the pretty-boy, puppy-dog look down pat, but he was one of the most lethal killers in Gideon's arsenal.

Both were Jacks, trumped in rank only by Gideon's Kings and the Ace of Hearts himself.

They had been assigned to my detail for the past year and a half after a Six of Clubs tried to get handsy with me in the courtyard. My guards at the time weren't fast enough to react, but I was. My skin had singed the hand of the Club so badly that he had permanent nerve damage. Gideon had also promptly exiled him from the Cards. The Club was lucky he wasn't executed.

Same with my guards. But they'd been demoted to perimeter detail, and Kenji and Laykin were assigned to watch me and my boring life. Typically, Queens were assigned Eights, but I was a unique case at this compound. I was the only Queen—hell, the only Silver—whose silver was a living, breathing electricity radiating from her skin. After I'd burned the Club, Gideon had thought it prudent to assign higher-ranking guards with additional silver rations for their personal use each week. It made them stronger. More easily able to heal from any potential burns.

Neither of my guards ever complained about their post as my watchdogs. I think Kenji preferred it to hunting and slaughtering rival gang members. Laykin, well, Laykin missed the kill. He never said it outright, but sometimes he got this hungry look in his eyes, and I just knew. He would love for one of the Cards to try to cross a line with me. He'd relish the excuse. So far, none of the new recruits had been so stupid. By now, they'd all been warned about my reputation.

The Silver Queen who could spark.

Not like a match. Like a bomb.

"Time for breakfast, boys," I announced. "Karadin has ordered me to eat."

"Thank god," Kenji groaned, kicking off the wall. "I'm fucking starved."

He'd eaten a little over an hour ago before we'd walked to the clinic, but I wasn't going to argue. He was a head taller than me and built like a machine. He did that walk thing where his arms swung wide while he took his steps only because his biceps were too large to fit comfortably at his sides. It wasn't his physique alone. Each of Gideon's leads, his suit Cards, were given a generous ration of silver each week, which tended to speed up the metabolism. Increased strength, increased healing, and increased stamina all required increased energy. The silver could only supply so much.

We walked from the clinic onto the lawn of the compound. It was built atop a jutting cliff that had been a key factor in the Cards' success over the years. When you had a forty-foot drop bordering 75 percent of your territory, enemies didn't stand much chance of sneaking up on the place. The drop ended with volcanic rock and crashing waves. I'd watched men thrown from the cliffs in the past as a punishment. Mostly captured rival gang members. It was one of the kinder ways Gideon chose to end people.

The compound itself had once been a mansion for some rich oil tycoon who'd had too much money on his hands and nowhere to put it except into a lavish house with fifty-six rooms, four guest houses, and a hangar for his helicopter and cars all on one property.

I was told the walls of the mansion were once white. Not that anyone actually remembered the color. Thanks to the flair of the Cards, the walls were now tagged—completely covered in graffiti art from grass to the roof above the third floor. Of course there were suits and playing cards, but there were also pictures. Some were cartoonish, like the one of a woman's red mouth biting her lip seductively or one of an orange monkey holding a mug of tea. Others couldn't be described as anything but works of art. There was an eye with long fanning lashes and the iris painted in a rainbow of colors and detail that always made me stare a bit too long trying to uncover her thoughts. Or the image of a black hand and a white hand clasping wrists, holding on to one another as crimson blood leaked between their fingers. It was as if, together, they could stop the other from bleeding, one saving the other's life.

The walls of the compound were alive with art and images. When I looked at them, I felt how it must have felt to walk in the museums of old they wrote about in books. I understood the way that light and colors and shapes could embody emotion.

As we walked, I lifted my heavy cloak to keep it from collecting bits of earth and grass. It really wasn't cold enough, even with the sea breeze, to justify wearing the cloak all day, but I liked how it felt against my skin. And I liked even more the things I could hide within its layers.

Laykin and Kenji followed me up the dirt path to the front entrance of the compound. Two leather-clad Spades holding automatic rifles nodded to us as we walked inside.

Where the outside of the compound was color and art and vibrancy, the inside was a stark contrast of white marble floors, charcoal-gray walls, and shimmering silver banisters lining the double staircase.

It was bright inside, given that it was barely morning. The natural light of the day was filtering in through the large windows at the back of the house. But once the sun began to wane, the soft glow of evening would give the interior a somber, studious feel. It was nearly sterile.

But that was how Gideon liked it.

It was easier to see when there was blood that needed cleaning, and there was often blood that needed cleaning. The only hint of color allowed inside. Well, that and the red embroidery on the Cards' clothing.

The kitchens were on the first floor, through the entry room, past a sitting area, into the living room and then we reached the dining area off to the right. A full staff was on hand twenty-four hours a day in rotation, always prepping, cooking, and cleaning. In a steady rhythm, they served up the most decadent foods.

This morning for breakfast, the counter was laden with soft boiled eggs, an assortment of sausages, steaming potatoes, roasted vegetables, a platter of fruit, and of course, pastries. So many pastries in assorted shapes and sizes they would have put that mustached baker at the market to shame.

My stomach twisted at the thought of that man.

For a moment, I was crawling through the mud with tossed pastries growing soggy around me in the streets. Tayna's burnt and bloody face was just out of reach as silver—my silver—sparked at my fingers.

"What'll it be, Lissa?" Kenji asked, cutting the line of Cards waiting for food and grabbing a plate, heaping on a spoonful of potatoes. No one even scowled at him. Suit Cards had priority in all things on the compound. It was just the way of things around here.

But I shook my head, taking a step back from the spread.

"Hey." Kenji pointed the now-empty serving spoon at me. "Karadin's orders." He flicked the spoon from me to the food in a "come on" gesture.

"We're going to actually agree on this one," Laykin said at my ear, giving me a gentle push forward. "You don't eat enough as it is."

"What are you, my guard or my mother?" I grumbled but stepped forward, swiping a pastry from the tray and giving the others in a line an apologetic grimace for holding up the line. The pastry was one of my favorites, a flaky croissant filled with pistachio cream and topped with crunchy roasted nuts and raspberries.

"Protein." Kenji handed me a sausage, and I scrunched my nose in disgust at the flesh-colored tube of meat.

"A man like that knows what he's talking about," my favorite of the cooks, a rosy-faced middle-aged woman named Millie, called to me as she walked by with a pan of bread rolls ready for the oven. "Get something in your belly, and then come see me after. I have something for you, Miss Queenie," she said cheerily.

That had me perking up and shoving the sausage into my mouth, chewing and swallowing without actually tasting it. It wasn't that bad. Okay, it was delicious if I felt like being honest. And when had I gotten so picky about food?

But I would give anything, pay any amount of money, to eat a cold french fry after a long night on the streets again if it meant Tayna would be here.

I took a bite of the pastry instead, this time focusing on chewing so I didn't focus on my thoughts. Not yet. There would be time for that later.

Kenji, Laykin, and I took a seat at one of the round tables near the windows in the dining room. It was more of a dining hall than a room, with ten tables spread out across the space, surrounded by windows and one-eighty views of the ocean water stretched out before us. A few other Cards were in the dining room, but my heart sank when another Queen entered with her guards close at her heels. Not just any other Queen, but Enver Jeffries, Queen of Diamonds, who might as well have been Queen of this whole damn compound.

Whereas I had woken up, braided my chestnut hair down my back, and called it a day, Enver looked like she had woken up early to spend hours in front of the mirror. There was no way a person could be so flawless otherwise. Her long hair fell to her lower back in luscious waves. Its silvery-blond color matched her silver eyes as the full embodiment of the title. She'd painted a delicate line of black above her eyelids and kept her lips a neutral, glossy blush to highlight her natural features. She'd forgone her heavy black cloak today, opting instead for a satin lavender dress that swished around her hips while she walked and was cinched at her delicate waist.

She piled fruit on her plate and selected a single egg before making her way into the dining room.

When her eyes caught mine, she seemed just as unenthused to see me as I was to see her.

"Lissa." She flashed a grin that didn't meet her eyes.

"Enver." I sighed. "Where are your groupies?"

Enver was rarely alone at the compound. She was usually surrounded by a flock of Queens and their guards, their noses turned high unless they were looking down them at me.

"It's draw day," Enver said, as if that were answer enough. "Karadin reserves the first slot for me so I can get it over and done with since I have such a packed schedule."

"Yes, all those hours in front of the mirror must be exhausting."

She gave me a flat look.

And that should have been the extent of our interaction. That was about all of Enver I could manage.

Except she walked over and sat down at my table.

Even Kenji sat up a little straighter at her arrival. Laykin fist-pumped Enver's guard, an Eight of Spades I didn't know well. I grinned at him and took another large bite of my pistachio croissant, not even feeling a bit of embarrassment as a glob of the cream center smushed out the side and fell onto my plate.

Enver's eyes tracked it as it fell.

"Gideon's returning tonight," she said.

"I'm sure you'll have a busy night, then." I took another bite of the pastry. I wasn't even hungry. It was just something to do other than make up a conversation with Enver, who could have sat anywhere else. There were plenty of open tables.

Her gaze tracked to Laykin, shocked at my statement, and then back to me.

She cleared her throat. "I'm not here to gossip with you about my night," she quipped. "Rumor has it, he's bringing back a truck full of new recruits."

"You can call dibs," I said dryly. "I'm not interested."

Her fork clattered to her plate. "Can you at least try to be civilized for a moment?" she snipped. "Instead of sitting here and implying I'm a whore when we both know where *you* spend your nights?"

I flinched.

Because I was the sniveling street mouse who had wormed her way into Enver's territory. Well, Enver could goddamn go to hell. Because it was just as much her fault I was here as it was my own. Those Queens I'd seen on market day? The ones looking at the pastries. That had been Enver and another girl at the compound named Ariya. They'd been at the market that day. And they'd both just watched as the Cards had snatched me from the streets and left Tayna to die.

Enver could look down her nose at me all she wanted, but at least I had the decency to hate this place instead of pretending like it was a goddamn holiday. At least I wasn't throwing myself at the Cards like they were heroes.

Instead of saying that to her face, I clenched my teeth and said, "What do you want, Enver?"

"You know what?" She stood from the table, slamming her hands down. "Never mind. It was a bad idea anyway."

I sat back in my chair, crossing my arms over my chest, not caring that I had flaky pastry crumbs down my chest, stark against the black of my cloak.

She gave me another look of disgust. "And you wonder why you don't have any friends." She shook her head. "I just wanted to see if you wanted to donate some silver to the bonfire tomorrow after the—"

Kenji perked up. "Bonfire?"

Every so often, the Queens hosted a bonfire for the men after they returned from particularly hard or long missions. By sprinkling some silver over the flames, the Queens lit giant flaming pits along the cliffs that burned a silver blue all night long. It had become a sort of tradition on the compound. A gift from the Queens to the men. As if we didn't already give enough with our weekly donations of silver.

I'd never attended a bonfire, which meant my guards, who usually took turns rotating shifts at night, had to take turns attending.

"You're on shift tomorrow, man." Kenji patted Laykin's shoulder.

"No, Kenji." Laykin shook his head. "Tomorrow is all you. I covered for you at the last bonfire."

"Come on, man! You don't even drink."

Laykin gave him a flabbergasted look. "Therefore, I don't like having fun?"

"Exactly!" Kenji said with a casual shrug.

It got him nowhere, as Laykin said again, "No."

Kenji turned his eyes to me, waving a hand between Enver and me. "One night of silvered fun won't hurt, right, Lissa? You can go back to pretending you hate us all in the morning, but can you please just decide to have a little bit of fun for once and go to the bonfire?"

"No," I said, glaring at Enver, my tone just as flat as Laykin's had been.

Her lips thinned, and she gave me an, "Of course," before she turned on her heels and left, taking her dainty plate of fruit with her. Over her shoulder, she said, "See you there, Layk."

Kenji sighed and raised his eyebrows at me.

I held up my fork, stabbing it in his direction. "Not a word."

He held up his hands in surrender, though I knew I hadn't heard the last about this bonfire.

Truth be told, I wasn't entirely against the bonfires. It didn't sound altogether miserable. And none of the Queens had ever even made an attempt to invite me before, even if it was only because they wanted some silver from me.

It was... nice. To be invited.

But I could still feel the warmth of the vial next to my ribs beneath my cloak. I'd given five vials today already, and though a little extra here and there wouldn't hurt, I needed the little extra I did give. Every bit counted, and I'd be damned if I'd give Enver so much as a drop.

5

Lissa

After breakfast, I left Kenji drinking juice and Laykin sipping tea to find Millie.

She was pulling bread rolls from the oven, red-faced and wiping her brow with a towel as the stove's heat surrounded her—all of it powered by Silvers. Not my silver, though. That, Gideon kept for himself. He had a particular fascination with my blood, insisting that it was more potent.

Leaning against the counter, I waited patiently for Millie to finish her work before she said conspiratorially, "They're ready for you."

I beamed. It was the first thing today that truly made me feel like smiling. I said a little breathlessly, "Where?"

She side-eyed me as she went to the tall, steel refrigerator and stuck half of her body inside as she began rummaging around in the back. "I had to hide them," she explained. "'Cuz lord knows those boys come back here sometimes and raid this fridge even harder than they raid the cities."

I flinched at her attempt at a joke.

She withdrew from the fridge with a small Mason jar, holding it out to me.

"Dill," she said, "as requested."

Inside were a dozen or so perfectly quartered and brined pickles. I clutched the Mason jar to my chest and hugged her tightly.

"You sweet, sweet woman," I said as I squeezed her.

She chuckled. "Happy five-year anniversary, Lissa."

"Don't remind me." I pulled back. "Or I might stop calling you sweet."

Millie rolled her eyes at me. That was normal on the compound. I was too idealistic, too much of a dreamer that I didn't see the big, bad world outside, realize how good we had it here, and just shut my mouth and beam with happiness. Everyone else managed to do it. And while I was grateful for a full belly and a safe place to sleep at night, I knew I had traded my soul to the devil in exchange for these small mercies.

It would never feel right. My mother had given her life to ensure I never ended up in this place, yet here I was, a pampered captive but a captive nonetheless.

And I would give anything, anything for one more night in that lumpy, makeshift bed on the floor with Tayna.

"I'm going to savor these," I promised Millie before returning to the dining room and collecting my guards. We had an errand to run.

Laykin drove us down to the square. The Humvee rumbled to a stop as we neared the city center, and people stopped to stare from the streets.

Their haunted eyes and hollow cheeks reminded me of me all those years ago.

They shrank away as we emerged from the truck, their eyes darting to the shoulder of my cloak and then away quickly. I hated the fear there but had also come to expect it. I pulled my hood up over my eyes as we headed toward the rows of tables and stands.

Five years ago, the market only happened weekly, aside from the barely surviving stores like Tea and Trinkets that operated weekday hours. Now, the market was thriving. Gideon had seen to it that this place was a haven for the farmers and the fishers and the bakers and the crafts people, who worked hard to support their families. As Gideon would say, there was no use ruling if you had no one to rule. And that meant people needed to eat. Stands were now set up daily with breads and vegetables and fried fish and even fruit.

I weaved through the stands, stopping only briefly to buy a few loaves of bread and some fried fish. Kenji and Laykin refused to help me carry all of my purchases. They said it kept them from getting to their weapons if there was an attack, which made me promptly roll my eyes and walk ahead to the rickety front door. A bell tinkled as I opened it, Laykin stepping forward to hold it as I struggled with my full hands.

I shot him a glare of annoyance that he had deigned to help, but Phenola was already racing to the front of the store. I saw her mass of curls before I saw her russet face and deep brown eyes, which were serious today. She scooped a few of the bread rolls into her arms.

"It's good you came today," she said, her voice low as she set the bread and the fish on the counter. "It's been a bad week. I almost sent word for you at the compound."

"It's a good thing you didn't," I muttered back, glancing to where Kenji and Laykin had taken up posts by the door. I knew they would guard me with their lives, but their loyalty was to Gideon and the Cards above all else. They guarded me because their Ace demanded it. "Make them some tea," I said. "The food is for you. I won't be long."

She put a hand on my cheek. "You're good to us, Lissa. Bat will be glad to see you, even if she pretends she isn't."

Our eyes met for a few heartbeats before I said to Laykin and Kenji, "I'll be quick."

They knew this routine by now. They'd only pushed to accompany me the first time. After they realized I wasn't trying to escape but only visiting with a friend, they allowed me my space.

Gideon hadn't even allowed me out of the compound during my first couple of years there. It took time to build his trust enough to be afforded that privilege. Even then, I wasn't allowed out without both my guards close at my heels.

At first, when I'd been allowed out, I'd started plotting my escape from the Cards, only to realize a short while after that I had nowhere to go. My mother had given her life to keep me from the compound, only for it to end up being the only option I had left. It was that or hide in alleyways by myself. And I wasn't dumb enough to think I could survive on these streets for long alone. There would be no sleeping. Not unless I wanted to find myself drained of all my silver blood when some desperate junkie managed to catch me off guard.

So I was satisfied with my weekly trips to the market and told myself repeatedly that this small taste of freedom was enough. Helping Phenola and Madam Cartenoth in this small way was enough.

At the back of Tea and Trinkets, through a thick wooden door, was a small living area. It was all of a kitchen sitting area, a bedroom, and a bathroom. It smelled vaguely of rat piss and cooked beans. There was mold growing on the sink. A deflated mustard-colored couch sat in the center of the sitting room, and a wooden table with mismatched chairs barely fit next to it.

I walked into the bedroom. It was a closet of a space, and an antiseptic smell burned into my nose. The room was lit with orange light. The patchwork knit blanket on the bed was tucked around Madam Cartenoth, whose frail body looked nearly mummified beneath the sheets.

Still, she shivered. She was even thinner than the last time I'd come. I understood why Phenola had looked so frantic. She'd moved in to help with Tea and Trinkets when Madam Cartenoth, her grandmother, first fell ill two years ago. The old woman had progressively gotten worse since then.

It wouldn't be much longer.

"Hey." I breezed to the side of the bed and pulled another blanket from the side chair, draping it across her frail body.

She seemed to settle with the added layer, and her eyes found mine. Her cheeks were hollow, and she smacked her lips and croaked, "Water."

A small cup sat on a chipped wooden side table. I pulled the vial of blood from my cloak to put a few drops of it into her cup.

She halted my hands. "No use wasting that on me."

"It'll help you sleep and ease your pain," I said.

But she just shook her head. "Give it to Phenola for the tea."

"There's plenty for the tea and for you. And I can always bring more next week."

"No." Madame Cartenoth clamped her hand over the vial. I hadn't even seen her move, and the fact that she could act so swiftly, even in her condition, startled me into submission.

"You always were a stingy old bat," I said with a shake of my head, putting the vial away and bringing the cup of water to her lips so she could take a few gentle sips. It was exactly why Phenola had given her the nickname. She always called her Bat, never Grandma.

Once she'd finished sipping her water, Madam Cartenoth fell back into the bed as if the effort had utterly exhausted her.

"What's the Ace doing these days?" she asked, her voice slightly clearer than it had been before the drink.

"Nuh-uh." I shook my head. "Don't you get your gossip from me."

She kept her eyes closed, but a smile graced her lips. "What else am I supposed to do while stuck in this bed all day?"

"I've brought you books, and you have yet to read a single one."

She scoffed. "Fiction bores me."

"You haven't even given it a try!"

"Try telling me something real." Madame Cartenoth waved a bony hand.

"I don't have anything real to offer," I said sullenly. "I'm a prisoner at the compound. No one tells me anything."

"Then you aren't using your ears." Madame Cartenoth cracked an eye to glance at me.

I offered her more water, but she waved me away.

"Are you hungry?" I asked instead.

She just shook her head. "You could be so much more than a prisoner."

"So you've said." I sighed, knowing I wasn't going to escape this lecture, but I still asked, "Can we not do this today of all days?"

"Oh what? Because it's your five-year anniversary at that place, you think you've earned the right to be a hopeless mess? You're a hopeless mess every day. Today isn't any different."

I tried not to flinch against her blunt words. "And I'm supposed to be happy about my condition?"

"You're supposed to use it to your advantage, girl," Madame Cartenoth snapped, a hint of her fire returning. "You have a choice. You keep letting your troubles break you, or you allow them to forge you into something new. You've had five years to grieve for him. It's time to make a different choice. He wouldn't want this."

"Tayna wanted a farm or a ship or a tree house." I scoffed. "He was a dreamer, not a realist. And now he's dead."

The silence stretched on between us as I reined in the ache in my chest. Madam Cartenoth's breathing evened out as she began to fall asleep, and I tried not to sigh too loudly in relief. She was always hassling me, always pushing me.

But I was surviving. I was surviving without Tayna. Wasn't that enough?

Once I was sure Madam Cartenoth was asleep, I unstoppered the blood and was about to pour a few droplets into her water when she said evenly, "If you put that blood in my water, girl, I will make sure you never step foot in this store again."

Caught.

It seemed the old bat had one eye open, even on her deathbed.

Teeth clenched, I restoppered the bottle.

Not because I was scared of her threat. She'd been threatening me for over five years since I first stepped into the shop. No, I respected her too much not to listen to her request, even if I disagreed.

"You're in pain," I said, my last-ditch effort.

"This whole world's in pain." She sighed.

"Well, I can't save the world."

"You can't save me either, girl. I'm ready to go." And then she added, "But you could save a good chunk of it with that gift of yours, and you know it."

Silver blood could help in so many ways, healing wounds and easing pain. But it couldn't stop death. Especially not when it was so close at hand. Old age combined with the sickness in her veins meant the silver would only delay her suffering.

Madam Cartenoth instead preferred to save it for others, slipping it into her teas, which she gifted to the poorest in this city. Never enough that they would realize what she'd done. She was careful. I trusted her and Phenola to be careful. They used just enough to ease a hunger-cramped belly or a hacking cough or a festering wound.

I stared down at my fingers, surprised not to find them glowing silver. My heart beat erratically, pressing into my ribs. The silver always acted up beneath my skin when my emotions were high.

"Even if I wanted to help more people, I don't know how," I admitted.

"Even though you don't know it, you already have."

My eyes flashed to her. "What is that supposed to mean?"

She just shrugged. "I think I'd like to sleep now."

"Madam Cartenoth," I demanded, "what are you talking about?"

She began to faux-snore loudly, and I had the urge to launch myself at her. Now, the silver did flare at my fingertips just before I tamped it back down.

But I knew it was time for me to go. I needed to be alone and get myself under control. Her words had niggled something deep within my gut, stirring emotions I didn't want to feel and thoughts I didn't want to contend with.

Not today.

Or tomorrow.

Or the endless years that stretched before me.

"I'll come back next week," I said, but she continued to snore. Loudly and fakely.

When I made my way back to the front of the shop, I found Kenji sitting at one of the small tables, leaning in closely to Phenola. Close enough that my eyebrows shot up.

She heard me enter the room and blushed a deep and beautiful rose as she clutched her teacup. They'd finished the fish between them and had made good work on one of the loaves of bread.

I cocked a brow at Kenji, and he said quickly, "She offered!"

"It's fine, Lissa," Phenola said, standing.

"Can I talk to you?" I asked her tightly.

She followed me into the back sitting room, her gauzy dress swishing around her ankles. I had to work to keep my voice low as I said, "She's in a mood today, isn't she?"

Phenola sighed. "What did she say this time?"

In answer, I held up the silver between us. "Well, she's now refusing this. And she made some vague reference about how I've already been helping people in ways I don't know about. Do you want to tell me how I've been helping people, exactly?"

Phenola didn't meet my gaze.

"Phenola." I said her name low and in warning.

"Look," she said so quietly I wouldn't have heard the word if I hadn't seen her lips move. And then she took a deep breath before continuing. "There's a new group in this city. They don't agree with how things have been done around here for the past seventy years, and they want to do something different. They've been asking for support and supplies."

The dread crept along my spine and down my fingers, where I could feel my silver coiling at my palms. I clenched them to try to control it. Now was not the time to lose control.

But I was already on edge today, and I didn't have it in me to deal with anything else when I was trying so hard just to keep my silver coiled tightly within my veins.

What Phenola said wasn't anything new.

Every few years, some rebel group or another tried to band together to make a stand against the gangs. And every time, Gideon and Olita Ravidian—the matriarch of the Veiled—made it an unspoken competition to see who could kill them all first.

Deciding on the most important piece of information, I said, "Supplies?"

Phenola glanced at me quickly before looking away again, and I knew. I knew what Phenola and Madame Cartenoth had done.

"Phenola." Her name came out in a disbelieving plea. "Phenola, please tell me that the blood I've been giving you to help your sick grandmother and sick friends has not been going to some new wannabe gang that thinks they can challenge the Cards?"

I'd give her credit that she didn't back down from my stare. "This one isn't like the others, Lissa."

My gaze darted to the door to make sure it was still shut securely, and Kenji and Laykin were soundly on the other side.

I hissed, "You're out there flirting with Kenji when you're secretly using my blood to try to tear down everything he stands for?"

"Kenji isn't like that," she said, surely. "I like Kenji. I like you. Laykin, well, he's got this look—"

"That's not the point!" I gritted my teeth. "Do you know what Gideon would do to me if he found out my blood is going to some rebels?"

"They're not just some rebels!" Phenola countered. "And they're not a gang. They're more of... a movement. And they're gaining traction. They believe in the old ways where everyone had a say. They've got this whole saying. It's like 'For the people.' It's incredible what they're talking about doing. You could see for yourself. They host meetings down in the—"

I covered her mouth with my hand, shooting my gaze to the door.

There were footsteps just outside the door.

And then a knock. "Phenola?"

It was Kenji.

He slid the door open just as I pulled away from her.

"Uh," Kenji said. "There's some guy here who wants help finding some kind of remote?"

Phenola, at least, was quick. She'd already slipped the silver from my fingers and tucked the vial into the pocket of her dress. She cleared her throat and breezed past him to go see to the customer.

Little thief.

I had no way of getting it back from her without causing a scene in front of Laykin and Kenji. But that was the last she'd get from me. I wanted to help Madam Cartenoth, but I had no desire to help some rebels get themselves killed.

I would not get involved.

Kenji looked at me. "We should go."

And I nodded, following him out. As we passed Phenola, the ruddy-faced man she was helping froze, staring from the red Q on my cloak up to my silver eyes and back again to my cloak.

I drew my hood up and said low to Phenola, "I'm not sure I'll make it next week," before stepping out onto the streets.

6

Gideon

I valued honesty and integrity.

And when those failed me, I valued blood.

Preferably silver blood. Preferably silver blood from a certain snarky little Queen, who would be waiting for me back at my compound. Well, I couldn't help but chuckle to myself. She wasn't really waiting for me. At least not in that pining sort of way. No, my little Queen would never deign to pander. But she'd miss me all the same.

The same way I missed her.

Ached to touch her.

Ached to taste her.

Ached to feel her blood in my veins while I claimed the deepest parts of her.

The red blood pooling along the concrete toward my black leather combat boots made my nostrils flare as I drove my heel into the stomach of the man laid out on the pavement in front of me. He didn't stir. Not anymore. His stringy hair was covered in dirt and grime that streaked across his pale face.

Pathetic.

The four men I'd taken on this trip and the handful of new recruits we'd collected along the way simply watched in stoic silence as I continued to drive my foot into the man's stomach until his chest began to squelch beneath my shoe.

The man was a gutter rat, so addicted to silver that he'd lied to me. He'd pointed me toward "rebels" in the north. Rebels that didn't exist. A fucking goose chase waste of time. It was a lie that had kept me another week from my compound, from my Queen. He'd dared to lie. To me. The Ace of the fucking Cards. The goddamn top of the food chain in this deplorable excuse for a city.

But I had made it my mission to see this city reborn.

My father never saw the potential of this place. He cared about power, and he cared about the silver blood that gave him that power. He would have lorded over a city of beggars and addicts.

I had bigger dreams.

Dreams of rebuilding this city to its former glory.

I would make it better.

And my little Queen would be by my side to see it through.

She was an essential part, after all. She didn't understand her place in this city. Not yet. But she would. Soon, she would know that the silver in her blood and the electricity she harnessed at her fingertips were not a curse but the greatest of gifts. Her unique silver abilities meant she could protect the Cards and this city from anyone who would dare threaten us. She was the next phase.

As it was, her abilities scared her. And I understood. I truly did. She'd had a girlish crush on a street rat that had ended with him dead, after all. Burned by her silver and bleeding his red blood along the dirty cobblestones. But she was never meant to be a street rat.

She was always meant to be mine.

And together, we'd create an empire, the likes of which this ruined city—a testament to the failings of the democracy that came before—had never seen.

7

Lissa

I wandered down the streets, Kenji and Laykin trailing just behind me. The path gave way from the crumbling concrete sidewalks to a dirt walkway that bordered the ocean. It was just near sunset, and orange light painted the sky in a line where the ocean met the horizon.

I wondered what Tayna would do if he were here living my life instead. He was always so brave.

He would have an answer for Phenola and Madame Cartenoth and even Gideon and the Cards. One piece of this was obvious: I couldn't give Phenola any more of my blood. Smuggling her vials was already dangerous enough, let alone smuggling her vials to give to some idealistic rebel gang. Especially when they would be dead by next month, their camps raided by whatever gang was victorious in finding it first.

Rebel groups were a dime a dozen in this city. All of them spouted their words of hope and vision for the future with beautifully spun prose. And then Gideon cut them down where they stood. Beautiful ideas were nothing compared to his control of this city and his willingness to use violence in order to maintain that control.

I stopped walking when I came to the rusted park bench beneath the dead remnants of a once-large tree. Pulling the cloak from my arms, I let the cool ocean breeze of the evening dance over my bare shoulders. I wore only a loose-fitting black shift dress.

Kenji and Laykin gave me space. They'd been to this park bench with me before.

At least, they gave me space when I pulled out the jar of pickles from Millie. Laykin stepped forward as soon as I pulled out the bottle of tequila I'd smuggled from the kitchens. Queens were forbidden from drinking. Couldn't have their blood tainted. But I'd donated today and wouldn't be due for another draw until next week. Maybe, maybe the amount of tequila I planned on consuming would be out of my system by then.

"Lissa..." Laykin's voice was a low warning. A vein pulsed in his pale throat.

I popped off the cap and took a deep swig before he could snatch it away.

Kenji put a hand on Laykin's chest to stop him from reaching for the bottle. "We'll be over here." Kenji pushed Laykin back and gestured behind him, where the crumbling wall still stood with the ace of hearts tagged across the surface.

"Thank you, Kenji." I raised the bottle at him in a mock cheer and crossed my legs beneath me.

Laykin glared at Kenji but stepped back with him, relenting.

I took another swig, trying to drown out my anxiety about Phenola and Madam Cartenoth.

More people who would be dead because I couldn't protect them. *Fuck.*

The silver crackled at my fingers, so I took yet another swig of tequila.

It had been there ever since that day at the market. The silver was now a living, breathing pulse right under the surface of my skin. I could always feel it sparking its way through my veins. That day at the market when I'd... killed Tayna... had cracked something open within me so profound that I'd never been able to spool it back within myself. The silver was part of me now. I was the only Silver who was able to use their abilities rather than simply be used by whoever could drain their blood. I didn't understand it. I could hardly control it. And I wished I could get rid of it.

I took another long, deep pull from the bottle.

The tequila was already going to my head. Drinking the same day as a blood draw would do that to a girl. But it was what I wanted. It was shitty tequila. Not quite the stuff in the plastic bottles but close. It burned as I swallowed. I only relished the pain and used it as an excuse to let the first tear fall down my cheek.

Brushing it away, I put aside the tequila and carefully unscrewed the jar of pickles. I smelled them first and smiled at the tang of vinegar and garlic and dill. Not quite like the ones Tayna would bring me from the club, with their briney musk and lime-green color. But these still made me feel that nostalgic longing deep within my gut.

I tilted my head to the sky as another tear tracked down my cheek.

We never got to eat those pickles on that last night on this bench.

Tayna and I had left so much unfinished.

Now, I slid one of the quartered spears from the juice and took a big bite, savoring the crunch and sharp flavor. It only made me cry more. That night, we'd dreamed about a farm and a full belly and getting out of this city. But I'd give up everything, *everything* I had for one more night on this park bench with an empty belly and Tayna by my side. I'd do anything to go back.

I took another swig of tequila.

One, two, three... it still wasn't enough.

All of the tequila in the world wouldn't be enough to heal the hole in my fractured heart.

When Tayna and I were together, there had been hope and possibility. The dream of a better life didn't feel entirely out of my reach. We could escape into our books, and we could imagine the adventures we would have. There was so much possibility that seemed to offer us a way out.

But that was not my reality anymore.

The first year or so I'd been at the compound, I'd thought of nothing but escape. I planned all the ways I would run away. I even made it out one night only to reach the compound gate and be dragged back inside by the guards.

Eventually, I'd convinced my guards in those early days to let me return to the warehouse. In my mind, if the warehouse loft still existed, then maybe, maybe there was a world where Tayna still existed too. Perhaps I would find him there waiting for me to return.

But it was over two years before Gideon finally agreed to let me go, only to find the loft just as Tayna and I left it.

A light layer of dust had covered the table. The bed was unkempt. The lamp and refrigerator had long run out of silver and sat unused. The books were the only things that had any life in that place. And the stuffed turtle. I carried all of them back with me. All thirteen of them with the turtle resting on top, my most treasured possessions. They were the threads that still connected me to Tayna in some small way. I could read those books and, for the briefest moment, remember what it was like to dream.

I took another swig of tequila and was surprised to find Kenji coming to sit beside me.

Laykin stood on my other side, and his form swayed slightly in front of me, just a hint out of focus.

"I think that's enough," Kenji said gently.

I nodded, but then took another drink.

"Come on." Laykin put out a hand for the bottle.

"Do you think there are pirates out on the ocean somewhere?" I asked him, blinking up through the haze in my eyes.

"Lissa..." His voice was a warning. Not that he'd ever hurt me, but he would, maybe, drag me to the car. As Jacks, they both received enough silver that they weren't scared of the sparks at my fingertips. Even if I did manage to burn them, they would be able to heal themselves quickly.

"Do you want a pickle?" I offered.

Laykin glared down at the Mason jar as if personally offended. "Those things are disgusting."

"You don't know what you're missing." I shrugged, fishing out another one for myself.

Kenji reached around me and grabbed one, giving Laykin a pointed look. We crunched on our spears in silence, and I appreciated that neither of them commented on my tear-streaked face. As my guards, they'd seen me at my most vulnerable countless times. Kenji had a habit of forgetting to knock and had caught me in the midst of changing on too few occasions. Laykin got spooked easily at the slightest hint of danger and had even barged in on me in the bathroom in one instance.

That memory made me chuckle softly. And then start crying again. Because it was a selfish thought on such a shitty day. And Tayna wasn't here to talk to about any of it.

The crease in Laykin's brow deepened as he silently watched my tears.

They both looked like hulking brutes, but I knew them at this point. And, well, they *were* hulking brutes. But they were also kind in a way I hadn't known Cards could be kind.

Kenji knocked into my elbow. "What's so funny, you tipsy Queenie?"

"I'm not tipsy." The words were thick on my tongue.

"No." Laykin looked down at me. "You're drunk."

He did snatch the tequila bottle from me then, and I scoffed. "Watch out for my pickles." I scooped the Mason jar into my arms, afraid his quick movements would shake the bench enough to spill them.

I looked around for the lid but couldn't find it.

"It's right in front of you," Kenji pointed out dryly.

"I know." I picked it up from the bench, but it was surprisingly difficult to line the grooves back up with the glass rim to close it. I brought the lid closer to my eyes. If I could just focus, I knew I could get it.

"Okay," Kenji said with a smile, folding his hands over mine and taking the jar from me. "Now you're the one who's going to spill them."

"I'd never spill them," I grumbled, but let him put the lid on nonetheless.

Once the jar was secure, he tucked it back into the pocket of my cloak and said, "Come here." He cradled my face tenderly in his palms and wiped the tears from my cheeks with his thumbs. His hands were so large he could probably cover my whole face with just one.

Then he helped me to stand and draped the cloak back over my shoulders, securing the pin at my neck.

"Time to go," Laykin said. "The riffraff is crawling out of the gutters."

Indeed, a group of people were watching us warily from the side-walk. A guy was smoking a cigarette, and the puffs carried into the air above his head. The other three were women. Well, girls, really. Their dark makeup only seemed to highlight their sunken eyes and malnourished frames.

"They're not riffraff," I said to Laykin.

Before either of them could stop me, I walked toward the group.

"Lissa," Kenji hissed, but I was out of reach and already marching.

"Hi!" I called to them.

"Lissa," Laykin yelled at me now.

I ignored him.

One of the young girl's eyes widened at me, but she didn't look away. She was the only one who didn't look away. Her hooded gaze was clouded with wary curiosity.

"Do you like pickles?" I asked her, holding out the jar.

"Pickles?" she asked, her voice soft.

"Yeah." I grinned, offering them to her. "They're dill flavored. Probably the best in the whole city."

Laykin reached my side now and grabbed my arm.

The man with them sneered at him up and down and flicked his cigarette. He wasn't a small man, per se. Not by normal standards, but

I thought about telling him he shouldn't make that face at Laykin. He wouldn't stand a chance.

Instead, I focused back on the girl whose eyeliner was too dark for her big blue eyes. "Take them."

She tentatively reached out a hand, and I pushed the small Mason jar into her chest, just as Laykin yanked me back, gripping my upper arm tightly.

I gave the girl one final smile over my shoulder before letting Laykin drag me toward our Humvee, Kenji close at our heels.

8

Lissa

There was commotion when we returned to the compound.

The drive back had sobered me up to the point that I only wanted to fall into bed. My mouth was a cotton ball, and my stomach began to feel watery. Plus, the Humvee was always so bumpy on the crumbling roads.

Apparently, it had been a nice night to be out of the compound because our car wasn't the only one waiting at the gate. We waited in a line of three cars ahead of the guard stand.

We never had to wait.

I groaned, and Kenji shook his head from behind the wheel. He peered at me through the rearview mirror. "You good, Queenie?"

"I knew that tequila was a terrible idea," Laykin muttered. "Open the door if you're going to vomit."

"Do we have to wait in this line?" I whined.

Peering out the window where I sat in the back seat, I could see men patrolling outside. They walked evenly in clusters on the lawn through the white light that illuminated the grounds at night, thanks to spotlights strategically placed overhead.

All the movement and light hurt my eyes.

Even the Queens still seemed to be up. A group of them huddled near the entrance to the mansion, their cloaks wrapped tightly against their frames.

It all meant one thing: Gideon had returned.

He'd been gone for a month now, on a mission to the outer banks of the city where there'd been rumors of civilians spotted taking up residence. Gideon had informants throughout the city, mostly people who were so addicted to silver they would give him anything, *anything* he asked for just for a hit. He had eyes everywhere and saw any new groups as a threat to his control.

Our Humvee made it to the gate, and Kenji rolled down the driver's side window.

"Checking back in," he said, handing over our IDs, which were just playing cards laminated with our pictures and vague details the Cards had deemed important, like rank, joining date, height, weight, and membership number.

The guy at the gate didn't seem all that interested, barely glancing at us as he took our IDs and said, "Names?"

"Kenji Jones, Laykin Longbury, and Lissa Metarro."

That got the guy's attention. "The Queen of Hearts?"

I hiccuped from the back.

Kenji snorted. "The one and only."

"Gideon's been asking about her," the guard said. "She's to report to his office immediately."

I groaned and fell back against the seat.

"Tell him she's on her way," Laykin said, shooting me a glare over his shoulder.

"Queenie," Kenji said as we drove through the gate, "you've got about fifteen minutes to sober yourself up."

I let out the most pitiful scoff.

"Here's what's going to happen, Liss," Laykin said, turning around in his seat and looking at me so I knew he was serious. "We're going to park in front of the house. You're going to go to your room. You're going to change, brush your hair, and for the love of God, brush your damn teeth—"

"My teeth are fine!" I scoffed.

Kenji laughed. "You smell like vinegar garlic and the bottom of a tequila bottle."

I stuck out my tongue at him and crossed my arms.

"Hair, clothes, teeth," Laykin said, listing them on his fingers as Kenji pulled around to the front of the house.

"I'll get her some water," Kenji offered, pulling into the parking spot. "You get her to her room."

Before I could even track their movements, Kenji sprang from the car, and Laykin was already around the side, opening my door. I slid from the seat, and he wrapped a hand around my upper arm.

"I'm fine." I tried to jerk away but only stumbled into the side of the car.

Shit.

It wasn't my fault the driveway was uneven.

He gave me a look that said he wasn't even going to respond and kept his grip firm on me.

We couldn't avoid the other Queens at the front of the house. Enver and Ariya were among them, and their lips curled at the sight of me.

"The street mouse is in trouble," Ariya sneered.

"Stop it, Ariya."

My eyes widened when I realized that statement had come from Enver.

She stepped up to Laykin. "I'll help."

Ariya and the other Queens snickered behind Enver as if this were all some sort of joke. I flipped her off over my shoulder as Laykin nodded, grabbing me and leading me inside.

Enver followed us up the double staircase and down the hallways lined with black and silver oriental rugs. All of the Queens kept residence in the same hallway of suites. There were nearly twenty of us in residence at the compound. While some women shared rooms, I'd been given one at the end of the hall, all to myself. When I'd first come to the compound, I'd shared a room but, well, I'd had a nightmare and become a living ball of lightning. By the time I woke up, I had singed my bed down through the mattress and scared my room-mate nearly to death. Gideon made the decision then that I would room alone.

Laykin opened the lock on my door and threw it open to reveal the space.

I swayed inside, and Enver followed.

"I don't need your help," I snapped, trying to sound as confident as possible, but my lips were thick, and the words jumbled out in a childish garble.

Laykin just eyed me up and down again and said, "Five minutes," before shutting the door with Enver inside.

My room was small but cozy. The rest of the house may have been decorated in black and white only, but my room was a splash of color. The furniture was rich mahogany wood. The bedspread was a deep emerald green. The chair in front of my desk was a magenta velvet, and I'd draped the lights with gauzy orange and yellow curtains to give everything a low glow that reminded me of the lighting at the loft. I'd also brought in plants. They dotted every corner and spare place in the room. Gideon even brought me a few as presents when he'd traveled far away. They made this place feel like less of a prison, which was exactly why he did it—bribery and manipulation at its finest.

Enver didn't waste any time helping herself to the walk-in closet and rummaging through my belongings.

"I don't want your help," I called to her but found myself stag-gering and flopping onto the bed. My face smashed into the stuffed turtle I always kept in the center.

"Right." She came from the room with a laugh and handed me a navy dress I knew was so long it would drag at my feet.

"I'll kill myself in that thing. Even sober," I said.

"Put it on," she insisted. Moving into the bathroom, she asked, "Where did you even find alcohol?"

I shrugged and pulled my black shift over my head. "In the kitchens."

"You mean you raided Gideon's personal stores," she said, emerging from the bathroom with a comb in hand.

"Are you going to snitch to him?"

"Why would I do that?" she deadpanned.

"Because you *love* the Cards." I sang the word "love" for good measure.

She just sighed, her delicate nostrils flaring.

I couldn't wear a bra with this dress, so I pulled it off along with my dress, unashamed of my nakedness in front of Enver. I'd long since grown comfortable with my body, with the womanly curves that had formed themselves into my frame over the past five years. Once, I'd been only limbs and hollowed bones, but five years of solid nutrition had seen my body blossom into supple, soft lines.

The navy dress fell over my breasts and the curve of my hips in a way that only flaunted my figure, cascading down my legs to the floor where the flowing fabric pooled.

As soon as the dress was over my head, Enver pulled out the tie on my long braid and began loosening the pleats, running the brush through the ends as she did until I could see from the mirror at my desk that it fell in soft waves around my face.

"Are you helping me because you want my silver?" I asked her, the alcohol making the questions loose on my lips.

She sighed. "We should talk at some point. But, for now, you need to brush your teeth."

I stood but grumbled, "Why does everyone keep saying that to me?" I walked into the bathroom to dig out my toothpaste and brush.

Once I was done, I splashed some water on my face, and Enver applied a light coat of mascara to my eyelashes.

Just as she was spraying a misting of perfume on my neck, Laykin opened the door. "It's time."

With a heavy breath, I nodded.

I looked over my shoulder at Enver before I left. "Don't steal my books."

She shook her head and rolled her eyes, and then I was following Laykin down the hallway.

Gideon's office was on the other side of the house. Kenji met us and fell into step beside me, handing me water to sip on as we kept a brisk pace. Or as brisk a pace as I could manage, given the dress around my feet and the tequila in my veins. I kept stopping to hike up handfuls of the skirts. Maybe Enver had done this just to spite me. Eventually, Kenji ended up just carrying a fistful of the fabric behind me while I held up the front.

"Did you have to wear this dress?" he asked, eyeing the plunging neckline and the low-cut back.

"It was Enver's idea," I snapped. "Talk to her."

"Oh, I have questions about that," he said.

"You and me both," I grumbled.

"Be careful with that one."

But Laykin said, "Quiet. Both of you. She was just trying to do something nice."

And that stopped both Kenji and me short. We shot side-eyed glances at one another but didn't say another word. I did, however, purse my lips against a giggle as Kenji mouthed, "Oh my god," with his big wide-eyed stare.

Gideon kept a whole wing of this giant mansion as his private quarters. He had his living space, which was a suite in and of itself complete with a lounge area and a dining room, not to mention the largest bathroom I'd ever seen. But he also kept a conference room for strategy meetings and his personal office in this wing as well.

A lot of the gangs were unsophisticated in the way they operated but not the Cards. Gideon had set it up to run like a corporation, and he operated more like a CEO or a general than a flippant, power-hungry leader. He was those things, but he was also ruthless and cunning and intelligent. More than anything, he was willing to do what needed to be done to stay on top.

Laykin knocked on the door of the office.

"Come in." The male voice was a deep caress that had me shuddering with recognition.

"That's your cue." Kenji gave my lower back a little nudge.

I glared back at him but stepped through the door Laykin had opened for me. Then promptly closed it behind me as soon as I was inside. I glanced back at the door, feeling for the wisps of my dress to make sure none of them had snagged. I smoothed the fabric down my front and found my hand tracing up to my collarbone to make sure the top was securely in place.

When nothing was left to fuss over, my gaze finally tracked to the center of the room.

The office was decorated entirely in black, with different materials as the only accents against one another. The black marble floor had a large fur rug on top. A black iron bookshelf was lined with leather-bound books. Even Gideon's desk at the far end of the room was a black wooden monstrosity with gaudy Roman carvings along the perimeter. Windows lined the wall behind the desk, and the billowing curtains had been closed. They looked almost like black smoke as they wafted slightly against the breeze from outside.

The room was kept so dim, there was only the hint of silvery light from a lamp on the desk table, but I could clearly see the outline of the man leaning against the front of the desk, his arms and ankles crossed. He had obviously spent time outside while he was away. His forearms were a deep bronze where he'd pushed up the sleeves of his shirt to his elbow. Tattoos traced down the expanse of one arm. The hint of chest I could see, thanks to the few open buttons of his shirt, revealed the golden color of his skin descended farther, too. He looked like a statue made for this room, all carved lines and dark shadows highlighting a sculpted frame. He was watching me through lowered lashes, and a lock of his black hair fell across his forehead into his eyes. It was longer than when he'd left but pushed back from his face as if he'd just showered.

"Welcome back," I said, breaking the silence.

He pressed his tongue against his perfectly white canine, his full lips curving into a wicked grin that danced in his eyes. "Miss me?"

"No," I said flatly.

His grin widened. "Come here." He crooked a finger at me.

I crossed my arms over my chest. "I don't like orders, *Ace*." I emphasized the word as if it were a curse.

"Clearly, I was away too long," he said, pushing from the desk, but his eyes lit with the challenge. "You've forgotten your place."

"I never agreed to that place." I met his stare.

"It doesn't require your agreement." He shrugged, running a casual hand along the desk like he was picturing what he would do to me on top of it. "Now..." His voice was so, so calm. "Come. Here."

"No." I dug in my heels.

He crossed the room in only a few purposeful strides. I didn't have time to take more than a step backward before he was pressing into me. My back slammed against the wall hard enough that I sucked in a sharp breath. The bookshelf beside me rattled with his force. His hand gripped my chin. His hips pinned mine as he caged me against his body.

I forgot how massive he was. His entire frame engulfed me, and even though he bent, I still had to gaze up to meet his dark, gray-blue stare.

"God, I missed that venom in your eyes," he said.

And then his mouth was crashing into mine. His kiss was a reclaiming as he forced my mouth open with his tongue and drove inside me. He kept a grip on my chin, holding my face steady even as I jerked against him.

Fire tore through me. My anger was hot and burning, but my impulses were dulled from the alcohol. All I could do was feel the rage as it settled into my stomach. My hands pressed against his chest, my nails digging into his skin, but he only continued to claim me with his mouth and his tongue.

He didn't even flinch as my silver sparked, burning his skin and his shirt. He'd consumed enough silver that, if it weren't for his shirt, you'd never know I'd hurt him.

I let out a ragged scream. I could feel him smile against my mouth before he grabbed my wrists and pinned my arms overhead with one hand. His kisses became languid, slow things. I knew what he was doing. He was showing me just how much power he held over me. He could take his sweet time, and no matter how much I begged, I was his.

His fingers drifted across my lower lip. His hips rolled into mine. And the fire, the fire in my belly turned into a deeper sort of ache. My breath hitched, and he pulled away just slightly, pleased with himself.

I didn't want to feel anything but hate and disgust for this man. I wanted to burn with the rage and agony of the day. He couldn't take that away from me. The passion and the sensual slowness of his kisses made me feel like we were lovers. And we were not. He was my enemy. His kiss could never, would never be like the kiss I'd shared with Tayna. That was separate and pure and kept in a small place that I would not allow anyone to have or touch.

And so I launched myself at Gideon, forcing the kiss to be frenzied. Our teeth clashed.

He seemed surprised at my force for only a moment before he met me in the kiss. I bit his lip, drawing blood, and he rolled his hips into mine until I was crying out.

"Careful, little Queen," he murmured. "I'll bite back."

His mouth returned to mine, hungry and consuming. He didn't break the skin, but by the time he was done with his claiming, my mouth felt bruised and swollen. My skin prickled everywhere he touched, and I worried I might start glowing with silver at the intensity of it all.

He moved to my neck, his hot breath trailing across my skin. My breathing was heavy.

And then he pulled out a small switchblade from his pocket, flicking it open and holding it to the space just above my collarbone.

I stilled.

"Lissa." His voice was low against my skin where his tongue still licked across my neck. "Have you been drinking?"

9

Lissa

Those words and the knife were enough to bring me wholly back to myself.

"No," I said quickly. Too quickly.

He kissed me again, his tongue delving into my mouth deeply as he kept the knife poised steadily near my throat. He hummed as he pulled back again. "Tequila, I think."

My heart became a nervous flutter in my throat as Gideon slid the flat part of the blade along my collarbone until the tip reached the very center of my throat.

The fear didn't stop me from saying, "I guess I have nothing to offer you tonight."

Two years ago, it started with my blood. I'd been sent to his office when he'd been shot in the side out in the city. He hadn't wanted his men to see how badly he'd been injured. My blood, for whatever reason, had always been stronger than the others. It worked more quickly and gave heightened abilities. So I was the Silver chosen to aid him that day.

But it hadn't ended there, and my blood was far from the only thing he wanted from me now.

His dark eyes tracked to mine and held. The gray-blue pupils were as steady as his hands around the small blade. He flicked it closed and tucked it into his back pocket.

"Come here," he said, lowering my arms and grabbing my hand, pulling me toward the center of the room.

"You're not going to punish me?" I asked, letting him lead me toward the desk.

Over his shoulder, he flashed a smile that was all white teeth. "Do you want me to punish you?"

I shook my head.

I knew the alcohol wasn't forgotten, but for the moment, it seemed Gideon was in a playful enough mood to let it go. And I sure as hell wasn't going to be the one to push the issue, so I let him lead me to his desk. He directed me to sit in his black leather armchair, and I sank into the plush seat. It folded around my body, and I almost, almost let out a sigh of relief.

"Close your eyes," Gideon told me.

Instead, my eyes narrowed at him skeptically.

"Close your eyes, or I won't give you what I brought you," he ordered, his tone darkening only slightly.

He did this—brought me presents from his travels. Sometimes it was plants. Sometimes it was books. Once, he'd brought me a sparkling necklace. The entire chain was paved with small diamonds to make up the links.

It was not lost on me that he brought priceless possessions to give to his favorite priceless possession, which was exactly what he considered me. Even before he'd started taking me to his bed two years ago, he would use words like "mine" and "own" and "everything" to refer to me. It wasn't enough that the Queen of Hearts had been grated into my skin with a red-inked needle. He had this desire to mark an even deeper part of me. It was a part I kept locked away from him, even if I would allow him to have pieces of my body.

So I did as he instructed and closed my eyes. I heard a bag unzipping from somewhere over my shoulder, and I balled my hands into fists to keep from pulling them into my lap.

I jumped when something brushed against my bottom lip.

"Open," Gideon told me.

My mouth popped open at his command, more from surprise than anything. He slid something onto my tongue, and I tasted chocolate. I'd had chocolate before. That wasn't new, but something hard was underneath.

"Chew." He laughed near my ear.

Again, I obeyed. Only to find the thing slightly hard to break with my teeth. My eyes flew open as I crunched on the chocolate-covered thing in my mouth. The flavor was sharp like wood and earth, and my immediate reaction was to spit it into my hand, but I forced myself to keep chewing. Crumbled bits of the thing stuck into my teeth.

He saw the uncertainty and hesitance on my face. "No?"

The thing in my mouth was growing mushier like mud the longer I chewed it, but the flavor wasn't entirely unenjoyable. There were almost notes of fruit within the bitter taste. The sweetness and creaminess from the chocolate seemed to take the edge off the harsher notes.

"I think I need to try another one," I said, swallowing roughly.

Gideon laughed but brought another of the things—I wouldn't call them treats yet—to my lips. I opened, allowing him to place the second on my tongue before I began chewing, more confident in it this time around.

"What do you taste?" he asked.

I mulled over his question. It seemed like there were a lot of flavors within it. "It's like fruit that isn't sweet," I finally said. "But also maybe a bit of wood? Or spice?"

"It's all of it," he said, still smiling as he watched me contemplate the flavor.

"What is it?"

"A bean some farmers have started growing in one of the northern territories. It was apparently once even more popular than tea. It's called coffee. They roast it, which is what gives it those strange and complex flavors. They can make it taste like all sorts of different things."

"Like what?" I'd heard about coffee in books I'd read. I always thought it was like a bitter tea that made people feel more awake. But this bean was nothing like any tea I'd ever tasted before.

"Caramel or vanilla or smoke or berries or flowers or spices." He listed them off as he gave me another chocolate-covered bean to chew on. The little flecks of it were stuck in my teeth like tiny pieces of gravel or wood.

"And you can drink it?" I asked, using my finger to pick at a particularly annoying particle in my back molars.

"If you steep it, yes. But it's a whole process. You have to grind it, heat the water, allow it to steep, and then strain out all of those fine particles. The chocolate-covered ones seemed like a much easier gift to bring back."

"And where did your travels take you this time?" I asked.

He sat on the floor in front of me, tossing one of the beans into his mouth and leaning back against the leg of the desk before answering. "North. It was the farthest north I'd traveled in over a decade. My sources warned me about a new compound forming that way."

Gideon was in his mid-thirties but barely looked older than his late twenties, thanks to the silver he consumed on a regular basis— my silver. He kept his dark stubble close-cropped along his face but visible, and I knew it was because he felt like it somehow made him look more commanding. It reminded me that a piece of him was always wild and untamed, even in this crisp, black-and-white life he'd built.

"Did you find them?" I almost didn't dare ask, but I had to know.

"No." Gideon traced a hand between the layers of fabric of my dress until he found the bare skin of my ankle and ran a lazy finger up my calf. "But that doesn't mean they aren't there. Multiple people have told me of a new rebel group forming in that area."

I thought of what Phenola had revealed to me today and trained my eyes on where his hand traced up my leg. I let him think I squirmed in my chair because of what he was doing under my skirts. That was part of it, to be sure.

"We'll go back to scout again in two weeks," Gideon added.

"You'll leave again?"

His hands traced up to my knee, his fingers light against my skin. "You *did* miss me," he said, squeezing that sensitive spot at the top of my knee until I jerked and squealed from the tingling sensation he'd elicited from the pressure point.

He sat up on his knees, his eyes meeting mine as his fingers stilled above my thigh. His hand gripped just below the apex of my thighs. I sat up a little straighter, awareness creeping along my skin as I stared down at him, watching him watch me. His gaze lingered over the low cut of the dress, skating along my body, taking in the details of my curves.

I swallowed. "Why does it matter if there's another group forming in the north? As long as they don't come here?"

His other hand snaked under the fabric of my dress, and he pressed his body between my legs. They opened wider for him as his hands settled on either side of my thighs. The fire had returned to his gaze.

"People are never satisfied with just enough," Gideon told me. "This group may claim they will keep to their territory, and maybe they will for a year, two years, ten years. But then they will come. Eventually, they always come. I won't risk your life or the lives of the people in the Cards for the chance that this group will be the exception. They may be. I don't care what they want. For you, I'd ruin them all."

His hand moved to the apex of my thighs then, moving aside my panties to run a finger down the very center of me.

My head tipped back into the plush chair.

"I knew you'd be wet for me," he growled.

And I was. There was no use denying the blatant desire.

He pressed a finger inside me, and my back bowed against the chair. He worked it in all the way, then withdrew and added another. I bit my bottom lip to keep from screaming, but a groan slipped free when he began using his thumb to circle my clit. My hips rolled, and delicious pleasure shivered down my spine and across my limbs.

"Look at me," he growled.

And I did, forcing my eyes to meet his where he knelt before me.

He worked me like that, two fingers sliding deep within my core while his thumb drew lazy circles over my clit, never once breaking eye contact as I began to squirm in earnest, my hips taking on a life of their own. It had been too long, too long since I'd felt his touch like this. My body knew it and craved it. With the alcohol and the pleasure, I was too far gone. I could admit that to myself, at least, if not out loud.

Luckily, he didn't demand it. He just moved his fingers inside me, withdrawing his other hand from my skirts to pull down the strap of my dress, revealing one breast.

"So goddamn beautiful," he said, marveling at the peaked nipple and tracing the curve of my skin until his fingers pinched the center and twisted.

I cried out, my mouth gaping open at the pleasure twisting through me.

He didn't stop, only pulled down the other strap and did the same to my left breast. The way he knelt in front of me put him at perfect eye level with my chest.

By the time he'd finished with my nipples, I was panting, my forehead pinched as his fingers continued their steady rhythm in and out of my core. Wetness coated my inner thighs, and I gripped his shoulders, writhing against his fingers.

"Gideon." His name on my lips was a plea.

"Such a good little Queen," he said, and the sound of his rough praise as he pressed his thumb into my clit sent me over the edge. The orgasm had me rocking into him, my forehead falling into the crook of his neck as I let the pleasure consume me. We stayed like that until the high began to subside.

For a few moments, nothing was between us but our breaths, both heavy from pleasure. Mine soothed, his still wound tightly like a bowstring.

Slowly, he withdrew his fingers from me and gently kissed my cheek. "Happy five-year anniversary, Lissa."

He remembered the date.

And it was almost tender, the way my head rested against his shoulder. The way he knelt between my legs. The way he cupped the base of my head as if to hold me to him. As if I might slip away if he let go.

But then he said, "Now take off your dress."

"What?" I turned my head. The exhaustion had begun to seep into my limbs.

"Did you think we were done?" His eyes turned dark with his words. His jaw set in a hard line. "Did you think I would forget about the alcohol?"

His words sent up an icy flair through my veins.

"Gideon—" I pressed my hands into his chest to push myself away, but he stopped me, his grip bunching at the fabric along the rib cage of my dress.

"No more asking twice, Lissa," he said before ripping the dress down the front.

The fabric pooled around me in the chair, and I stood abruptly.

But the words I was ready to hurl at him died on my lips as he followed me up, spinning me and pressing my front into the desk so I was folded on top of it. The wood was cool against my stomach and my already sensitive nipples. My hips dug into the carved pattern that bordered along the top. His hand fisted into my hair.

I cried out at the impact. It didn't hurt as much as it startled me how quickly he'd turned, fueled by silver and desire.

He pulled the knife from his back pocket. I couldn't see him fully, but I heard the swish of the blade as he flicked it open. And then I felt the cold metal slide underneath my panties.

"Don't move." His voice was a low command behind me.

Two quick flicks of his wrist and the fabric fell from my body, leaving me completely naked and bent in front of him.

Once he was done with the blade, his hand traced over my spine until he reached my backside, kneading my flesh until I released a gasping breath.

I wanted him as much as I hated him.

It was a sick game we played, this back-and-forth. There was no denying my body's response to this man. My desire for him was, at some moments, consuming. And it was no wonder. Even without the silver, Gideon was a sight to behold. There was attraction and chemistry, yes, but he had strength in other ways that I envied. He had the confidence of a man who grew up with choices and the intelligence of someone who had seen the world and was not afraid.

But my arousal warred with my contempt. It made it so much easier to turn off my brain when he pushed me like this. He demanded, and I resisted, but deep within my core, I knew it was so I could justify it to myself in the morning. The way we were together meant I could hold on to my hatred for him even as he consumed me body and soul.

If he stopped now, it would take everything in me not to beg for it.

From the corner of my eyes, I could see him unbuttoning his shirt with one hand. His wrist flicked seamlessly at each of the black buttons, revealing the sculpted muscle of his abdomen inch by inch.

His gaze had turned dark.

"I'm sorry, Gideon," I murmured and meant it. The man who knelt in front of me, worshipping me with his hands beneath my dress only moments ago, was gone.

"I know, little Queen," he said.

He thought I was talking about the alcohol. But I was talking about my ragged soul. I would never be able to give it to him, not fully, not like he wanted. It was cracked when the Cards had killed my mother and fully shattered that day Tayna had died because of my silver. I had nothing left to offer anyone except my blood.

Gideon shrugged out of his shirt, only loosening his grip on my hair for a moment so he could pull the sleeves down. When I moved to press myself up, he was there again, pressing me fully into the desk. The warmth of his palm between my shoulders had me sucking in a breath.

His chest was all carved lines and broad planes. As I suspected, every inch of his tanned torso glowed. His tattoos started at his shoulder and ended at his wrist. The Ace of Hearts on his shoulder was the only piece with any color. The rest were black swirls and designs looping over his skin, some in languages I couldn't name. Scars, as well as the tattoos, flecked across his body. Some were new cuts, though they'd already healed over, thanks to the silver.

He placed the pocketknife next to me on the desk, and I jerked at the noise of it hitting the wood with a smack.

I heard the clatter of his belt as he pulled it free from the loop and tossed it to the floor. The sound of his zipper coming undone was the only warning I got before the head of his cock was at my entrance. I gasped as he ran the tip through my slick folds, teasing along my center.

He was gloriously naked. His shoulders were rounded over me, one hand gripping my hair, pressing the side of my face into the desk, while the other gripped his length.

His eyes flared with determined desire when they met mine, aligning our bodies along the desk until they were perfectly flush. My backside pressed against his hips. My spine curved along his stomach. His breaths hot against my cheek.

And then he rocked so deeply inside me that I knew nothing except him.

10

Lissa

My body ached the following morning when I woke. It was not the delicious sort of after-lovemaking soreness. It was the complete-and-utter-mess soreness that left me groaning as I rolled onto my side.

The sun was already well into the sky, and I blinked against the rays that filtered through my yellow curtains.

My head pounded from the goddamn tequila. My lips were dry and rough from the stubble of Gideon's beard, even though the scratched part had healed. I could feel the rat's nest on top of my head that was my hair. The mascara Enver had applied caused my lashes to stick together as I tried to blink them open. And the evidence of my night with Gideon was dried on my thighs.

The silver healed injuries, yes, but that didn't stop all discomfort. After my first time with Gideon, I'd been terrified I would remain a virgin forever. Turned out, the silver in my veins was smart enough not to heal certain injuries. Nor could it fix dehydration after a night of alcohol.

I felt at my shoulder, just above the Queen's tattoo. At least the small cut he'd made had healed.

Gideon had fucked me before drawing my blood with that small switchblade so he could take from me in other ways, licking the silver from the small slice. He hadn't cared one bit about the tequila in my blood. And once his body practically glowed from the power of my silver, he'd fucked me again.

Afterward, I'd snuck back to my room—the scraps of my dress clutched around me like a makeshift blanket. Every shadow from the Queen's wing in the mansion had me worried someone would witness my walk of shame. The Queens already whispered enough behind my back about Gideon's silver pet. I pictured Ariya's laughing face outside of the compound when she'd realized I was drunk and "in trouble."

Fucking Ariya.

But the halls had been blessedly quiet. Save for Kenji, who'd been waiting by my door and pushed it open without a word.

I was grateful he was on duty tonight. It spared me from the judgment I knew I'd find in Laykin's eyes—that cunning, curious gaze that dared me to justify sleeping in my enemy's bed.

Well, rather, fucking in my enemy's bed.

Gideon and I never had sleepovers. He asked. Sometimes he even pulled me into his chest and held me there. But it was too intimate. Staying the night with him felt like too much of an admission that I did, as he insisted, belong to him.

What would my mother think?

The sudden, unbidden image of her made anger bubble hot, my silver sparking at my fingers. It was rage at myself, at my own stupidity for landing in this goddamn situation.

My mother had refused to bow to the gangs. She'd refused to be one of the Cards. And they'd killed her for it.

"Run, Lissa," she'd whispered to me, shoving me out the back door. "Run!"

And I'd obeyed. Not a hint of my silver sparked at my fingers then.

No, I was useless and helpless as a child. I'd trusted my mother to protect me and to protect herself.

But I'd looked over my shoulder just in time to see a man in a leather jacket with a King emblazoned on the sleeve hit my mother so hard across the head, her silver blood had sprayed against the glass of the window.

And when she'd launched herself at him, he'd grabbed her by the throat. Squeezing and squeezing and squeezing.

I'd tripped over a rock then.

Hit my head on a sharp edge as I fell.

By the time I'd regained consciousness, it was well into the night. Not even her silver blood sprayed across the window remained. No doubt, one of the Cards had wiped what they could to take it with them.

I'd waited.

I'd waited weeks for her to return, hiding even at the sound of the ravens fluttering in the trees.

My mother hadn't returned.

And I knew.

Even at ten, I knew.

She was dead.

The King might have dealt the fatal blow, but Ishmael had ordered her death. Ishmael had hunted her down. Ishmael had coveted her silver.

And no matter how many times Gideon said he wasn't his father, insisted even that he had despised his father and only avenged his death out of a desire to protect the Cards, I couldn't fully give myself to Gideon and the Cards. I wouldn't. For my mother, I would never.

I would rather see it all burn.

Dragging myself to the bathroom, I didn't even bother looking in the mirror as I ran the water in the tub. I brushed my teeth. That was the first stop, bent over the sink like someone who'd just returned from a desert island.

The bathroom was all white tile so, naturally, I'd covered it in plants to try to liven it up. I ran my fingers over the pothos ivy I'd strung from the ceiling. It had grown nearly out of control, like a curtain around the front of the porcelain standing tub. The light from the small windows spaced high around the walls filtered in like rays of morning gold.

When the tub was full of steaming water, I slowly curled my body into the warmth, groaning at the near-pain of the temperature. Just how I liked it. After living on the streets for eight years, hot water never stopped feeling like the most precious of gifts.

I was just sudsing up my washcloth when there was a knock on the door.

Kenji poked his head in, his eyes cast to the floor. "I'm not looking. I promise I'm not looking, but you missed breakfast, so I brought you something." He placed a pastry on the counter. "Oh, and something else from Karadin you may need." He placed two pills next to the pastry that looked like the ones for pain relief. "Oh, and something else you'll definitely need." He placed another pill next to that. A contraceptive.

He closed the door just as quickly.

I would have yelled at him if he hadn't brought me a pastry and if my head weren't pounding so badly.

Instead, I sank below the water and stayed there until it felt like yesterday, and the memories of my mother had burned away from my skin.

Finally, I couldn't deny the day any longer. There was a bonfire to prep for, after all. And someone I needed to see.

Throwing on a simple cotton dress and my cloak, I met Kenji in the hallway and grumbled, "Thank you for the pastry. We will not speak of the rest of it ever again."

He snorted. "Yes, ma'am. As per usual, Queenie."

And then spun on his heels to avoid my scowl.

It was Laykin's day off, so Kenji and I wandered the grounds together in relaxed company. Kenji fist-pumped most of the Cards we passed with cheerful recognition. A lot of them were part of the company that had returned just last night with Gideon. It was a relief, even to me, that all of them had returned. It was just as much a relief that they hadn't found anything—no rebels to challenge them in the northern mountains. No blood on their hands, at least this time.

Karadin wasn't alone when we entered the clinic.

Another Silver was there for his weekly donation. Male Silvers were less common than females, but Gideon took them all in. The male Silvers donated once a week just like the rest of us, but they were also expected to join the ranks to defend the compound. I gave him a small smile but didn't know him well. He didn't smile back, just looked at his guard as if I might explode into a ball of silver right then and there and kill them all. I thought about telling him that it only happened when people made me exceptionally mad so he better stop making that face... but then I thought better of it.

Kenji fist-pumped a couple of Spades who were leaving, their rations of silver blood clutched in their palms.

"You're welcome," I grumbled when they left without even looking at me.

"If you want people to like you, you've got to loosen up a bit, Queenie," Kenji said, elbowing me and gesturing with his chin to my crossed arms. "You look like you might stab someone's eye out if they dare talk to you."

"The urge only strikes when I'm around you," I snapped, but he just laughed.

"You're definitely a heart." He sighed. "A viper in the hen house."

"In the rooster's bed," I said with satisfaction.

He balked at me. "You did not just make that joke. One, you said you didn't want to talk about it ever again. Two, I should probably report you just for saying that."

I waved a hand. "Go ahead. I'd say it to Gideon's face. He likes my *fire*." I rolled my eyes.

"Hellcat's more like it." Kenji twined his fingers behind his head and leaned back against the wall. "You're lucky I like you, you know that?"

"You're lucky I like *you!*" I countered. "Otherwise, you'd be a charred little silver pile of ash by this point."

He laughed so hard he snorted. "Let's hope little scaredy pants in there can't hear you. Otherwise, he won't sleep tonight."

The Silver emerged from the clinic room as if on cue, and Karadin followed close behind, a pursed look on her face which suggested they could, in fact, hear us in that room. The Silver—some Club—didn't look back as he left.

"Sorry." I shrugged at Karadin, only slightly sheepish for being overheard.

"You're lucky I like *you* both." She waved a finger between us. "What do you need?"

I cringed. "I think that means I'm probably not on the right foot to ask for a favor. But I need a favor."

"I already gave you two favors this morning," she said dryly. "And one yesterday."

The vial of extra blood. The pain medicine. And the contraceptive.

Right.

"I need another vial of blood?" My voice tilted up at the end as if asking a question as I gazed at her sideways.

"Absolutely not, Lissa," she hissed.

"Not even a full one!" I countered. "And it's not for anything"—I looked at Kenji—

"nefarious. It's for the bonfire tonight. I want to help."

"You probably still have tequila in your blood." She crossed her arms.

I glared at Kenji and said tightly, "Word sure does travel fast here."

He threw up his hands. "How do you think I weaseled the pain meds!"

"Karadin," I said evenly, "I don't need a full draw. Even half a vial would be great. And no one's going to drink it. It's for the bonfire, so even if there's still tequila in my veins, it'll be fine."

I didn't add that Gideon had had a taste last night, too, and was still breathing as far as I knew.

Her nostrils flared. "Did you even eat breakfast?"

"Yes!" I nodded eagerly. "Kenji brought me breakfast!"

I tossed him a look that hopefully conveyed that he should not ruin this for me by telling her it was only a pastry.

His brow cocked only slightly, but he said nothing.

"And you swear you won't drink tonight?" she asked sternly.

"On the Cards," I agreed, more than willing to curse the Cards but also pretty sure I'd be swearing off alcohol for a long, long while.

"Half a vial?"

I shrugged. "If you think that's all that's safe."

"I think that's all that's safe." She nodded.

"Half a vial it is," I said, pressing onto my thighs to stand. The room went black at the edges as I stood, blinking against the twinging headache. Stupid hangover. But I was not about to be the one to ruin this.

The pounding behind my eyes passed after a few seconds, so I followed Karadin into the clinic room.

11

Lissa

We left with a nearly full vial of blood, and I clutched it happily in my palm.

"You gonna explain?" Kenji asked as we walked onto the grass.

The day felt warmer around us than yesterday. Was it truly almost springtime? The breeze off the ocean was chilly, but the sun promised a beautiful day. The smell of fresh-cut grass stung my nose as I inhaled. The world felt more alive today, somehow, than it had in weeks. Or maybe that was just the hangover wearing off.

"I just want to help out at the bonfire tonight." I shrugged.

"Since when?" Kenji asked.

"Since now."

Large barracks tents were being set up on the lawn. There was a warehouse building where a lot of the men slept, but between the returning Cards and the new recruits they'd brought with them, the compound was limited on space. Only suit Cards like Kenji and Laykin were allowed beds inside the mansion. Even then, they shared a room.

"Why does this feel like it's going to end badly?" Kenji sighed, his head falling back toward the sky.

"You said you wanted to go," I countered as we reached the door to the mansion.

He held it open for me, the space inside smelling like leather and floors freshly cleaned with pine.

"We don't have to go," I added.

"That's not the point, Lissa," he said as he began marching up the staircase behind me. "The point is, I don't trust you."

"You didn't stop me from drinking that tequila."

"The tequila was less of a concern than the pickles you handed over to some street hookers and their pimp."

I froze at the top of the staircase.

And that stopped him short.

"Lissa—"

Silver burned at my fists as the hollow look in that girl's haunted eyes loomed in my swaying vision. She and I weren't so different really. That easily could have been my life if the Cards hadn't taken me. If I hadn't been born a Silver. If Tayna hadn't found me after my mother died. Even now, our paths were more parallel than it seemed on the surface. Yes, I lived a life of privilege where she did not. But I also lived a life with limited choices, just as she did. We did what we had to do to survive. Though her opportunities for survival were significantly more dire.

"Lissa," Kenji snapped, grabbing me with his monstrous hands.

And I gasped as I heard the snap of my silver energy and felt the release of it with his touch.

"No—"

But it was already too late.

"Did I hurt you?" I grabbed his hand.

He pulled it away. "It's nothing. Just a little burn."

"No, I—" I reached for him again.

But he shook his head. "I still have my silver ration from this week."

I opened my mouth to object again, but the guilt stopped me from saying more. I clenched my fists at my sides, tucking them beneath my cloak. My neck burned with the shame of my silver. There was a good reason people around here were afraid of me. I hurt people—especially the people who loved me most.

But then I realized I was holding a vial of blood. And Karadin had taken more than she'd said she would. I held an almost full vial. Kenji could have just a little of it. I opened my palm between us and extended the vial in offering.

"No, Lissa..." Kenji said.

"You can just take a little," I said, noticing he still shielded his hand from my view. "How bad is it, Kenji?"

"I shouldn't have said that, Queenie," he said instead. "I didn't mean that."

"It doesn't matter. I should never have let my silver slip like that."

"I deserved it."

"Kenji," I growled.

But he shook his head again. "I'll enjoy your silver during the bonfire." He grinned, one of his locks falling onto his forehead.

I thought of the Silver Card at the clinic who'd been terrified to be in the same room with me. He wasn't wrong. We'd made fun of him, yet my silver *was* volatile. I hurt people, and it didn't matter that I didn't do it on purpose. I was a freak, different from the Silvers. Other. Dangerous. Wild.

I stared resolutely at Kenji for a few seconds longer, wanting to press the issue to make it right, somehow, that I'd hurt him. He was a few stairs below me and still nearly as tall as me.

Finally, I gave in, turned, and continued toward the Queen's corridor. "We'll talk about this later," I said over my shoulder.

Though I'd never been to it, I knew which room belonged to Enver. She shared with Ariya, and they'd had the same room for as long as I'd been at the compound.

The large black-painted door was closed, so I knocked.

The distinct sound of scuffling rattled the space behind us, but no one answered.

I looked at Kenji. He shrugged.

I knocked again.

Silence.

"Enver?" I called, pressing my hands against the door to get closer to try to hear.

There was more scuffling.

Did she need help?

The door flew open, and I nearly fell onto her as she held the door ajar and poked her head out. She looked how I'd felt this morning.

Maybe I wasn't the only one who'd found themselves a tequila bottle.

Her silver-blond hair was tied in what used to be a braid but strands of it fell haphazardly around her face and the hair at the top of her head was pushed forward, making it fluff up in the back. She looked like she'd just been rolling around on the ground.

"Lissa!" she said surprised, her large silver eyes going even wider.

"Hi." My response was hesitant as I wondered if I'd made a huge mistake. Sure, she'd helped me last night. And she'd even stood up for me when Ariya had made those nasty comments, but that didn't mean we were friends. My face felt heated. Was I getting lightheaded again? "I just—"

There was a clatter over Enver's shoulder.

"Is everything okay?" I asked, trying to peer around her.

She hugged herself closer into the doorframe. "Totally fine! I'm just doing some cleaning. Everything's messy."

"Oh, come off it," Kenji said, easily reaching over my head and pushing the door. "You're not even doing a half-decent job at covering for him."

He forced the door wider until Enver was forced to let it go. It swung open, revealing a shirtless Laykin, struggling into his black cargo pants.

I failed at hiding my shock. My jaw fell open as a laugh cracked in the back of my throat.

"Quite the day off, I take it," Kenji yelled to him. I smacked him in the chest and then quickly recoiled my hand. After the stairs, I shouldn't be touching anyone. But Kenji was laughing, and the silver wasn't sparking at my fingers any longer.

Enver's blush was a pretty pink on her cheeks. "Well"—she sighed—"I wanted to talk to you about it last night, Lissa, to make sure it was okay with you that we were getting to know one another. But then you'd been drinking, and it just didn't seem like the right moment with Gideon…"

"Oh"—I put up my hands—"I don't mind!"

So many things were starting to make sense. She'd been trying to talk to me because of Laykin. She'd been buttering me up with that bonfire offer, hoping it would make me more likely to accept their relationship.

"It's so sweet of you to ask our permission," Kenji said, his words syrupy thick as he leaned forward near the crook of my shoulder.

"I don't need your fucking permission, Jones," Laykin snapped at Kenji from the bedroom.

"You just seem so close with them," Enver said quickly to me. "I wanted to be respectful. And Laykin speaks so highly of you…"

"I bet he does." Kenji snorted.

"Of course I do," Laykin barked, coming up behind Enver.

"Stop being an ass," I growled at Kenji. And then I looked at Laykin. "Really sorry we interrupted. We didn't know—"

"Then what are you doing here, Liss?" Laykin asked.

"I—uh—" I produced the vial of blood. "I just wanted to help," I explained, looking at Enver whose already wide eyes had gone even wider with surprise, "with the bonfire tonight. And say thank you for last night."

Enver seemed shocked into silence for a moment, but then she said, "That's really, really nice of you, Lissa."

"Great. Well, here you go." I extended the vial to her. "We'll leave now."

"Actually," Enver said, pushing the vial back to me. "Why don't you keep it?" I waited for her to tell me she didn't want my dirty silver blood anyway, now that the secret was out about her and Laykin. But instead, she said. "You can use it to start the first fire tonight. That much of your silver will have it burning all night."

It was an honor, of sorts, among the Queens to start the first bonfire. It was a symbol of status. It was almost always Enver who lit the flame. She was extending me yet another kindness—another attempt to include me.

And I realized I wanted to be included. I didn't even care that her motivations for being nice to me may have started with Laykin. She was extending an olive branch.

So I nodded and tucked the silver back into my pocket. "Tonight then."

She grinned. "Tonight."

Laykin gripped the door. "This was lovely," he said. "Now go away."

And slammed the door in our faces.

It only made me smile more until I turned and caught a true look at Kenji's hand.

The side of his palm was so red that it was almost purple. It was blistering and shiny where it was oozing a clear fluid.

I cursed and pulled out the silver, leading him toward his room. "Drink some of this right now, Kenji."

He shook his head, shrugging me off and walking ahead of me. "It's fine, Queenie."

"It's not fine," I said, unable to keep the panic from my voice. I had seriously hurt him. Yes, he'd said something dumb, but that didn't mean he deserved to have his hand fried for it. "Take it." I shoved it at him. It was the only way I knew how to truly make amends for what I'd done. Giving him my blood was the least I could do.

"Lissa, stop." He pushed it away again.

"What is wrong with you?" I asked. "Why won't you take it?"

"I have some back in my room. It's not that bad," he assured me.

I didn't believe him for a second. "Kenji, what the hell?"

We reached the next corridor over where the men kept their

quarters. It was the hall for the Queens' guards. Kenji and Laykin were three doors down on the left.

I snatched Kenji's key from his hand and opened the door myself so he could continue cradling his blistered and pussing hand. God, he needed the blood quickly to ensure it wouldn't heal with any bacteria inside it.

"Maybe we should go to the clinic," I said, closing the door behind us as he went to the mini fridge next to the single, simple desk. The room was sparse. Oak furniture and two full beds. I'd been in here dozens of times. It always smelled like sweat and lemon and cedar.

"You're fussing, Liss." He rolled his eyes, pulling open the fridge with his good hand.

"Why won't you take some of my blood?" I asked again. "We should at least clean it before—"

Kenji withdrew a small vial of blood, popped the lid with one hand, and downed the contents.

He closed his eyes as if in relief as the blood began to work its way into his veins. It happened quickly. Within a matter of seconds, I could see the burn beginning to give way to new skin.

"See," he said. "Just a little blister."

"Don't avoid my question." I glared. "Why wouldn't you take my blood?"

"Queenie, come on." He sighed, sitting on the edge of his mattress covered in a sage green quilt. "Just let it go. You needed it for the bonfire."

"I can tell you're hiding something."

"If you want to make up for singeing my hand, you'll stop pestering me," Kenji leaned back on the bed until I could see the muscles of his abs flexing through his gray shirt. He kept the hand that had been burned tucked across his stomach.

"Why won't you tell me?" my voice grew quieter as I realized there was a secret here that I would not like. But I couldn't let it go.

"Gideon would have my hide." His response held a hint of remorse.

"But it's something about *my* blood."

Kenji flopped onto the bed, scrubbing a hand over his face. I understood I was asking him for a truth he wouldn't give me. I was his Queen to serve. But he was a Card above all else, which meant he was loyal to Gideon.

"Fine. I'll ask him myself."

12

Lissa

I spent the afternoon in my room, re-reading *The Count of Monte Cristo*, one of my favorites.

But I'd finally had enough and moved to the window to watch the bonfire preparations. I had the perfect view from my window, overlooking the water. Men walked back and forth from the trucks carrying large armfuls of wood. The pits were set up along the cliff's edge, the wood piled so high atop each one that the fires could burn all night, even without the help of silver.

I spotted Enver pointing at one of the piles and ordering around some lower-level Diamond. She would have made a fantastic mistress for this mansion when it was in its prime. I could imagine her wearing her fancy clothes and ordering servants around while she spent her days planning events just like Mercedes in my book.

Kenji lounged in the chair near my bed, reading *Pride and Prejudice*. His large frame was curled into the plush armchair, his back resting against one arm with his legs slung over the other. A turquoise pillow was propped behind his back. He'd draped his jacket over the back of the chair, leaving his Jack of Hearts tattoo on full display. It was the only one he had. The deep red ink nearly blended with his skin, which only made the tattoo somehow more striking.

He set down his book, shaking his head. "Why would Charlotte agree to marry that idiot Collins guy?"

I laughed, turning away from the window. "She felt like she didn't have a choice."

"People back then were so freaking weird." He set the book aside.

I looked back at the window where Enver was now fixing one of the wood pits herself. "I don't think a lot has changed."

Kenji opened his mouth but then paused, cocked his head and shut it again. "At least we got rid of the whole marriage for property thing," he finally said.

That was true.

People still had children, of course, mostly by accident. Certainly not on purpose if they were part of the Cards. Gideon sent pregnant women and children away from the compound. It was rare, but it did happen every so often. The Queens, well, the Queens were expected to take precautions. This was not the place for a baby.

Some people outside of the gangs chose to share their lives together. It made sense. It was the same reason Tayna and I had banded together as children. There was safety in numbers. It was easier to survive with someone to help.

But love?

Love was complicated and not worth the hassle for most, especially not the men of the Cards. They went to the clubs at night and found pretty women willing to get on their knees. Females always flocked to the Cards, especially the ones who needed money or who were addicted to silver. Those were a dime a dozen. A night of pleasure was enough for both involved and then back to work the following morning.

People were still weird.

But Mr. Darcy and romance was decidedly dead.

Before I could think about Tayna, I moved to the door, swinging it wide. "Time for me to start getting ready," I said, gesturing Kenji to the hallway.

He stood but let his shoulders drop, and his mouth opened in a whine, "Door duty."

"I let you read in here all afternoon," I countered.

"Only because you felt sorry for burning my hand," he said, walking into the hallway.

I leaned against the door and smiled. "Take my pity while you have it, and be grateful." I closed the door with a soft snick.

"At least give me the book!" he called through the door.

So I did, opening it just enough that I could reach my hand through the crack and drop the book on the floor.

Just because I was feeling generous, I added, "I'll be quick."

"You always say that!" he said, but I'd already closed the door again.

Then I got to work. I used hot rollers on my hair, an old set that had been in the house. I'd experimented with them for weeks and wasted a ton of silver before getting just the right waves in my hair. Large enough that they fanned across my face when I ran a brush through them. What else was I supposed to do to kill time in this place? Now, the process was easy, and my fingers expertly wrapped the strands until every piece of my hair was tucked in the rollers.

While they cooled, I did my makeup. I was much less skilled at that but managed to apply a ring of black around my eyes and a crimson-red lipstick that matched the color of the tattoo on my arm and the crest on my cloak.

I chose a simple black knit dress and flats. It wouldn't matter what I wore underneath the cloak. It would be too cold tonight to take it off, even with the fires burning. Plus, the Queens would be expected to arrive in full attire. All of the Cards would be showing off their suits tonight, especially the high-ranking members. And, though my clothing was simple enough, I clasped the diamond paved necklace Gideon had given me around my neck. I liked the idea of it sparkling against the blaze of fire.

By the time I took the curls out and ran my fingers through the strands, it was dusk. The noise from outside was beginning to grow. Bottles clinked. People laughed. And I could hear music from a speaker starting up on the lawn. It was a song with a heavy bass that made me think of the bodies I'd seen moving together at the club all those years ago.

I opened the door to find Kenji sitting against the wall, his legs stretched out and braced on the other side of the hallway. He was slumped and reading, nearly finished with *Pride and Prejudice.*

"You can't possibly be ready," he groaned. "I only have four more chapters. It's the good part!" And then he got a look at me, and his eyes went wide. "You look—"

"Let's go, lover boy." I laughed and said with an old-world flourish, "Your Lady Lizzy will wait. Your Queen Lissa will not. I have to light the bonfire, after all."

"Right, fine." He closed the book and stood quickly. "Look at you, looking all put together and fancy. Two days of friendship with Enver has done you some good."

"We're not—"

I thought of how she'd come to my aid over the past few days. She'd most likely done it to impress Laykin and get on my good side, but I didn't begrudge her for it. She invited me to participate in the bonfire and helped me get ready when Gideon arrived home last night. No one had ever extended kindness to me like that. Female friendship was something I'd only read about in my books, but I allowed a small smile. The idea of having a friend didn't sound so bad actually.

So instead of finishing my sentence, I said, "You know what? It has." And walked down the hallway and out of the house.

His cackle of laughter echoed behind me.

13

Lissa

Outside, the last of the sun was dipping behind the cliffs as the ocean waves crashed.

Enver sashayed over to me as soon as she saw me walk from the house. "I was just about to come up there and get you!" she said. "We have to light the fires soon."

She wore a silver dress beneath her cloak, and her silvery-blond hair was woven into intricately small braids that crossed over her head almost like they were forming a crown. She looked every bit the Queen.

"You've outdone yourself, Enver," I said, scanning the lawn.

At least ten bonfires were spaced evenly along the cliffs. The kitchen staff worked away on steaming grills of meat. Some brought out more plates filled with bread rolls and cheese and lettuce and tomatoes and onions.

I dragged my gaze away to look at the bar counter, where beers were already being passed around from kegs, and the music I'd heard upstairs was so loud that I could feel it beating in time with my heartbeat.

Enver clapped her hands together. "I know!" she squealed. "Isn't it amazing? And the night's just getting started."

My eyes landed on Gideon then.

He was impossible to miss. Where everyone around us was dressed in black, he wore a cloak of deep red. A pearl white "A" with a heart underneath bordered along one of his shoulders. But it wasn't just his outfit; Gideon was a magnet in the crowd. His dark hair fell around his face, only framing the cut of his stubble-covered jaw. He laughed, and the flash of teeth was enough for my heart to skip a beat. He practically glowed. And maybe it was from the silver, but I couldn't seem to look away.

He caught me watching and held up his glass to me in greeting. His eyes tracked over me before he mouthed, "Later."

He was talking with his second, Dia, the King I avoided at all costs. Tall and lithe, Dia was like a snake in the grass, his green-yellow eyes tracked up my body in a way that made me shiver and pull my cloak around my shoulders. I'd never liked him and mostly managed to avoid being around him. If Gideon was the executioner, then Dia was his blade, always happy to strike. Dia led the recruits on the compound, training the new guys and handing out their assignments once they'd proven themselves.

Yes, Gideon and I would talk later when Dia wasn't hanging around. I had questions for him, after all. Specifically about why Kenji wouldn't touch my blood.

In the meantime, I let Enver lead me to the pyres built along the cliffs.

"It's time," she said to the DJ booth as we passed, and the Card controlling the speaker began to lower the volume of the music. Enver grabbed a microphone.

My stomach dropped with the urge to run as hundreds of eyes began turning to focus on Enver and me.

I glanced at Kenji, clenching my fists to keep from panicking. The last thing I needed was to burst into a Queen-sized ball of silver in front of everyone.

But then Enver clasped my hand, and I realized she wasn't afraid of me at all. Not even Kenji dared to touch me most of the time, but Enver squeezed my fingers like we'd done this a million times.

She didn't say anything. She simply turned on the microphone, and said, "Hello, hello!"

Her smile was so bright, I felt compelled to follow suit and forced a grin to pull at my lips, even though I was looking out at a sea of faces that made my stomach flip under my cloak. As a former street rat, I took comfort in the shadows rather than in the spotlight. Crowds made me itchy, and being the center of attention made me feel like running.

"For those of you who are new, the bonfires are a way for us to celebrate the safe return of our Cards," Enver said, her silver eyes dancing as she made eye contact with some people. She seemed to know them all, whereas I knew almost no one. "It's a small token of our thanks to the Ace and his suits for keeping us safe. It's also a welcome celebration for those of you who have been given the opportunity to join our community."

A few men let out whoops from the crowd.

I resisted the urge to roll my eyes at that. Keep us safe? More like, kidnap us from the streets. It was one of the reasons I'd always had an issue with Enver. The Cards were anything but saviors.

But I bit my tongue. She'd helped me last night. I would do the same for her tonight and not ruin her moment.

"Tonight, Lissa Metarro, our Queen of Hearts, has graciously agreed to light the first flame with her silver—"

A deep male voice in the crowd grumbled, "Better back up."

And my smile faltered.

Kenji whirled to try to see who had spoken.

But Enver just squeezed my hand more tightly and said, "Let's get this party started!"

Cheers erupted, but my eyes tracked to Enver.

Maybe this was a bad idea.

Whoever had spoken was a dick, sure, but he also might have been right.

"Go for it." Enver nodded toward the wood pile over her shoulder.

I looked back at Kenji but couldn't find him in the crowd, so I gave Enver a nod, uncapped the silver, and poured it over the wood.

The moment of truth.

Enver handed me a matchbox.

I struck a flame.

And threw it into the fire.

The blaze rose instantly, heat blasting across my face. The flames licked skyward, silver and blue, thanks to the blood.

Now I did take a step back.

But the flames settled into a slow melodic dance to the beat of the wind coming in from the sea. It burned hot and stretched higher into the sky than any normal fire, but it wasn't out of control. It was beautiful. I felt my heart dance with the flames as I watched it reach into the sky.

Enver laughed, and then other Queens stepped forward around the cliff's edge, emptying vials of silver onto the piles of wood and lighting those, too. Ten silver and blue bonfires danced into the sky in a matter of minutes.

The DJ began playing music again, and the party came alive as people dispersed to dancing and drinking and eating and, well, more private things.

Laykin came up and offered me an awkward high-five. "Good job." He nodded.

"Thank you?" I looked over my shoulder. "Where's Kenji?"

Laykin shrugged. "I told him I had your back for a minute. Probably wants food."

"Should we dance?" Enver asked, excitement lighting her eyes.

I'd never actually danced before. Sure, once or twice around my room when I was sure I was alone. But never in a crowd.

I watched the throng of swaying bodies, their hips connected and arms raised. The silver and blue light from the bonfires cast long shadows against the ground. The music was so loud, it drowned out all sound of the waves, and the warmth from the fires had me sweating and itching to pull the Queen's cloak from my shoulders. I hesitated.

Enver's gaze slid to me, tilting her gaze as if beckoning me, her hips swaying to the rhythm of the music.

"I need to speak to Gideon first," I finally said.

I'd been waiting to talk to him ever since the weirdness with Kenji this morning. He'd been holed up in meetings all day with his kings. There was no way I would have dared to barge in on them. I was brash but not suicidal. During the day, Gideon was business. Tonight, he owed me an explanation.

"I'll walk you," Laykin said quickly.

I didn't bother objecting but said to Enver, "Sorry. I'll make sure he's back quickly."

She waved me off. "Go, go. There's plenty of time for dancing, and I'll hold you both to it."

Either Kenji or Laykin were required to watch me at all times outside of my room. It was for my protection. It was their duty. Really, it was all just overkill so Gideon could flaunt how well he took care of his Queens. Enver's guards stood over her shoulder even now as she danced her way backward. Their eyes scanned the crowd as she was swallowed up between writhing bodies.

Laykin and I broke through on the other side of the dancing, heading in the direction I'd seen Gideon and Dia earlier.

The space was empty now.

I looked at one of the guys nearby. "Have you seen Gideon?" I asked.

His eyes widened as he realized who was speaking to him. He shook his head, his cheeks shaking with his jerky, nervous movement.

I sighed and moved closer to the house.

"Did Gideon go inside?" I asked someone else, who shrugged.

"He's around back," a high-pitched female voice purred from the shadows.

Ariya was leaning against one of the marble beams around the house. Her arms were crossed over her chest from beneath the layers of her cloak. Her silver eyes glinted in the night like a cat's. The graffiti on the walls behind her was lit neon against the light of the fires.

"Thank you." I sighed and began to walk around the house.

But she called after me in a singsong voice, "I wouldn't go back there if I were you."

"What?" I stopped short, Laykin nearly running into my back.

"It's probably a bit messy by now." She smirked, and it wasn't pretty or friendly.

Was he with someone else?

Ariya's words only made me quicken my steps around the expansive mansion. I passed men who were adding new tags to the sides of the exterior walls and others who were huddled in shadows, vials of silver glinting as they tipped them into their mouths.

As I rounded the corner of the mansion and got farther away from the DJ's music, I could hear strange noises. Dirt sliding. Grunting.

Was that... moaning?

"Lissa..." Laykin's voice was a low warning. He'd heard it, too.

But I wasn't about to turn back now, not with Ariya's cryptic taunts.

If Gideon was hiding things from me...

I imagined him with another Queen, pressed up against the side of the mansion, touching her like he touched me. It made my insides twist and my silver flare at my fingers. The feeling was primal, and I hated it, but it only pushed me to walk faster.

The back of the house came into view, and Laykin put out a hand to stop me.

"Don't—" I skirted his fingers before he could touch me.

It was too late anyway. I'd already seen the horrific scene laid out in front of me.

14

Lissa

I kept walking toward Kenji, who held a beefy guy by his arms while Gideon struck him, landing blow after blow.

The guy's jacket had been stripped from his body. The sleeve of his shirt was cut away in ragged strips. Blood flowed down his arm from where his Card tattoo had been carved from his body. The cut was so deep, I could see the ravaged muscle. He was slumped in Kenji's arms. I wasn't sure he was conscious anymore.

And still, Gideon hovered over him, repeatedly driving his fists into the man's torso. He was already littered with damage.

"What the fuck!" I demanded, lifting my cloak and skirt to run toward them.

Damn these flats I'd worn. They just got in the way of running.

But my voice had been enough for Gideon to halt. He wiped his upper lip with his forearm. Red blood was sprayed on the side of his face. Not his blood.

He was high on silver. His eyes were pure rage as they landed on me. His pupils were so wide and dark, I couldn't even make out the flecks of blue in his gaze. It felt like I'd interrupted a feral animal in the middle of an attack and had now drawn its attention.

The silver meant Gideon's blows would have landed on the man that much harder.

Kenji dropped the man, who fell to the ground in a heap, and said, "Here we go."

"Go back to the party, Lissa." Gideon was on me in a second, grabbing my shoulders and spinning me around. The absolutely insane first thought I had was that he was probably getting blood on my cloak. The next was that my silver was burning in my chest. Or maybe that was my heart, another piece cracking free.

"Don't touch me!" I whirled around and shoved him, realizing too late that silver sparked at my fingers.

Horror struck me.

But Gideon didn't burn. He didn't even seem to feel it as he absorbed the electricity at my fingers. He was so high on silver himself that it was acting as a sort of shield.

He didn't even take a step back, and I found myself looking up… and then up some more to meet his dark gaze. His hair clung to his forehead, where sweat beaded along his brow.

I didn't like what being this close to his face made me feel, so I shoved him again and then ran toward the man on the ground.

Kenji caught my arm with a gloved hand before I could kneel to touch him.

I couldn't even tell what his Card rank had been. Gideon or Kenji had cut the tattoo out so meticulously, only bloody flesh was left.

Digesting the utter shock of it, I realized I might be sick. I moved to cover my mouth, but my limbs were shaking so badly I froze.

Being at the compound for five years, I'd seen violence. This wasn't the first time or the last I would see the blood of a Card on Gideon's hands. Hell, I'd seen Gideon throw Cards from the cliffs if their sins were bad enough. There were certain things Gideon did not allow: Lying was at the top of the list tied with hurting one of his Queens. But men were foolish and power-hungry, and there were always those willing to test the limits.

"Why?" I uttered.

I found myself turning from the horror to look between Gideon and Kenji, seeking some reason in their gazes to explain this violence.

"Because he doesn't know how to keep his mouth shut." Gideon spat on the man. Literally spit on him and then kicked him for good measure. The man grunted.

"Stop!" I yelled.

It was hard to tell his age between all the swelling around his face and neck, but he had a full-grown beard that maybe once had been blond before all the blood.

My knees buckled, but I forced myself to stand.

"Lissa," Kenji said, his voice surprisingly stern. "You need to go back to the party."

Laykin grabbed my shoulder. "Ace, I didn't know—"

"Do not apologize to him!" I cut Laykin off. "I deserve an explanation."

Suddenly, my questions about my blood seemed so trivial and small.

The man on the ground groaned and rolled over onto his shoulder. "Don't you dare fucking move," Gideon warned him sharply.

I pulled from Laykin's hold. "Explain yourself," I snapped to Gideon.

"I don't have to explain anything to you," he sneered.

"This was supposed to be a celebration!" I threw out my arms. "This was supposed to be fun! And you're back here beating a man to a pulp? Is that your idea of fun, Gideon?"

He stalked toward me and grabbed my chin with one of his large hands, jerking my face up to look at him. A flash of that feral creature had returned to his eyes. "Who do you think keeps this place safe so you can have your *fun*, huh? You read your books and eat your pastries and judge me all you want, little Queen."

"I didn't ask to be here," I seethed, my voice low. "You took me, Gideon. You kidnapped me from my life, from my—"

"Oh right." He laughed, actually laughed, the sound so crisp and clear in the night's air. "Because you had such a life before! Living on the streets and starving."

"You had no right!" I screamed. "If it weren't for you—if it weren't for you—"

But the words died. Because they were untrue. I wanted to blame Gideon for Tayna's death, but it was me. It was my fault. If it weren't for *me,* he'd still be alive.

"Pathetic." Gideon shook his head, his grip loosening. "I see how you burn with hate even though you are safe and well-fed and well-fucked. I see it. But at the end of the day, I make the hard choices. For you. Even still. Because if some prick in the crowd makes a jab at you, he isn't just insulting you. He is testing my control. He is drawing a line that makes me question his loyalty. And if I can't trust him, he can't be a Card. Period."

His words dropped into my soul like coins in a mental bucket, each one hitting with a shrill *plink* into my skull.

I do it.

For you.

Some prick in the crowd makes a jab at you.

I looked down at the man again, still groaning, blood and saliva running from his mouth.

This was the man who had told the crowd they "Better back up." It was this man.

"You're a monster." I pushed at Gideon's chest. "Let me go."

Surprisingly, he did, dropping the hand gripping me.

I went for the man, to help him. I could give him my blood.

But Kenji stopped me, stepping in front of my path. "Go back to the party, Lissa."

I shook my head. "Let me help him."

The anger I felt made my throat feel stuffed with cotton.

"You can't help him," Kenji's voice was low. "Even if you give him silver."

And I knew they were going to kill this man. They would kill him, and Kenji was trying to spare me from seeing.

But I couldn't leave.

"Come on." Laykin came up behind me, placing a tentative hand on my shoulder.

"No," I said. "I'm not walking away from him."

It was about so much more than this man. At this moment, it was about who I wanted to be and what I wanted to stand for. I didn't want to be the girl who ate pastries and read books and did nothing when I could help someone. As Gideon said, I'd been that girl for far too long.

If only someone had done something the day Tayna died.

"Lissa." Gideon's voice was a low warning.

"No!" I said more forcefully, and silver sparked at my fingers.

"Dammit, Queenie," Kenji said.

But Gideon had had enough. His eyes were raging at my defiance, and I knew I was pushing him, but I didn't care.

I didn't care.

I felt just as wild as he looked, and I was not going to back down.

I locked eyes with Gideon again. "No."

And that fast, he had me pressed up against the back wall of the house, my cheek pressing into the graffiti art that spanned the wall.

"And what are you going to do, little Queen?" Gideon's voice was lethal calm. "Huh? You gonna blow this whole clearing with your silver? Kill me? Kill Kenji? Kill Laykin? All for this asshole piece of shit?"

And I faltered.

The silver sputtered at my fingers as my resolve sputtered with it.

He was right. What could I do? I couldn't control the silver in my veins. It was a wild, untamable thing that only erupted and caused damage in its wake. I couldn't save this man, not without killing everyone behind the mansion with me, which just so happened to be the three men I cared about most in this world.

Even if I hated them all at that moment.

My hands relaxed and the silver fizzled completely.

"Good girl," Gideon said against my ear before releasing me.

Kenji's shoulders visibly sagged as he said, "Fucking hell, Queenie."

I choked on a sob, realizing he had reason to be afraid. I'd been on the edge of fully letting loose. For a minute there, my control of my silver was tenuous at best.

I began shaking with holding the force of it in.

And so I ran, panic settling into my chest.

At some point, the flats fell off my feet, and it didn't even matter. The sand and grass on the cliffs weren't rough. But my feet were soft from so long tucked in cozy socks or under warm sheets or within pretty shoes. It had been so long since they'd been cracked and bloody because my sneakers were too small or I didn't have socks to wear.

At the edge of the cliff behind the clinic and well beyond where the bonfires had ended, there was a rocky path that switchbacked down to a small cove of beach sand. It was surrounded by the rocky cliff face on either side. It had once been a private beach for the wealthy residents who owned this mansion. Now, hardly anyone ever went down here.

Except me.

Kenji followed me. I knew he was following me, always close enough to keep an eye on me as I pushed through the crowds of people and zigzagged through the dancing. I didn't stop running until I reached the rocky path to the beach. Then I regretted not having my shoes, but it didn't stop me from gripping the railing and continuing down until the bonfires and the light faded. At the bottom, it was just me and the moonlight and the waves.

Kenji stayed at the top of the cliff face. He would wait for me there.

The cove was the one place I could be alone, aside from my rooms. It was safe. Safe for me to be and a place to keep others safe from my silver. The waves on either side were too treacherous for boats and the cliff face above was surrounded by Cards. With the sound of the crashing waves around me, drowning out all other sound, silver light streamed from my fingers as I fell into the sand and choked on a cry.

I truly was a useless fool.

This silver at my fingers was a curse. Tonight, I'd wanted to use it to help someone, to save a man's life when the reality was that I had almost ended numerous lives instead. I would have decimated a 10-foot area. That man, and anyone else within it, would have been burned beyond help.

I'd called Gideon a monster, but he was only the monster my silver allowed him to be.

Kneeling fully into the wide sand of the beach, I tipped my head back and screamed, knowing the silver would be streaming from my skin into the sand in ribbons of power. I'd seen that power gleaming in Gideon's eyes tonight.

What would he have done if I had used my silver?

The thought was like a dagger to my gut because I knew he wouldn't have hesitated to do what he felt was necessary, just as he hadn't hesitated to beat that man to a pulp.

Gideon had mocked me for being a spoiled Queen, who ate pastries and read books and did not make hard choices.

And he was right.

I was a coward, afraid of my own silver.

I was a useless prisoner.

But maybe...

I thought of my conversation with Madam Cartenoth. She believed in me. She believed I could be more than a Queen for the Cards. I thought of the rebel group Phenola had talked about. I thought of Tayna's dreams and a world beyond this city.

Tayna would be ashamed of me if he could see me. I was ashamed of myself.

I had made a mistake these past few days. For a moment, I had allowed myself to belong. But I did not belong. And maybe Madam Cartenoth was right. Maybe I didn't have to live like this.

Maybe there was another option beyond this compound.

And maybe I wasn't brave enough to use my silver tonight.

But maybe I was brave enough to make another choice for myself.

By the time I stood from the sand, the silver had fully drained from my veins, and I was exhausted. My limbs felt heavy as I dragged myself to the steps back up the cliffs.

But the makings of a plan began niggling at my mind.

And, for the first time in five years, I began to dream.

15

Lissa

In the days after the bonfire, I avoided Gideon, and he didn't seek me out. I didn't let myself admit that his seeming indifference stung. But I only allowed the sting to serve as further proof that I had fallen so far from the girl I'd been on the streets. That girl wasn't a street rat; she was a feral cat who would have clawed out eyes if it meant protecting herself and Tayna.

The small bite of rejection should be nothing compared to the aching realization that I should be so much more than the house cat I had become. Sometimes hissing but lacking any real claws.

The most frustrating part of the realization was the waiting. The continued pretending.

But I told myself it was just the first move in this game of Cards I had decided to begin playing.

It wasn't so bad. It wasn't all pretending. I'd gotten over my anger at Laykin and Kenji. We hadn't discussed the night of the bonfire, but I knew they felt bad. What could any of us possibly say to make it okay? At the end of the day, they were soldiers following orders with no more control than me.

And I didn't want to spend my final days at the compound hating them.

So I fell into an easy rhythm with Enver and Laykin and Kenji. We ate meals together. Enver painted my nails while I read her the first act of *Othello*. I even acted out the voices as if I were on a stage. She'd only scrunched her nose and said she didn't understand half of it but had liked how it sounded. It was a start, I supposed.

The worst part was the guilt that started to slowly gnaw away at me for enjoying all of these little moments. Who was I to share a pastry with Kenji and discuss the ending of *Pride and Prejudice* on a Tuesday afternoon while people down the road were dying of starvation? The laughter had died on my lips and the pastry had crumbled on the dryness in my mouth.

Days passed like this: the highs of friendship and the lows of my own gluttony. My every action left me feeling like a fraud.

Finally, on the sixth day, I couldn't take it anymore.

Enver and I were in my room. I was curled in the chair reading, and she was sitting at my vanity organizing my jewelry, which was just an excuse for her to try it all on.

"I can't even fucking believe he gave you diamonds," she said, her fingers stroking over the paved necklace like it was a lover. The reminder of the gifts from Gideon had me tensing. "I have a ruby from the—"

"Does it bother you?" I blurted.

She stilled with her shoulders hunched over the box.

"I just—" I found myself wishing I could take it back. It was so much easier when we were just pretending and trying on jewelry and gossiping about which Cards were interested in which Queens. But I said, "I just sometimes feel like none of it matters."

She closed the jewelry box and turned to me.

And then I realized this may have been a glorious mistake because she could also go running straight to Gideon. If he knew I was thinking about life outside of this compound, he would have me under lock and key. My already-tight leash would become a shackle to this place.

She folded her hands into her lap. They sank into the fabric of the pink summer dress she wore today. It was hardly even spring, but it had been sunny out today, and I'd learned that for Enver, fashion was life.

But... was it enough of a life for her?

She sighed, her bright-painted lips pursing. "You know I'm not from the city?"

My eyebrows rose. I'd never known someone who wasn't from the city. Or at least, hadn't known them in the way that I could talk to them as I so desperately wanted to talk to Enver.

She nodded. "I grew up on a farm about three days south from what I remember. My parents grew oranges and grapefruits and some pecans, I think, too. Gideon's father, Ishmael, offered them enough money to support the orchards for at least a decade. I was six. My family was a big family, which is rare these days, I know. They had four other children, and I was the middle child, and the only Silver, and I was always getting into trouble anyway, so..."

She didn't need to finish her sentence. Her family had accepted Ishmael's offer and sold their daughter to the Cards.

She paused for a long moment before she said, "I still remember the farm. I remember lying in the dirt, staring up through the trees at the sun and watching the white petals from the flowers on the trees fall around me. I've never seen snow. But that's what I imagine snow looks like." She shrugged, the small gesture revealing a fragility closer to the surface than I'd realized. "I'm happy here. I have friends and Laykin"—she blushed—"and good food, and I get to throw parties and wear nice clothes, and that never would have been my life otherwise. But I've been here for twenty years, and I know that money has run out by now on that farm. And sometimes... I wonder."

"Did you ever go back?"

She shook her head. "It wouldn't... It wouldn't be a good idea. My father was a religious man. He didn't approve of the Silvers. He thinks we're abominations of God's will. My mother didn't let him hurt me. And he left me alone for the most part. But I think they were relieved, honestly, to see me gone."

"I don't remember my dad," I admitted. "My mother raised me until she died when I was ten. She was a Silver, too. She loved science. I remember she had all these science books around the house. Tons of them!"

"I guess that explains why you love reading," Enver said.

But I laughed. "Absolutely not! Those books were so freaking boring. But she loved it. And she kept this huge garden in our backyard. It wasn't a farm, and we weren't rich, but we did okay. The Cards killed her. She refused to join a gang so Ishmael sent a group of his men to our house. I lived off the garden she'd planted for as long as I could. I waited in the house by myself for weeks. I kept hoping she would return, like her death was all just some big misunderstanding. But, eventually, the plants began to die so I had to leave. Tayna found me a few weeks later digging through a trash can."

Enver and I sat in silence for a while. My book was forgotten next to the chair.

I thought of that day when I'd first met Tayna. He'd seemed larger than life—like Peter Pan jumped from the pages of Neverland. It felt like he could do anything. I was the one with silver, but Tayna was the one with dreams. He'd offered me his hand, told me it was okay, and gave me a chunk of bread. I'd taken the bread. And then his hand. And it had been just that simple to trust him. It had been the most natural thing in the world.

"I—" Enver started, and I looked at her, only to find her eyes bright with pain and unshed tears. "I remember that boy," Enver said to me, a tear slipping down her cheek onto her full lips. "I still have nightmares about your screams sometimes." And she was crying. "I'm so sorry for it, Lissa. I'm so, so sorry. I think I avoided you for all of these years because I couldn't bear to look at you. It made me feel too awful, and I'm just so sorry. And you asked me if it bothers me, this life, and I can stomach the life. But I will never, never be able to stomach the choices I made that day in the market. I wish every day that I could change it."

I found myself wiping away my own tears. All I could do was

shake my head, the words were so clogged in my throat as I felt more tears spill onto my face.

"Maybe," my voice was raw. "Maybe none of us get through this without getting a little bit broken."

Her smile was wet. "I think that's why I want to be your friend," she said. "We broken things need to stick together."

I nodded, let out a pitiful laugh, but then nodded again.

And I still felt the deep desire to leave this place. But this day, this day did not feel like a waste.

16

Lissa

The next day was another draw day.

As I arrived at the clinic with Kenji and Laykin at my heels, Karadin met us in the lobby with a raised eyebrow.

She looked at Kenji and Laykin and said, "You two, stay." Then back to me. "You. With me."

"Yes, ma'am," I said, grinning as I followed her.

She'd already laid out the syringe packages and butterfly needle in a neat row on the counter, the vials for collection stacked behind that. I was just one of many Queens who would be in today for their weekly draw.

"You look good today," Karadin noted as I pulled my cloak from my shoulders and settled into the straight-backed chair, propping my arm up on the rest.

"It's all the pastries and tequila," I noted wryly, and Karadin shot me another dry look that had me saying, "Kidding, kidding!" The last thing I needed was a report on Gideon's desk that I was unable to draw on schedule.

We still hadn't talked since the bonfire.

I watched him leave in one of the trucks yesterday afternoon with Dia and a couple other high-ranking Cards. If they'd returned, it had been well into the night after I was asleep.

It wasn't abnormal for us to go days without seeing one another when he was at the compound. We weren't a couple... we were... well... We'd never discussed it. I never wanted to, and he never pressed the subject. It was a symbiotic relationship. A release. Even if it was one born from anger and malice. It was either sleep with him or kill him, which wasn't entirely off the table, either.

My rage still simmered from the bonfire.

But the thought of him niggled something deeper within my chest, too, and I resisted the urge to rub at it. He was a tyrant. He was a murderer. He'd killed that man. I knew, after I ran, he'd killed him. It was a heavy weight I now carried on my shoulders. But there was also hurt. Hurt that he'd so easily let me run away, as long as I was close enough that he could reel me back when he needed something.

And that hurt, yes, and the hurt was terrifying.

Because it meant Gideon didn't just have control over my body and the blood in my veins, but a deeper part of myself that I didn't want to give to him. I'd never intended to give it to him. Yet...

Karadin secured the band around my bicep with swift fingers and then opened the needle from the packaging.

"Do you want to watch?" she asked.

"Yes," I said.

And she eyed me before eyeing the veins in my arm. "Pastries indeed," she grumbled, feeling for the vein. "There she is," she said before easily slipping the needle into my skin.

I always expected it to hurt more. My body always wanted to react to that initial sting as if it would only get worse from there, but it was gone as soon as the needle had settled into my vein. The first vial began filling with blood.

"Reading anything good?" Karadin asked.

"Just *The Count of Monte Cristo* again." I sighed.

"Have you read the entire library yet?"

She attached the second vial.

"Most of the fiction section," I admitted. "Though, I don't like those fast-paced mystery books. The women are all the same. And so are the plots."

She laughed. "I haven't read them."

"Don't," I said. "What are you reading?"

"A book about the history of the human species according to early 21st century philosophers." She shrugged. Karadin was a non-fiction reader, which meant we shared book titles but not book conversations.

Third vial.

"Any good?"

"They got quite a bit wrong. It seems they truly believed humans were simply a linear species."

"And we're not?"

"Oh, not by a long shot."

Fourth vial.

She moved to pull the needle from my arm, but I said, "One more."

Karadin hesitated.

From the moment after the bonfire when I'd fallen onto the beach sand and screamed at the sky, I'd known that I would no longer be a grieving Queen locked in a mansion. That meant starting to secure a stash of my blood and willingly agreeing to help Phenola and Madam Cartenoth with their cause.

"Please Karadin," I pressed. "One more."

"Lissa," she sighed. "I can't keep helping you."

"One—"

She pulled the needle from my arm before I could argue further and covered it with gauze. It would be healed in a matter of seconds.

"I'm sorry." Her lips were pressed into a thin line as she leaned against the counter. "It's too risky out there right now. The Cards are monitoring everything so much more closely with this new rebel group Gideon's concerned about. Now is not the time to get caught with an extra vial on you."

"I would never tell them I got it from you," I promised, keeping my voice low.

She sighed and leaned back against the counter, crossing her arms over her chest.

"They're not letting anyone leave the compound right now anyway," she said.

And I sat up straighter. "Wait, what?"

She nodded. "I just got word last night." A piece of her hair had fallen into her face, and I realized that while she'd said I looked good, she looked tired. Her ponytail sagged on her head just like her shoulders. Doctors were rare commodities, and she had the most medical knowledge at this place.

"Did something happen?"

"Lissa..."

"Did the men come back last night?" suddenly I worried they hadn't. What if they were still out there and that's what had everyone so worried?

But she nodded. "They got back late. They're fine. Nothing a couple of vials of silver couldn't fix, at least."

"So there was trouble?"

She pressed the hair back from her face. "You know I don't know details about what happened out there."

"But you know something,"I pressed.

"Gideon is fine, thanks to your silver." She quirked an eyebrow at me. "But Dia had a deep gash in his side. Baxter took a bullet to the arm. Reggie had a couple of bullet wounds in his chest. He's lucky he lived."

"Where are they?" I stood from the chair.

And swayed.

I reached out a hand to steady myself on the counter.

"Whoa," Karadin put a hand on my shoulder. "Slowly," she cautioned. "Let me get you some juice."

She left the clinic room.

Which is exactly what I hoped she'd do when she thought I was lightheaded.

Without missing a beat, I slipped a needle and two empty vials into the pocket of my cloak.

When she returned, I had just got them tucked away and out of sight, as she handed me the small paper cup filled with orange juice.

"Thanks," I murmured, taking a sip.

"Breakfast," she said in response.

"Promise."

"And the Cards are fine," she added. "Resting in their rooms. It was a long night."

"Get some rest yourself," I told her.

She snorted. "Find another doctor, and then maybe I can sleep."

Technically, doctors didn't exist anymore. There weren't colleges to study at. No one gave aptitude tests or residencies to put a student's knowledge to the test. No, Karadin relied on her books and her practice. She'd been mentored by a doctor before her, who had taught her most of what she knew.

"You should train an apprentice, at least," I said.

She sighed. "If these Cards would stop getting injured, then maybe I'd have the time."

I smiled at her and tossed the gauze into the disposal bin. The wound on my arm had healed. Only a small mark of silver blood on the cloth. "Or you could just stop trying to save them." I shrugged.

She gave me another one of her dry stares. "Don't tempt me," she said, and I thought I saw a glint in her eye that wasn't entirely joking. "Go eat some breakfast. I'll see you next week."

"Right." I headed for the clinic door.

But she grabbed my arm before I could leave and hissed in my ear, "And if anyone finds that needle and those vials in your pocket, you stole them. Got it?"

My eyes widened at her. She knew I'd taken them.

I bit my lip against a grin. "Of course."

The door opened before I could grab the handle, and Laykin stood in front of me. His eyes narrowed at Karadin and me, our heads bent together for only a moment before he said, "Gideon's asking for you."

And my heart seized.

But I said, "No."

"Lissa—" Laykin stalked into the room like he might drag me out. He paused before reaching me.

Karadin took a small step back.

Silver crackled at my palms as my anger flared. "I don't want to see him."

Laykin's nostrils flared. "Goddammit, Lissa, you're going to get me thrown off the cliffs."

17

Gideon

"She... what?"

My voice was level, relaxed even as I tented my fingers and leaned back in my office chair, meeting Laykin's eyes for the first time since he'd stepped into the room.

He was all formality with his chest puffed out, his hands clasped behind his back, and his shoulder blades pinched together. I bet if I stacked the pile of papers on my desk on top of his head not one would fall to the ground.

I normally didn't elevate the brownnosers in my ranks. I liked my men to be independent thinkers, not lap dogs. Especially my suits. Laykin had been one of the rare exceptions. As uptight as he was, he made up for it as if he were a self-sharpening blade in the palm of my hand. Both his mind and his muscles were well-honed, making him an ideal guard for my little Silver Queen. He wasn't afraid of the power that sparked at her fingertips and that made him unique. Valuable.

Yet he stood here in front of me now. A disappointment.

"She has declined to see you, Ace," Laykin repeated.

"And you... what, exactly, Laykin? Agreed to play her messenger boy instead? I gave you an order."

"Sir, her silver—"

I rose from my chair.

Not quickly. Or even suddenly, really.

But I had to bite back my chuckle at the quick flash of uncertainty that lowered in his eyes as I rose. Not quite fear. No, Laykin wasn't one to feel fear. But close.

He knew he'd failed me.

"Did you forget to take your silver rations today, then, Layk?" I drawled.

"No, Ace, I never forget—"

Of course he didn't.

"But she's angry, and I think it might be a good idea to—"

Before he could say another word, my fist connected with his face. I felt the crunch of his nose beneath my knuckles. And god, it felt good. His blood spurted, and he barreled over at the waist. But he really took it like a champ, especially considering the amount of silver I'd consumed that morning. He didn't even unclasp his hands from behind his back, just took a second to catch his breath before straightening out in front of me again. His head held high even as blood dribbled over his mouth and down his chin.

"You better not fucking be here when I get back," I barked, stalking around him and out the door.

A few Queens mingled with some of my guards at the end of the hallway. None that I particularly cared to recognize. They froze when they saw me marching toward the Queens' wing of the mansion, watching with wide eyes as I passed without acknowledgment. Their gazes tracked me until the shadows of the hallway swallowed me, and then the whispers began.

Let it be a show, then.

If she was going to disobey, then she'd get a spectacle out of me.

Laykin's blood was already beginning to dry on my knuckles. It cracked against my skin as I flexed my fingers. My neck strained against my rage. I'd had enough of Lissa's tantrums. It was time for her to let go of her past and take her place by my side, where she belonged.

I'd been patient.

When she'd come to the compound, she was barely a woman. And she was so thin and breakable. I'd known she was special. She would be a key ally for my Cards. But as she'd gotten older, as she'd grown into herself, as her defiance hardened into a fierce sort of fire within her soul, my desire to have her as my greatest weapon turned into a desire instead to have her as so much more. It was more than the fact that I'd taken her silver and her silver alone over the past five years. A piece of her had woven its way into the very fabric of my soul. She was no longer that scared little street mouse. She was my Queen. The only person who somehow managed to make me bow, even as I was ready to rage at her smart-ass for refusing my orders.

Kenji saw me coming down the hall from where he stood watch by her door, a book in hand.

"Ace—" It was all he got out before he was stepping to the side as I threw open the door.

It crashed into the wall, which had Lissa scrambling from the bed.

"What the fuck do you think you're—"

I caught her wrist as she tried to run. It wasn't like she had anywhere to go in this space.

One of her plants was caught in the tussle, though, knocking the pot sideways as dark soil spilled across her bright purple chair and onto the carpet.

"Gideon!" Her voice broke as I hauled her into my arms, tossing her over my shoulder so her round ass was next to my face.

I paused long enough to run my hand over her backside, growling softly as desire mingled with my rage. It took every ounce of my self-control not to run my hand beneath her shift dress and bury my fingers into her exposed, wet heat.

She squirmed against me, wriggling her hips, but I held firm to the backs of her thighs.

"Put me down!" she screeched.

"You should have listened, little Queen," I tsked, whisking her from the room while she continued struggling against me, her fists driving into my shoulder blades. But it only made me chuckle.

Until her skin began to burn, crackling with silver electricity.

"Dammit, Lissa!" I swore, dropping her onto her ass as the back of my shirt began smoking.

Enver opened her door to peek out into the hallway along with a few other Queens who were bold enough to watch along with their guards.

No one dared speak.

Lissa glared up at me.

My jaw clenched, tamping down on my anger.

I took a breath.

And smiled.

I let the smile turn into a flash of teeth that had fear lighting in my little Queen's eyes as I grabbed her upper arm and hauled her to stand, not even flinching as her skin burned against my palm.

"Big mistake, little Queen," I murmured close to her ear before yanking her down the hall back to my rooms.

18

Lissa

"Well, you clearly haven't forgotten our bonfire conversation," Gideon snapped as he slammed his office door closed and finally released my arm.

I turned on him, ready for this fight. My silver still flared at my skin.

Gideon's dark hair was mussed, his shirt unbuttoned at the top, still smoking at the shoulder, and there was blood on his knuckles. He looked feral. He looked like hell.

Good.

"Conversation?" I seethed. "You mean when you murdered a man?"

"I've murdered lots of people." Gideon shrugged, beginning to roll up the sleeves of his shirt as I took a tentative step back.

Even when he looked like hell, Gideon was formidable. It was in the set of his shoulders and the knowing glint in his eyes. It was the way he studied me so thoroughly and kept his chin slightly upturned.

"You don't get to shrug this off and avoid me until you think I'm over it."

"I'm not avoiding you." He leaned back against his desk, looking every bit like the panther playing with its food. "I just stormed into your room to collect you, didn't I? Made quite the spectacle in front of all your friends."

"Yes." I bowed dramatically in front of him. My bare toes slid across the carpet as I curtsied. "At your service, *Ace*." I only called him Ace when I was sneering it at him like a curse.

"Yet, here you are, defiant as ever." He quirked a brow.

"I have my priorities, too." I shrugged.

And he grinned, letting the monster show in the glint of his midnight eyes and the flash of bright teeth. "Mmm, I see. Not about an apology, then. You want something."

"I don't want anything from you."

"What is it, little Queen?" He leaned back in his chair.

Part of me wanted to demand what was stirring in his mind. Did he regret what he'd done at the bonfire? Was there a part of him that had understood why I hadn't wanted to walk away? If he would just let me in, maybe I could make sense of this life and justify staying here.

But he didn't. And he wouldn't.

He was stone in front of me, unrelenting and unforgiving. Even if a part of him hated what he had to do to lead the Cards, he would never admit it to me.

So I relented and said, "I've been told you're now requiring approvals for anyone who would like to leave the compound. I'd like to leave for my weekly trip to the market."

"No," he said shortly, his eyes turning from wicked to dark with anger.

It made me realize he had recently taken silver. No wonder he'd been up all night.

"I'll take Laykin and Kenji."

"Out of the question," he said sharply.

"Then I won't ask the question," I snapped, my tone growing sharper to match his. "I'm leaving."

It was as if I wanted to bait him. Maybe I did. My anger was bubbling hotly under my skin. Not just because he was preventing me from leaving but also because he didn't seek me out after the bonfire. He didn't try to explain himself or justify what he'd done to that man. He'd seen no problem with his actions and clearly hadn't called me here because he'd wanted to work things out.

He did more than just look at me then. He pushed off from the desk as I stood my ground in front of him. The large mahogany table stretched behind him like a dark ocean, and he was the wave cresting toward me.

"Do not test me, Lissa." His tone turned wicked as he leaned into me, mirroring my stance yet towering over me. "It's been a long night."

"So I heard."

His hand snaked out to wrap around my throat, just tight enough to hold me in place. "Why do you always have to challenge me?" he growled, his breath whispering across my cheek.

"Because you've caged me and put me on a leash."

"Now that's a tempting image." His words were a bark of laughter.

"Gideon—" I tried to pull away, but he held me. This wasn't what I wanted. I wanted to stand up for myself, not be reminded why it had been so easy to fall into lust with this man.

He'd hurt me. What happened at the bonfire had hurt me. And he didn't seem to care at all as long as he could still strip me naked and taste whatever part of me he desired. Most of all, I hated myself for wanting it.

"Please stop," I practically begged him as he moved around the desk to stand in front of me. His hands swept beneath my cloak, sliding it from my shoulders.

"I'm not the Prince Charming in your story, Lissa," he murmured as he began kissing and licking at my neck, bunching up the fabric of my dress as he sucked at my skin. "Don't ask me to be."

"I've always known you weren't," I murmured, feeling like he was plunging a dagger into my heart, regardless.

He tried to pull the dress over my head, but I pulled it back down until we both struggled with the fabric.

"Let go," he said in my ear. "Or I will rip this fabric and send you back to Laykin and Kenji in your undergarments."

"Wouldn't be the first time," I said through clenched teeth.

"Do you like that?" he murmured, still clutching the fabric tightly as he held my body close, at the precipice of his cresting lust and rage. "Do you like that everyone in this compound knows you're my little whore?"

I gasped and slapped him across the face.

He laughed, which only made my anger flare hotter. But I was pleased to see a red welt appear across his cheek for a flash before fading, thanks to the silver in his blood.

"I am *not*—"

He cut off my outrage then by grabbing my wrists. The suddenness stole my breath as he yanked me into the leather armchair, shoving me to sit.

"Stay," he ordered.

I stood right back up, following him. But he beat me to the door and opened it just wide enough to say to Kenji and Laykin, "You are both dismissed. I'll see to our little Queen today."

"Gideon!" I tried to move around him. I was not staying here with him today. Absolutely not. Not after everything he'd done and said.

He slammed the door and locked it.

"Gideon!" I objected again, but he grabbed my forearm, the dam of his control breaking. He held me in that vise grip and stalked to the door that connected his office to his room. "Stop!" I shrieked as he pulled me along with him.

He whipped me around so unexpectedly that my jaw snapped, my teeth clacking. He yanked me in close, leaning down so we were almost nose to nose.

"You seem to have forgotten a few things." His eyes were pure black. The beast was rearing its head, fueled by the silver. "So you and I will spend some time getting them sorted. It isn't up for nego-tiation."

"I want to leave."

"Lesson one: I own you." He spun me around and marched me through the door to his room.

As he shut the door behind us, I staggered back into the sterile space. Where his office was black, his bedroom was white. White carpets, white four-poster bed, white sofa in the corner, all accented with dark silver like the blood that gave him so much power.

"Lesson two." He yanked my dress down my arms, the fabric pooling at my feet as I gasped. "What you want doesn't matter."

The room was cold, and goose bumps pebbled my skin, my nipples already hard.

"Lesson three." He pulled off his belt, and I began backing up in earnest. Fear and, yes, arousal, spiked as he stalked toward me. The back of my legs hit the bed, and I braced myself against one of the four poster beams to keep from falling. He advanced on me, his pupils blown wide, but his steps unhurried. Still, he was on me in a matter of seconds. Each of his steps was about two of mine. "Lesson three," he repeated, grabbing my wrists and looping the belt over them until they were securely bound. "You are so much more to me than your body or your silver blood."

My eyes flew to lock with his, and his touch was gentle as he traced my lips with his thumb. His hand wound into my hair, and he gripped it tightly, forcing my head back as he kissed along my neck.

I let out a breathy gasp at his words and his fingers, all of it over-whelming.

"What am I, then?" I dared to ask, my chest tight. We were tiptoeing a dangerous line. It had always been that way with us. I kept my hate so close to my heart that it seemed they got mixed up with one another somewhere along the way. Fucking him was fine, but it was never supposed to be about intimacy. Now, he had stripped me bare, and I scrambled to keep clutching my anger. I didn't want him to take my anger. He'd taken everything from me. He couldn't have that too.

He made me feel like a fool every time I gave in to him, then threw it in my face at the bonfire. I couldn't keep living like this. It wasn't enough to have a full belly. It wasn't enough to be his. It wasn't even enough to have friends like Enver and Kenji and Laykin. Not if having it meant I spent my days doing nothing but wearing pretty clothes and reading stories and eating pastries and fucking at Gideon's whim.

He gripped my chin and brought our eyes to meet again. He said, "Stay with me," as if he could read my mind and knew where my thoughts had gone.

But my mind drifted as if I was outside myself. Seeing myself standing in with Gideon, tied with his belt, naked and vulnerable, and yes, aching for him. Despite all of it, I wanted him.

It made me want to cry.

But then Gideon swept me into his arms, one hand beneath my shoulders and one under my knees. He placed me on the mattress and said, "On your stomach. Hands above your head."

"Gideon—"

"Do it, or I'll make you do it."

I shivered but obeyed, rolling onto my belly and stretching my arms up, the sheets cool against my bare skin. He sat behind me on the mattress near my hip, and I jerked as his hands ran along my lower back and then up to my shoulders, gently massaging.

I groaned. I couldn't help it.

And then his hand landed on my ass with a sharp crack that had me screaming and bowing off the bed. His other hand between my shoulders pinned me in place. I struggled to get away from him on the bed, but he landed another blow, just as hard on my other cheek.

I sobbed against the pain with a strangled, "Gideon!"

He smacked me again and said, "Shhhh," as my tears began flowing in earnest.

I pressed my face into the mattress, muffling my screams as his hand landed on my inflamed skin in a steady rhythm. The pain became the only thing I could focus on. It was the only thing I knew. It was the first time he'd spanked me like this, but it wasn't the first time he'd used pain to get my attention. It felt like every time we were together, it wasn't enough for him just to have my body. Gideon wanted me—mind, body, and soul. When he said I was his, he meant every part of me all the way down to my thoughts.

The pain continued, but there was something else: desire. Gideon knew me. He knew exactly what I'd respond to, even when I did not. He'd pulled me back to this room and to him with his touch. The steady slap of his hand across my flesh was all I could focus on, and it was so easy just to give in to it. I found myself floating on a feeling of euphoria, even as my cries of pain continued.

When he finally stopped, I moaned into the bed. My body was sweaty from exertion and wet with need. Pieces of my hair clung to my forehead. My breaths came in small, heady gasps. The burn in my ass only fueled the ache low in my belly. I could feel the wetness coating my inner thighs as my backside tingled while my silver worked to heal the reddened marks.

Gideon pressed two fingers inside me, and I groaned. I didn't even have it in me to feel embarrassed.

"That's right, little Queen," he said as he rose from the bed.

I bit back another cry as he withdrew his fingers, leaving me empty. Was he leaving? But I turned my head to find him stripping instead.

He let me watch as he pulled first his shirt, then his pants from his body, the hard length of him on full display. My mouth parted slightly as I took in his cock from the thick base to the engorged tip, already leaking with precum. I couldn't drag my eyes away from the pure, masculine sight of him, even as my stomach clenched in fear as he stalked toward me. He crawled onto the bed, tenting over me until I could only see his powerful thigh over my shoulder.

He sat back on his knees, settled between my legs, and let out a groan of his own. "Fuck, you're beautiful." He leaned into me, leaving a trail of kisses over my sensitive, inflamed skin. "Though I wish your silver wasn't healing those marks I left so quickly. If I had it my way, every time you walked, every time you sat, every time you got dressed, you would think of me for a week." He ran a hand up my thigh, massaging my backside.

My flesh was still tender, and I let out a small cry of pain, but buried my face into the mattress as it turned into a sigh of pleasure.

"Look at me," he demanded.

It was a strain to turn my head to see him. My hands were still bound, but I managed to lift myself onto my forearms so I could watch him as he gripped the base of his cock and lined it up at my entrance.

He pressed into me slowly, gliding through my wetness inch by inch so I felt every part of him as he claimed me. It was blissful torture that had me pressing back, seeking, but it was a final rock of his hips that had him fully seated inside me.

The cry at the stretch of him barely left my throat before he was on top of me, gripping my neck. He held himself inside me. His legs pressed between mine, his stomach lined up along my back. One arm caged around me as the other held my throat, hovering over the bed.

"Lesson one?" he said into my ear.

"You own me," I rasped without hesitation. I didn't even think of denying it, not with him pressed into me so fully and stretching me so completely. There was no thought except for him and the pleasure of my body.

"That's right, baby," he said and began to roll his hips into me. The pace he set was languid, keeping my release close but not letting me go over the edge.

I gasped, trying to create more of that delicious friction, but my body was pinned beneath his hips as he ground his length deep within me.

"Lesson two?" he purred against my ear.

Anger flared in me, and I clenched my teeth against the rising plea in my throat.

"Don't make me ask again," Gideon said, his voice a whisper of breath tickling across my ear.

I gritted out, trying to keep my desperate pants at bay as he moved in and out of my body. "What-What I want doesn't matter."

"This is not going to be over quickly." He kissed along the side of my jaw, capturing the lobe of my ear with his teeth. All the while thrusting shallowly within me. "And if, *if* I let you come, it won't be until you're a puddle on this bed with nothing but my name on your lips and thoughts of my cock in your head. Do you understand?"

I choked on a sob but nodded mutely. I was aching for release.

But I knew with the silver in his blood, he wasn't lying when he said this wouldn't be over quickly. He could take me like this all day and still want more by the end. My body, too, would get tired, sure, but I would heal just as quickly. He could do whatever he wanted to me, and I would still be ready for more.

He would use me to his heart's content. With that realization, I relaxed into his hold, going limp on the bed, but he stilled. He stilled and then drove into me roughly enough that I gasped.

"Oh, little Queen," he said. "You're forgetting lesson three."

And then his hands reached around to toy with my nipples.

This. This alone would make me come. I felt myself cresting toward the edge and nearly sobbed with relief.

He pulled back just as suddenly. "Lesson three, Lissa?"

This was the hardest one for me to voice. It cut in a deeper part of my soul.

I shook my head, just trying to focus on the feel of him so deep inside me. That was enough. Right now, the feel of him pumping in and out of me was enough. It was all I wanted to focus on.

But then he stopped that too, leaving me empty.

"No." I gasped before I could stop myself.

He chuckled darkly, running a hand over my nipple again. "Lesson three, Lissa."

My body shook with need. My hips pressed back, searching for that delicious feel of him.

He only held himself farther from my seeking body.

The cold, empty air licked over my skin.

"Please," I whined.

He laughed, low and delicious.

Breathing heavily, I finally said between panting breaths. "I'm more to you... than my body... or my silver blood."

Just like that, he pressed back inside me, filling me once again, and I clenched around him. His body bowed into mine, his sweat-slicked skin sliding along my backside. I was so, so close to coming. God, I was close. He gripped the side of my face, tilting my head up and around for a claiming kiss while he continued driving deeply inside me, rougher now. His hand wrapped around my throat to hold me in place as his tongue swept into my mouth while his hips held me at the mercy of his length.

He pulled away just long enough that my eyes fluttered open, finding the blue of his irises watching me with rapt attention.

Our gazes locked as tightly as our bodies. The storm blue of his gaze filled my vision.

"You are everything," he breathed.

And it was his words—his words and his deep voice against my lips and his body pressed so securely against mine that sent me tumbling over the edge, falling into something without knowing what the end would hold.

But I knew, I knew that if I stayed at this compound any longer, he would own me completely.

19

Lissa

G ideon was true to his word.

He kept me in bed all day. He was inside me for most of it, but we did pause just long enough to have food sent up. We ate the spread of meats, cheeses, olives, and crackers in bed, not bothering with clothes.

I sat cross-legged, piling cheddar onto one of the salty crackers before shoving the whole thing in my mouth.

Gideon took one look at my puffed-out cheeks and lost himself to a fit of laughter, which only caused me to start laughing and spew cracker crumbs across the bed. Nothing made my heart flutter more than seeing Gideon's genuine laughter. It felt like witnessing something rare and precious and... mine.

"Whoa!" he said, covering his face with his arms to avoid the spray.

And I only laughed harder.

It took me minutes before I could swallow, and then I sputtered, "Your... fault!"

He launched himself across the bed at me, and I squealed as he rolled on top of me, kissing me deeply, his tongue dancing into my mouth. "Mmm, salty," he said finally, still grinning until his eyes were shining with so much blue that I lost myself to them. I traced my fingers up his arms and over his chest as he held me beneath him. My nails followed the path over the ridges of his shoulders, across his pecs, and down the hard ridges of his stomach.

"Gideon—" I ventured.

He rolled off me. "Don't, little Queen. Don't push this."

I sat up. "Please, Gideon. Please just let me go out like I do every week."

"No." He met my pleading gaze. "Can't you just trust me? For once, don't make me be the bad guy. Just let it go."

And I realized something: Gideon was afraid. Whatever had happened last night had been enough to truly shake him. It hadn't occurred to me before that this rebel group was anything more than an annoyance—another game for he and the Veiled to play. I thought he was being overly cautious, but maybe I was wrong.

"What happened?" I asked. "Explain it to me, then."

He buried his face in his hands. "It's—"

He stopped himself from saying *It's nothing.* And I waited.

"There's more of them than I thought," he finally admitted. "And they have more silver than any of the other groups I've seen so far. I don't know where the hell they're getting this stuff. It's powerful. It like—fuck." He shook his head. "I wasn't prepared. And we almost died out there. Reggie's body was littered with bullets. Dia took one in the arm. We didn't have time to pull the bullets out, so they had to drive back like that. It's war. They're declaring war on my Cards."

Gideon's fists were clenched, and he had a faraway look as if he could see exactly what was coming, and it wasn't going to be pretty.

"There's a group out there who wants to kill us, and the best way to get to me is through the Queens. It's through you, Lissa. I couldn't live with myself if you—just give me time to get this under control. I need time."

I crawled toward him on the bed until I was on my knees behind him. I traced a hand up his back, and he tensed as if I'd startled him. I pressed a soft kiss to his shoulder, above his Ace tattoo.

"There's always going to be threats, Gideon," I said softly.

"Not like this." He shook his head.

"I can do more than eat pastries and read books," I pressed. "I can take care of myself."

"That wasn't fair of me to say," he admitted. It was as close to an apology as I knew I would get. "I want that for you, Lissa. I want you to be here. I want to know that you're safe. Out in that world, sometimes the thought of you here is the only thing that—I need it."

My throat closed in on itself as he pulled me onto his lap to straddle him. What could I possibly say to that? Here he was, opening up to me and being more vulnerable than I'd ever seen him. But those words *I need it...* But what about what I needed? I couldn't stay here, locked away. Not anymore. It was never what I wanted. It would never be enough for me.

But Gideon would not give me permission.

And if I couldn't get permission to leave for the market, how could I possibly get away with more?

I knew nothing I said would make him change his mind. He would be the bad guy if need be. He'd made that clear.

So I let it go. I cupped his face in my hands and kissed him gently until the worry lines on his brow smoothed away, and I felt him harden beneath my naked body.

Then I took his hand and led him to the shower.

Once inside, under the stream of hot water, I lathered soap into his hair before making my way down his broad torso and to my knees.

He was already hard.

I wrapped my lips around his length and got lost in the taste of him until the water ran cold.

Finally exhausted, we both collapsed into bed. My hair was still wet, but it didn't matter. He pulled me onto his chest, and we lay like that until the sun set.

Only then did I pull back, untucking myself from the bed.

He gripped me harder, keeping me in place.

"Stay." That one word was as close to begging as Gideon Valmontry ever got.

I hovered over him in bed. He was truly beautiful. The sharp angle of his nose. His high cheekbones with the hint of color in them. Thick eyebrows that matched his wild mass of dark hair. My eyes tracked over each of his features to his jaw. His tongue flicked out to graze his bottom lip, and I couldn't help myself. I fell into him. Our mouths connected, and he pulled me closer.

But this was not a kiss to begin something.

This was a kiss to say goodbye.

Because I couldn't stay. Staying would mean making a different sort of choice. I couldn't be what he wanted, sitting at this compound day after day, waiting for him. I couldn't be his docile little pet without choice and without a purpose aside from my blood.

I couldn't stay here eating pastries and reading books and playing dress-up. Not when I could do more to help people outside these walls. I could be something better for Madam Cartenoth and Phenola and other kids like Tayna and I had once been. I would never forgive myself if I let go of that rediscovered dream. I couldn't accept it or ignore it anymore.

I had rediscovered my claws.

"Stay," Gideon said again.

But I shook my head. "I can't."

And he let me go. He let me slip from his bed and wrap myself in my cloak as I moved to the door.

The hallway outside was dark and quiet. Gideon had dismissed Kenji and Laykin. And just as I'd hoped, he didn't think to call them back as I left.

The first stop I made was to my room. I needed to draw more silver from my veins. I hadn't done my own draws in years since I was using those crappy needles in the loft with Tayna. But I would need to work quickly to ensure I had as much time as possible.

My vanity became my makeshift blood draw station. I unwrapped the needle and two vials I'd swiped from Karadin's clinic that morning, carefully laying them on top of the wrappings to keep them clean.

I didn't have an elastic band so I wrapped a hair ribbon around my upper arm instead, feeling for the vein against the dim light of my room.

The trick to inserting a needle into your skin was to fool your mind. It didn't hurt. Not badly, at least. It was more a mental game than anything. Stabbing yourself required you to get through a lot more mental hurdles than simply placing the needle on your arm. So that was the way I started. I placed the needle on my skin, right where I knew the vein was. From there, all it took was the slightest bit of pressure, and it slipped under the skin.

An exhalation of breath was the only indication I gave of any pain.

The hardest part was done.

I attached one of the vials to the butterfly needle and watched it fill with blood. It refracted against the dim light of my room. The dark blood glistened with its telltale silver sheen.

Once it was as full as possible, I switched to the second vial.

By the time I removed the needle from my arm, mere minutes had passed.

I held up one of the vials. I needed all the silver I could get for what was ahead. Pleased with my draw, I stood.

And the room swayed.

I gripped the vanity and cursed. I hadn't eaten enough today for two blood draws. If only I had a leftover pastry in my room. Normally, I did, but my day with Gideon had thrown a wrench in my routine. I didn't dare risk a trip to the kitchens. If I ran into someone, they would wonder where my guards were, and my plans would be dead before they even began.

My only choice was to wait for the room to level out before packing my small sack with the vials of blood, a few of my jeweled necklaces to sell, all of the coins I had, a change of clothes, and a blanket, just in case I needed to sleep on the ground. With the final space in the bag, I packed the few precious books I could carry: *The*

Count of Monte Cristo and *Where the Red Fern Grows*. I looked around the room at all of my plants. Hopefully, Enver would care for them. Maybe they would even give her this room to herself. And Laykin could become her guard.

And I'd have to leave the stuffed turtle behind, too. The books from the loft and the turtle were almost enough to make me rethink my plans. They were the only memories of Tayna I had left. Could I leave all this behind for the dreams of a couple of lonely street rat kids on a park bench?

Yes.

I could do this.

That thought gave me enough courage to walk out the door and not look back.

I left my Queen's cloak behind, folded on the bed. That would be enough of a note for Gideon. Instead, I opted for one of the large wool shawls, a dress of thick cotton, and my black slippers. I wished I had a pair of sturdier shoes, but I'd never needed them at the compound, so the slippers would have to suffice until I could find a different pair.

Guards patrolled the mansion grounds. I watched them from the corner of my window, waiting until they'd just passed the front door to begin sprinting.

I raced down the hallway to the double staircase, keeping my steps light as I flew down the stairs.

The front door clicked open with a soft snick, and I held my breath for any noise. Hearing none, I bolted out the door.

I ran onto the grass, lifting the hem of my dress so I could keep a steady pace without tripping.

The white glow of the overhead spotlights illuminated the lawn. My heart pounded in my ears from adrenaline, making my hearing unreliable. I glanced over my shoulder twice, sure I'd heard footsteps approaching, only to find empty space and dark.

I made it to the side of the mansion where the Cards kept their vehicles in a large hangar warehouse. The Humvees here mostly ran on silver, so they wouldn't need keys to start the ignition. I'd never driven one before, but it couldn't be that hard. I'd seen Kenji and Laykin do it a million times.

Except it was that hard.

I slid into the front seat and wasn't even sure how to turn the car on.

I tried to remember what I'd seen my guards do. Did they push a button? Or maybe turn a dial on the side? I tried that, and the windshield wipers began to flap. And then I couldn't figure out how to turn them off. And I ended up turning the headlights on instead.

I slammed my hands against the wheel, which only beeped the horn.

All of the guards on shift would now be alerted to someone in a vehicle.

I cursed—out loud—glaring at the wheel. What did more noise matter at this point, anyway?

This was just great.

The door next to me flew open.

"Fu—"

Kenji covered my mouth with a hand. His hazel eyes were wide. "What in the hell are you doing?" he hissed.

I glared daggers at him because I couldn't very well explain with his hand pressed tightly over my mouth.

He reached around and turned the lights and the windshield wipers off before looking over his shoulder and carefully lowering his hand.

"Are you insane?" he demanded.

"Maybe..." I admitted sheepishly. My plan had been far from solid, after all. It was made in the spur of the moment, lying in bed with Gideon. I realized that if I didn't leave now, I could stay in that bed forever and allow myself to be the perfect little house cat he wanted. When he was on top of me, inside me, it was too easy to give in to him.

"Let me guess"—Kenji sighed—"you were planning an escape to a certain shop with tea and trinkets."

"I can't stay here anymore, Kenji. I can't be Gideon's little pet my whole life. And Madam Cartenoth and Phenola need my help," I pleaded, trying to make him understand.

He swore under his breath. "I knew you were giving them blood." He shook his head. "How much?"

There was no use denying it at this point. "About a vial a week," I said, my voice small.

He swore again. "Gideon has killed many people for much less, Lissa."

I pictured that guy on the ground that he'd beaten to a pulp for making a sly comment about me. Of course Kenji was right.

Aside from killing a Card or a Queen, sharing silver outside of the compound was just about the worst offense I could think of. Whoever controlled the city's supply of silver controlled the city, and Gideon did whatever it took to stay in control. It was why he hadn't glanced twice at Tayna's mangled body the day he'd taken me.

That thought alone made me even more resolute about leaving.

"Please just let me go, Kenji," I begged.

"And what exactly is your plan, Queenie?" Kenji quirked an eyebrow at me. "If you can even get the car started, that is."

"I know the route there!"

"Uh-huh." He nodded. "And you were just going to drive and wave at the guards on duty at the gate and, what, hoped they missed when they pulled their guns to shoot your tires?"

"I thought these trucks were bulletproof," I grumbled.

"The windows and frames are bulletproof," he clarified. "The tires are just regular old rubber, I'm afraid."

The frustration boiled over in me then, and I gripped the steering wheel and shook it as if I might break it off the car. "Dammit!" I screamed. It wasn't so much that my plan was full of flaws, as Kenji so eloquently pointed out. It was that I seemed to be incapable of doing anything except getting myself caught.

"Watch it," Kenji warned. "Don't want you blowing up the whole car."

And that was when I realized I wasn't helpless. I had my silver. I had my power.

I gripped the steering wheel again and let the tiniest hint of my silver flow from my hands into the wheel. It wasn't hard when I was already so worked up.

The car sparked to life, the engine rumbling, and I laughed, glancing excitedly over at Kenji only to see his expression fall.

"Queenie," he sighed.

"I can do this, Kenji," I said before he could say anything else to sway me to get out of the car. "Please let me do this. Just let me go."

Instead, he said, "Slide into the back. You're not fucking driving. If you want to learn to drive, we can tackle that on a different day. For now, I need you to hide."

I stared at him dumbfounded, trying to process what he'd just said.

But then he said, "Move," and I crawled into the back, huddling behind the passenger seat. "And if we get caught," he added, looking back at me, "I realized you were gone and was dragging your ass back here. Understood?"

I nodded vigorously, and he shifted the car into reverse.

"I just fucking know I'm going to regret this," he said, pulling out of the compound and toward the guard's station.

My heart began beating erratically. I was actually going to do this.

I was leaving.

I was *leaving*.

20

Lissa

The compound was quiet. Only the expected patrols were outside. The headlights illuminated the gate and the four men at the guard stand ahead of us. One stepped into the road as we neared. He had his hands looped around his black jeans.

Kenji slowed as we approached and rolled down the window.

"No one's allowed out," the man called.

"I'm a Jack," Kenji called back. "Suits have exception." He rolled up his sleeve to show his tattoo. "And I need to do reconnaissance after the attack today. It can't wait."

"Reconnaissance?" the guard asked.

Kenji looked the man up and down. His lip curled. The guy was a Four of Spades, which meant he was hardly worth a second look around here. He'd barely begun to prove himself.

"What's your name?" Kenji asked the guy, who, to his credit, stood a little straighter once he saw Kenji's tattoo.

"Briars," the guy said.

"Well, Briars, if you want to call your commanding officer, I'd be happy to discuss the details with him. You, however, don't have the clearance."

The guy seemed to realize he'd gotten himself into trouble. And it wasn't good for a low-level Card to get on the bad side of a suit. Those guys didn't tend to last long around here.

"It's fine," Briars said, looking back to the others. "You're right, sir. Suits have exception." And then he called over his shoulder, "Open the gate!"

I sighed with relief, keeping myself hidden behind the seat even as Kenji drove out onto the main road. He didn't say anything and neither did I. Through the tinted windows, the world outside took on an eerily shadowed hue against the car's headlights. The cliffs above turned into trees and brush below as we descended into the canyon leading us into town.

Once I was sure we were well out of the eyeline of the compound, I crawled into the front seat. "Well, that was easy, thanks to you and your big macho suit tattoo."

Kenji didn't take the playful bait. His thick eyebrows were pinched together, his hazel eyes studying the road. I looked back out in front of us but didn't see anything that would make him so distracted.

I tried again. "Kenji, I'm so—"

"What the fuck is this, Lissa?" Kenji demanded.

I opened my mouth but couldn't form an answer. Kenji had always had a fire and a keen intelligence beneath his playful banter. And I knew he was dangerous enough to kill people. Hell, I'd watched him hold that guy at the bonfire while Gideon had pummeled him. But that ire had never been directed at me.

He was angry.

Suddenly, our adventure into the city didn't seem so exciting as it did full of nervous tension.

"What did I just risk my entire position—my life—to do for you, huh?"

My voice turned quiet as my chest constricted with the guilt worming its way down my spine. "I know. I know, Kenji. You've risked a lot to help me. Thank you."

"No." He slammed his hand on the steering wheel. "I want you to tell me why, Lissa. Is this because you and Gideon had a little tiff, so you're trying to make him pay?"

"No!" I blurted. "No! Of course not. This isn't about Gideon at all."

"You've practically been a ghost since you got to the compound. Half of my job as your guard is just an effort to get you to smile in a day. And now, in the past week, suddenly you have this look in your eyes like you're seeing the world for the first time. Ever since your anniversary, it's like something lit a fire under your ass, and now you care. And now you're, what, running away?"

"I always cared." My voice seemed so fragile in the silence of the car. It was the best I could do. He was right, though. This new, frenetic need within me left me feeling itchy and unsettled. It had started with Madam Cartenoth's words at Tea and Trinkets. It was propelled by that helpless, desperate moment at the bonfire when I'd left a man to die by Gideon's hands. And it was sealed tonight when I lay in Gideon's bed, realizing that if I didn't leave, his mouth against my body would convince me to stay. So I didn't know what I wanted. I just knew that I couldn't stay at the compound. I couldn't be the simple little Queen anymore, safely locked away.

"Why?" Kenji challenged me, pushing even still.

"I just, I want more," I said.

"More?" Kenji scoffed, shaking his head. "That's not good enough, Queenie. I'll turn this car back around, I swear," he said. "It's time for you to start being honest with me and with yourself."

"What do you want from me, Kenji?"

He slammed on the brakes.

"No!" I panicked, realizing he was about to flip a U-turn. "No, I-I have to leave because if I stay any longer, I think I might want to stay, and that scares me! It's terrifying to think I might accept this life."

Kenji took a minute to digest my words. The Humvee was silent. Then he began driving forward again, not once looking at me.

"And why don't you want to accept this life, huh?" he pressed. "Most women would kill to be a Queen and have the comforts you have."

"I can't stomach trading my soul for a full belly anymore," I muttered as I thought about all of the hollow-eyed girls and starving boys and people addicted to silver with no choice but to die in the streets.

"And what are you going to do about it?"

My head snapped his way, trying to see the answer he seemed to desperately want from me. But he was just staring out at the road.

"Tell me, Lissa," he said.

"I don't know!" I said honestly. "I just know I can't stay with the Cards. I definitely can't fix anything there."

"And what needs fixing?"

"Everything!" I threw up my hands.

"No." Kenji shook his head. "No, tell me what's wrong."

"I don't know what you want from me!" I snapped.

He smacked the steering wheel. "This isn't a joke!"

"I can tell!"

"So give me a straight answer. What's wrong in this city?"

"The gangs," I finally said. "The gangs are wrong."

He rolled his eyes as if that were the obvious answer.

"People without food is wrong," I continued. "People addicted to silver is wrong. Girls expected to sell their bodies is wrong. All of it!"

He sighed.

So I added, "Gideon is wrong! The Cards are wrong! People without choice is wrong!"

I slapped my hands over my mouth as if I'd uttered a string of curse words.

That got his attention. Finally, that made him turn and look at me, the slightest hint of a smile curling at the corner of his lips.

"And what else, Lissa?" he said, his eyes glistening against the lights from the car.

"Making Silvers give their blood is wrong," I said. "Keeping me a prisoner is wrong."

He just nodded and looked back out at the road.

And finally, finally, I added, "Doing nothing is wrong."

My voice was so quiet I wasn't sure if he'd even heard the words.

The fog was rolling in across the pavement. It swirled between the canyon roads, casting an eerie glow against the trees as we continued our drive.

Kenji hadn't gotten angry with me for saying those words about the Silvers, but he also hadn't agreed. My skin felt prickly with tension as though maybe I'd made a grave mistake in trusting him. Gideon needed every Silver too much to truly harm one of us. We were the keys that kept him in power, after all. But that didn't mean he couldn't do other things to me if he found out my loyalty wasn't to him. It never had been.

Yes, I could understand why he made the choices he made. I didn't even fault him for them, for the most part. He protected himself and his Cards above everything else. But he also loved the power and control it gave him to be that person, the Ace. It was as addicting as the silver.

But in the books I'd read, people hadn't always lived like this. Sure, no system had ever been perfect, but there were times when people at least had a choice. There was a time when governments made sure that people had things deemed as basic human rights. And it might not have been a perfect system, but it was at least something. At least it meant that one person could not own another person.

Lesson one: You are mine.

I shivered at the reminder of Gideon's words, and the memory of the feel of his hand as it landed on my backside. There was so much about Gideon to hate. He had taken everything from me. But I also couldn't deny that I understood him on a deep level, which scared me sometimes even more than his actions. He made me feel things I hadn't even known when Tayna was alive.

"Kenji?"

"Hmm?" he asked as we rounded into the first blocks of the ruined city streets.

"I hate him," I admitted. But in an even quieter voice, I said, "But I think I also might love him."

After a moment, he nodded. "I know exactly what you mean. But you have to pick a side, Lissa. You can't love him but also work to destroy what he stands for."

"I don't want to hurt anyone. But I especially don't want to hurt him."

Kenji's small smile was sad. "I used to say the same thing."

It was then I realized that Kenji and I were the same. Maybe we came from different backgrounds and had different things tattooed on our arms. But we had both been doing what we had to do to survive. And we both had learned that simply surviving wasn't enough.

I knew he'd gotten into this car with me because of that feeling.

I knew I'd drawn my blood in the darkness of my room tonight for that reason.

But now I had to figure out what it meant to actually begin living.

21

Lissa

The shop was closed for the night, of course. We'd arrived well past nine. But Kenji and I took the path down the side alley that I knew led to the living quarters in the back. The street was wet from the sea air around us, and I lifted my dress to keep it from dragging in the muck. It smelled like fish guts and stale pond water.

I rapped on the door, not surprised when no one answered.

So I knocked again.

Still nothing.

The door was bolted shut. The lights were off inside.

"Phenola," I called, daring to speak among the quiet alley streets. From my days as a street rat, I knew it was never a good idea to draw attention at night, but I didn't have much choice. After everything that had happened tonight, there was no other option. She had to answer. "It's me. It's Lissa."

Finally, the bolt on the door began to jiggle. A moment later, the door opened, just a crack, a security lock still protecting the hinge from swinging open fully.

I could see a sliver of Phenola's face. Her hair was wrapped in a colorful scarf, and she wore a long-sleeved flowing dress with purple and red flowers.

"Lissa?" she asked. "What's going on?"

"It's okay, Phen," Kenji said behind me. "Everything's fine."

"I'm so sorry we're here so late," I added.

She began unlatching the rest of the locks before opening the door to Kenji and me. "We heard the Cards were in lockdown. I didn't expect to see you this week."

I looked at Kenji before saying, "I almost didn't make it," as we walked inside.

She led us into the hodge-podge sitting area, and I settled into one of the mismatched chairs at the oval table.

"Bat's already asleep," she explained before offering a drink in a dark decanter up to Kenji and me.

"Uh, I'm good." After last week, liquor was the last thing I needed.

"Same," Kenji said.

"Tea then, I suppose," Phenola said, moving to the stove and beginning to heat a pot of water.

"Don't waste silver on our account," I said, but she waved me off and lit the burner.

"How is she?" I asked, looking at the bedroom.

Phenola sighed. "It's only getting worse. She sleeps a lot now. She's barely eating."

"What about the silver?" I asked.

Phenola just shook her head. "She doesn't want it, Lissa. It doesn't do much good, anyway. Maybe eases her pain a bit, but her body has started to shut down. Not even silver can keep the body from doing what it was made to do. We all face death one way or another."

I waited to pull the vials of silver from my pocket. I had questions first about these rebels. I needed to know I could trust them, that they wanted to do the right thing.

"I..." Where to even begin? "I don't want to go back to the compound," I said. "Kenji helped me get out tonight. Gideon doesn't know I'm here. I can't go back."

Phenola pulled three mugs from a cabinet. One was missing a handle. The other had a chip in the side, worn but usable. She didn't seem startled by my words, but rather, a sort of resignation settled over her.

She put the mugs on the cracked tile counter, then looked at Kenji. "What did you tell her?" she asked.

My eyes widened as they, too, turned to Kenji.

"I haven't told her anything yet. She came to this conclusion all on her own, just like we agreed," Kenji said, his eyes fixed on Phenola. "But it's time."

"What are you talking about?" I looked back and forth between the two of them.

I thought about the way Kenji had looked so contemplative in the Humvee. He had pressed me for answers like he wanted me to admit something to him. And then there was Phenola. The last time I was here, she'd talked about this new rebel group. A group she'd claimed was different from the rest. And Madam Cartenoth had said I was already helping people in ways I didn't know.

I pushed back my chair and stood from the table just as the kettle began to whistle throughout the room.

"What, exactly, is going on?" I demanded, wondering if I'd made a mistake coming here.

Kenji hadn't explained how he'd known it was me who would be in the Humvee. It could just as easily have been another Card.

"Sit down, Lissa," Kenji said.

Phenola began casually spooning herbs into satchels and pouring hot water over them. I thought I heard her sigh.

I looked at Kenji. "Who are you?"

"I'm your guard and your friend," he said. "And if you'll just sit down, I'll fill you in on the rest."

I considered my options. If I ran right now, could I escape? And where would I go? Back to the compound? Or maybe somewhere else? How long could I survive on the streets before the Cards or another gang hunted me down? A rogue Queen on the streets couldn't stay hidden for long.

But the most important question was whether I trusted Kenji. My lovable, pain-in-the-ass guard who seemed so loyal to Gideon and the Cards. A huge chunk of my reality was shifting on its head, and it all depended on how much I actually trusted him.

The answer was surprisingly simple.

I sat back down in the rickety wooden chair.

"Thank you," he said, seemingly understanding the deeper decision I'd made.

"Please have something to say that will keep me in this seat." My words were bordering on desperate.

Phenola placed two mugs of steaming tea in front of us before she grabbed hers. She sat opposite me in a lime-green-backed chair and gently blew on the tea.

"Why don't you start, Kenji?" Phenola tipped her head to him. "I'm curious how you'll tell it."

He gave her a dry look but said, "Phenola and I are—" He sighed and reached across to take her hand in his, leaning forward across the table. She gave a faint smile, and her slender fingers slipped between his. "Phenola is pregnant."

My mouth popped open. Of all the things I expected to learn around this table in this small living space, that was not among the list. Phenola's gaze was soft as she lifted it to Kenji, and I wondered how I'd missed that shared look before. Sure, I'd known there was a flirtation, but I'd never guessed it had gone deeper than that. Now, looking at them, it was so clear they were in love.

"When—" I stuttered, "How—"

Kenji nodded, pulling his hand back from Phenola's to grip his mug of tea. I picked up mine as well and took a small sip of the steaming chamomile. It was perfectly hot and spiced with cinnamon and cloves and something vaguely sweet. I instantly felt calmer. The tea here always had that effect, like coming home.

"That's where this all gets very, very long and complicated," Kenji began. "I wanted to join the Cards, Queenie. I was fifteen when they brought me to the compound. Gideon had just taken control of the Cards and was rounding up whoever he could to build his ranks. My family fished in the ports just off the sea here. I grew up in the city. I saw it as a chance to build a better life for myself and my family. Gideon pays the Cards well, and I was good at—I learned quickly and did what I had to do to gain his trust. But I never believed in what he did. I never liked hurting people, and I hated that we took Silvers. I never thought that was okay. But I did my duty. I was always loyal.

"When I was assigned to guard you, it all changed when I met Phenola. The moment I saw her, I knew there would never be anyone else for me. I began coming to the shop on my off days, and I slowly started telling her about my reservations with the gangs and the Cards and the way Gideon ran this city.

"She listened, but it took her a while to trust me in return. It wasn't until about a year ago that she told me about a group of people on the outskirts of the city who wanted a different option. They call themselves the Whigs. Some term or another from the history books. But what they represent is freedom, Queenie. They believe in a world where everyone has a say. They want to establish a government in this city where gangs don't rule, but everyone has a voice. It's pretty revolutionary."

"I know about democracy," I said between sips of my tea, thinking of the books I'd read where that idea of a government and voting and liberty had been so ingrained in the way of life.

"Then you know it can work," Phenola said.

"Not without a war," I countered. "You would have to completely overthrow the gangs. Gideon and Olita have too much power over this city for that to be a feasible plan."

"They only have power if they control the Silvers," Kenji argued.

"I'm just one," I reasoned. "The gangs have hundreds between them."

"You aren't just one," Kenji said. "You know you're different, Lissa. You have a power separate from your blood."

"It's unpredictable." I shook my head. Tonight was the first time I had used it intentionally when I'd started the Humvee's engine. Even then, it might have just been luck that I didn't blow up the whole engine in the process.

"But you can clearly learn to control it. And if you could control it, Queenie, you would be unstoppable. No one could tell you what to do."

Admittedly, I hadn't considered it. My head began to feel light. The day was taking its toll. Between the extra two vials of blood I'd drawn, the lack of food, and now this sea of information, I was exhausted.

I took another sip of tea.

"Do you remember the other day when you burned me, and I wouldn't accept your blood?" Kenji asked before continuing. "Gideon has forbidden anyone but him from consuming your silver. He hoards it all for himself."

"What?" I scrubbed my eyes, trying to process the information. I knew Gideon kept my blood for himself, but no one had told me it was outright forbidden for other Cards.

"He knows your blood is more powerful than the others, and he won't even let his own men have a taste of what your silver can do."

I looked at Phenola. I'd given Tea and Trinkets my blood for years.

She said, "We keep a little of it for ourselves. The rest goes to the cause. It's powerful stuff. Kenji's right that it's different. It's more potent, and it lasts longer."

I stared down at my arms, at the veins running just below the surface that I didn't want or ask for. My skin was pale against the dim light of the room. Phenola had been using my blood to help a rebel cause I'd known nothing about until a week ago. My blood had already fueled a war.

As I took another gulp of tea, I thought of Madam Cartenoth's words. *Even though you don't know it, you already have.*

She knew Phenola had been giving my blood to these Whigs.

And Gideon and his men had almost died last night because of it.

It was all I could do to move from the table. I was going to be sick. The room swam. It was too much. This was all too much. I had decided I wanted to be useful, but I couldn't do this.

"Lissa," Phenola said, standing too.

I braced myself against the table. Everything was a haze. I shook my head.

Gideon could have been killed. And it would have been my fault. It would have been another person dead because of my silver. And not just another person. It would have been Gideon.

I didn't want to be different or unstoppable or powerful. And as much as I knew I had to leave the Cards, hurting Gideon was the last thing I wanted to do.

"Lissa." Kenji's tone was a low warning. "Deep breaths."

I couldn't. I couldn't breathe. The air was getting trapped in my throat, and everything was spiraling. The room swayed in and out of focus, and I realized this wasn't just from blood loss or from the information Phenola and Kenji had given me.

My gaze connected with the mug of tea on the table just as I felt my knees give out.

Strong arms caught me from behind. "It's okay, Queenie," Kenji said in my ear. "It's going to be okay."

And then the darkness swallowed me.

PART III

THE PLAYS

22

Lissa

My neck hurt, and my throat was so dry it burned.

Those were the first thoughts I had as I regained consciousness.

Everything was black. I realized something was covering my eyes as I blinked them open, my eyelashes brushing the fabric tied securely around my head.

I groaned as I straightened my spine. I was sitting upright in a hard chair. My hands were bound tightly behind my back, which explained my stiff and aching shoulders. It felt like some kind of rope, which dug into my skin, rubbing it raw. Even I couldn't heal myself if something prevented the wound from clotting.

I opened and closed my jaw a few times, wetting my lips, but my tongue was like sandpaper in my mouth. My lips were cracked from dehydration and whatever drug Phenola had put in my tea.

"Thirsty?" a deep male voice asked.

I didn't recognize the tenor. It wasn't Gideon, and I wasn't sure if I was relieved or not. It wasn't Kenji, either, though that didn't mean he hadn't backstabbed me and returned me to the Cards to face punishment for trying to run away.

A cup was pressed to my lips, and I drank greedily. The water hit my throat, and I coughed, sputtering out the liquid as it burned its way down. The small amount I managed to swallow wasn't nearly enough.

"More," I begged roughly, but that only got me a deep chuckle in response.

The blindfold was pulled from my eyes, and I blinked rapidly against the sudden light that hit my pupils. Dark spots swam in front of my vision. I couldn't blink them away fast enough as the blurry frame in front of me became a man.

Even as my vision cleared, the hulking form that stood only feet away was a shadow. He was tall and broad, but that was about all I could discern of my captor. He had on black trousers tucked into knee-high black boots that buckled over each ankle. He wore a long brown coat with a hood pulled over his eyes, and a black mask covered his nose and mouth. He didn't have a suit of Cards embroidered on his shoulder.

The two biggest dogs I'd ever seen in my life sat by his feet. They were nothing like the mangy and feral street dogs in the city. Those would sooner bite you than sit anywhere near a human. I'd never seen dogs like this. They were more like the photos I'd seen of wolves with their large stature and gray-and-black coats. They gazed at me patiently as they sat as if waiting for orders.

Still, I watched the beasts warily, not sure if I was more scared of them or the man. I leaned back in the chair, and the ropes around my wrists strained against my skin, causing me to wince.

"Where's Kenji?" My voice was raw, but I pressed out the words anyway.

The man laughed again, a surprisingly light sound that made me think laughing came easily to this man. He patted one dog on the head. It stayed sitting as the man approached me.

"Kenji is fine. Probably back at the compound by now covering for your mysterious disappearance." He brought the cup to my lips again. "Drink some more. You clearly need it."

I obeyed, swallowing a few more mouthfuls. It wasn't as if refusing had even crossed my mind since I was so desperately thirsty. I figured it wasn't poisoned. What would be the point of dragging me here just to kill me?

He seemed to sense my thoughts. "I'm not planning to hurt you, but I expect you to control your silver. Otherwise, I'll be forced to knock you out again, and I'd hate to delay this conversation."

Once I'd drained the cup of water, I looked around where I was being held. It was a barn of some sort. An old one with bales of hay strewn around and covering the ground. It smelled like animals, though I didn't see any other than the dogs in here with us.

Some chips in the wood along the walls gave way to the bright daylight that streamed inside, which meant it was most likely the middle of the afternoon. The light almost looked like it was reflecting through glass, the way it was shining and refracting around the large space. If I turned my head at the wrong angle, I would found myself blinded by light, which kept me disoriented in the space.

How long had I been out? My stomach was cramped with hunger and thirst.

"Where's my bag?" I rasped, thinking of the few precious belongings I'd packed with me. The books most of all.

"Here." He kicked at the sack, which I'd missed on the ground next to a hay bale. The man swooped low in one fluid movement and snatched the book from the top of the bag. "Eclectic reading taste, I have to say." He idly thumbed through the pages of the hardback. "Wait and hope and all that."

Did this man just quote *A Count of Monte Cristo*?

"Who are you?"

The man tossed the book on the hay bale and stood to his full height.

"Apologies for the theatrics." He clapped his gloved hands in front of him and then opened his arms wide as if he were, indeed, introducing a theatrical show. "But you're a Queen. Well, not just any Queen, right? You're Gideon's Queen."

I was very aware of the shawl covering the Queen's tattoo on my shoulders. Had he looked at it while I was asleep? He clearly knew who I was.

"He thinks I am, yes," I said cautiously.

"You've been with him for the past five years, haven't you?"

"Yes," I breathed.

"You share his bed?"

"Excuse me?" I was more shocked than offended that he would ask such a bold question.

But the man only pressed the point. "He doesn't just take your blood, right? He fucks you. Only you, in fact."

"That's not your—"

"And he won't take anyone else's blood, either. Isn't that right?"

"He—"

"So you'll forgive me if I understand why he *thinks*"—the way he said the word dripped with derision—"you're his Queen."

"How dare you—" I could feel the silver sparking along my hands.

The man put up a gloved finger in front of my face. Not close enough to touch, but close enough to suggest he wasn't as afraid of me as most.

"Remember. We had a deal," he said.

I took a few shaky breaths, and the silver began to sputter away.

"Very good." He sounded like he was smiling beneath that mask.

So this man wasn't a Card. And I certainly wasn't at the compound. There weren't any barns on the cliffs. And there most definitely weren't any wolf dogs.

That could only mean Kenji and Phenola had handed me over to the Whigs.

Gideon had been searching for them in the northern outskirts of the city. There were rumors they had created their own compound in the mountains. Was that where I was now? The air did feel distinctly colder. I imagined I could almost see puffs of my shaking inhales and exhales.

"I willingly left Gideon and the Cards," I tried for reason. "If Kenji's the one who brought me here, then he must have explained that."

It was in my best interest to get this man to trust me.

"Yes," the man mused. "After five years, you woke up and decided you didn't like being a blood pet anymore. How nice for you that Kenji provided you with another option. My job is to determine whether you deserve that option. I'm not convinced, Queen."

"Who are you?" I demanded again, looking for any clues along his shrouded frame.

"Right now? I'm the man who decides whether you stay or you go." He shrugged. "Let's talk about your Ace. Do you love him?"

The word "no," faltered on my lips. It was right there, yet I couldn't bring myself to say it even though I knew it was what the man wanted to hear.

The man shook his head. My hesitation was all he needed. I could tell even with his mask that he was disgusted. He stood over me, and I strained to look up.

"Gideon is a complicated man," I said, breathlessly trying to search for the words to explain. I knew it was wrong to love him. It made no logical sense. He was flawed. More than anyone, I saw his flaws. But he was so much more, too.

This man couldn't possibly understand.

"Complicated?" the man barked. "Kenji tells me he killed your friend. Or did you choose to forget that?"

The mention of Tayna had me reeling. Why had Kenji told this man about Tayna? It made my breath come in quick gasps as the silver sparked at my fingers, and the words got lodged in my throat.

"Oh, that hit a nerve." The man still sounded amused. He moved back across the barn, sitting down on a folding chair set up a few feet from me. He leaned forward, resting his elbows on his thighs and tenting his gloved hands in front of him as he watched me through the shadowed hood.

I bit back on the rush of tears as I said hoarsely, "Gideon didn't kill Tayna."

"No?" the man asked. "Left his body in the streets while he snatched you from the market?"

"Fuck you," I breathed.

The man only laughed and bent closer. "Did you even fight?"

"You don't know what you're—"

"But you didn't try to escape?"

"I—"

"Just watched him die and moved on?"

"I-I didn't—"

"Seems like you'll give your loyalty to anyone, even a murderer."

"Gideon didn't—It was an accident—"

"Gideon? The way you even say the Ace's name is disgusting. How many people have you watched him kill?"

"Stop!" I choked on the sob, thinking of the man he'd beaten at the bonfire and straining against the bindings. Silver snapped at my fingertips. "You have no idea what I've—"

"And how long after this 'accident' did you start fucking the Ace?"

I didn't care if this man was the damn salvation come again. He could not speak to me that way. I focused the silver on the ropes binding my hands behind my back, and it burned away.

I didn't hesitate.

I launched myself at the man.

"Fuck you!" I screamed as I clawed at his face. "I will kill you!" The silver burned at my fingers. "You have no idea what I went through losing him! I died! I died, too!"

My silver singed through his clothes, and I pulled at the mask across his face just as something clamped down on the back of my dress and hauled me backward.

I'd forgotten about the damn wolf dogs. The one who had grabbed me had a mouthful of my dress, dragging me back, while the other stepped over my prone figure. It growled low in my face, and I raised my arms to shield myself, sure it was about to rip out my throat.

Silver sparked along my fingers in a dangerous cacophony.

"Ann, Dan, leave it," the man called, and both dogs backed down.

All of the blood rushed from my face. It felt like the floor had dropped from where I lay.

Ann and Dan.

Where the Red Fern Grows.

I scrambled to sit up, my wrists slipping on some of the hay, barely noticing as it tore into my palms.

The man was sitting up now too, the dogs back at his side. I'd managed to pull the mask from his face, and the hood had fallen from his forehead. I'd burned a few places on his arm with my silver, and they weren't healing. The patches of red were beginning to rise into mean-looking blisters. Not on silver, then.

My eyes scanned up slowly from the tanned skin of his chest, landing on his face.

His deep chestnut hair was cut short. His skin was a honeyed brown from the sun, even in the early days of spring. There was a long scar slashing through one eyebrow and into his eye.

Nothing else existed except for those eyes.

I crawled toward them.

Those eyes.

His eyes.

They haunted me when I closed my own. I'd forgotten his voice and pieces of his face and the way he moved when he walked, but those eyes...

The only thing driving me was a deep need to see them up close. I needed to see them closer.

He didn't move as I got so close that we were nearly nose to nose, even with my silver still feeling so volatile beneath my skin. I didn't touch him as he let me look at every inch of his face. I studied each detail, cataloging the face that had filled out with age, the hint of stubble along his jaw, the slightly crooked nose. And his eyes.

His golden eyes—like the sun as it broke over the horizon.

I lifted my hands to touch his face but hesitated.

He couldn't be real.

I'd spent so many moments of my life during the past five years thinking about everything I would give if I could run my fingers across his face one more time. I'd thought about the years of my life I would give if it meant I had more time with him. I'd thought about the moments I would trade just to be face-to-face with him again for seconds, minutes, breaths.

Maybe whatever Kenji had given me had made me hallucinate, and I wasn't here at all but still in Phenola's shop sleeping soundly.

But my fingers tentatively caressed across his wide jaw, over the ridges of his nose, and along the bow of his lip.

A smile curved at the corners of his mouth, and deep dimples appeared in each of his cheeks.

I traced the lines again, sure he would disappear beneath my fingers at any moment.

But he was solid and remained solid as he let me touch him.

Tears ran in rivers down my cheeks as I said tentatively, "Tayna?"

"Hi, Liss." He grinned, his mouth moving over my fingers from where they hovered at the corners of his lips.

I gasped.

He embraced me, wrapping me in a hug that was somehow so new but also like coming home. His frame was nothing like the starving, lanky kid I remembered. Beneath me was a solid man who had filled out over the years and was clearly not starving anymore.

He smelled like fresh-cut grass and sweat from a long day. I buried myself into him, only managing to ask, "How?" against his chest as my tears left damp spots along the crook of his shoulder.

"I've waited five years for this, Liss," he said into my hair, cupping the back of my neck with his hand. "For five years, all I thought about was you. I thought you were lost to me. I thought you'd forgotten me."

"You don't know, Tayna." I sobbed at all of the hurt and the pain and the things I had done. I cried for the person I had become without him, and the girl who had died, too, on that day she was taken. "You have no idea."

"It's okay," he said, breathing me in. "It's okay. We'll get there."

And I understood. For now, it was just enough to take him in.

Feeling the press of his body against mine made me all too aware of every inch of my exposed skin. The shawl had fallen from my shoulders, but I was warm tucked into Tayna's embrace.

It wasn't exactly comfortable, but nothing could get me to move at that moment. The stubble of his cheek rubbed roughly against my forehead. My arms cramped from the blood that had rushed into the muscles after being bound, but I didn't drop my grip from his neck. The sole of one of his boots dug into my calf. And the hay on the ground poked mercilessly into the thin fabric of my dress, spearing me with small pricks where I sat.

Yet everything seemed perfectly and completely right.

I was holding Tayna.

And he was holding me back just as tightly.

We sat like that in the barn, our bodies folded together, tears dampening the fabric of our sleeves, until we exhausted ourselves and the sun began to set.

23

Lissa

By the time Tayna and I stood from the barn, it had been nearly a full twenty-four hours since I'd had anything to eat. And my knees gave out as he held out a hand for me.

He caught me, concern furrowing his brow. "Are you okay?"

"Just hungry, I think. And maybe still a little woozy from whatever Phenola put in my tea," I admitted sheepishly. "And I've given a lot of silver in the past couple of days."

"Food, fuck." He laughed, sweeping me easily into his arms. His strength was staggering. "How could I forget how much you like to eat?"

I wrapped my arms around his neck, savoring the feel of him. I didn't want to stop touching him or staring at him. I was too afraid if I blinked, he would disappear.

"Um..." I ventured. "I have a lot of questions, but... where are we?"

He laughed again, and I basked in the rich sound.

"You'll see," he said, sweeping me from the barn like I was lighter than one of those hay bales, which I knew I most definitely was not. I, too, had filled out in the years we'd been apart. Where Tayna might have gotten muscles, I got curves.

Still, he held me like he intended to keep me against his chest for the rest of our lives. It wasn't a bad idea. Until I thought about Gideon, at least. He would know by now that I was gone. He would have the entire compound searching for me. His rule that everyone stay put would have been null and void the second he discovered me missing. There was a pang of guilt.

You are everything.

But I couldn't be everything to him if I didn't even know who I was myself. I had left because it was the right decision for me, even if it had also broken a piece of my heart.

Instead, I ran my fingers down Tayna's chest, reminding myself what I had gained by leaving. Tayna was here. He was alive. I was in his arms. This was home. Or, at least, he had been once upon a time.

Now, as happy as I was to see him, a strange sort of unease settled over me. We were both different people. Yet it felt good to be in his arms. It felt too good in a way that had my stomach knotting with my betrayal. Leaving Gideon's bed only to be held by another man the next day left me reeling with uncertainty. Even if that man was Tayna, *my* Tayna.

So the fingers that trailed down his chest became a push as I lifted myself from his arms, forcing him to set me down.

"I can walk," I said. "It's okay."

He set me just outside the barn doors, and I looked at the sweeping expanse around me. Acres and acres of farmland stretched in front of me. Fields of crops drifted in the evening breeze. Everything was lush and green and sprouting with the promise of the spring.

Houses were dotted between the fields of wheat and corn. Chickens roamed, and horses were stabled. I could make out what I thought were cows grazing in a far-off field. People worked around the crops. A group of women pruned branches from a grove of citrus trees. Two men were digging lines in a patch of dirt. Still others were dumping buckets of what looked to be food scraps in a large bin for a couple of pigs.

And there were children. Not the hollow-eyed, skinny ones I saw on the streets of the city. But thriving. Two kids ran through a field chasing a butterfly. Another older boy was mucking the horses' stalls. Still another young girl sprinkled seeds for the chickens.

"Tayna," I breathed, taking in the sight of people living and working together in a thriving neighborhood. "Tayna, it's a farm."

Ann and Dan prowled from the barn and sat on their haunches, surveying the land as if proud of what they saw. I looked at Tayna to find his face reflecting the same sort of pride.

"*Where the Red Fern Grows.*" I felt another wave of emotion threatening to spill over into tears. "You did it. You actually did it."

Because I knew it was him. Deep within my soul, I knew he was responsible for this place. My hand found his, our fingers twining together as if he could anchor me in the reality of his dream come to life.

The children chasing the butterfly ran past us, their laughter floating on the breeze. And I saw the little boy's eyes as he glanced at me curiously. His eyes were silver. They were silver.

"He's like me," I said, smiling at the sight of him running and laughing with other children.

Tayna returned it, his dimples deep. "There's a few of them here now. They'll be excited to meet you. But first." He squeezed my hand. "Dinner."

We walked toward a large building that looked like a main house. It looked like it had been reconstructed at some point. Unlike the dilapidated buildings in the city, this home was freshly painted white with gray paneling. The slats in the wraparound porch were neatly spaced, and the windows free of broken corners.

Tayna led me up the front porch steps, and the wooden stairs were sturdy beneath my feet. I looked back at him in wonder as I took in the house in front of me.

"Grant and I spent two summers renovating this place," Tayna said by way of explanation.

"Grant?" I began, but then an older man stepped from the house, scooping me in a hug. He was a large man with a red face and a brown-and-white beard that was more white than brown. He was smiling at me with a face full of crooked teeth, and he appeared to have grease down the front of his shirt, which didn't stop him as he wrapped his large arms around me and held me tight.

"Welcome! Oh welcome!" he said, shaking me a little before setting me back on my feet.

I staggered a bit, trying to find my footing as Tayna held me upright.

"We've just been waiting for you for so long," the man beamed. And then his gaze landed on Tayna's arms, where patches were burned. "Seems like the reunion went well enough. We should get those bandaged."

My blush was hot on my face as my eyes met golden-brown ones.

"I—"

"I deserved it. She didn't know it was me. And they're fine."

"Rixa gave me some silver just this morning that you—"

Tayna held up a hand. "Absolutely not."

"I could—" I began.

"No." Tayna was firm. "They're minor."

"Right." I forced a small smile back at the man, finally tearing my eyes from Tayna. "I take it you're Grant?"

"The one and only." Tayna seemed grateful for the change in topic. "Can we do introductions after a bowl of stew? I may have accidentally starved our new guest."

"Oh, of course! Of course!" Grant said, moving to usher me inside, but Tayna placed a steady hand on my lower back. Clearly, neither of us was ready to give up contact after being apart for so long. My gaze swept his face again, desperate to memorize his features like he might disappear again at any moment. His full lips turned up at the corners as we followed Grant.

"I guess that explains the burns," Grant said over his shoulder, perfectly happy to fill the silence. "I'd start burning things on an empty stomach, too, if someone forgot to feed me." He let out a low chuckle and playfully knocked my arm with his like we were old friends. And it felt like, just that easily, we were. He wasn't afraid of me in the least. He wasn't horrified that I'd burned Tayna. He wasn't staring at the silver in my eyes as if it were a foreign and alive thing. He was welcoming me as if I were, indeed, a long-awaited guest.

Ann and Dan found a patch of grass by the porch and lay down like sentries guarding the place.

A living room greeted us just inside the entryway, complete with a blue plush sofa and a fireplace. Someone had picked wildflowers that were overflowing in a jar on the side table. Just inside to the right was a sprawling kitchen.

There was an island in the center with polished wood counter-tops. Pots hung from a rack in the ceiling, and the walls were lined with cabinets and three giant refrigerators.

The farmhouse was nowhere near the size of the mansion, but it was a cozy space that fit plenty of people all the same. There were at least five already serving themselves in the kitchen out of a giant pot on a gas-burning stove.

"We try to use silver as little as possible," Tayna explained. "We prefer all-natural methods wherever possible." He handed me a bowl.

The word, "Clearly," died on my tongue, but I eyed the burns. Tayna hadn't been lying when he said they weren't bad. They weren't the worst I'd caused, at least. But they still looked red and angry.

"Food, Liss." Tayna nodded again toward the bowl, and I took it. My eyes were drawn from Tayna to the steaming concoction inside the bowl he'd handed me. It smelled delicious.

"How many people live here now?" I asked.

"Just over three hundred," he said, "though we have friends that help us in the city as well. People like Phenola. And more are joining our cause every day."

"Your cause?" I asked, spooning around the soup in the bowl to try to cool it. It was a chunky thing, full of carrots, potatoes, hunks of meat, and what even looked like spiraled pieces of pasta.

"We'll get to that part," Tayna said, ripping a piece of bread from a loaf and handing me a wedge. I took a bite and began chewing before dunking the rest in the stew. I had to stifle a groan. The bread was fresh from the oven. The outside was crisp and chewy while the inside was filled with some kind of seeds that gave it a nutty flavor I'd never experienced.

Tayna also filled two mugs from a wooden jug near the back, handing me one.

"Wine," he explained. "I think we could both use a glass after today."

"Oh." I put up my hand. "I'm not allowed to—" But I stopped myself. I wasn't at the compound anymore. So I cleared my throat and asked, "As part of staying here, well, if I stay here, do you require weekly blood draws?"

Tayna nearly choked on the wine he'd just swallowed. "Lissa, no. No. You decide how to use your silver here, if you even want to use it at all. The farm is self-sufficient. We don't require silver here. Ever."

"Okay," I said and tentatively took a sip of the wine. I'd only had wine on a few rare occasions in my life. Mostly, I'd snuck sips of the hard stuff since it was the most concentrated and easiest to get my hands on. But I found I enjoyed the flavor of the wine with the food. It was like the coffee Gideon had given me, complex and rich, and the more I had, the more I liked it.

We found a corner where we could sit and eat in the kitchen. It was a small table in a little nook next to a washroom. But it was enough to give us a bit of privacy among the bustle of activity.

I took a big bite of the bread, which had soaked up a good helping of gravy from the stew, and Tayna laughed at the expression on my face of pure joy. I set about finishing the bowl.

The sun had almost entirely set by now. The last slivers of pink and orange outlined the sky. More and more people were coming in from the fields to share a meal, and I watched them for a moment. They all seemed to know one another, embracing and laughing.

I found Grant among them. He was eating a bowl of stew while standing and talking to another middle-aged man and woman. The pieces of silver in his hair reminded me of the silver in my eyes. A built man stood next to him with his hand around Grant's waist, talking animatedly, clearly amid a wild story.

"That's Grant's husband," Tayna said, following my gaze. "You should avoid him if you can help it. He's ornery, that one."

"Husband?" I asked, wondering if that was just an expression for partner.

But Tayna nodded explaining, "People get married here, actually commit to one another. Grant and Alaric have been married for four years now, though they've been together for about a decade."

"How?" All of the questions were there, in that single word. "How are you alive, Tayna?"

He sighed. "The short answer? After... well, after the Cards took you, and I was well enough, I left the city. I had nothing and no way to get to you, so I fled. Most nights, I slept in the woods, but it finally got cold enough, and I was desperate enough to go into a house."

"And that was Grant?" I guessed, chewing my bread more slowly to savor the final bites.

"No!" Tayna laughed. "That was a woman who beat me senseless with some kind of racket while yelling at me about being a thief. Grant and Alaric happened to see me running away and also thought I was a thief, so they grabbed me by the scruff of my neck, intent on shaking me down. Once they realized I was just a street rat with shit luck, they took pity on me and brought me to their house for dinner. I've been with them ever since."

I set down my spoon, my food finished. I wanted more stew but not as badly as I wanted my questions answered now that I'd had a bowl. "Tayna, what happened? That day, I mean. You were... I saw your body in the street. You weren't moving. I couldn't wake you up."

It was an effort not to get lost in his face every time I looked at him. It was difficult to comprehend that he was in front of me, and we were sharing a meal. I had pictured his face a thousand times in my mind, and still, nothing could have prepared me for the sight of him today—his sharp jaw and warm skin and sparkling golden eyes. There was so much the same, yet so much changed. I wondered if it was the same for him as he met my gaze.

"Madam Cartenoth saw everything that happened in the streets," Tayna explained. "As soon as the Cards left with you, she dragged me inside and gave me the silver you had left at her shop that day. I guess there was just enough life left in me that it worked. I stayed with her until I was strong enough to leave. It's the only time I've willingly taken silver."

I dared to voice the thought that niggled at the back of my mind. "You left."

I couldn't meet his eyes then. What I didn't add was the word "me." He left me. He hadn't waited for me to return to the city. And Madam Cartenoth hadn't told me he was alive. Sure, it had taken me nearly two years to gain Gideon's trust enough that he allowed me to leave the compound, but Madam Cartenoth hadn't said anything even then.

Tayna shook his head as if in sorrow as he replayed the memories. "At first, I planned to join the Cards," he said. "I was going to enlist as a new recruit. Whatever it took to get in that compound and get to you. But then what? I knew we wouldn't make it out of there. Not then. I knew if we had any chance of creating a life beyond that city, I had to make something of myself. I needed to be able to challenge Gideon."

"And what about me?" I couldn't help the bite in my tone.

"You were a Queen," Tayna said. "You were Gideon's pet. By the time you emerged from the compound, you were one of them. I didn't know if I could trust you anymore. Madam Cartenoth and Phenola said you gave them blood when she got sick, but they also said you were *with* Gideon. I couldn't risk the people here on my hunch that you would choose me."

"You wanted to know I wanted to leave on my own." I thought of that car ride with Kenji, how he'd challenged me by demanding to know what I wanted. I'd wanted a different life in that truck.

I think it's time.

I hadn't understood what Kenji meant when he'd said those words to Phenola. But now it made perfect sense.

"I won't help you start a war with the Cards." I shook my head, pushing my empty bowl away.

I might have known that I needed to leave Gideon, but that didn't mean I wanted him dead. And thinking about Laykin and Enver and the people at that compound, none of them deserved to die in some war for a supposed new world. I just wanted out, a fresh start.

"Lissa," Tayna said, "this all started for you. All of this began as a way to get you back, but it's bigger than that now. We have a real chance to change things in this city. The people here believe in our mission. The war has already started. There's no going back."

"I won't be part of it, Tayna." I shook my head.

"You already are, Lissa." He slammed a fist on the table, and I jumped. He seemed to catch his flare of temper and settled a bit. "You already are. Your silver is too powerful for you not to matter. Gideon will come for you."

He was right. Gideon, no doubt, was already looking for me.

"Then we run!" I said.

"To what end?" Tayna was still shaking his head. "Lissa, I'd run with you to the ends of the earth, but it won't stop the fighting that's already started. He'll still destroy us if he has the opportunity. You may be the key to winning this war, but you're not the only catalyst for it. This is about what's right."

"Gideon only wants to protect the Cards," I argued. "If your men stop picking fights with him, he'll leave you alone."

"You can't possibly believe that." Tayna's voice turned darker, and I realized he hadn't touched most of his stew. The half-eaten bowl was growing cold. The bread was getting soggy in the gravy. "Gideon will destroy anyone he deems a threat. He's done it dozens of times already."

I wanted to defend him—to explain he wasn't a monster without cause, but even I knew that wasn't entirely true. Gideon was ruthless. Hell, he had no problem beating a man to death for a stupid, sly comment at a party.

Tayna sighed and pushed his stew at me.

But I shook my head.

Even my appetite had soured.

Music started up outside. Someone was playing a guitar, and I realized we'd sat in this corner, hunched over our table, while the rest of the house had enjoyed their meal. A young woman rounded up a group of children and shooed them out the door as she sang, "Bedtime, bedtime!"

"Come on." Tayna stood, offering me his hand. "We can talk more later."

Though I had a million things I wanted to say and ask, I took his hand. Because twenty-four hours ago, I thought I'd never hold this hand again. And now he was leading me out into the night to listen to music among the starlight.

24

Lissa

It wasn't just a woman playing the guitar, but a small band set up near a blazing fire. The woman at the center was beautiful, though. Her curly hair gleamed orange with the flicker of firelight. True firelight, too, not silvered. It was dancing deep orange and red at the center of the blaze. The woman's full mouth was puckered as she concentrated on the flames and the notes that lifted into the night.

"How do you keep the fire like that without silver?" I asked Tayna.

"Oh, it's all natural, baby," he said with a wink. "Just good old walnut wood piled high. It's amazing what fresh air and clean wood will do for a fire."

I thought of the silvered bonfire on the cliffs at the compound and Gideon's fists landing blow after blow into that man's bloodied face, closing my eyes as if that would help me escape the memory.

At the end of the day, I make the hard choices. For you. Even still.

Gideon's words from that night struck me as the heat of the blaze in front of me licked across my face, warding off the cool night's air.

Well, I'd made a hard choice for me, too.

I snaked my fingers down Tayna's forearm, sliding my hand into his, reminding myself he was real. He smiled down at me, leaning in closer until our sides brushed against one another. I was as aware of the heat from his body as I was of the flames in front of me.

It calmed my erratic heart, panicking upon finding itself suddenly torn in two directions. But tonight, I was with Tayna—the first night we'd had together in five years—and I refused to let thoughts of Gideon ruin this moment for me.

Dozens of people had gathered around the fire, some dancing and holding each other closely. Others talked in quiet pockets off to the side and still more sat, enjoying the night's peace and the stars scattered overhead.

The children had gone to bed, shuffled off to one of the buildings next to the main house, which seemed to be a bunk room for the littles old enough to have their own beds. I knew nothing about children and bedtimes beyond my memories of myself as a small child. My mother would read to me at night before I fell asleep. Sometimes I still heard her voice in my dreams, laughing through rhyming lullabies.

The woman played the guitar as she strummed the final notes of an upbeat melody. Her gaze met Tayna's, and she smiled softly. Her eyes stayed glued to his even as the last vibrato of the guitar faded, giving way to the sounds of crickets and the crackling blaze.

Something spiked within me at their shared look.

It was enough to remind me that Tayna had built a life with these Whigs. A life without me that I did not yet understand. The flare of jealousy was quickly followed by sinking guilt. Because I'd built a life without him, too, in the years we'd been apart. And why shouldn't he? He should be allowed that. It would be silly of me to expect he'd gone five years without any sort of companionship. Yet... I'd been forced to move on, hadn't I? I'd thought Tayna was dead. He'd moved on knowing I was still in the world. Did that mean he'd never wanted me the same way I'd wanted him? Yes, we'd been close. But childhood crushes fade. Of course they do.

For some.

Tayna watched the woman back for a long heartbeat, longer than the last note of the song.

It made me feel like shrinking into the shadows. Maybe it was time to call it a night. It had been enough of a day by that point, anyway. If I discovered anything else today, my silver might just burn me from the inside out.

I gently released our twined fingers.

But Tayna didn't let go of my hand. Instead, he pulled me to the center of the dancing as the next song began. I was grateful for the shawl that hid my shoulders and the Queen's tattoo on my skin. People gave me wary glances. I sensed that under normal circumstances, I would have been an untrusted outsider. But as a Card, these people had every right not to like my presence, especially if the war had already started in earnest as Tayna suggested.

Grant winked at me from where he sat by the fireplace with Alaric, and Tayna tucked me close into his arms. I'd had just enough wine that this place and the newness and uncertainty and jealousy all faded maybe more than it should.

The feel of Tayna's broad chest pressing against mine and his hands wrapping around my back made me feel like I might get lost in this night and never return the same. Dancing this close to him was also a chance to marvel at the man he had become. It was unfamiliar and new, the feel of the ridges beneath his shirt. But I truly lost myself in his eyes. They sparked like the light of the fire as he gazed down at me, taking me in in the same, desperate way I was staring back.

Tayna.

Tayna was alive.

What did it matter if his feelings for me ran deeper than friendship? It shouldn't matter. Not now. Not when I should just be happy to be close to him like this again. I could let that be enough for tonight.

I wrapped my arms around the back of his neck and pulled him in close, burying my face into his shirt just so I could breathe him in.

There was still so much to discuss and so much to unpack about what it meant for me to be here in this place with him. But for now, I was content just to enjoy the feel of him and to revel in the fact that he was alive, and we were together.

We were together.

I was running my hands across the hard planes of his chest, over his ribs, around his defined waist. I wasn't really dancing with him so much as exploring.

Did he remember the kiss we'd shared in the loft on that last night?

The thought made me glad my face was buried into his chest so he couldn't see it on me. The innocence of that memory struck something deep in my gut. The eighteen-year-old girl who'd blushed and knocked her mouth against his was now a woman. Five years ago, Tayna was my protector. But with the Cards, I'd learned to protect myself. My skin had grown harder, my dreams had grown tamer, and my anger had cut deeper.

Tayna felt my body tense but only held me tighter.

I fisted the fabric of his shirt but shook my head lightly as he swayed with me, his hips brushing my stomach as we moved together.

The woman playing the guitar began singing with the notes she strummed. Her voice was a haunting prayer sent to the stars that filtered in with the music as if she was simply another string inlaid on the instrument. It was a sad, unearthly melody. Her harmony danced with the notes like the fire danced on the wood, and I found my eyes drifting closed. The wine buzzed through my veins, the song filled inside my chest, and Tayna was warm around me.

"Are you sure you're real?" I murmured against Tayna's shirt.

"I'm real." He tightened his grip on me until I could feel my collarbone pressing along the planes of his chest.

We stayed like that under the stars until my feet began to drag, and the fire was reduced to embers. At the final song, I realized only a few people remained around the fire, and Tayna and I were the only ones still dancing.

"It's been a long day." I pulled away and the breeze filtered between our bodies as if waiting to find the cracks, all of the unspoken things still to say.

But Tayna took my hand. "Let me show you to your room."

My room.

Not ours.

Of course, I hadn't expected we'd share a room. We weren't kids sharing a loft anymore. But that strange, foreign feeling of change still crept beneath my skin, and I glanced once more to the woman who'd played the guitar. She had set the instrument down and was watching us. Her gaze still lingered on Tayna as she worried at her bottom lip.

Turning my gaze back to Tayna, I let him lead me back into the house, only to come face-to-face with Alaric standing in our path. Where Grant was soft lines and large smiles, Alaric was edged with barely restrained contempt, and his lips turned down at the corners in well-honed skepticism.

"So this is Gideon's little pet," he said, looking me over.

"Alaric." Tayna stayed between me and the man, his voice a warning. "Lissa made the decision to leave the Cards."

"Is that so?" Alaric took a step toward me. "And how do we know she isn't a pretty little silver bomb sent here by the Ace to kill us all?"

Grant approached us and gripped Alaric's arm with a warning, "Hon..."

But Alaric shrugged him off.

"I don't want to hurt anyone," I said, ashamed of myself for ducking into Tayna's shadow but also not trusting that this man wouldn't lunge for me. And if he did lunge for me, I would become that exact little silver bomb he was so concerned about.

"This is a war, girl," Alaric snapped. "And you're a Silver. Not hurting anyone isn't an option for you."

We were drawing attention from the people around the fire.

"Enough, Alaric," Grant said with more venom than I expected from the jovial man. "She deserves a chance, same as you got all those years ago."

"I wasn't fucking the leader of the Cards," Alaric spat.

"Well, you might as well have been." Grant rolled his eyes.

"You were a Card?" I asked around Tayna's shoulders. Maybe that was why something was vaguely familiar about him. The man was old enough to be my father, but still maybe the strongest-looking man I'd ever seen in my life. It made sense the Cards would have wanted someone like him on their side.

"Oh," Grant sighed. "This man wasn't just a Card. He was Ishmael's second."

"Enough, Grant," Alaric snapped, the firelight flickering across his face and highlighting the deep lines in his forehead.

"What?" Grant shrugged. "You get to judge her and not give her any information about yourself. This isn't how it works around here, my dear sweet hubby." He leaned into me conspiratorially. "Sometimes I call him Spadie just to piss him off."

Ishmael's second? The image of my mother standing before those Cards that had come to our house flashed before my eyes. I was fairly certain I'd never seen Alaric before, but could he have information about my mother's death? Was he there when Ishmael ordered her to be found?

"When—" I stammered, reining in my silver. "When did you leave the Cards?"

"A long time ago, Queen," Alaric glared.

"It was before, Lissa." Tayna's voice was low, meant only for me. He knew exactly where my thoughts had gone. His fingers traced down my spine as he leaned close to my ear. "Over a decade before they would have come for her."

A nod was all I could manage.

It was then I realized the rest of the talking had stopped. No one was even attempting to hide the fact that they were staring at us. Most of the people at the fire seemed just as interested in an explanation as Alaric was. But now I had even more questions. I'd never heard of a Card who'd abandoned the gang and lived to tell about it.

"Why did you leave?" I asked Alaric.

His lip curled in response, and he spat, "Because I fucking wanted to. Why did you leave?"

I glared at him and deadpanned, "Because I fucking wanted to."

Alaric's eyes narrowed to slits while Grant chuckled.

"Enough." Tayna put up a hand. "That's enough. Everyone's had a long day. We can hash this out tomorrow. I'm sure Lissa would be happy to speak with you, and anyone else who would like to say hello and have a pleasant conversation about why she's decided to join us." He looked around at the faces lit by firelight. "But if anyone wants to question if she has a place here"—Tayna glared back up at Alaric—"they can come talk to me."

Tayna was slightly shorter than Alaric and, as tall as he was, that was saying something. But he glared at the hardened man as if he were the superior, and Alaric, surprisingly, backed down with a nod.

"We'll continue this conversation," Alaric agreed. "Bring her to the council meeting."

"Would love to." Tayna sighed and then took my hand with a squeeze. Over his shoulder, he said, "Good night, y'all," before leading me back inside the house.

"What's the council meeting?" I asked, my voice low as I continued to avoid the furtive glances in my direction.

"The leaders of the Whigs meet weekly," Tayna explained, "to discuss matters concerning the compound. It's where decisions are made. Majority rules."

"And why do you get to make the decisions?" I asked as he led me past the living room and the kitchen to a wood-paneled hallway at the back of the house.

"Because we were elected to make them. The people who live here chose us as representatives."

Stained glass floral sconces lined the path, lighting the way to a nondescript wooden door.

Tayna pushed it open.

Not locked then.

Inside was simple but clean. There was a bed barely big enough for two covered in a green quilt. A small desk sat in one corner with an old wooden chair.

And there were books.

Stacks of books.

Even a stack of books next to the bed with a lamp and a cup on top like a makeshift nightstand.

"This is your room," I said, turning to Tayna.

He scratched the back of his head and shrugged. "Space is limited here. I'll crash on the couch."

We'd spent years sleeping next to one another in the loft, and I ached to feel his body next to mine again. But it also felt so strange and unfamiliar, as if the idea were more nostalgic than realistic. Plus, this didn't feel like it had when we were kids. Innocent, that is. The idea of asking him to stay felt too intimate. I'd just found out he was alive, after all. And that last night we'd spent in the loft together... Well, it hadn't been innocent then either. Maybe it hadn't been for a while. The tension had been building in that small space we shared.

It still hung heavy in the air around us.

But he couldn't possibly stay. My mind was too fractured to think rationally after the day I'd had. Between leaving Gideon, being drugged by Kenji and Phenola, finding out Tayna was alive, and now trying to decide where I stood in a war between the Whigs and the Cards, I had enough to deal with.

Tayna and I could wait to sort where we stood with one another.

And then there was Gideon. But he was a piece of my heart that was mine alone to sort.

So I just nodded to Tayna. "Goodnight, then."

He didn't look disappointed or surprised. He was simply taking me in against the yellow light of the lamp as he said, "Good night, Liss."

But as he turned to leave, I couldn't help but say, "Tayna?"

He turned back to me. The scar down his eye was stark against the light. His eyes shone as they met mine.

"Please still be real in the morning," I said, a small smile playing at the corners of my lips. Because more than intimacy, I feared he might disappear again if I let him out of sight. It still felt too new to be real that I was here on this farm, and he was alive.

"Promise." He grinned back, the dimples showing in his cheeks.

"Shirts and stuff are in the drawer if you want to change. They'll drown you, but they're clean. Bathroom's down the hall. Help yourself to whatever you need."

"Okay," I said, balling my fists to stop myself from asking him to stay.

He hesitated for one more moment, one more breath as if waiting for the question.

But then he closed the door and didn't return.

25

Gideon

Thirty-four hours.

She'd been gone for thirty-four hours.

"The sixes finished the sweep of the cliffs. There's no trace of her. Not even a shoe print, Ace."

Kenji's words were even, bordering on nonchalant, except for the slight upturn in the way he said my title. It almost, almost turned the statement into a question.

It wasn't laced with fear, not like his words should be. It was worse. In that statement, I heard pity.

The wedge that had been driven into my heart twisted into a slow burning rage. I stretched my neck from side to side as if that could relieve some of the pain in my chest. The burn only grew.

And I stayed silent as I contemplated his words, toying with the used butterfly needle I'd found on my little Queen's desk.

Her rooms were undisturbed. Everything in its proper place.

Until now.

Until I'd searched it from top to bottom, her books scattered across the floor and the diamond necklace I'd given her tucked into my pocket.

At first, I'd thought she'd snuck from the compound only to prove she could. This was her way of pushing me because, when she'd asked, I'd told her she wasn't allowed to leave. My little Queen had never done well with boundaries. I reveled in the ways I would push her limits when she returned.

But when the day had passed without any news of her, not so much as a sighting in town, I'd realized this was more than a game.

Stay.

I'd almost ordered her that night.

I can't.

And I was the bastard who had already taken so much from her that I'd allowed her to have that choice. I thought it was a choice to sleep down the hall instead of in my arms. But it was a deeper sort of betrayal. She hadn't simply denied me access to her sleeping body. She'd denied me access to her entirely.

She'd left.

"It appears two dresses, a shawl, and a pair of her slippers are missing, Ace," Laykin said from the closet where he'd been rifling through the garments. "And a couple of her books."

In addition to the used butterfly needle, I'd found a knotted hair ribbon on her desk. The little liar had even taken some vials of silver with her.

Had she intended to be gone this long, or had something happened to her once she'd left my protection?

The only message she'd left was her Queen's cloak, laid out neatly across her bed, as if to say, "Never again."

The butterfly needle pricked my finger. I relished the distraction of the pain and wanted more, so I squeezed it in my palm until the blood dripped from between my fingers. My blood, still laced with her silver.

"Ace."

Kenji's fucking pity again.

I ignored him, jaw tight, not dropping the needle as it wedged its way into my palm in the same way my little Queen had wedged her way into my heart.

Kenji fucking Jones was lucky to be alive right now. He'd realized she was missing that night, and instead of coming to me directly, he'd gone out looking for her himself. We'd lost the entire night because of his insolence. I hadn't settled on his punishment just yet—had barely stopped myself from pommeling him to death if only because I knew Lissa cared for him. There was still time to throw him from the fucking cliffs for his neglect. But demoting him to patrol duty along the cliffs with the sixes had seemed a fitting first step.

My glare tracked to Dia, where he leaned in the doorframe, looking for all the world like he didn't give a damn as he eyed Kenji. His tree trunk arms were crossed over his chest. My second rarely cared about anything. The only time I ever truly saw life in his eyes was when he was killing or maiming. He was a useful, loyal weapon in that way.

"Find her," I said to Dia. "Take whatever men you have to. Do whatever needs to be done. But find her."

And he smiled a wolf's smile, his eyes shining with his ration of silver.

"You have my word, Ace."

I knew Dia, at least, was not a liar.

26

Lissa

D espite my exhaustion, I found it impossible to sleep.
As soon as I started to doze off, I sprang awake again as if I were falling. And then I had to wait for my eyes to adjust to the darkness, confirming I wasn't back at the compound with the Cards. When I could make out the smooth contours of Tayna's wooden bed framed around me, a whole other sort of fear crept over me.

I wasn't at the compound anymore.

Gideon would know I wasn't there by now.

And Gideon would come for me.

There was a certain knowing within me that he wouldn't stop until he'd found me. In the dreams I did have, after more tossing and turning, his words were front and center.

Lesson one: You are mine.

Lesson two: What you want doesn't matter.

Lesson three: You are so much more to me than your body or your silver blood.

You are everything.

And I couldn't even call them nightmares because a deep part of myself burned with those words like they were promises seared on my heart. The game of hate and love we had played for so many years had festered through my soul until he was wound into the fabric of it in a way that truly terrified me even as I ached for him.

Maybe it had been a mistake to come here. Perhaps Alaric was right. I'd put everyone with the Whigs at risk by being here. I hadn't known; I hadn't realized what it would be. I thought it would be another gang. But it was so much more than that. Even in the small slice I'd seen, I could tell this place was different. Phenola was right. This wasn't a compound. This was a community, and these people were family. There were children here. Families.

Tayna had built something special because Tayna was special. I knew he looked after these people the way he'd looked after me for all those years. He cared about people more than anyone I'd ever known in my life, so I knew he would have dedicated himself wholly to protecting this place.

And to Tayna, protecting this place meant destroying the gangs, starting with the Cards.

I wished I could be so black and white in my convictions. But I saw the shades of gray. I saw Gideon both as the monster and as the protector. He would do anything to keep me safe. He would do anything to keep the Cards safe.

Which was why he, too, would do everything in his power to destroy the Whigs.

And yet, I couldn't go back. No part of me wanted to return to the compound. It was the right decision to leave, and I would pull the prongs Gideon had clamped around my heart, one by one, no matter how long it took.

I stared at the pine ceiling as the sun began to creep up through the small square window in the room. My mind felt foggy, and my eyes were heavy-lidded with lack of sleep, but I dragged myself from the bed.

There was no point in staying in this room if all it meant was more worry.

I found a black jacket in the closet. It was a long cotton thing that fell just above my knees and zipped up the front. It smelled like Tayna, like maybe he hadn't washed it among the other things, but I reveled in the scent of sweat and grass. I grabbed *Where the Red Fern Grows* from my bag and left the room.

Tayna was sleeping on the couch when I walked into the living room, and I stepped lightly to avoid disturbing him. His soft breaths filled the space. It was cold in here. He had a small thin blanket pulled up to his chin. With his face relaxed in sleep, he looked so much like the boy I remembered. His mouth slightly parted instead of pressed into a thin line, his brow soft instead of creased in thought, and his cheeks slightly red from the cold.

He was beautiful in a way that made my heart ache. Because I'd missed seeing him become this man who was now in front of me. How had he changed so much from the scrawny, smiling dreamer I'd grown up with to this strong, commanding man?

I settled another blanket on top of him, unable to keep my hand from trailing along the curve of his face. I wanted to curl up next to him.

But then my stomach soured with guilt. Thoughts of Gideon muddled my mind. So I forced my hand back to my side and left Tayna sleeping as I ventured outside.

Dan and Ann were still on the stairs. They jerked upright as I exited the house, their ears perking.

I froze.

They froze.

But then the one with one floppy ear took a tentative step forward. When I didn't back up a step, the wolf dog took another step and then another until it was level with my hands.

"Please don't eat me," I murmured, but the pup simply licked my palm, then sat near my feet.

The other, I was pretty sure it was Ann, seemed less inclined to make a peace offering. She was the one who'd grabbed me by the scruff yesterday, and she seemed to eye me like she'd do it again given the slightest provocation.

Dan leaned a bit of his weight against my leg, and I tentatively reached out a hand, running my fingers through the mane of hair near the back of his neck. The fur was coarse, but underneath it was a fine layer that felt silky beneath my fingers.

"They won't bite," a voice said on the porch to my side, and I whirled to find Grant sitting in a porch swing, sipping from a steaming mug. His face was even redder than I remembered it last night, thanks to the morning chill.

"I've never seen dogs like this," I admitted. "In the city, they're all feral."

"Dogs are meant to be with people," Grant mused. "Take them away, and it's no wonder they're unhappy. Same with the people. Creatures like to care for other creatures. When you strip away that option, well, the dogs in the city are a great example of the result."

"Where did these two come from?" I asked.

Ann sauntered closer to Grant, clearly preferring his company to mine, which was fine with me. He scratched her haunches as she neared.

"Alaric and I raised their mother in our home in the city. We'd found her as a puppy in one of the dumpsters. No family in sight. She must have gotten frisky one night because a few years after we found her, we were surprised with a litter of 'em. Big ole things. By that time, Tayna was living with us, and he begged to keep these two. Not that we could have separated him from them if we tried. That boy was born to care for creatures in need."

I snorted, knowing that all too well.

We seemed to be the only ones awake at this hour. There was a hint of mist along the tree line. The light made the crops in the distance glow golden. The dawn air was quiet, though I sensed we were on the verge of a flurry of activity. This didn't seem like a place where people wasted daylight.

"I'm sorry about Alaric," Grant said. "He means well. But he's as protective as Tayna about this place. And you have to understand, we've never had someone like you come to this community. It's why

Kenji and Phenola drugged you the way they did. We couldn't risk a Card, let alone a Queen, knowing directions to this place."

"I'm not a Card." It was my gut reaction to deny it. I'd spent five years denying that I belonged at that compound. It never felt like my home. Yet, in my last few weeks there, there had been something different about that place. It had started to feel, well, maybe not right but comfortable. I'd begun to find a sort of peace.

Which was exactly how I'd known I needed to leave.

Grant nodded his chin to my shoulder. "Your arm would seem to suggest otherwise."

"Alaric has one, too, I would guess."

"Alaric has his own demons." Grant sighed, leaning back in his seat and narrowing his gaze out at the misty morning. "Things he wishes would stay buried have a way of always finding him again."

"I didn't want the tattoo," I said. "It wasn't given with consent."

"Oh, I believe that," Grant mused. "Alaric would say the same. But you drank the proverbial punch at some point. I can see it in your eyes."

"I left, didn't I?"

"Not sure you've actually left yet." Grant shrugged, taking another sip from his mug and standing. "We better get started on breakfast."

"We?" I ventured. So much for a quiet morning spent reading. To be honest, I liked the idea of being useful, but I wasn't sure about my skills in the kitchen. I'd never cooked anything in my life, aside from warming up soup in the microwave in the loft I'd shared with Tayna.

"Everyone's expected to do their part around here. It's different from your gang in that way. Will that be a problem for you?"

"No." I shook my head. "Absolutely not."

I didn't plan to sit around and waste my days here, after all. At least this was a start. So I followed Grant into the kitchen. He handed me an empty basket and directed me to the chicken coop. Once I'd dodged a few angry hens and filled the basket, he'd shown me how to make scrambled eggs, adding a bit of cream and a healthy pinch of salt and pepper.

That part wasn't so bad.

The eggs cooked slowly, little by little as I stirred them constantly.

Grant fried bacon next to me. The long strips sizzled and sent little spats of grease flicking onto my arms as I stirred the eggs. The smoke of the meats made the kitchen hazy.

At some point in my cooking, I glanced over my shoulder only to realize the space was full of people. A bleary-eyed child added a scoop of eggs to his plate. A woman ran a hand through the boy's floppy hair and began buttering toast. Still more were pouring cups of a steaming dark liquid. And, as if called by my gaze, Tayna walked into the kitchen, meeting my eyes and smiling. His face was still ruddy with sleep, but he grabbed a plate and two mugs and found his way to me, weaving through people to reach my side.

"Your eggs are burning," he said with a cheeky nod of his head.

I cursed, hurrying to pull them off the heat as Grant had shown me.

"Damn," I said, seeing the brown bits.

But Tayna just laughed and held out his plate. "I'll eat them."

I looked at him like he was crazy. "I ruined them! They'll taste like rubber."

He shrugged. "I don't mind. Still good protein. None of that should go to waste."

I couldn't argue with him there. It was the shared reminder that we'd been starving kids on the street not that long ago who would have given anything for hot burned eggs to eat in the morning. So I loaded them onto his plate.

"Coffee?" he asked, handing me the mug.

"This is coffee!" I gasped, looking into the steaming cup. It smelled vaguely like smoke and nuts and enticing in the same way Millie's pastries filled the air with richness as they baked.

I took a big swig and wished I hadn't. I looked for a place to spit, but there was nothing. It was bitter and sharp like an underripe berry. It was heavy on my tongue. It took everything in me to swallow, and then I began coughing.

"You look like that night we drank tequila." Tayna laughed, shaking his head at my horrified expression.

Gideon really had spoiled me with those coffee beans. Those must have been as fine as he'd claimed because they tasted nothing like the muck in this cup.

"You need some sugar and cream." Tayna nodded to the pitcher on the counter. "It'll get better. Just keep drinking it."

I handed the mug back to him. "No, thank you."

And he just chuckled.

Alaric entered the kitchen then, chewing on a piece of bacon as his gaze found mine and held. He looked like he'd been up for a while. His face was ruddy as if he'd been working outside, and his boots were muddy. He pointed at Tayna and me with bacon-greased fingers and said, "You two. Let's move."

"Now the real fun begins," Tayna murmured, placing a light hand on the small of my back that had me sucking in a breath.

I couldn't tell if he meant that statement seriously. Alaric seemed like the opposite of all things I would consider fun. And I hadn't even eaten breakfast yet.

"I got this," Grant said, taking over with the egg pan.

If I was being honest, I missed Millie's pastries at the compound, but I settled for a piece of that nutty bread with some jam as Tayna led me out the door. Alaric was already stalking up the hill back toward the barn.

The mist from the morning had given way to a sunny day outside. The air was growing warmer, and I wished I'd changed out of Tayna's jacket and back into my dress. I hadn't anticipated the day starting so quickly so I shoved up the sleeves of the hoodie the best I could, sweating just from the climb up the hill.

Inside the barn, folding chairs had been set up in a semi-circle around a whiteboard that was faded with colors from markers that had been used too frequently across the space.

Alaric stood, his arms crossed over his chest, watching as we filed in.

Five others were taking their seat around the semi-circle. Most of them couldn't have been much older than me. It was rare to see middle-aged people in the gangs like Alaric and Grant. Most were kept on while they were young and then cut loose.

I wondered if that was the real reason Alaric had left the Cards. And, if not, why had he left? Kings were treated like, well, royalty at the compound. I had no doubt Alaric would have had access to as much silver as he wanted, along with just about anything else. Ishmael was known to be a brutal man, but he was a loyal man with those he trusted. Just like Gideon.

The woman from last night, the one who had played the guitar and stared at Tayna, was already in the barn. She put a hand on Tayna's shoulder and said something to him under her breath. I watched her red lips as her mouth moved but couldn't make out her words. A light dusting of freckles dotted the skin of the arm that was resting on Tayna, and I resisted the urge to swat her hand away. Her blue eyes settled on me for the briefest of moments, and I no longer needed to wonder what they were discussing. I had a feeling I would be the center for a lot of conversation today.

Tayna caught me staring, and his eyes seemed to brighten. "Lissa," he called, beckoning me over.

My smile was wobbly as I approached Tayna and the redhead. I stuck out my hand to her in a jerky, awkward gesture. God, I had no idea how to forge a new friendship. My one with Enver had taken five years, and even then, it hadn't been my doing.

"I'm Lissa," I said, but then I couldn't help but add, "the new topic of gossip around here."

Her eyes only lit in amusement at my quip, though. "You have certainly made things around here more exciting." She took my hand. "I'm Clary."

I couldn't help but notice how her shoulder brushed along Tayna's in a casually intimate way. It made the hair along the back of my neck prickle. I had no right to feel possessive over him. I'd been in another man's bed only a few nights ago. Tayna and I had just been reunited yesterday after five years apart. Of course, he had every right to find someone, to be happy. I had no claim to him. We hadn't even been a couple when we were together before.

But, well, we were kids before and so young, we had no idea what we were doing. At least, that was how I'd felt. "Together" felt like too simple a word for what we'd been to each other before. But I had no way to articulate it beyond a deep and certain knowing in my gut that he belonged to me, and I belonged to him.

Now, we were strangers.

But that tug to him still ran deep within my belly. It made the toast roil in my stomach as it yanked me in two different directions. I couldn't help the attraction to the man in front of me, yet there was a hole in my heart from the man I'd left behind.

I swallowed the nausea. "You're part of the council, Clary?"

She shrugged. "I help organize things around here. We've got a rotation for the chores that need to be done, and we keep a list of the skills people have so we can optimize our resources. The council voted to make my position an official one at the start of winter."

"She's our chief of staff around here," Tayna said with a hint of pride dancing in his eyes.

Clary just beamed right back, a small hint of color tinging her cheeks. It made my chest feel tight. Maybe Tayna hadn't wholly returned to me after all. Perhaps his heart was still lost. Or maybe the person I'd found alive wasn't my Tayna at all anymore. He'd grown from a boy to a man. It wasn't just his build that was different but his presence, too. He was more confident and commanding as he stepped up in front of the group as everyone gathered to sit.

"Thanks for being here today," he said to the ragtag band sitting in the circle of folding chairs.

There was a woman with the sides of her head shaved short, her dark hair piled in a high ponytail. Clary sat next to her, followed by Alaric. Then a stern-looking guy with a white-blond beard and his arms crossed over his chest. A beefy guy with a shaved head and rich brown skin. And finally, a woman I'd seen at dinner last night. Her hair was a long ebony braid down past her lower back, and I realized now that her eyes were silver. She was like me.

She seemed to notice my staring and gave me a small smile before turning her attention to Tayna.

Tayna continued, "We only have one topic to kick off our agenda." He looked at me. "Lissa Metarro, former Queen, has left the Cards. Kenji Jones and Phenola Cartenoth brought her here. It's up to our vote to decide if she stays."

27

Lissa

The blood rushed to my head.

"You're going to vote—" I gripped the chair to keep myself seated.

I hadn't realized there would be a formal vote to decide my fate with the Whigs.

"This is how things are done around here," Alaric said, giving me the side-eye as if he expected my protest. "We represent the interests of this community. It's up to all of us to keep the Whigs safe."

"Let her speak, Alaric," the man with the shaved head said.

"I—" I looked at Tayna as the breath left me. "I don't have anywhere else to go."

Tayna looked like he might reach for me but held his ground instead.

"The bigger issue," Alaric said, his boots crunching in the hay as he stood, "is that the Cards will come for her. By allowing Lissa sanctuary here, she is putting everyone in this community at risk."

"Or giving us the edge we need against the Cards," Tayna argued. "She's also a Silver, let's not forget that. And not just an ordinary

Silver, either. Lissa has the ability to use her power as well as gift it through her blood."

"Silvers can use their powers however they'd like," the Silver woman said. "She's not bound to give us her silver if she stays."

"Well, maybe this one should be," the blond man said. "If we're going to take the risk to protect her and all."

"That's not how this works," Tayna said sternly. "We won't ask people to give up their liberty to be part of this community."

"Yet she's asking all of us to put our lives at risk?" the blond man demanded.

"Rumor has it her abilities are quite uncontrollable," the man with the shaved head mused.

"From what Tayna's told me," Clary spoke up, her voice soft but strong, "Lissa left of her own free will but had no idea Kenji and Phenola would bring her here when she did. So she hasn't asked us to risk anything. Not knowingly, anyway."

"Knowing or not doesn't mean the risk is any lower," Alaric said. "Gideon will not stop until he's found that one." He pointed at me.

Tayna shook his head. "All of the Silver who live here have—"

But I cut him off with a low, "Tayna." I remained seated and took a deep breath, bracing my hands on my thighs before I said. "Alaric's right. I'm a risk to all of you. In the short time I've been here, I see what a sanctuary this community is. I can tell this is a special place. You have every right to want to do everything to protect it. I agree. It wouldn't be fair for me to stay. I'd just ask for a few days to get myself sorted on a plan and maybe some food for the road. And then I'll leave."

I'd never truly been on my own, but I could do it. I knew I could survive. Maybe I could head south where it was warmer. I'd never been much of a gardener, but I was my mother's daughter. I could learn. I could do this. And then maybe—

"If Lissa leaves, I leave," Tayna said.

"Absolutely not." I did stand then. "Tayna, this place needs you."

At the same time, Alaric said, "Don't be a fool."

And the Silver woman with the long braid stood. "Enough."

I realized now she was older than I'd first guessed, maybe in her thirties. Her features were strikingly sharp as she surveyed everyone in the room.

"This isn't even an argument. I know all of you," the woman said.

"Rixa..." Alaric growled.

"Oh, sit down, Alaric," Rixa barked. To my surprise, he did, but not without a dramatic sigh as he leaned back in his chair and crossed his arms. "None of you are going to actually vote to send Lissa out by herself. Except maybe you, Alaric, but only because you're a grumpy old ass. You wouldn't actually let her leave. It's not who we are, so this is a ridiculous discussion. She stays. Anyone want to pretend they have any more objections?"

"I have an objection." It was the woman with the sides of her head shaved who stood. "She isn't just an ordinary Silver. She's Gideon's pet, and that makes her more of a risk than this community should be willing to take."

"A risk that could be a turning point in this war for us," Grant mused, and I realized he'd been leaning against the open barn door, watching us argue. Breakfast must have ended. "Lissa could be taught to use her abilities. She could learn and become a vital ally for this community. You're being shortsighted, Felina, just like my dear husband."

"I won't kill anyone," I said. "But I am willing to help, however I can otherwise."

No one from the group said anything else. Tayna let the silence settle.

Finally, he said, "Does anyone else besides Felina and Alaric oppose Lissa staying?"

No one said anything.

"Then it's settled." Tayna nodded. "She stays."

"This is suicide!" Felina interjected.

"It's done." Tayna's tone was sharp, and Felina settled back into her chair, arms crossed and glare on me.

"Now that that's done," Tayna said, "let's move on."

As the council launched into a discussion about funneling fresh water for the spring crops, I fell into the seat in relief, Tayna's sweater billowing around me. A bead of sweat collected at the baseline of my hair, the barn growing warmer as the morning sun moved further into the sky.

My gaze tracked to Tayna, who stood before the group, leading the discussion. I tried to match the broad, commanding man in front of me with the scrawny, scrappy street rat he'd been just five years ago. And it was there. That boy was there. It was in his dimples. It was in the dusting of freckles scattered across his golden skin. It was in the easy, relaxed way he commanded the room. But it was in his eyes most of all. They were still the eyes of a dreamer. In his gaze, I saw hope and passion and sincerity.

And when his gaze tracked to mine, it was in the way my very soul quieted. It was as if I had been screaming a question into the universe for the past five years, and it was only in seeing him again that my soul found its answer. Even the silver in my veins stilled.

But then he spoke. "Alright, final topic on the agenda today." His golden gaze didn't leave mine. "We need to discuss what we're going to do about Gideon."

Gideon's name made my heart beat to a near frenzy just as quickly as it had quieted.

"Lissa, we need to ask you some questions." Tayna's lips pressed into a thin line. "Is that okay?"

All eyes turned to me. Keen eyes. A council curious to learn the secrets I could give them about the Cards, their strategy, and what information they had about this small community.

I knew Tayna had done this strategically and for my benefit. He made the council vote on my status within the Whigs first to confirm I was safe. Even if I refused to answer these questions, I would be allowed to stay. This was my choice.

"Gideon didn't involve me in the strategy with his Suits," I hedged.

"But you know he's scouting for our location, right?" asked the man with the bald head, whose name I learned was Vinza.

I finally dragged my gaze away from Tayna to the others around the room.

"Yes," I allowed. "He's looking for you."

"Where has he looked?" Vinza pressed.

I glanced back at Tayna, who nodded his encouragement. He was trying to give me an out, but he was just as eager for these details.

I swallowed the lump forming in my throat. "He thinks you're in the north. He's been searching in the mountains. I'm not sure how far he's gone, but he'll leave for weeks at a time."

I didn't like talking about Gideon. This conversation made me even more unnerved than the argument about my fate in this community. I might have decided to leave the compound, but by telling the secrets I knew about the Cards, it was the final level of betrayal. It was the final decision that I was no longer allied with them. With Gideon. It was a bigger choice than simply handing over some information. It was a choice I didn't feel prepared to make. Gideon had protected me, even if I hadn't asked him to. Was I willing to sell him out to the Whigs?

"And where will he search after the north?" Felina asked.

I shook my head. "I don't know. But he won't give up. Gideon's ruthless."

Felina snorted. "Especially now that you're here, right Queenie?"

"No," my silver spiked at the derision in her tone. "Gideon never stands for rebels. The Cards and the Veiled practically make a sport out of who can kill new rebels first. But this time, with you, it was different. I've never seen Gideon as nervous about a threat as when he was speaking about you."

"Thanks to this one." Alaric clapped Felina on the shoulder. "Gave 'em a real run for their money a few night's back."

"You were responsible for the attack?" I couldn't help the slight tremor in my voice.

She grinned. "Really thought we had that bastard."

The thought that he'd almost died by this woman's hands made me feel sick. I clamped down on my silver as I felt bile rise in my throat at the reminder of Reggie's injuries and the desperation I'd felt to see Gideon unharmed.

"They never leave without a large stock of silver," I managed to say.

"Good to know," Vinza said. "Means we can steal it next time we get the jump on them."

"Next time?" I asked, my stomach roiling.

"This is war, girl," Alaric said. "Of course there'll be a next time."

The conversation continued, but I found myself shrinking in on myself. This betrayal felt like a step too far. Sitting in this room and hearing them discuss the plans they had to ruin the Cards made me lightheaded.

The heat on my skin built beneath the sweater.

It felt tight against my neck.

Tayna stood. "I think we can break. We've asked Lissa enough questions for one day."

The group stood, and I had to slow myself to keep from running from the barn. I didn't allow myself to meet Tayna's eyes. I caught just enough to see Clary reach for Tayna before I pushed through the doors and into the clear air. The breeze hit me, and I choked in a breath as I turned toward the back of the barn and made a beeline for the trees.

There had been so few moments since I was a child when I had truly been alone. Yes, I'd had time in my rooms at the compound or nights in the alley while Tayna was working at the club, but there had always been people just around the corner. There had always been a need to keep one eye over my shoulder.

Now, I tore into the woods, content to get so lost that I would be well and truly alone.

Large oak trees reached out to me in all directions, their branches old and ancient with tufts of green creating a canopy above and around me. These trees stood well before the Silvers even existed in this city, and I ran my fingers along them as I slowed to a walk. My chest ached from running, but I could no longer hear any noise from the compound.

My breathing finally slowed.

The earth beneath my feet turned rocky, opening up to a creek, which I followed until I reached a natural pool of sorts, surrounded by volcanic rock. Boulders peaked from the center of the water, scattered throughout the surface. The water was a clear evergreen and only a few feet deep from what I could see.

My slippered feet slid along the rocks, and I eventually kicked them off, leaving them on one of the taller boulders, along with Tayna's sweater so I could feel the sun on my skin. Content in just my bra and the oversized shorts I wore, I found a flatter rock face and stuck my feet into the pool, surprised when dozens of tiny tadpoles scattered at the ripples I created.

The air outside the barn was cool, but the sun and the warm rock I lay on were just enough to keep me comfortable. I closed my eyes against the glare and sighed, content to stay in this place for a while. There was a sweet relief in the simplicity of the noises around me. The wind echoed softly through the oaks. The creek ran in a tickling melody. And a bird cawed occasionally from a nearby tree.

This place was mine to call home if I wanted to claim it.

Home.

I'd had many of those at this point in my life, though not one since Tayna. And not a home that was a building since my mother had died.

But maybe I could have had one at the compound if I'd stayed for a bit more time. I shook off that thought, refusing to admit I missed Gideon. Enver and Laykin and Kenji, yes. I missed them. But Gideon had burrowed into a different sort of ache in my chest. I supposed that was why I knew it was time to leave. It was never meant to be my ending place. I'd never felt peace enough there to want it to be permanent. But was that what I wanted? Peace?

Gideon had offered me a sort of safety.

No, it wasn't safety. That wasn't the right word. He'd offered me a sanctuary from the chaos of my life. He'd offered me a place to read and think and, yes, be angry when my grief had felt overwhelming. I was allowed to be that person at the compound. And it worked. For a while, I'd made my anger and my resentment and my hurt work in my favor in that place.

But then it hadn't been enough anymore. Madam Cartenoth had hit a nerve. She'd been right when she said I should be so much more. There was that desire within me, too, to be more than a street rat and more than a Queen. What could I become with the Whigs?

For the first time, the answer didn't seem to be limited. And that, at least, felt like a significant improvement.

I smiled against the sun, and it warmed my face.

Sitting up, I climbed down from the rock face and explored the pool a bit more. Once I found a patch of soil far enough away from the water that it was dry, I bent down to my knees in the earth, running my hand just under the cool surface of the grains.

With the smallest bit of focus, I sent a stream of silver into the earth. The small saplings that had sprouted around the dirt, shocked by the electricity, wilted under my touch. I singed them just enough to leave a mark but not enough to kill them.

Delicately, oh so delicately, I controlled the flow from my fingertips.

It was thrilling to know I could harness this power inside me. And that, more than anything that happened in the past week, made me feel like I could forge a new future that was mine alone.

28

Lissa

Tayna stood just outside of the treeline when I emerged some hours later. He had a hand slung in his pocket, his hair in his eyes as he watched the horses graze in the distance while waiting for me. When he saw me, his eyes lit up, and he held out a piece of buttered bread and a few slices of what looked to be cured meat.

"You missed lunch," he said, watching me as I stepped over a particularly large rock. "We need to find you some more suitable clothes." He eyed my slippers skeptically, and I imagined I looked ridiculous in his oversized sweater and long shorts, paired with my delicate flats from the compound.

"Better than my Queen's cloak." I shrugged, which earned me that pinched look between his brows as he continued to study me.

I realized I wanted him to touch me. I wanted to feel those strong arms wrap around me, cocooning me in some of that hope he seemed to carry in abundance. He seemed so sure of himself and his place in this community. If only I could borrow some of his confidence.

Instead of reaching for me, he fell into step next to me as we walked toward the main house. The only contact was the slight brush of his arm against my sweater.

"What were you doing back there?"

Again, I shrugged. "Clearing my head a bit. It's been a weird couple of days."

"That's an understatement." His eyes gleamed, and those damn dimples appeared on his cheek.

I ripped off the end of the bread with my teeth and chewed it like the street rat he remembered. He laughed at my open-mouthed, loud chewing. "It's not exactly fresh!" I said in my defense around the wad of bread in my cheek.

That only made him laugh more. "It's good to see you're not a starved, scrawny girl anymore."

"Same to you," I said as I pushed the locks of hair from my face so I could study him again. He was broader than even Gideon, I would guess. He clearly hadn't been dumpster diving in a long while, and working on the farm all day, paired with fighting out in the streets, well, it had turned him into more warrior than street rat.

"Was that scar from me?" I dared to voice the question before I lost my nerve, inspecting the raised red slash through his eye.

"That day wasn't your fault, Lissa."

And I knew it was. I remembered the cut on his face. It had been so deep. Even with silver to heal, a cut like that would leave a mark.

"I have a lot of scars now," he said. "I don't regret any of them."

I pointed at one I could see on his arm. It was a long, raised gash. "What about that one? No silver?"

"Actually, it was from a silvered pocket knife." He sighed. "My own damn fault. It happened two years ago. I was out scouting with Alaric and Felina. We stumbled on a group from the Veiled who had a Silver girl with them. Five of them. They'd clearly beaten her badly, and she was so pale like they'd almost drained her dry. It was amazing she was still conscious. We didn't intend to let anyone know we were there that night. We planned to observe and then leave. But I couldn't walk away when we saw that girl with them.

"So I didn't. But we weren't prepared for a fight. Felina took a bullet to her side that day. Alaric broke his collarbone. I got this. We were a wreck and didn't have any silver with us to heal."

"And the girl?" I asked.

"It was Rixa."

Rixa. The ebony-haired woman who'd stood up for me with the council.

I pursed my lips and nodded, daring to ask, "And Clary? How did she find her way here?"

"She was born in these mountains. Her parents live in one of the houses on the farm property. When Alaric, Grant, and I found this place, they were one of the first to welcome us in and encourage us to create a home here."

"And have you made a home? With Clary?" The words slipped out on a breath before I could stop them.

But he heard every word.

"Jealous?" Tayna smirked sideways at me.

"No," I said quickly. Too quickly. I didn't have a right to be jealous. But in this world, right and fair didn't matter so much. It didn't stop me from feeling that frantic niggling in my chest whenever he looked at her.

Tayna sighed. "We've both lived a lot of life in the time we've been apart, Liss. Clary and I were easy in the same way you and I were easy. Sometimes, on hard days, we found ourselves together. But we've never discussed our time together beyond that."

It struck me like a dagger that he'd compared us.

"Oh." That was all I could manage in response. The back of my eyes burned, and my cheeks flamed with embarrassment and rejection.

No relationship had ever been like my relationship with Tayna. It was sacred to me in a way that allowed me to survive the dark parts of life, knowing that one bit of light existed in my time with him somewhere in this world. It made me wonder if it existed for him in the same way with Clary because he'd managed to find two people in this shitty, fucked-up world who lit his heart on fire. Or was it that his feelings for me had never been as all-consuming as mine?

The questions lingered. I'd already asked more than I had a right to know. For now, it would be enough. To be here on this farm with him alive was enough.

It had to be.

Because as soon as my desire for Tayna sparked, Gideon was in the back of my mind, reminding me he owned me, body and soul. But if Gideon owned my soul, then Tayna still held the fractured, messy pieces of my heart. Even after all these years, the thread of that connection was alive and real.

We walked back into the house only to find a scattering of kids huddled in the living room. About eight of them gathered, perching along the couch or the rug.

A young girl read out loud from where she sat at the mantel, and I quickly recognized the book. "*As the days passed, the dog-wanting disease grew worse. I began to see dogs in my sleep. I went back to my father and mother. It was the same old story. Good hounds cost money, and they just didn't have it.*"

They'd found my copy of *Where the Red Fern Grows*. I'd left it in the kitchen this morning after coming inside to help Grant with breakfast.

"Sorry," Tayna murmured, "they're fiends for any new stories."

I gripped his arm, quickly shaking my head. "It's okay."

His eyes traveled from where I'd grabbed him up to my face. Our gazes lingered.

Held.

The words read aloud transported us back to a small loft with piles of moth-eaten pillows and blankets. And two kids who had huddled next to a small, silver-fueled lamp to escape to a world that no longer existed.

Only now... Tayna had built that world.

We were standing in it.

And it felt like déjà vu. That this place could be real. That this dream could be real. That *he* could be real.

And who cared, really, what had happened over the past five

years? None of it mattered. All of it was worth it if we could be here. Now.

It was like within Tayna's golden gaze, I could see all of those memories reflected at me. We were suspended in the past, held hostage by the moments weaving themselves together until it was as if we'd never been apart. Stories and dreams and hope—it all existed between us.

I only managed to tear my eyes away from Tayna when the small girl paused, looking up at us and asking, "Do you want to hear the story, too?"

"I'd really like that," I said.

Tayna and I settled onto the floor, our backs resting against the baby-blue couch, small feet hanging next to our shoulders as we listened to a story we knew all too well become new once again.

29

Lissa

In the days that passed, I lost myself to the routine of farm life.

In the morning, I made breakfast with Grant, then spent a few hours working on the farm, doing odd jobs like feeding the animals or helping to plow the lines for new crops in preparation for spring.

After lunch, the time was mine, and—when I wasn't listening to the children reading stories in the living room—I spent most of my afternoons at the rock pool. Sometimes I read by myself, and sometimes I swam, but most of the time, I trained. Using my silver in small spurts, I tried to control the direction or the amount I released from my fingers.

I knew the real test would come when my emotions were high, but I began to truly see the potential in my silver abilities. I could be a real asset to this place. I knew Tayna didn't like to use silver. He'd always avoided my blood when we were younger, but he'd have to see the potential now. I could power farm equipment, allowing us to produce so many crops this year. Plus, my blood could help the workers stay strong and feel rested. And maybe I could even help on these scouting trips Tayna mentioned.

Life in this community was quiet and peaceful, and it was easy to settle into this place. In a week, I felt more a part of this community than I had in five years at the compound.

Tayna and I didn't interact much outside of normal chores and routines. I continued to sleep in his room, and he continued to sleep on the couch. It wasn't that we were avoiding one another; it was just that my mind got so muddled around him.

I still felt that pull to be near him. It was like a silver energy between us that belonged to us alone. When he entered the room, I could feel the crackle in the air. When he glanced my way, I felt the shiver run through my body.

I felt his absence even more accurately when he left the community for short errands. It was a hole of fear in my chest that didn't allow me to breathe normally until he returned. That pull had been there when we were kids and was still there now.

The problem was, I didn't know what to do with the feeling.

I'd given myself to another man. Gideon loomed large in my mind, even as the farm felt more and more like a home. I'd already betrayed him by leaving and sharing his secrets with the Whigs. To give my body to another, to explore things physically with Tayna, well, just the thought felt like another betrayal.

Plus, Tayna hadn't exactly expressed interest in me that way. I knew he was attracted to me. But he was always around Clary or she was never far away. He laughed with her often and had clearly downplayed his relationship with her. They were together. She looked at him like she knew every inch of his body and couldn't wait to discover something new over the planes and lines of his chiseled form.

The ground in front of me sparked and burned where I'd been practicing my abilities at the rock pool. I burned the earth more than I intended with my silver, killing the small sapling I'd only wanted to singe. I realized then I'd also killed all the plants in a two-foot radius around me.

"Clearly, that control is tenuous at best," a clear male tenor called behind me.

I cringed and glanced over my shoulder at Alaric. "At least I'm making progress."

"I thought you said you didn't want to kill," he mused, looking at the scorched earth.

That hit a nerve, and my pulse spiked along with my silver. It shot from my skin in a sudden wave, already primed for a trigger, thanks to my focus on the plant. I clamped it down, but not before a small jolt hit the earth again and sizzled.

The killing was one of the biggest things I struggled with when it came to my silver abilities. I felt proud that I could heal and protect myself. Nothing had felt quite as invigorating as that moment I'd started the Humvee on the compound and realized freedom was within my grasp. But I was only too aware of the damage my abilities could cause. *Had* caused. I could hurt people.

Worse.

I could kill them.

I had killed.

There were others at the market that day besides Tayna. Three people had lost their lives that day. Technically, my silver would have killed Tayna, too, if Madam Cartenoth hadn't cured him before it was too late. I thought it had killed him.

"You shouldn't be here," I said to Alaric.

"Afraid you'll singe me to my bones?" he asked, taking another step forward.

"You make me feel like I'm not in control," I admitted. "Which is not what I need when I'm trying to get this under control."

"Hmm," he mused, still walking toward me. "You see, I think it's exactly what you need."

"I could hurt you."

"Nothing a taste of your blood couldn't help." He shrugged a bulky, sun-worn shoulder. My gaze couldn't help but fall to the King of Spades tattoo on his shoulder. His skin there was weathered like he had intentionally spent as much time in the sun as possible, as if that would fade the mark.

"No," I said flatly. I wouldn't even consider allowing Alaric to help.

First of all, there was nothing he could do. I was a Silver, and he was a red blood. Sure, he was strong enough, but that didn't mean he could hold up against my silver. And second, I just didn't like the man. He triggered all of the worst of my emotions.

"Come on." Alaric looked like he was eyeing a new weapon, and I wondered what he was playing at. "It'll give you an excuse to hit me."

"I have no desire to hurt you or anyone else here."

"No?" He cocked an eyebrow at me. "Not even a little bit."

He'd neared enough now that I stood and said into his face, "Not even a little bit."

His chest was close to mine, and he was still grinning down at me.

I took a step back, and Alaric laughed, his teeth gleaming.

"Come on." He beckoned me forward again. "I'm just a red blood. Not a threat to you." He stepped into me again.

"Stop." I stumbled back, my breath catching in my throat.

He was goading me. Maybe he was hoping I would hurt him so he could use it as a reason to see me kicked out of the community.

"Don't act like you're a weak little mouse." Alaric kept advancing on me. "That's a bunch of bullshit." He shoved me. Actually shoved me. Not hard enough that I fell but hard enough to make me gasp and stumble.

Now, it was all I could do to shake my head.

"Come on, Queen," Alaric taunted.

And he pushed me again.

And again.

I did fall backward then. My foot caught on a rock and had me stumbling down to my bottom.

"No more baby—"

I launched myself at him, shoving him with a, "Stop!" that rang clear and commanding through my chest. I hardly recognized myself.

But I did recognize the flood of silver that streamed from my fingers at the impact. My body was not physically strong. The muscles along my arms were small and soft. Yet the blow I landed sent Alaric tripping backward and falling to the ground.

It happened in a blur of movement.

As soon as the power passed through me, I panicked.

"Alaric?" His name was a breath, a plea, as I crouched down beside his sprawled form.

For a moment, all I could think of was Tayna's broken and limp body in the streets of the market. The Cards had not broken him. I had. Just as I was now responsible for Alaric. Yes, he'd pushed me, but I shouldn't have allowed myself to lose control like that. I could never allow myself to lose control.

But Alaric sat up on his forearms and gave me a sloppy grin. A small cut was bleeding at the corner of his lip but healing.

"Are you okay?" I studied him. He had a gash on one arm where he'd hit the edge of a rock, but I couldn't see any other injuries. None from my silver even as his shirt was smoking.

"Rixa gave me a vial before I came out here," he explained, following my gaze. "I'm silver-proof for now."

"Fucking asshole," I gritted between my teeth and stood as soon as I realized he was uninjured.

"That wasn't half bad, Queen." He smirked, standing with me and licking at the blood on his lip. The cut was sealing itself closed.

"Don't call me that," I snapped. "I'm not a Queen anymore."

"You don't know what you are anymore," he said, leaning into me. "That's part of the problem."

"I don't know why you keep saying things like that to me." My anger was spiking again. "I left Gideon, didn't I? I'm here, aren't I? What do you expect from me?"

He shook his head. "You're still trying to walk on both sides. Sure, you left Gideon, but you only tell us the bare minimum about the Cards. And I can see it whenever anyone mentions Gideon's name. You get all stone-faced and protective. You may have left, but you're still his Queen."

Running my hands into my hair, I faltered. He wouldn't understand.

"This is war, girl," he continued. "You don't get to play both sides. Not here. That's why I don't trust you. Well, one of the reasons I don't trust you. You're unpredictable. If Gideon were to show up right here, right now, I don't know what you'd do. I wouldn't put it past you to turn on all of us to protect him the way you protect him with your words."

"I don't want there to be sides. I don't want a war. And I don't want to hurt anyone." I slumped down onto the ground.

"Sounds like a pretty little picture," he quipped, "but not reality. So if I can't trust you with your loyalties, then I might as well be sure I can trust you with that silver at your fingertips. I worked with your lot when I was with the Cards."

"Did you meet others like me? Who could use their silver?" I pressed.

"Only one." He nodded. "Only one."

"What happened to them?" There wasn't anyone like me at the Cards when I was there. Someone who could use their silver rather than just hold the power in their blood.

"She died," Alaric said, getting to his feet and brushing off the dirt. Then he offered me his hand. I tentatively took it, and he pulled me to stand.

"Is that why you left the Cards? Because she died?" I asked, wondering how much he'd be willing to tell me about his time with the Cards. I didn't know much about Ishmael, only that he was reputedly even more brutal than his son.

"I left the Cards for a lot of reasons. Most of all because they're bastards." I opened my mouth to ask more questions, but Alaric shook his head.

"Enough chatting," he said. "Hit me again."

30

Lissa

I was training with Alaric by the lake on a particularly sunny afternoon when Tayna emerged through the trees with Dan and Ann at his heels. He had on a loose white shirt and his brown riding boots as if he'd been about to take out one of the horses. He looked like the farm version of a man from a Jane Austin novel, clasping his hands behind his back as he approached. Sure, maybe younger. And yes, with a few more scars. But his hair had grown longer, the wind sweeping it across his brow. His eyes were shining as they met mine through the midday sun.

The sight of him made me pause.

Which only meant I didn't block Alaric's arm as it swung into my stomach.

I doubled over as I heard Alaric grumble, "Shit, Queen."

And then strong hands braced me. Tayna's gold gaze was so close to my face that it made breathing even more difficult.

It made me remember that night in our loft when I'd leaned in to kiss him. My gaze tracked to his lips, framed by a hint of chestnut stubble.

"Are you okay, Liss?"

Those large hands trailed their way from my shoulders to my neck as he gently guided my gaze back to his golden eyes, examining me for signs of injury.

No.

God no, I was not okay.

Because, at that moment, as I took in small sips of air trying to get my lungs to remember how to work properly, all I could think about was his mouth moving against mine.

We'd barely even hugged in the weeks since I'd been at the farm. Instead, I'd avoided him like a coward, confused by my feelings, which consistently oscillated between missing Gideon and wanting to fall into Tayna's arms. Preferably naked.

So no, I was not okay.

I quickly shrugged off Tayna's grip with a spluttered, "I'm fine. I'm fine."

Sweat stuck to the hair at the back of my head, and I could feel the stray strands from my braid sticking to my neck. I braced a hand on my hip, still catching my breath.

Tayna took a step toward me, but I held out a hand. A sliver of silver trickled across my fingers in a wave of my abilities to warn him back.

I just needed a minute to breathe and get my head straight.

"She's getting good." Alaric grinned, his white hair also gleaming with sweat.

"You two spend all your time training," Tayna said. "I just thought you might like to go riding. The weather's perfect today."

"I've never been on a horse before." I shook my head hesitantly.

"Exactly," Tayna said, offering me his hand. "You'll love it."

I looked down at my oversized T-shirt and cargo pants. Finding suitable clothing had been difficult at the farm. I didn't care so much what I looked like, but I didn't think it would be comfortable riding in clothes like these.

Tayna seemed to sense my hesitation. "Rixa already said she has some clothes you can borrow. And I've found a pair of boots that should work just fine. Come on." He stuck out his hand a little farther and looked at me with pleading eyes.

Not that I'd ever been able to refuse him. This was the first time he sought me out in weeks. So I took his hand and said to Alaric over my shoulder, "Same time tomorrow?"

He nodded and wiped the sweat from his tanned brow. "Good work."

We hadn't become friends per se in the days we'd spent training together, but we had come to a sort of truce. And I had to admit, he was a surprisingly good teacher. He was patient with me even though he pushed me until I was red in the face with exhaustion and frustration. He made me train to the limits of my silver until my body and my mind were exhausted. Everything from using my silver to using my body, all of it meant to hone me into a tool. Alaric would say a weapon. I would say a power outlet. More potential than certain danger.

Tayna and I stopped by the main house so I could change. Rixa had left out a pair of thick black leggings, a sports bra, and a fleece riding jacket that was a bit snug along my chest but fit well enough.

Tayna looked approving when I emerged in the outfit, surveying me with a sweep of his eyes that definitely lingered over the tight places. I tugged at the sleeves of the jacket, feeling self-conscious. The boyishness was gone from his gaze.

A man watched me.

A man who took a step toward me, leaned down, and said, "You're perfect." His lips grazed along the shell of my ear.

Then, as if we were still those street rats running in the night, he took my hand and led me to the stables while my heart struggled to keep up. His teasing touches were no longer satisfying my traitorous body, only making me more and more aware of how much I wanted him.

But I tried, *tried* to focus on the task at hand.

I liked the horses at the farm. I'd observed them from afar on a few occasions, even volunteering to muck the stables just to see them up close. They were beautiful creatures with their shiny coats and strong, muscled bodies. But the idea of climbing on one? I looked at the huge beasts as Tayna led them from the stables and out to a wooden post in the sunshine.

Tayna carried a blanket and a saddle out to a brown mare, his arm muscles flexing as he hoisted it onto the center of her back. She tossed her neck, the long hair of her mane swishing as she shook off the flies.

"Are you sure I can't help?" I asked.

"Horses can sense fear," he explained. "Your nerves will only make them jumpy. It's more important you all get used to one another."

Tayna ran his hands gently down her side, then her leg, checking her hooves. He placed the bit between her teeth and scratched her nose for good measure.

I sat on the wood railing of the stall, watching him as he repeated the same pattern with the horse next to the brown mare—this one a sandy-colored stallion with a shiny black mane. The horse watched me as Tayna worked around him, our eyes meeting and holding. He seemed to be studying me, and I felt the distinct impulse to impress this horse as if he were judging me.

"Did you tame these horses from the wild just like in the books?" I asked.

He snorted and shook his head. "I may have turned country, but even I'm not that skilled. No, these came from one of the families who joined the Whigs in the early days. They've cared for them generation after generation. In fact, we're hoping to breed these two in a few months."

The brown mare shook her head as if in challenge, like she dared the sandy horse to try.

I laughed. "She might need some more convincing."

Tayna walked in front of me, his hands gripping either side of the railing and pressing closer to me than I expected him to come. "And what about you?" he asked, his honey skin shining as he smiled along with me. "Do you need more convincing to stay?"

It was hard not to get swept up in him when he was this close. My adrenaline kicked up, causing my pulse to thrum. The hairs along my neck seemed to rise as if my body was warming against the sun.

Gideon hadn't been far from my mind in the weeks I'd been here. Whether it was worry that he would find me or worry that he would forget me, thoughts of him always wormed their way in.

But Tayna had occupied the same amount of space.

I didn't like seeing him and Clary together. That much I knew. I couldn't stop watching him. It was like the silver spiked in my blood whenever he was near.

And now that he was pressing so close, it took everything in me not to lean forward until our lips connected. With me sitting up on the fence, I was at eye level with him. The gold in his eyes shone brightly, and his mouth parted slightly as he watched me. I'd like to kiss him again. I'd like to know if it would feel as thrilling as it had that night in our loft.

"I like being here," I said finally. "This place feels like a dream."

"It was our dream, wasn't it?" His voice had dropped an octave, and my eyes again went to his mouth.

"We had a lot of dreams when we were starving kids on the street," I murmured, breathing in his earthy smell.

"We weren't so young, you know." He shrugged.

"It feels like a lifetime ago."

"I remember every minute."

I felt my body falling forward into his. He rose to meet me. We were so close that our breaths mingled in the small space between us. I was aware of every twitch of his lips. He seemed to be waiting for me to make the final move, to close the space between us.

But I pulled back. It was a last-second reaction that had me hot with embarrassment and desire. "We should probably go, shouldn't we?"

He dropped his head and pushed off the railing. His hair fell into his eyes as he shook his head to clear it away with a grin.

"Yeah, Liss," he said. "Let's get you on a horse."

He picked me up by the hips, his hands firm around my waist as he lowered me to the ground. On instinct, I put my hands on his shoulder to brace myself. He didn't pull away right away, nor did I. It felt too good being close to him again.

He twined our fingers and led me to the brown mare, running his free hand down her neck as she pressed her nose into his shoulder.

"This is Misty," he told me. "She's gentle. Perfect for your first ride."

I nodded and reached a hand out to her nose, running my fingers down her bristly snout. She let out a contented huff.

"See?" Tayna said. "She loves you already."

"Maybe I should watch you first," I said, eyeing the saddle warily.

"No way." Tayna tapped my side. "You've got it. I'll help you up."

We moved to the side of the horse, Tayna keeping his hands along her neck the whole time so she knew where we moved.

Once we were at the horse's side, he said, "Ready?"

Before I could answer, he lifted me into the air. I landed on the saddle and gripped the horn to steady myself.

"Now swing your leg around," he instructed.

But I found myself too unsteady to move. Misty shifted beneath me, and I held tighter to the saddle.

"I've got you," Tayna promised, and he brought his hand up to my right thigh to brace me. My eyes tracked his fingers, digging softly into my skin. His grip was firm on my body and decidedly distracting.

His fingers slid higher, pressing into my leg.

I swallowed.

"Leg, Liss," Tayna said with a smirk.

"Right." I nodded and hoisted my leg around and over the horse. It wasn't the most graceful maneuver. My foot got momentarily stuck on the horn, and I lurched back and then forward again, afraid I was going to go careening off the other side of the horse.

But Tayna was true to his word, keeping his grip on me secure with arms that I was pretty sure were larger than his waist had been when we were teens until I had righted myself on the saddle.

"I did it!" I said. And then to Misty, I added, "Thank you for not tossing me off," giving the side of her neck a light scratch.

"Remember what we talked about?" Tayna said, untying the horse from the post. "Nudge right with your thigh to go left and left with your thigh to go right. Pull back to signal her to stop."

Tayna hooked his foot into the stirrup and gracefully pulled himself into the saddle.

"Show-off," I grumbled under my breath. He just spun his stallion around and winked at me. "Misty." He clucked with his tongue, and my horse began to move.

On instinct, I tensed and pulled back on the reins, which only made her pause.

Tayna looked over his shoulder and must have seen the wild panic in my eyes because he said, "Give her a little squeeze with your legs. She knows where to go."

So I did, just a gentle press of my thighs, and Misty smoothly began to walk.

Tayna guided me patiently as we walked into the trees at the edge of the fields, following a small dirt trail that branched off opposite the rock pool I'd claimed as my training grounds.

Once I'd gotten the hang of directing Misty and felt a bit more comfortable on her back, Tayna called over his shoulder, "Want to speed up?"

"No, I—" But he was already clicking his teeth into motion as his stallion gained a bit of speed.

Misty followed suit, and I found myself bouncing along uncomfortably, gripping one hand on the reins and one on the horn as I cried, "Tayna!"

He slowed, grinned over his shoulder at me, and I nearly cried with relief.

He circled back around to me so our horses were sidled up next to one another. "You okay?" he asked, that mischievous spark still in his eyes.

"I don't think I like that." I shook my head.

"You're too tense. You have to let your body move with the horse. If you try to fight it, you'll bounce until you bruise your pelvis."

"Right," I grumbled, thinking it already might be. Thank god for Rixa's padded leggings.

"Come on." He motioned with his head, swinging his horse back around. "There's a place up ahead I want to show you. We can stop there for a bit."

What Tayna hadn't mentioned was this place was up a hill. A steep hill with a thin trail that snaked back and forth the higher we climbed. Even Misty seemed resentful of the climb, but as we reached the top, I realized I could see in all directions around me. It was a clear day, and the approaching spring meant everything was on the verge of blooming.

In the distance was a sliver of ocean. On the other side, the ruins of the city stretched before me. A few of the giant buildings still stood, looming in the sky in the distance. At its height, the city had been known for its many neighborhoods that offered different lifestyles for different people. Now, the remnants of those neighborhoods stood out like gray boils on an otherwise green and lush landscape.

Tayna helped me off my horse, and we found a place to hitch them to a tree while we took in the view.

"Where are the Cards?" I couldn't help but ask.

Tayna pointed off to the north. "They're actually farther up the coast than we are. This place is tucked inland between mountains and canyons. It was a great place for farming, even at the height of the city. And a great place to hide from the gangs, it turns out. Thanks to you, we know Gideon isn't onto our location."

It went without saying and me asking. Tayna trusted me enough to show me this place. He was allowing me to see where we were positioned in relation to the rest of the city.

I turned back to him and met his gaze. I was pretty sure I could spend the rest of my life staring into his eyes and never tire of memorizing them. In the five years we'd been apart, I'd forgotten them little by little. I wished I were an artist so I could draw them. I didn't even have the paper and pencils to try.

"What are you thinking?" he asked.

And I answered honestly, "That I almost forgot your eyes, and I'm scared of forgetting them again."

"That won't ever happen."

I looked down at his chest, at the broad planes I could see beneath his white shirt. "How do you know?"

"Because I'll never leave you again."

At that, I heated. "You shouldn't say things like that."

"And why not, Lissa Metarro? I mean it. I've been trying to give you space, Liss." His words were low and the only thing in the air between our mouths. "But I don't want to give you space anymore."

"And what about Clary?" I asked, unable to stop staring at his mouth, forever tugged upward into that hint of a grin.

"I had a discussion with Clary yesterday," he said. "She and I have agreed to remain friends. But nothing more. I tried..." Tayna moved the slightest bit closer until I could feel each of his words against my lips. "I know you've been through a lot, Lissa, and I've tried to be patient. But I don't want to keep you at arm's length. I hate this. I didn't know you could suffocate from space until the past couple of weeks."

"Oh." It was all I could say as I swallowed down a rush of adrenaline and excitement and, yes, fear at his words. This was uncharted territory for Tayna and me. Before, it was the two of us against the world. I wanted so badly for it to be that way again.

"Tayna—"

"No, Liss. Me first. I didn't say it to you before, and I spent five years thinking about it every day. Liss, you and me, we're everything. Every thought I have, every move I make. It's all for you. None of it makes sense without you. You're everything to me."

I gasped and stumbled a step back.

You're everything.

I felt like I might be sick.

I stumbled another step, and Tayna caught me. "What?" he asked. "What did I say?"

But I shook my head.

"I know you feel the same, Lissa," he said, nearly shaking me with his desperate words. "I know it's always been the same for you."

"It's not that." I tried to clear the image of Gideon haunting me.

"Then what is it?" Tayna pleaded. "Because I can't do it anymore. You've been here for weeks. It's all I've dreamed about, and you're here. But you still feel so far away."

"You have no idea what it's been like to find you alive, Tayna. It doesn't feel real. I keep thinking I'll wake up and all of this will be gone. These weeks with the Whigs have meant so much to me. I didn't know life could exist like this. I didn't know life with you could exist anymore. Tayna. It's all I want..."

"But you love him?" Tayna's voice turned low.

"I—" I faltered. "It isn't that simple, Tayna. You and me—It's always been you and me. You mean so much to me, too."

I reached for him, but he visibly flinched away.

"But I'm not your everything anymore?" His voice was dark. "I don't understand how you can feel anything but hate for him." His eyes narrowed against the pain of the realization. "You know what a monster he is."

Part of it didn't have to do with Gideon at all. Part of it was about me. I wasn't sure any man could be my everything again, not the way Tayna had once been. I was no longer that scared little girl who needed to depend on him for everything.

"It isn't—" I faltered. "Gideon will do anything to protect the Cards and the people he cares about. You two aren't so different in some ways."

"Don't—" The anger flickered to life in him. His nostrils flared, and the smirk and his dimples were smoothed out into an icy rage. "Don't say that to me."

"It isn't an insult, Tayna. It's the truth."

Now, he was the one stepping away from me.

"Tayna, please—"

But he had turned away from me, heading back to where the horses were waiting.

I tried again. "Tayna—"

"We should get back," he said.

31

Lissa

Tayna wasn't at dinner that night.

He didn't join the bonfire later, either. Clary was there, and she smiled softly at me when she saw me watching her as she strummed her guitar. I returned it weakly, wondering if Tayna regretted ending things with her after our conversation on the hill.

The ride back to the stables that afternoon had been stilted and silent. Once we'd arrived, I'd tried to help unsaddle the horses and get them brushed.

He'd dismissed me with a curt, "I've got it."

The anger and hurt in his eyes had been enough that I hadn't pushed it.

Even the next day, he showed up at breakfast but wouldn't make eye contact with me. Grant looked between us with raised eyebrows, but I shook him off. Tayna had just stalked from the kitchen, which only infuriated me to the point that I almost said something in front of everyone gathered for eggs. He had no right to be so angry with me. I didn't owe Tayna my heart. I thought he'd died. And I'd done my best to survive in his absence. He might not like Gideon, but it wasn't for him to say what was wrong or right of me to do while I was with the Cards.

After breakfast, I went to find Alaric for our training session. I desperately needed the release of silver. But Alaric was in the barn rather than at our usual meeting spot by the tree line. When I found him, he was pulling down a backpack complete with a couple of canteens and his weapons lined in a neat row on top of a bale of hay.

"No training today, Queen," he told me when he saw me. "We're off on a scouting mission. I'll be gone for a few days."

"We?" I asked, "Who's we?"

"Tayna, myself, and Felina," Alaric ticked off the names. "We head out this afternoon."

He didn't even bother looking up from his backpack as he shoved a rain jacket to the bottom.

Tayna.

Tayna was leaving. After everything he'd promised on our horse-back ride, waxing poetic about never leaving me again, he was walking away. I knew he was upset about our conversation, but I assumed he just needed some space. It would have been easy to lie to him and tell him that Gideon meant nothing to me. But I didn't want to lie to Tayna. We'd never had that type of relationship. On the streets, we told each other everything, and it was the right thing to be honest with him now. My feelings for Gideon were built on years of complicated experiences that I wasn't going to deny.

Still, silver sparked at my fingertips at Alaric's words that Tayna was leaving. He was leaving me. After everything... he was leaving.

Well, he'd at least have to look me in the eyes then and tell me himself.

I didn't even bother saying goodbye to Alaric. Our relationship wasn't built on pleasantries, and I knew there was a good chance he wouldn't even notice I'd left.

Stalking from the barn, I willed my breaths to even out and my silver to dissipate. I'd gotten good at controlling it. Alaric had pushed me in all the ways I possibly could have imagined at the rock pool, yet the emotions I felt about my situation with Tayna put me on loose ground.

On the one hand, I was angry. How dare he leave me after telling me he would never leave me again? On the other hand, I was hurt at how easily he'd pushed me away. He said he'd built the Whigs all for the sake of finding his way back to me, and at the first sign of a challenge between us, he was just going to back out? It was a stab to my already fragile heart.

So I stomped into the main house, breezing past the kitchen.

Grant was prepping lunch and, seeing me, got out all of an, "Oh, Lissa—" I stormed past him and didn't make out the rest of his words. I didn't bother stopping as I breezed through the living room, down the hallway and threw open Tayna's bedroom door.

There was a backpack on the bed. The bed where I'd been sleeping in the weeks since I came here.

Tayna was pulling clothes from the closet, and his eyes widened and then narrowed when he saw me.

Good.

I slammed the door shut behind me.

"Scouting?" I demanded. "You're going scouting?"

Every word was clipped, my anger barely restrained just like the silver at my fingertips.

Tayna's jaw tightened, and he grabbed some clothes to stuff in his backpack, his focus locked on the task.

"Kenji sent word that Gideon's men are getting closer." He turned his back on me as he added a sheathed knife to the bag, then went back to the closet. "We need to figure out their location and make sure they don't find the community."

"And were you planning on telling me or just leaving me here to figure it out on my own?"

"Did Gideon report to you when he was leaving?"

"You ass," I seethed. "Don't treat me like I'm some toy you're mad you didn't get to play with first."

His eyes flashed hot. "The problem is not who played with you,

Lissa. The problem is which side you're playing on. You need to make a choice."

"I'm here!" I practically stomped my foot. "I've been right here with you for weeks."

"But your heart is somewhere else!" His voice boomed throughout the room as he finally focused on me.

"Fuck you, Tayna!" If he wanted to have this out, then fine. "I tried! I tried to move on. I tried to find some semblance of happiness without you. It took me years, but you know what? You're right. I found it. I found it with some of the Cards. I found it with Gideon. And you don't get to be angry at me for that. You fucking died, Tayna. And I couldn't mourn you forever. So I found a way to move on. I found a way to move forward. And I had *just* started feeling like I could live again. And now you're back, and it's killing me because I—because I—"

"Say it, Lissa." He threw the shirt he was holding on the bed and stalked toward me. "Say it!"

I put my hands out to stop him from advancing, but he brushed them out of the way as if the silver crackling with my fury was nothing.

"Get off me!" I tried to wrench myself from his grip, from his body as he pressed closer to mine.

"Tell me what you *want*, Lissa. Tell me what's going on in that head of yours." His frame took up every inch of space between us.

"Stop it!" I balled my fists against the silver, struggling to tamp it down as I finally pulled free of his grasp and raced toward the door. I had to get out of this house. I had to get outside before I lost control.

Tayna was on me faster than I could register. His front pressed into my back, my palms hitting the bedroom wall.

But then he froze. His mouth hovered near my temple, his chest heaving so fast that the fabric of his T-shirt grazed along my shoulders where he bent above me. The space between us was losing its fire just as the silver in my palms dissipated and settled deep in my belly instead.

A calm passed between us, blanketed by our shared breaths. It was a quiet intimacy that raised the awareness along the back of my neck and down my spine until it dissipated deep within my belly.

"Because you what, Lissa?" Tayna asked me again, softer this time. His heavy breaths were hot in the space between us.

I shook my head, my forehead rolling against the wall.

Seeing my silver fizzle, he put just enough space between our bodies that I turned to face him, biting my lip as I worked up the courage to meet his gaze and face this truth.

"Tayna." His name was a plea. He'd always been too good at reading me. And he already knew. He already knew what I was going to say.

He snaked a hand between us, lifting my chin to meet his eyes, still blazing with the intensity of our fight. My head rested against the wall where he held me gently.

"Because you love me, Liss," he said in the breaths between our lips. "You never stopped loving me."

I was angry with him for that most of all. I swallowed, fighting the rising emotion clogging my throat. It was all so tangled— this trust and friendship for Tayna and the deep protectiveness and loyalty I still felt for Gideon.

"I know," Tayna said. "Of course, I know."

He took his time closing the space between us then. His fingers twined in mine, bringing our chests together. He lifted our bound hands to press a delicate kiss against the back of mine, all the while watching me with that golden gaze, as if asking a question at each turn.

He found his answer as my body responded.

Yes.

And then his lips melded into mine. My eyes fluttered closed as his tongue pressed gently between my teeth, asking again for permission.

I opened for him, returning his kiss. My body began to follow the dance he'd started as we explored each other. Mouths, tongues, lips —each piece taken in turn, the feelings savored.

Never had I been kissed like this. This slow, sensual exploration was like the rising tide as my desire became an overflowing, heady thing spreading from my belly to pool in my core.

My body burned hot where it touched Tayna's skin, but a different sort of heat from my silver. My fingers dug deeply into his as I both braced myself and pulled him closer. But he didn't pull away, didn't even hesitate in this kiss that felt like coming home.

He kissed me in a way that folded over me, overtaking me in a slow rush of warmth. It both reminded me of the kiss we'd shared in the loft and also felt entirely new. The feel of his lips was familiar and so, so satisfying, but the body that moved beneath me with such a sensual understanding felt wholly and completely different. Tayna kissed me as if he was relearning every piece of me, and my body bent to it. My knees buckled, but he wrapped a firm arm around me, keeping me upright and flush against his frame.

I moaned into his mouth, and he swallowed the sound.

"I'm sorry," he said, kissing me between the words. "I'm sorry I'm such an ass. Fuck—"

But then he was gripping my hair, his tongue slipping between my lips again as if he couldn't get enough.

With a sigh, he pulled away from me as if it physically pained him, reaching his hands up to pull at the tousled strands of hair above his ear.

My breathing came in heavy pants, my mind whirling at the feel of him. I braced my palms against the wall, slumping against it as I tried to get ahold of myself.

Tracing the lines of my mouth, I watched him as he began rocking, a distressed half-pace in the small room.

"Fuck, Lissa—" he said. "You're all I want, you're all I think about, and I'm fucking this up. I just want it to be easy like it was when we were kids, but everything's gotten so complicated."

He looked so young with the way his face crumpled into vulnerable misery.

But I didn't have anything to give him to smooth the pain. He *was* being an ass. This *had* gotten so complicated. And I'd chosen to leave the compound, but that didn't mean I'd abandoned my feelings for Gideon entirely either.

Yet...

That kiss.

Gentle but no less passionate, his restraint only heightened my desire for him.

My fingers lingered on my lips.

His mouth had seared into a part of me that made it hard to focus on anything else. The want was a palpable pull in my chest. I felt like that teenager again who couldn't remember how to breathe.

"What I said—" Tayna was still rambling. "God, Lissa. I won't be like him. I won't treat you that way. I won't leave you behind, and I swear I'll work for as long as I have to to earn every piece of your heart that you'll give me. I'll take every shred you'll give me. It's enough. You, here. It's more than enough. I'll—"

I leaned into his body, pulling his face down until our lips pressed against each other again. My hands balled into his shirt, pushing it up to his chest so I could run my fingers over the bare planes of his exposed skin.

Just like that night in the loft, I just... needed him.

And his words had been so right, his apology so sincere. He was trying. And yes, things were complicated and messy and definitely not like when we were kids. But I wanted it. I wanted *him*. The rest... I would figure it out.

But right now, I just needed his mouth on mine. That certain knowing wasn't complicated at all.

His surprise melted, and his body responded, folding into me. He twined his fingers into my hair, choking on a noise that sounded like some kind of relieved groan in the back of his throat.

Neither of us broke the kiss, even as my hands explored under his shirt. Even as I took control and pulled him toward the bed.

His core clenched as I brushed the tips of my nails up the ridges of his abdomen. His chest was smooth skin layered over hard-earned muscle. He groaned again as the pads of my thumbs skated across his nipples.

My breath hitched as his hips rolled into me, pressing his body even deeper into mine until my legs were pinned between his body and the mattress.

He cupped the side of my face, trailing kisses across my jaw, down my neck, over my collarbone until he reached the sensitive flesh between my neck and my shoulder and lightly ran his teeth over the spot. Heat flooded my veins, and my head tipped back in ecstasy as he ran his hands down my arm until he was twining our fingers together, holding me in place. He bit down hard enough on my throat to make me gasp.

My hips jerked into him, so he did it again, nibbling along my collarbone. My cheeks heated in arousal and embarrassment at my obvious need, but I was too far gone to care enough to stop.

"We'll go as slow as you want," he murmured. "Just tell me to stop."

"Don't." I shook my head.

One hand moved up to cup the side of my neck as he continued to suck at my flesh.

"Tayna—"

I wanted him now. I didn't want him to take his time.

His mouth moved from my neck, and the cool air over my sensitive skin made me shiver. He claimed my lips again, and his tongue delved deeply as he moved his hips against me in time with my own. His hands ran along my lower back, his fingers tracing at the edges of my pants, promising more.

I was desperate for him.

It took every ounce of control I had—even more control than it took me to rein in my silver—to say, "Take me with you."

He paused. His hand feathering over my too-sensitive skin.

He pulled back just slightly, still cupping my neck as his bedroom eyes met mine. His thumb swept delicately across my throat.

"You want to go on the scout?" he asked.

I nodded, my face falling to his reddened lips. Mine felt just as swollen from his kisses. His hips were still pressed into mine, and I wished our pants weren't in the way.

"I could be useful," I said, my voice full of the heady need I felt. "I mean." I cleared my throat. "Alaric's been training me, and I'll have my silver if anything goes wrong."

"It won't be an easy trip," Tayna studied the lines of my face. "We'll be sleeping outside on the ground. Food will be rationed. We'll hike for most of the daylight. And that's not even considering what could happen if the Cards see us."

"You forget." I smirked. "I may have grown up, but I'm still a street rat. I can handle myself."

"I've always known you can handle yourself," Tayna said, his voice serious. And then he nodded. "Okay. We'll need to pack you a proper bag. And we'll need to see Grant to get some more food."

He pressed a gentle kiss to my forehead. It sent a shiver racing over my spine. My body was still primed for more. I still wanted more from him, but he took a step back. Resisting the urge to sink into the mattress like jelly, I braced myself against the end of the bed.

Tayna laughed and scooped me into his arms, lifting me from the floor. "Oh, Lissa," he said, cradling me to his chest before setting me gently onto the bed. "I'm going to have you. I intend to take my time with every inch of your body and your mind until I'm the only man you want. But right now, as much as it absolutely pains me to say it, if you're going on this scout, we need to get you ready, and then we need to get some sleep. And if I get you naked now, we're definitely not doing either of those things."

This time, I did groan, pressing my head against the mattress.

"But god"—he smiled and leaned over me, his strong arms braced on either side of my head—"I fucking love watching you squirm on my bed."

He kissed me again, too quickly for my liking.

And then he pulled me from the bed, handed me a backpack, and got to packing.

I wished I'd waited until after he had me naked and did all the things he promised before asking him if I could go on the scout. But the fact that he'd apologized and trusted me enough to let me join meant more to me than any kiss ever could.

And the promise of what was to come for us was enough.

For now, it was more than enough.

32

Lissa

We left on foot with the sunrise.

Felina drank a small vial of silver, but both Alaric and Tayna refused when she offered them some as well. I wished it would benefit me in the same way it did for red bloods, but drinking another's silver would only make me ill for days on end. It was a weird anomaly with the Silvers. We didn't mix well. It had to be pure in order to be effective, which meant I only had my own strength and endurance to get through this scout.

Horses would have been the most convenient way to travel but not the stealthiest so they stayed at the farm. Dan and Ann, however, were close at Tayna's heels as we hiked to the edge of the Whig's community.

Unlike the compound, there were no high fences here. Only a small rickety watchtower that was rarely occupied. The dogs were the quickest and best alarm for the community. Someone from a watchtower would need to run to the house to alert the community if there were visitors. It wasn't practical. Plus, the community rarely had visitors, and none that weren't expected. The best weapon was the property's concealment within the mountains.

If the Cards were narrowing in on the location of the Whigs, all the more reason to send out scouts to make sure they weren't heading on a course that would lead them directly here. That was our mission on this trip.

"And what if they *are* headed toward the Whigs?" I asked Tayna while watching my step down a particularly rocky embankment. I'd worn the boots Tayna had found for me for this trek. They were well-worn and comfortable but maybe not the best options for tread and distance. Rixa had given me a coat to wear, though the spring sun was promising the warmest day we'd had this year.

"We do our best to avoid confrontation," Tayna said.

"The Cards don't do well at avoiding confrontation," I argued, thinking of the injuries Gideon and his men had suffered shortly before I'd left.

Felina snorted up ahead like she knew that only too well. Her hair was pulled back in a braid down her back today, showing off the shaved side of her head.

"Then we do what we have to do to protect the Whigs," Tayna said. "Is that going to be okay for you?"

He asked it in a way that wasn't judgmental but rather genuine concern. I understood it. He needed to know he could trust me if things got ugly. He couldn't have me getting in the middle of a fight trying to protect both sides. Even more, he couldn't risk me using my silver in a way that would put the Whigs at risk.

So I said, "No. No problem."

And mostly meant it.

I wouldn't put the Whigs at risk. But I also expected Tayna to do everything he could to avoid hurting someone. The Cards were mostly young guys with chips on their shoulders out to prove themselves and provide for their families. Sure, I didn't particularly like most of them, but that didn't mean they deserved to die.

I added, "As long as you promise to only do what's necessary."

To which Alaric looked over his shoulder and snapped, "This is war, Queen. Survival means playing dirty."

Alaric would be the one to draw his gun first. I knew that. I'd seen his loaded firearm in the barn. The bullets were silvered, meant for maximum damage. Felina also had a gun strapped to each of her thighs in holsters that made them easy to access. Tayna had a rifle slung across his shoulder. These weapons weren't just for show. I carried nothing but a small pocket knife in my backpack, though Alaric had shown me how to shoot one of his pistols this morning. Just in case.

The lesson was okay, but I felt uncomfortable carrying a gun myself. I wished I could see the world as they did. The Cards were bad. The Whigs were good. But it wasn't that simple for me. I'd lived both sides of this fight.

But Gideon would never allow another faction to gain power. Even if the Whigs were well-intentioned, he viewed them as a threat to his control and his people. Threats were eliminated.

"We should be better than the Cards," I told Alaric.

"We are." His voice was a low warning as if daring me to say otherwise.

"We are," I echoed, "which is why we shouldn't shoot first unless our lives are at risk."

"Agreed," Tayna said.

"There won't be much choice if they're heading toward the Whigs," Felina said over her shoulder.

I stumbled on a loose rock outcropping but managed to right myself. Dan nudged the side of my leg as if warning me to focus on my steps instead of the conversation. The dog stayed by my side during the hike, and I found his presence oddly reassuring.

"Then let's hope they're farther off course than we think," Tayna said. "There's a good chance they're not even close."

His steps were smooth and graceful along the rocks. His long legs served him well, but he also seemed to have a sixth sense for where to place his feet next. I tried to follow in his footsteps but failed to match his long gait.

I knew I was moving slower than this group was used to. It wasn't that I was tired or my muscles were sore. I simply didn't have the confidence they had moving between these trees yet.

We walked like that, on the downhill, for hours until the sun beat well overhead.

Our group stopped for lunch, and I peeled the jacket from my arms, unsurprised to find it slick with beads of my sweat. The slight breeze in the air cooled the damp on my arms, which felt like sweet relief to my heated skin.

Tayna passed me a skein of water, and I took a grateful gulp.

"About another mile and a half and we'll be down the slope," Felina promised.

"Then what?" I asked.

"Then we head west." Felina nodded her chin up ahead. "The scouts were reportedly looking around about seven miles northwest of our camp. Thanks to the information you gave Tayna, we know the Cards think our community is farther north, but it seems like they're slowly making their way closer and closer. The idea is that we camp tonight, then find them in the morning. If we can circle around and distract them from the north, we can lead them back the way they came."

"Misdirection." I nodded. "Keep them thinking that you're retreating farther north so they stop heading into the mountains west."

"Exactly," Tayna said. "It's worked so far."

He handed me half of a pecan butter and strawberry preserve sandwich. The bread was hearty with seeds and soggy in the middle from sitting in a warm backpack all day, but I ate it all in only a few bites. My body needed the fuel.

"Shooting them is also a viable option if the misdirection doesn't work," Alaric said between bites of his sandwich.

I glared at him.

"Oh, quit bein' so unrealistic, Queen," he said. "You live in an idealistic world."

"And you live in a black-and-white one," I grumbled.

"And how would you have the world, Lissa?" Felina asked me. "As someone who has seen both the Cards and the Whigs?"

"I don't understand why we can't coexist," I admitted honestly. "I don't understand why it always has to be such a fight for power."

"Peace is only an idea. You have to give people a say to truly achieve peace," Felina said. "But peace can't exist when a tyrant only wants it for the few."

She was talking about democracy.

"How do you think the city should function?" I asked.

"We vote," she said as if it were the simplest idea. "We give power back to the people who live here and let people have representation."

"The gangs would never agree to it." I stood from the rock where I'd eaten my sandwich and found my legs were beginning to stiffen, the muscles fatigued already. I inwardly cursed the years I'd spent at the compound for making me so soft.

"The Tanks already have," Tayna said, also standing and stretching.

"The Tanks?" I whirled on him.

He nodded. "They've allied with us. They've agreed to our system. Each gang would be allowed a set number of representatives based on their population. We would also agree to give a small percentage of income to support the function of this council."

"And what would the council do, exactly?" I asked Tayna skeptically.

"Lots." He shrugged. "But the first priority would be to help the city rebuild. We need to build infrastructure, support people to sell their goods and services and advance technology with the help of the Silvers."

"The first priority should be education," I countered. "If you don't raise your children with knowledge, then there is no hope. Kids should go to school."

Tayna's smile widened. "You think we should build schools?"

I nodded. "With libraries. And it should be free for all children."

"Now you're starting to sound like a Whig," Alaric said, slinging his backpack over his shoulders and beginning the steady walk down the rocky terrain once again.

And I didn't miss Tayna's dimpled smile of approval.

33

Lissa

My body could hardly handle the effort of rolling out my sleeping pad and bag that night. If I hadn't trained every day with Alaric over the past weeks, I was sure I wouldn't have made it down that mountain. My backside was so sore that I could hardly sit for our dinner of dried meats and cheeses without bracing myself first.

Tayna was unrolling his sleeping bag next to me and snorted as I hobbled my way around the bed. Dan and Ann had found a place near a large oak tree to settle in for the night. Tayna had given them each a stick of dried meat for dinner, and they were gnawing away happily.

"Shut up," I groaned.

"Your silver doesn't work on your muscles, then?" He arched a brow.

"It makes them more resilient, I suppose." I sighed. "But no, it doesn't speed up the healing. Apparently, lactic acid is a different sort of pain response. Otherwise, I wouldn't be able to build muscle."

"Just wait until we have to hike back up." He chuckled, his hair falling over his forehead as he crouched on the ground to carefully lay his sleeping bag over the pad so it wouldn't get dirt in it.

I glanced over my shoulder, where I knew the mountain we'd scaled loomed in the distance, and groaned again.

"I think you're just going to need to leave me here," I said.

"You forget"—he tapped a finger on my nose—"I'm never leaving you again, Liss."

Liss. I liked that he called me that. He didn't call me Queenie or my Queen or Silver or Card or Whig or girl or street rat. It was always my name, like he saw me. He saw through the tattoo on my shoulder and the silver at my fingertips and the curves of my body. And maybe I was too idealistic and loved too freely and didn't fully understand the strange silver that coursed through my veins, but Tayna made me feel like the bundle of me, all of it, was worth the fight.

Alaric and Felina had set up their bedrolls in other corners of the clearing around our simple camp. A small fire at the center burned low and hot against the chill in the night air, crackling faintly and echoing through the trees. The stars overhead were glorious. The sky was white and cloudy in some places from so much light clustered together.

The city had always seemed so gray and empty to me. Even the sky there was hazy black. But here, tucked against the mountain, the world looked more vivid than I'd ever seen it, full of rich color and vibrancy even in the dark.

"Good night," Felina called as she snuggled into her sleeping bag.

Alaric grumbled something from his side of the clearing that sounded like, "Stop your yelling." He'd packed himself a flask, which he'd enjoyed around the fire, passing it to the rest of us only once before he drained the contents.

Tayna's eyes were nearly as bright as the stars in the sky as he looked at me, his face framed by firelight, and I found my cheeks heating. I hoped he couldn't see it in the darkness. We hadn't talked about what happened between us yesterday, but his kisses were all I'd thought about today while I'd taken step after step.

Now, he sidled up his sleeping pad so it was flush against mine and whispered in the dark, "Is this okay?"

It was all I could do to nod, but then I realized he might not actually be able to see me clearly, so I murmured, "Yes." My voice didn't sound like my own. It was a throaty rasp that made my desire obvious.

As we lay down, he said, "Come here," and pulled my sleeping bag-wrapped body into his, kissing me so tenderly that it made me shiver against him. His lips were warm as they pressed into mine. "I've been waiting all day to do that," he murmured against my mouth, kissing me again more deeply.

My body went soft and pliant against him, and his tongue brushed against my bottom lip. I opened for him, letting him explore all the pieces of me that it felt like he already knew intimately.

His fingers found the zipper of my sleeping bag, and he lowered it slowly, keeping just enough space between us so he could work the zipper down and we wouldn't lose the warmth. But our breaths were hot between us. I found myself desperate to feel his skin against mine. His kisses only served to make me feel a frenzy of desire, but I was also all too aware of the others trying to sleep only yards away.

Still, I didn't stop as my fingers found their way to his sleeping bag and began sliding the zipper down. My hands were cold as they slid under his shirt and up his torso. His skin was warm and hard beneath me, a contrast to my own.

"Sorry," I murmured.

But he broke our kiss long enough to say, "Don't stop." His voice sounded as needy for me as I was for him. His lips reclaimed mine, his tongue dancing between my lips. My fingers continued exploring along the planes of his body, and I wished I could peel his shirt off entirely.

The sensations of our bodies were nearly overwhelming. Between his mouth on mine and my hands on the bare skin of his chest, I thought I might combust from his touch alone as he slid a hand under my sleeping bag to run down my arm. I opened my eyes only briefly to confirm I wasn't glowing with silver and hurting him. It felt like the same sort of electricity pulsing in my veins—hot and seeking release.

His hands found their way to the top of my pants, and he ran a finger along the waistband. I'd changed into a pair of his sweats I'd packed in my bag, which meant they were loose enough for him to easily pull the side over my hip.

He swallowed my moan with his mouth as his hand traced down to my center. He ran a finger through the wetness there, and I could feel his grin along my lips.

"God, Liss," he murmured, and I reached my fingers up to trace the dimples in his cheeks. My eyes fluttered open, and I found him staring at me, his eyes practically glowing golden in contrast to mine as they reflected my gaze.

He slid a long finger inside me.

I gasped, pressing my forehead into the side of his neck and biting back another moan.

"Tayna." His name slipped from my lips in a whispered breath as he added another finger and began working them in and out of my body in a steady rhythm.

"I can't wait to taste you," he whispered in my ear.

I choked on a cry, the hint of it escaping as I pressed my lips harder into his shoulder. I was very aware of the others sleeping only feet away, but I couldn't deny the desperate need of my body.

My hips rolled against him. I was helpless to stop it, especially when his thumb circled over the most sensitive part of me. Then my head did kick back, and he kissed me just in time to muffle the sound of my cries of pleasure.

"Mmm," he said as he continued kissing as if even the noises of my pleasure were delicious. His fingers continued moving inside me, kicking up my already panting breaths.

My body grew hot despite hints of the night's air licking across my exposed skin.

"You have no idea how desperate I am to have more than my fingers inside you," Tayna murmured as he increased their pace. His thumb continued stroking my clit in lazy circles. "God, Liss, I've thought about touching you like this for years. Next time, I'll taste you."

I bit back a moan.

"And then, once you're shivering from pleasure, just like you are right now, I'll press my cock slowly inside you so I can feel every bit of you squeezing me, begging me for more."

He slammed his mouth back on mine as if he'd known his words would send me over the edge. I crested with pleasure, my back arching into him as wave after wave of pure bliss washed over my body. I was no longer aware of the sounds I was making or the movements of my hips. There was only Tayna and the feel of his fingers seated deeply within my core.

As I came down from the high of pleasure, my breaths coming in gasps, he kissed me gently on both cheeks and then my neck, slowly licking along my collarbone before gently removing his fingers.

His free hand came up to clamp over my mouth as the withdrawal of his fingers caused me to gasp a final time. His answering laughter rumbled against my chest, which was pressed flush against him.

My eyes fluttered open. His were wide and pleased as he brought his fingers up to his mouth between us and slowly sucked them clean.

"Better than I imagined," he murmured.

My eyes went wide watching him, and I wanted to rip his clothes from his body right then and there.

That fast, my hands were back on him, going for his pants this time, but he grabbed my wrists, stopping me.

"Tayna—" My voice was foreign and low.

"There is no way we won't wake up Alaric and Felina if we do that, and I'm not going to allow any interruptions when I'm inside you. So unless you want an audience, we need to stop."

I was breathless from wanting him. I considered begging, telling him I truly didn't care. But I paused, my tongue flicking out to lick my bottom lip as I stared at the piece of skin I could see exposed at the top of his waistband. There was a deep v cut into either side of his hips that was enough to make another flood of liquid heat pool in my center.

How had we waited so long to kiss when we were together before? In the weeks since we'd been reunited, my body was constantly aware of him, continually wanting him. It was as if something in me recognized our connection and whispered "Yes. Mine." into my mind whenever he was near.

"Liss—" Tayna said in a low warning, seeing the conflict warring in my eyes. I knew if I pushed him just a little further, he'd have me pressed onto my back with his weight rolling into my hips. I imagined myself pulling down his pants just a little farther, knowing I'd find the length of him hard and ready. "Lissa," Tayna said, his voice sharper.

"If you two keep me up all night, I'm going to kill you," Felina called from across the camp.

That was like a bucket of water crashing over my head. I brought my hand up to cover my mouth, biting back the giggle that erupted up my throat. Tayna's answering chuckle reverberated against my chest.

"Sorry, Fel," Tayna called back, and she just grumbled as I could hear her roll over in her bag. To me, Tayna murmured, "Come here." He pulled me so I was flush against his body, my cheek pressed into the crook of his neck.

Contented, I drifted asleep curled against Tayna's chest.

34

Lissa

Just like the previous morning, we began hiking at dawn.

It was quick enough to pack up our things, clean ourselves up a bit, change, and begin walking once again. The muscles in my back and legs ached from yesterday.

Meanwhile, my core still ached for wanting more than Tayna's fingers. But I minded that ache a lot less than the stiffness of my muscles as we began walking.

We'd gone the majority of the distance we needed to cover yesterday.

Today, the focus would be to find the scouts and, if we had enough time, lead them away from the path to the Whigs.

But we didn't see or hear anyone as we made our way from the trees to the open terrain near the ocean. Just the crash of waves as the tide retreated with the morning.

By midday, Felina volunteered to climb to a higher peak to look out over a broader stretch of ground. While we waited for her, Alaric surveyed the area through binoculars. He called it glassing, which, apparently, was a term hunters used to spot their prey.

Tayna and I busied ourselves with looking for tracks on an old road that wrapped around the coast. Dan and Ann sniffed up and down the sand as if they too understood the mission.

But there were no signs of fresh tire tracks. No drips of oil that would indicate a recent stop. No boot prints that would signify a group on foot.

Nothing.

When Felina returned, she too reported that all was quiet in the surrounding area. She found no sign of the scouts.

Maybe the Cards had already given up and turned back.

Or maybe Kenji was wrong about the direction they were heading.

All in all, the day felt like a complete waste. Maybe the entire trip was a complete waste. At least we had confirmed all was safe in the surrounding area. There wasn't a human in sight, just the ocean and some gulls squawking in the distance.

Alaric found a place for us to set up camp for the night. It was inland from the road, a small, flat expanse within a hill surrounded by brush high enough to conceal us. We would camp for the night before returning to the community tomorrow.

Our rations were getting low, so we settled on some dried fruit and near-stale biscuits for dinner. Felina and Tayna spent the meal arguing about the best strategy to protect the community if the Cards were, in fact, getting close to its location. Felina wanted a schedule of around-the-clock surveillance, but Tayna was afraid of burning out the community so close to planting season. Around-the-clock surveillance, he argued, would cost the community more hours then they had to spare. He thought the dogs were sufficient for surveillance. They would hear any threats coming long before a human.

Alaric finally called off the conversation when it was clear the two wouldn't agree.

"We can take a vote when we get back to the council," he said, standing from the fire. "Tayna, help me feed the dogs."

And then it was just Felina and me sitting corner-to-corner around the small fire.

In the days we'd been together on this scout, I'd learned little about the fierce woman. She was cunning and skilled on the trails, but she didn't seem the least bit interested in me. Not that I was an expert in female friendship. Enver was the first friend I'd ever made, and even then, it was a credit to her persistence rather than anything I'd done.

But Felina didn't watch me with the same curiosity as the others in the community. Their gazes followed me like I was a marvel or something to fear. A Queen who had forsaken her throne to come and live with them. Felina barely spared me a glance at all, which was fine except her avoidance seemed deliberate.

Felina took the silver. I'd seen her drink some each morning. Maybe that would be my way in, so I said, "If you need more silver for the morning, just let me know."

Her grin against the fire exposed the tips of her canines, making her look predatory as she leaned back against the rock she was sitting on. "I'm good."

"It's just..." I started, wondering how starkly the silver in my eyes was shining against the embers of the fire. Maybe I looked like a cat in the night. "You drink the silver when a lot of people in the community refuse it."

"Why would I refuse it?" she asked. "It's a tool. It makes me stronger. I can travel farther, heal faster, and hit harder. And I'm not one of those idiots who will take too much and get addicted."

"I didn't mean—"

"I know," that feral glint in her eyes sharpened. "You weren't suggesting that. But you want to know why Tayna refuses it while I drink it?"

"I guess." I shrugged.

"Will knowing make you feel better or worse about the power that courses through your veins?" she asked, and I felt color stain my cheeks at the way she'd called out my internal struggle over my abilities. At my shrug, she added, "I see how you battle with your choices. Whig or Card. Silver as good or bad. Queen or street rat."

She didn't need to add "Gideon or Tayna." I knew that was what she was getting at.

"The truth is," she said, leaning forward and bracing her forearms on her thighs, "the choice isn't your problem. Your problem is you're scared to believe in anything."

"I..." I halted with my mouth hanging slightly. I wasn't sure how this conversation had started as my attempt to get to know her and had ended with her reading to the very center of me.

"Look, I get it. You've lived a ton of different lives already, and you're only what? Twenty?"

"Twenty-three."

But she just waved me off and continued, "Why believe in anything too strongly when it will be taken away, right? But I think you need to start believing in yourself, Lissa. Before you get us all killed."

"It seems like no matter what I do, people get hurt," I admitted.

"Which is exactly why I didn't want you at the community to begin—"

She halted, her head ticking up as she listened.

And then I heard it, too. A low rumble in the distance entirely separate from the waves crashing into the shore.

This rumble was mechanical. An engine rolling closer and then sputtering to a stop. The faint sound of voices as men walked along the darkness just beyond the hill where we'd set up camp.

Dan and Ann growled low, cutting through the dark. Alaric and Tayna dropped the bedrolls they were holding.

The men weren't even attempting to be quiet as they slammed doors and yelled about grabbing supplies.

Alaric ran to our smoldering fire and began picking up handfuls of sand to throw on it. I got down on my hands and knees, also gathering sand to help smother the small blaze. We were hidden behind the brush, but the light could filter through if they looked this way.

There was laughter as one man whined, "Come on, man," at whatever the other had said.

And then another hissed, "Be quiet, Sandrick."

Sandrick. I didn't recognize that name, but the other voice. I'd heard the other voice by my side every day for the past couple of years.

Laykin.

If he wasn't guarding me anymore, Gideon would have reassigned him, and it would only make sense that he'd be tasked to find me.

"Why, of all places," Felina said, crouching next to me to also begin tossing handfuls of sand on the blaze, "did they have to stop here?"

I shook my head, but as if in answer, Laykin said, "I thought it was just up here."

"Fuck," Alaric whispered. "We need to move."

We'd been spotted.

That was why they'd stopped.

Laykin had spotted the light of our camp from the road.

I stood, running to grab my bag.

"Leave the bed rolls," Alaric snapped as I moved to grab my sleeping bag. "We don't have time."

Tayna grabbed my hand, entwining our fingers and pulling me to his side.

Dan and Ann crouched near the trees, their noses to the sky as they waited.

Felina pulled one of the guns from the straps she wore on her legs and cocked it back to load a bullet in the chamber.

"You can't shoot them!" I hissed at her.

"Like hell." She glanced over her shoulder.

"No!" I tried to reach for the weapon, but Tayna pulled me back into his side. "One of those men is my old guard," I explained to him in a low voice. "He's a good man. We were—we were friends. He watched over me with Kenji."

Tayna grit his teeth and sighed. "Fucking hell." And then he hissed to Felina, "Stand down."

She looked at him incredulously, like she was about to argue. But then the voices came again, nearer this time.

"— looked like it could be a fire," Laykin said.

"It's the moonlight playing tricks on you," another said.

"Or the moonshine." Still another laughed, only for it to end abruptly as one of the other men, no doubt, lugged him in the stomach.

It sounded like at least five of them, though I knew most of the Humvees could hold up to eight. Either way, we were outnumbered.

At the front of our group, Alaric beckoned for us to run, and we quickened our steps along the side of the hill. We kept to the shrubs where possible, but mostly counted on the darkness to shield us. We were so much more exposed on this stretch than we had been in the trees.

Dan growled low, looking back as he and Ann prowled near Tayna.

Felina took up the end and didn't put her gun away as she, too, continuously looked back. Her footsteps were lithe even though she spent more time watching over her shoulder than looking at her feet.

As for me, I stumbled my way through the darkness, grateful for Tayna's hand wrapped in mine to keep me steady as I tripped over rocks and bushes.

For a stretch, all I heard was my breathing in my ears, the occasional shifting of rocks from our group, and the steady waves from the ocean to our left.

But then my foot caught on a root, and I tumbled, pulling Tayna with me as I fell. Air pushed from my lungs in a cry that tore through the darkness. Our hands were ripped apart.

My body was rolling.

I was vaguely aware of gunshots in the distance as I skidded on the dirt.

My shoulder smacked against a rock before my body finally stilled.

More shots rang in the night.

My mouth was full of dirt, and one side of my face felt sticky.

I needed to find Tayna.

I tried to stand, but the instant I put pressure on my arm, I knew something was wrong. I couldn't stifle the yelp of pain that burst from my lips at the agony in my shoulder.

But there wasn't time.

Those were definitely gunshots.

And I'd lost Tayna in the dark.

A flashlight beam landed on me, and I froze on my hands and knees in the dirt.

Laykin stood before me, a gun in one hand, his other bracing the weapon and holding a flashlight steadily.

"Lissa?" he asked, shock lighting his sharp features along with the flashlight beam.

Using my good arm, I pressed myself to stand, spitting dirt from my mouth onto the ground.

"Lissa." He pointed his weapon down, and he was helping me up before I'd even had the chance to speak. My arm was already healing, but I still gasped at the pain as he gripped me.

"My arm—" I swallowed air, trying to speak. "Laykin, you have to—"

A gun cocked behind me.

I whirled to see Tayna in the beam of the flashlight.

Laykin immediately had his weapon raised again.

"Tayna." It was all I could do to shake my head, stepping in front of Laykin's body.

"Lissa," Laykin warned, "get out of the way."

"You both need to stand down," I said, trying my best to keep my words from shaking.

"Your friends are dead or running," Tayna told Laykin. "It's just you. And me."

Laykin scoffed, "There's no fucking way you—"

But then Ann and Dan stepped behind Tayna. Ann's maw was red with blood, and she snarled fiercely at Laykin. Her low grumble reverberated through the darkness.

"What the *fuck*," Laykin breathed, and it was maybe the first time I'd heard fear in him.

"Please," I said to no one in particular. "Please just put your weapons down. Laykin, I don't want you to get hurt."

"You're *with* them?" Laykin demanded, and I knew that question was directed at me.

But Tayna answered, "Don't you fucking touch her."

"Laykin." I turned to him, only to find the gun directed at my heart. "Layk," I said a bit more softly. He was my guard, my protector, yet now he had a gun leveled at my chest. There were a few ways to kill a Silver. A bullet to the head or the heart would do just fine, and Laykin was an excellent shot.

"Gideon's been tearing up the city searching for you," Laykin said, holding the gun steady and level. "We've been out here for a week."

"Is he okay?" I asked softly, ignoring the way Tayna's eyes narrowed against the moonlight.

"He's a mess, Liss. What did you expect?" Laykin shook his head.

"You know that he—"

"That he, what? That he'd do anything to protect you? That he feels like you've betrayed him when all he wanted to do was keep you safe?"

"I couldn't be kept anymore, Layk. He tried to protect me by caging me, and I just... couldn't."

"Have you turned traitor, then?" Laykin's gaze swept quickly to Tayna and then back to me.

"Laykin," I said again, trying to keep my voice calm, "just please let me explain."

Over my shoulder, Tayna said, "Put the gun down, and we can talk."

Laykin looked between us for a moment more.

And then he lowered the gun with a heavy exhale.

Just as I was breathing a sigh of relief, I heard the gun go off behind me.

I turned to find Tayna, his weapon aimed. When I looked back, Laykin had staggered a few steps back. The flashlight and gun had dropped onto the ground, barely illuminating the small space where we stood.

But I could see he was bleeding.

"No!" I screamed, running toward my guard. "No, no, no!"

"It's just a flesh wound," Tayna said behind me. "He isn't dead. I just wanted to make sure he couldn't shoot us with that gun if he decided he didn't like what you had to say."

I realized then that the bullet had just grazed his arm. It was bleeding like crazy, but nothing that would kill.

Still, Laykin glared daggers at Tayna as he put pressure on the wound. The blood seeped through his fingers. "You fucking prick."

Tayna shrugged. "I could have released the dogs on you instead. I thought the bullet was kinder."

Laykin staggered to sit in the dirt, heaving in heavy breaths. I was slowly regaining mobility in my arm, but it would take hours, if not days, to fully heal. I was pretty sure it was more than just a sprain. Still, I reached for Laykin, sitting next to him and searching in my bag for the pocket knife I'd stuffed at the bottom.

"You shouldn't have come looking for me," I told Laykin.

"Orders are orders." He grimaced.

"I left because I wanted to leave," I said, fishing out the knife and flicking it open.

"You know that doesn't matter to Gideon."

"He has enough silver," I snapped, pausing for only a breath before slicing a thin line along my good arm.

"Lissa." Tayna's tone behind me was a warning.

"You"—I glared over my shoulder at him—"stay there."

I couldn't believe he'd shot Laykin. I also couldn't believe his aim was so precise. What if the wind had picked up, and he'd shot Laykin somewhere vital? Hell, what if he'd accidentally shot me? Though I could see from the precise placement of the bullet that Tayna had known exactly what he was doing as soon as he'd made the decision to pull that trigger.

"We're going to do this the old-fashioned way," I said to Laykin, lifting my wrist to his mouth.

He looked at me hesitantly, and I remembered Gideon was the only one allowed to have my silver at the compound. Kenji wouldn't even take my blood when I'd burned his hand badly enough to cause boils.

"Oh, come on." I scoffed. "You're bleeding all over the ground, Layk. You can't possibly be worried that Gideon will find out about this."

He gave me one more considering look before he brought his mouth to my arm, and I felt his tongue swipe across my skin.

"That's enough," he murmured. "I have more at the Humvee."

"The Humvee?" Tayna asked, incredulous. "You think you're just going to stroll back to your Ace?"

I glared at him over my shoulder again. Then back at Laykin, I said, "Of course you're going to return to the compound. But I want your word that you won't tell Gideon what happened tonight."

"His word?" Tayna demanded, still holding the gun aimed steadily at Laykin's chest.

I ignored him. "Obviously, he'll know there was an attack. But you can't tell him you saw me, Layk. He can't keep looking for me. I don't want to be found, and he can't destroy the city in the process. You know it isn't right. The only way to get him to stop is to give him no hope of finding me."

Laykin's eyes narrowed, studying me as the color returned to his cheeks as he healed.

"This is what you want?" he finally asked.

I nodded.

"I don't understand, Lissa," Laykin said. "You were finally—"

"There isn't time, Layk." I breathed, glancing back at Tayna. "You have to get out of here. But I need you to promise me first. Promise me you won't tell Gideon you saw me. Promise me you'll tell him you didn't learn anything from the attack."

After a moment, he nodded. "I'll agree to it."

I didn't question his motives. There wasn't time. I just had to trust him. The last thing I needed was for Felina and Alaric to find me here with Laykin and complicate things even more. I didn't think Felina would be happy with a simple bullet graze along the arm. Alaric would probably fire right along with her.

I sighed. "And you can't tell him it was the Whigs who attacked you."

"What the hell am I supposed to say?" His tone was aristocratic skepticism.

I shrugged. "Tell him it was a band of some randoms. Tell him you couldn't identify them."

Laykin's nostrils flared as if I'd just suggested he tell Gideon the group was attacked by flying fairies. "No one else would dare. He'll know."

"Well, then at least tell him you were attacked from a distance and didn't see anyone until it was too late."

Laykin's eyes met Tayna's over my shoulder, and I turned to see Tayna standing with his arms crossed, studying Laykin just as intently.

His eyes returned to me as he said, "Agreed. Are the others dead?" His gaze dropped again to Ann, who had settled a bit, sitting in the sand next to Tayna.

"At least two," Tayna said. "How many did you come with?"

"I will not tell you—"

Tayna put up his hands. "Doesn't matter to me," he said. "They're gone."

Laykin's nostrils flared again, but he nodded mutely.

"If I can save them, I will," I murmured.

But Laykin shook his head. "I know how this goes. Gideon sent me with a bunch of threes and fours. New and dumb. The others wouldn't dare show their faces again if they ran."

He was right, so I didn't push it. "How's Enver?"

It was the first hint of a smile I'd seen from him. "She misses you."

"Will you tell her... will you find a way to make sure she knows I miss her too? If you can."

"She thinks you're in trouble," Laykin said. "She's worried about you."

"I can't go back there, Layk." I didn't add that it was because my heart wouldn't survive. It was already torn between two men.

"He won't stop until he's found you. He's got Dia on the hunt. It doesn't matter what I tell him when I return."

Dia was the best tracker at the compound. Part of me was tempted to agree, to leave with him right then and there. If it meant saving the Whigs and others, I would do it.

Tayna seemed to sense my thoughts because he said to Laykin, "You should go."

Laykin nodded, standing. He left the gun and the flashlight without even attempting to reach for them. I also found my way to my feet, thanks to the hand Tayna gripped under my uninjured shoulder to help me up.

Laykin looked between the two of us, then nodded again. He turned to leave.

"Bye, Layk," I said stiffly.

"This isn't goodbye, Lissa," he said, his eyes tracking to where Tayna still held my arm. And I knew. A deep part of me knew he was right.

35

Lissa

"We should evacuate the children, at least," Grant argued. "And where will they go?" Tayna countered. "They'd run out of food in a week. It doesn't make sense to leave the community. No one knows we're here. No one followed us back."

We'd returned to the compound just this morning after two grueling days of hiking on very little sleep.

I was exhausted. But the others insisted we debrief the council first after everything that had happened on the hill.

There was still sand and silver blood smeared across my face. It was dried and crumbled, pulling the skin taut. I smelled wretched and felt uncomfortable beneath my dirty clothes. My shoulder had healed but was still sore even two days later. Whatever I had done to it, it hadn't been pretty. Probably a broken collarbone or shattered shoulder. Or both from what I'd surmised from the pain.

"We're putting all of our faith in some fucking guard," Felina spat, glaring at me. "He's a Jack."

My decision to spare Laykin's life and let him return to the compound hadn't done much to bolster a friendship between us.

Instead of indifference, Felina's eyes turned dark whenever they met mine.

"So is Kenji," I said.

That earned me another deadpanned glare.

So I added, "I trust Laykin."

"The issue isn't trusting the guard." Felina rested her arm on her knee. "It's trusting you."

"Felina." Tayna's voice was a low warning.

"What?" Felina dropped her arm. "Are we just going to pretend it's not a problem that she's still trying to play both sides? She asked us not to kill any of them. She spared her guard. She can't have it both ways."

"I don't want anyone dead!" I flinched at the reminder that three of the Cards had been killed. One had run. And I'd let Laykin leave. I hadn't wanted to know the details from Alaric about the ones who'd been killed.

"This. Is. War." Felina gripped the chair and leaned into me.

"But why does it have to be?" I couldn't live with myself if the Whigs hurt any of my friends. I couldn't live with myself if they hurt Gideon. The guilt was enough of a punishment for betraying him, and I would carry that with me. But not his death. That I could not accept.

"Enough." Alaric waved his hand. He sat next to Grant, who had a hand wrapped around his thigh as if he couldn't bear not to touch him now that we had returned home alive. "Lissa's a pain in the ass, but she got that guard to agree to keep our secrets. I think she's earned some trust. We can give her some space to sort the rest out, huh, Fel?"

I tried not to let the shock show on my face. Alaric had been one of my biggest critics when I'd arrived, and now, now he was... defending me? Not only defending me but understanding me.

"She should sort it out in a place where she isn't risking this entire community," Felina said, standing. "I'm not going to just sit here and let the Cards find us and kill us all."

With that, Felina left the room.

She'd clearly had enough, but so had I, to be fair. We were only going around in circles.

"Just give her some time," Grant said, pressing his hands into his thighs to stand as well. "Get yourselves cleaned up."

Rixa leaned into me. "It's good you're here. It's good. Our community should be a place for people like you. Don't get discouraged by Felina. She's tough, but she'll come around just like Alaric."

Tayna grabbed my hand then, pulling me to stand. "We can meet again tomorrow," he said, and the group dispersed.

Tayna kept hold of my hand and led me out of the barn. Spring was in full bloom around us, and the Whigs were busy with the planting season. At least three dozen people were scattered around the fields, turning the soil and planting seeds.

It was warm enough when we'd returned to the community that I'd opted to only wear my undershirt in the barn, and Tayna's eyes now drifted to the Queen's tattoo on my shoulder. I resisted the urge to cover it with my hand. I wondered if the red would fade over time. At least right now it nearly blended in with all of the dirt and dried blood on my skin.

Tayna pulled me into the house but only for a moment.

"Wait here," he said, leaving me in the living room.

"Tayna—" I started objecting. All I wanted right now was a bath, but he was gone before he could hear it.

So I grabbed a bread roll from the kitchen and munched on it. By the time I'd finished it, he was back.

"Come on," he said, wrapping our fingers together again. He carried a full backpack, and I eyed him suspiciously. He laughed, that grin of his making his eyes sparkle in a way that did weird things to my stomach. The dimples in his cheeks were dusted with dirt. It didn't stop me from wanting to kiss him. If I wasn't so filthy myself, I would have.

Tayna pulled me toward one of the trails behind the barn, and I groaned, "More walking?" I thought about sinking to my knees, but his hand was firm on mine, pulling me along.

"It's a short walk. Promise."

So I followed at his shoulder, pressing myself into him as we walked deeper into the woods.

We were near the rock pools where I trained with Alaric, but instead of stopping there, Tayna continued until we rounded the corner of one of the cliff faces, and I saw another pool surrounded by orange boulders. The sun beat down on us, making the sweat itch at the back of my neck.

"That water is freezing," I objected when I realized Tayna's intention.

He shook his head. "Not here. The sun heats the rocks, warming the water in this area. Touch it."

He found a dry rock near the pool and set down the bag, beginning to unpack the contents as I tentatively touched a finger into the water.

Tayna was right. It was warm, nearly like bath water. I slipped off my boots. The rocks beneath my feet were almost too hot to touch with bare skin.

I glanced back at Tayna to find that he'd packed soap, towels, and what looked to be a cozy change of clothes for each of us.

"You can go first." Tayna gestured with his chin. "I'll wait here for you."

Now it was my turn to grab his hand, entwining our fingers and pulling him. My voice was almost shy as I said, "It's definitely big enough for two."

I dropped his hand just long enough to pull my top over my head. I wasn't wearing a bra, and I let him see me for the first time. His eyes grew hot as they roamed over my curves. I peeled off my pants next. I could see the dirt on my skin, leaving clear lines around my ankles, but Tayna didn't seem to care as he took in all of me. Finally, I undid the elastic around my braid and uncoiled my hair with my fingers. It had grown longer since I'd left the Cards. It now trailed down over my peaked nipples.

"Goddamn, Lissa," he said. And my nakedness was all the encouragement he needed to strip off his own shirt and pants.

He was magnificent. Where he'd once been tall and lanky, now every bit of his frame was masculine carved muscle. My eyes traced over the v of his torso down to the length of him framed by strong legs. He was already hard, and I swallowed thickly. The dirt on him only seemed to define his honed body more as it settled into the ridges between his muscles. I bit my bottom lip.

My desire was so plain.

But we both needed to wash before we touched, so I sank into the water and sighed with relief to feel the warm stream rush over my skin. I immediately dipped my head under the surface, running my hands through my hair.

When I rose through the water and wiped the excess from my eyes, I found Tayna wading toward me, water dripping from his chest, glistening against the warm sunlight. His wet hair clung to his forehead in a way that made my core clench.

The scar through his eyes looked harsher against the sun, but I only wanted to trace it with my fingers.

He'd brought the soap with him, and as he got closer, he squeezed a generous amount onto a small towel and began lathering it up. I reached out to take some, but he shook his head with a mischievous glint that brought out his dimples.

"May I?" he asked, sweeping my body with his gaze. It was all I could do to nod, wanting nothing more than to feel him touching me.

He started with my arm, taking one hand and running the towel over my forearm, around my elbow, and up to my bicep. He was thorough, covering every inch of me with the soapy lather.

His gaze focused on each part of my body the cloth touched.

I bit back a moan as he reached my collarbone and my shoulder. When he moved to the injured one, he asked, "Is this okay?"

I nodded. "It's only a little sore now."

So he cleaned that one too. And then my other arm before moving to my chest. If I thought he'd taken his time before, now I was sure he was trying to torture me. He swept the cloth along both of my breasts before bringing his other hand up to draw slow circles around each in turn.

I choked on a cry as I tipped my head back, arching deeper into his touch.

He chuckled but pressed his body further into mine until I could feel his length against my belly. I gripped his biceps as he continued touching me, and I swear my hands barely wrapped around half of his upper arms.

I dug my nails into him as he continued alternating between using his fingers and the towel to touch my peaked nipples.

When he finally leaned into me and whispered for me to turn around, it was all I could do to open my eyes and whine out a breathy, "Nooo."

"Yes." He chuckled, gripping my shoulder to encourage me until I faced away from him.

But when his soapy hands began kneading my shoulders, my legs buckled under me, and I gripped one of the sandstone rocks in front of me, letting out a low groan. The rocks were hot against my palms.

"God." My hips pressed back as he kneaded the sore muscles, digging his thumbs into just the right spot next to my shoulder blades.

He pressed himself against me so his length ran along my backside. I wanted him. I wasn't against begging.

His hands drifted down over my waist, the soap getting lost to the water as his fingers explored my body, then dipped lower to run along the curve of my ass. He brought the towel back, running it between my legs until my hips were moving with his strokes.

"Please, Tayna," I said, wanting him right now. The rocks were rough between my palms as I braced myself against the sandstone so I could more fully press myself against Tayna's body.

"Not yet," he rasped near my ear. "I'm enjoying watching you get all worked up too much."

So I reached around and grabbed his cock in my hands, stroking it beneath the water until he growled, his forehead pressing into the back of my head as his hips began to jerk.

I turned in his grip, caged between the rocks and his body, and grabbed the soapy towel from where he'd draped it over his shoulder.

If he was going to tease me, then I could tease right back. I ran the towel across his chest, loving the feel of him. As I reached the spot where his neck met his shoulders, I looked up at him. His mouth was parted slightly, his breathing rough. His hair began to dry against the spring sun, and I ran my free hand through the strands. He closed his eyes, savoring my touch.

So much about him was familiar, yet this was entirely new. I knew his soul, but his body—this body—was something still to discover. I understood why he'd wanted to take his time exploring. We were relearning each piece of one another, and every piece was intricately fascinating, scars and all.

I ran the soapy towel down his arms, over his back, to his backside, and finally, settled myself for wrapping a hand firmly around his length again. I left the towel on the rock as I used my other hand to run my thumb over the tip. His hips jerked, and I captured his mouth with mine, kissing him deeply as I pumped him with my hand.

He moaned, a deep rumble in his chest.

"I want you," I murmured against his lips.

He caged me against the rock with his hands.

"I'm yours," he said, dipping to lick the water droplets from my collarbone. His forehead rested against my shoulder while I continued working him with my hand. "All of me is yours." He palmed my nipple, twisting it until I was arching into him. "Whatever you want."

He gripped my chin, lifting his head from my shoulder to claim my mouth.

"Oh fuck," a deep male voice said behind us. "Sorry! Sorry!"

"Kenji?" I gasped, ducking my head behind Tayna, who spun and tucked me behind his large frame.

Kenji stood at the edge of the rock pool, his chest heaving as if he'd run here. He waved a hand and turned away, collapsing his hands on his knees as he took in air.

"What the fuck, Kenji?" Tayna demanded, and his shoulders tensed like he might be resisting the urge to stalk from the pool and pummel him.

His back was facing us now, but I could tell Kenji was dressed in his Cards uniform. The Jack of Hearts patched on the shoulder of his jacket was the only red contrast against his all-black outfit.

"Sorry," Kenji said, as he stood and kicked his head back with a long breath. "Really sorry, but this can't wait. I came back as soon as I could only to find the two of you gone. Grant said he saw you two come out here... I heard the water... I thought... fuck. You should both get dressed."

Tayna looked back at me, his eyes flashing from angry to concerned as he said to Kenji, "Give us a minute."

And just like that, the air around us shifted from heated to concerned.

36

Lissa

We dressed quickly, which meant water was still dripping down my hair, dampening the clean T-shirt Tayna brought for me. There was also a wetness between my thighs that was decidedly not from the water. But, well, Kenji's sudden appearance had stalled my plans with Tayna this afternoon.

Now, there were more important things to focus on.

We talked as we walked back to the main house, Tayna and I close at Kenji's heels.

"It's Madam Cartenoth," Kenji said. "She doesn't have much time left, but she keeps asking for you, Queenie. She won't let it go. She said she has to see you. She won't tell Phenola or me why. She just keeps mumbling your name."

"No," Tayna said. "It isn't safe."

"You think I don't know?" Kenji said. "After what happened on the hill, the Cards are ready for blood. Gideon's been sending out triple the number of scouts. They're all over the city."

"Can we bring her here?" I asked, dodging the branch of one of the large oak trees.

Kenji shook his head. "Impossible. She's bedridden, Queenie, and there isn't a road that leads to the community."

"It's a non-starter," Tayna said firmly, squeezing my hand.

Kenji breathed, "Lissa, whatever it is... It's about your mother."

We broke through the trees behind the barn. The fields sprawled out in front of us.

"My mother?" I stopped walking. The pang of her loss hit me deep within my chest. My mother. Thinking of her always conjured images of misty mornings in the garden in front of our house. "What about my mother?"

"I don't know," Kenji said, frustration tinging his words. "But she kept insisting. Do you think I'd risk coming here otherwise?"

I turned to Tayna. "I'm going."

"Lissa—" The fear was plain in Tayna's eyes.

"What's going on?" Felina asked as she, Alaric, and Grant approached us from the main house, as if they'd been waiting. Kenji's sudden arrival had everyone on edge.

"Madam Cartenoth wants to see Lissa," Kenji explained. "She... she doesn't have much time left."

"Absolutely not," Alaric said.

And Grant sighed, looking around the fields at the others who had stopped their work to stare. "We should take this conversation inside," he said, nodding his head toward the main house.

By the time we were seated in the living room, the afternoon sun had begun to wane, sending golden light scattering across the blue furniture.

Tayna and I sat on the couch while Kenji and Grant settled into the floral chairs across from us. Felina leaned against the stone fireplace, and Alaric stood behind Grant's chair with his arms crossed. Grant had heated a pot of tea, which sat untouched on the center table.

"This isn't even a conversation, Kenji," Tayna said. "She can't leave. We nearly died on that hill. It's too dangerous right now."

"Laykin hasn't said shit," Kenji said, his eyes meeting mine. "He kept his word. And I talked with him. He... he's seeing the cracks."

"You said yourself Gideon's only gotten worse," Tayna countered.

"Yeah, but he doesn't know where to look. If he suspected us, Tea and Trinkets would already be rubble. I can get her in."

"There's no way I can leave right now." Tayna shook his head.

"I can protect her," Kenji argued. "I did it for two years, and I'm more than capable of doing it now."

It was the first time I'd seen them together, I realized. These two strong males, glaring at each other from across the living room. Yet there was a clear trust between them. They were brothers in this fight.

"And I can protect myself," I added. "I have my silver, and I know how to control it now." I said it for Kenji's benefit.

He raised his eyebrows at me. "The community's been good for you, then, in more ways than one." He smirked at Tayna, and I felt my cheeks get hot.

"It's not enough," Tayna said. "There are too many risks to allow it."

"But what if—"

"No." Tayna cut me off firmly.

"You can't just tell me what to do." I glared at him. "Or am I a prisoner here now, too?"

The question was a low blow, but it made Tayna's eyes flash hot. His voice was quiet as he said, "Of course you're not—"

"I'll go." Felina pushed herself off the fireplace stone.

"What?" Alaric looked as dumbfounded as I felt.

"I'll go," she repeated. And then looked at the men around her. "Oh, please," she sighed. "I'm the best tracker and fighter we have, even without the silver, and you all know it. I'll go. I'll watch our sweet little Queen and make sure she gets home safe and sound."

Tayna looked at me. In a low voice meant just for the two of us, he said, "I told you I wouldn't leave you again. I *meant* it."

"You're not leaving me." I brought my hand up to his cheek. "We'll go and be back by tomorrow night."

He shook his head. "I don't like it."

"If she knows something about my mother, Tayna, I have to know.

I have to know what's so important that she won't even tell Phenola or Kenji."

"Like I said, Queenie," Kenji piped in. "I wouldn't have come if I didn't think it was important."

Tayna dropped his gaze, pressing his forehead into mine and murmured, "Okay. Okay."

He was giving in. He was accepting my decision, and it made another tiny piece of my heart dislodge from where I'd kept it all these years. Maybe just for him.

"Thank you." I kissed his cheek.

"But Kenji will not leave your side." Tayna stared over at him, and Kenji nodded in promise. "And Felina will go with you, too. And you will be back by tomorrow night or I'm coming after you."

"Deal," I said.

"Agreed," Kenji echoed.

"I'll get supplies," Felina declared.

"I'll help." Kenji stood. "I have a Humvee parked in the usual spot for us once we can get on the road."

And it was decided.

We would leave tonight for the city.

I only hoped we wouldn't be too late.

37

Lissa

We hiked the few miles down to the road in steady silence. The last dregs of the day's sunlight served as our guide through the thick brush and tall oak trees.

The backpack on my shoulders bounced against my lower back on the downhill. I hadn't changed out of Tayna's shirt, and I liked that I kept smelling hints of him on my skin even though the shirt was way too big for me. Rixa had given me another pair of leggings to borrow, and they were comfortable and tight against my legs, tucked into my boots.

It didn't take us long to reach the truck Kenji had parked, concealed behind a thick cover of trees.

It was one of the standard models the Cards preferred, a shiny black vehicle with tires that sparkled like the blood in my veins. Hardly easy to conceal among the trees, but well, the Cards were more the flaunting types than the hiding types.

When I'd first arrived at the Whigs community, I'd been unconscious. Kenji and Phenola hadn't wanted me to know the location because they weren't entirely sure they could trust me yet.

Now, I watched out the window as we drove along the old highway through the canyons until we reached the ocean and drove south toward the city. I knew now that the route north would take us to the Cards compound. I could see the outline of the cliffside, jutting into the ocean against the setting sun, and shuddered.

No other cars were on the road.

Felina and I had taken the back seat just in case we passed a scout. The windows were tinted enough that we could hide behind the back seat, and Kenji could pass this off as a normal outing for the Cards. No questions asked or suspicions raised.

But we didn't see anyone on the drive.

The roads were quiet as darkness descended around us.

Felina downed a vial of silver from her bag, and Kenji's eyes kept flicking to the back seat, apprehension settled into the lines between his eyebrows.

"What's happening at the compound?" I asked Kenji as we neared the city, breaking the silence that had fallen over our car for the ride so far.

Kenji leaned his head against the headrest and gave me a sideways glance. His thin locks fell onto his forehead. "You want me to sugarcoat it, Queenie?"

"Of course not," I said.

"He's been going mad without you." Kenji sighed, looking back at the road. "He's sending out scouts. He's got Dia out in the city hunting and recruiting. The trainings have been brutal. I've been relegated to patrols. Everyone's up at dawn. The Silvers are guarded nonstop. No one can even get into the clinic to talk to Karadin without approval from their suit. And not Jacks. The Kings are the only ones with exceptions now. If you thought things were strict before, well..."

He didn't finish that sentence.

"Why can't he just let me go?" Maybe if Gideon would let me go, it would be easier for me to let go of thoughts of him, too. Because I wanted what I'd built with the Whigs. I wanted Tayna. God, did I want Tayna. But a part of me still wanted Gideon, too. And as much as I tried to push my feelings for him away, they were there, deep in my gut.

Felina snorted.

"What?" I snapped.

She shrugged. "Well, isn't it obvious? He's in love with you or obsessed with you. Or both."

"He's not in love with me. He's—" But what was the right word?

You are mine.

You are everything.

I swallowed around the hitch in my throat at the memory of him feeding me chocolate-covered coffee beans, of him asking me to stay in his bed, of those moments right before he claimed me when his eyes were so blue I could see my reflection shining in their depths.

Obsessed? Yes. But it was also more. More for both of us.

"He's insane," I finally said, shaking away the tears I felt pricking the corners of my eyes. My chest was tight.

"Insane, a narcissist, power-hungry—pick your word, Queenie," Kenji said. "Whatever it is, it's all come to a head without you."

"But Laykin isn't talking?" I managed to ask.

"Yeah." Kenji sighed. "Laykin's been tight-lipped. Said they were attacked from beyond the trees, and he never got a good look at who or where it was coming from. He did take Dia to the spot where it happened, though, and they spent a long time looking through the stuff you left behind. They were trying to find clues about your location."

"Fuck." Felina sighed, shaking her head and looking out the window at the approaching city.

It was as gray and ruined as I remembered. The headlights of the Humvee lit the crumbling sides of buildings and the scared looks of the haunted eyes that stood on the sides of the road. I saw a young girl, clutching a blanket to her chest with her small fists. A woman stood next to her wearing a skirt that was too short for the mild spring weather at night. Her dark eyeliner was smeared under her eyes.

I knew most of the people we passed were addicted to silver, addicted to blood like mine. They would drain me dry if given the chance.

Once we entered the heart of the city, Felina and I crouched in the back, sitting on the floor to be sure we were out of sight.

A few Cards milled around outside one of the bars, and Kenji rolled down his window to wave while Felina and I huddled, hiding in the back.

"Come have a drink, Jones," one of them called, holding up a beer, but Kenji waved them off and kept driving.

As we rounded the market street, I saw that some vendors were still packing up for the evening, but otherwise, the street was quiet.

Kenji rounded to the back, parking the Humvee in the alley where it wouldn't be easily spotted.

"Thank god you're here," Phenola said when she opened the screen door at the back for us. As she swung the door wider, I could see that she'd grown in the time I'd been with the Whigs. Her round belly stuck out even beneath the long, billowing dress she wore. It had been nearly six weeks since I'd come here with Kenji and told them I wanted to leave the Cards.

I hugged her tightly as we came inside.

"She's been asking about you," Phenola said into my hair. "She won't stop mumbling your name. But Lissa, she's not well. She's not always... coherent."

"I'll watch the door," Felina said, taking a position near the exit.

"Good to see you, too, Felina!" Phenola called as she held the door open for Kenji and me.

"Glad it isn't just me," I grumbled.

Kenji gave Phenola a soft kiss as he walked inside and pressed a hand to her belly. "I missed you," he murmured against her lips.

"Any trouble?" she asked, closing the door behind us and walking into the small kitchen and living area.

"All's quiet tonight," Kenji said, settling into one of the mismatched chairs at the worn dining table.

"Good." Phenola nodded. "I'll start tea. Lissa, you know where to find Bat. She's probably sleeping, but go ahead and wake her."

Madam Cartenoth was, in fact, sleeping when I gently opened her door. Her soft snores filled the space. It felt so quiet in this tiny room in the center of a once-large city. It felt so at odds to see a once power-ful, ever-moving woman now frail and still.

Silver could make her comfortable, but it wouldn't heal the sick-ness worming its way through her body.

That didn't mean I didn't want to try upon seeing Madam Cartenoth so feeble as she slept, her breathing ragged and hitching.

It seemed like her entire body was being leached of its color. Her hair was a stark white against her pale skin. Even her lips and eyelids seemed ashen. Only the tips of her fingers had any hint of color, and I realized those were purple at the nail beds.

Yes, death was close.

I knelt at the bed near her shoulder and gently put a hand on her arm.

"Madam Cartenoth?"

She jolted, then gripped my wrist with surprising force.

"Lissa Metarro." She cracked her tearstained eyes open. She said my name as if in deep knowing that I would come.

"Can I get you anything?" I asked, reaching for the water cup and straw by her bed.

She cocked her head up just enough to accept a drink, making small humming and grunting noises as she swallowed before sinking back on the pillows as if the small sips had been a great effort.

Her breathing was even more labored when she was awake.

"Is there anything else I can do?"

But Madam Cartenoth was already reaching for me once again. Her spindly fingers dug into the fabric of my shirt like a tree with roots burrowing into the ground until I gave way and leaned closer to her.

"Listen, girl." Her voice rattled around in her chest. "You need to listen."

"I know," I said. "That's why I'm here. I'm here to listen."

"There's so much…" She began to cough.

"It's okay." I put my hand on her shoulder again. "It's okay. Do you want some more water?"

She shook her head. "Listen." The word was a wheezing demand.

"I'm listening," I told her.

"Your mother was a Silver," she croaked.

I waited for her to say more, but she was gasping again.

"I know, Madam Cartenoth. I know she was a Silver."

"No," she rasped, "like… you."

"Yes," I said, "like me. I'm a Silver, too."

Had we come all this way for a fool's mission? Of course my mother was a Silver. I remembered her eyes shining with the same iridescence as my own. She used her blood to help the garden flourish. It was one of the reasons we never went hungry.

One of the most vivid memories I had of my mother was a simple moment in our gardens. She was bent in the dirt, her long dark braid falling over her shoulder. Her shoulders were hunched, a simple cotton shawl around her arms and a small kitchen knife in one hand. She'd sliced her palm open over the small saplings appearing through the soil. The blade had gleamed against the mist of the mornings just like the blood that welled in her palm. She'd cupped her hand, letting the blood pool, dispersing careful drops over each of the small plants in turn. I remembered the tiny leaves seemed to stretch toward her offering as if they, too, wanted to suck the life from the mother just like the people in the city.

Madam Cartenoth's tight grip pulled me back from the memory as she continued shaking her head. I thought she might leave bruises, but I didn't pull away. The marks would heal, and I was too transfixed by her next words. "She was the father's Silver. In here." She pressed a hand to my heart. "It's in here."

"The father? I don't understand…"

"Ishmael," she snapped, a hint of her old fire returning and then dulling as quickly as it had appeared as she sank into the pillows and coughed.

"Gideon's father?" Now she had my attention. "My mother was a Queen?"

"A Queen?" Madam Cartenoth laughed. It was a pathetic sound that had her coughing again. I brought the water to her lips, and she took a small sip from the straw, her lips moving like a fish trying to get more air when there was none to be had. When she fell back on her pillows she added, "Not a Queen. *The* Queen, girl. She was the original. And oh how they fought over her!"

"The original? The original what?"

But Madam Cartenoth's eyes were beginning to droop.

I shook her, and she stirred.

"The original what, Madam Cartenoth?" I insisted. "My mother was the original what?"

"Oh, Ishmael loved her." Her voice became dreamy in its rasping. Nearly a whispered song. "Plucked her from the Veiled like the flowers she grew. He loved her in the way his son loves you. Precious little jewels to be kept in boxes. But Naveera wouldn't be kept. No." She chuckled. "History is an ever-turning wheel, girl. Oh, how the wheels turn!"

"Madam Cartenoth!" I shook her again as her gaze began to drift. "Madam Cartenoth!"

"She ran. Oh, she ran. Into the night, she fled before they could know. She didn't want them to know. The king and the queen..." Madam Cartenoth smiled as if in a dream. "The king and the queen made a princess..."

"What are you saying?" I shook her again, realizing desperate tears trailed down my cheeks. "Madam Cartenoth, please." My voice broke.

"It's in here," she said, reaching for my heart again but not quite making it all the way before her hand dropped.

Her face settled. Her gaze grew unfocused.

"I've been waiting," she said, her eyes far away and not connecting with mine.

"No." I shook her shoulder, desperate to keep her with me. Why hadn't we gotten here sooner?

I knew there was more to tell. The bits she gave me were jumbled pieces in a puzzle that only she could put together.

She inhaled.

And on the exhale, she murmured, "In most games, a Queen trumps an Ace."

She didn't inhale again.

38

Lissa

Phenola and Kenji had run into the room shortly after Madam Cartenoth's last words. Apparently, my screaming cries were enough to alert them that something was most definitely not okay.

They found me hunched over her, holding her shoulders and crying onto her chest, begging her to come back.

Phenola knelt beside me, bracing a hand on her belly and gently closing Madam Cartenoth's vacant eyes. She kissed her cheek softly and wrapped a warm hand across my shoulders.

"Oh, Bat," she sighed, silent tears welling in her almond eyes.

"Maybe we can give her some silver to bring her back." I choked on another sob.

"She's been sick for a long time, Lissa," Phenola said soothingly.

But it was so much more than that. It was the whole of this moment that I found completely and utterly overwhelming. She said so much yet told me nothing. I knew there was more.

"She can't be gone," I cried. "She can't be gone."

Since I was a child, Madam Cartenoth had been a strange sort of comfort and protection in my life. But I'd clearly never known her at all. She'd had secrets. And I'd only gotten bits and pieces of them before she died.

It wasn't enough. I didn't feel like I had enough to adequately put the bits I knew together into a cohesive story of who I was. And I needed her to tell me who I should be in this world where I was torn between two sides.

"She didn't finish what she had to tell me," I said, catching my breath as the tears dried caked on my cheeks.

Kenji placed a blanket over Madam Cartenoth as Phenola and I stood still wrapped in one another's embrace. I reached out to press my hand into Madam Cartenoth's shoulder one more time. Her skin was still warm.

"Let's get some tea," Phenola said calmly. "We have time for a cup, I think, before you need to leave and I call the doctor."

"Her words were strange," I said as Phenola, Kenji, and I walked from the room.

We froze at the group of Cards standing in front of us, framed against the wide-open door.

There had to be nearly a dozen of them, all with weapons drawn and at the ready.

Dia stood at the front of the group, so large he looked like an over-sized giant in this space.

The metal on his boots clanked as he stepped forward and smirked in a way that made my blood chill and the silver spark at my fingers.

My silver crackled on instinct, and I used it, flinging the electricity toward one of the men, who was thrown backward as my silver zapped through his chest. A clever trick I'd been working on with Alaric. It wouldn't kill the man, only incapacitate him for enough minutes that we could get the hell out of here.

But there were too many.

"Ah, ah." Dia took another step toward me as I aimed at another. "None of that, my Queen."

I followed his gaze to the pistol one of the men steadily held less than two feet from Phenola's temple.

"Don't hurt her," I breathed, knowing her pregnancy would mean nothing to this snake of a man.

"Now," Dia crooned, taking a step toward me, "that's up to you."

My silver could wipe out all of these Cards in a matter of seconds. But would it be fast enough that this man wouldn't have time to pull the trigger just once?

No, it wouldn't.

So I raised my hands in the air, my eyes flitting to Kenji. He, too, raised his hands. His gun remained holstered at his side.

"Where's Felina?" I dared to ask.

"She's been taken care of." Dia stepped so close to me that I could smell the leather of his jacket.

I bit back the chill of his words. *Taken care of.* If I knew Dia at all, that meant she was no longer alive. Felina and I hadn't exactly seen eye to eye, but that didn't mean I wanted her dead.

God, Tayna had been right.

"Gideon will be so relieved to see you," Dia said, wiping the dried tears on my cheek with a gloved finger. I flinched away and curled my lip in disgust. He was clearly enjoying this moment, and I wouldn't be the cowering mouse before I was eaten by the cat.

"Fuck you," I spat at him.

He laughed. "I wouldn't mind it. Maybe we'd all like a taste. Gideon says you're quite the prize."

"Don't you fucking—"

Kenji was cut off when one of the Cards shoved the barrel of a rifle into his stomach.

"I'll go with you!" I said quickly. "I'll go with you without a fight. Just leave them alone. We both know Gideon just wants me. They don't matter."

"Ah, if only that were true, my Queen." Dia adjusted his glove. "But Gideon is also interested in Jacks who betray him—almost as much as he's interested in spoiled little Queens who run away."

Before I could even track the movement, Dia had slammed his fist into the side of Kenji's jaw. Blood sprayed.

Phenola was screaming.

Or maybe I was screaming.

But gloved hands were grabbing me. My neck was wrenched to the side.

Dia was still landing blows to Kenji—to his head and his stomach and his chest.

My silver sparked out, flaring into the Cards now at my back.

"Fuck!" I heard someone yell. "Get her down!"

I struggled, kicking out.

A needle was plunged into my neck, and I gasped against the prick of pain.

"No! No!" My voice had turned into a desperate squeak, just like that little street mouse I had once been, begging for Tayna's life.

Only now it was Kenji on the ground. Still, Dia continued to hit and kick him.

And as the drug entered my system, I could feel the pulse of electric energy die in my veins. I was powerless to stop them.

The thwack of flesh against flesh had turned wet.

"No." My voice was a breath. It felt like I was trapped within my own body. I wanted to fight. I wanted to help Kenji. But my limbs no longer worked.

Red splattered to the ground near my face where I was held against the wood floor.

The last thing I saw before I blacked out was Phenola's desperate eyes, wild with panic, as the Cards dragged her from the home where her grandmother had just died.

What was it Madam Cartenoth had said?

History was an ever-turning wheel.

If only I had learned more quickly.

39

Lissa

My eyes fluttered open, only to find everything was too white and too stark and too bright. So I closed them again, squinting away from the sudden pain in my head.

I tried to bring my hands up to shield my face, but they wouldn't move. They weren't working.

Everything felt heavy.

My head lolled to the side as I tried blinking my eyes open again. My eyelashes stuck together in the corners.

I was reclined in some sort of chair, lying propped against a cushioned surface.

But my hands...

"Just relax," a soothing voice said near my shoulder. "Do you want some water?"

I remembered giving Madam Cartenoth small sips of water right before she died. Right before...

I jerked, my body spasmed with the memories of the Cards and the gun to Phenola's head and Kenji's face as Dia punched him over and over and over.

My eyes flew open, blinded by the light, then slowly adjusted as the room came into focus.

I was in the clinic. The harsh sunlight of midday filtered into the large windows.

The room was hot with the spring.

I yanked maddeningly against the restraints on my arms.

Someone had changed me into a white linen dress at some point, but the sweat still clung to me.

My breathing was erratic, coming in small gasps.

My hands were pinned at my sides, strapped against the hospital chair. My palms were pressed face down onto the cushion, but still the silver sparked along my fingertips.

"Control yourself, Lissa," Gideon said from the corner of the room where he watched me calmly, one eyebrow quirked in silent scrutiny. He wore a black button-down rolled up to the elbows. The top buttons were left open, exposing part of his smooth chest. His black jeans hung low on his hips. His arms crossed over his chest, and his eyes midnight black.

Whatever he had planned, it wasn't good.

"Gideon, no!" My voice was shrill in my ears as I arched my back, struggling against the chair. "No!"

"Lissa, it's okay," Karadin said at my shoulder. "Just take some deep breaths." To Gideon, she said, "Her blood pressure's too high. She needs to calm down."

"No!" I cried, pulling on the restraints until I felt them biting into the skin of my arms. "No, no!"

My wild eyes darted around the room, but they snagged on Laykin standing by the door, watching with aloof coolness. Only a faint flicker in his eyes and the slight tightening of his shoulders indicated that he heard my cries.

"Laykin!" I sobbed. "Layk, please—"

All I caught was a blur from the corner of my eye before Gideon gripped my chin, squeezing my jaw between his gloved hands to the point of pain.

I cried out, my watery eyes meeting his depthless black pupils.

"You will behave, Lissa," he sneered. "I've been without your blood for over a month thanks to your tantrum, so we will do this draw, and then you and I will have a conversation."

My breathing rattled at his deadly calm tone. But still, I pursed my lips together and spit in his face.

He didn't even flinch as the sprays of it hit his cheek and ran down his chin.

He simply pulled back from me, wiped his face with the back of his glove, and said to Karadin, "Eight vials, please."

"But—" One look at him, and she stopped talking.

Eight was double the normal draw. That much would leave me fatigued and dizzy. I'd be lucky if I didn't pass out, assuming I could even stand.

"I won't forgive you for this, Gideon," I choked. "I'll never forgive you."

He only returned my gaze with dark calm. It was the look he gave the Cards who had betrayed him before he pushed them from the cliffs. He wasn't my Gideon right now.

The Ace.

The son his father wanted him to be.

He'd gone to that dark and separate place inside himself where I knew I couldn't reach him. He was my waking nightmare as he crossed his arms and watched me.

His detachment and the cool rage in his gaze wrenched at my heart.

"Go ahead." Gideon nodded to Karadin and her table of neatly lined vials.

Karadin returned her gaze to me, to the vein in my arm. My hands shook, and my breathing was ragged. The silver jumped erratically in time to the pulse I could feel throbbing in my throat.

Picking up the needle, Karadin flared her nostrils as she looked at me. Her tongue flicked her bottom lip in concentration, and I realized her hands shook, too, as she took off the needle cap.

She was scared.

Maybe even more so than me.

Her gaze tracked to my hands again, and I realized how close I'd been to losing control only moments ago.

I took steadying breaths, willing the silver to dissipate from my fingers. As much as I wanted out of here, I didn't want to hurt Karadin.

"It's okay," I said softly to her, trying to keep my voice from shaking for her sake. "It's gone. I've got it. I'm good."

Eight vials wouldn't kill me. I could do this.

"It's okay," I murmured again, offering her as much of a smile as I could manage. It pulled at the dried tears streaked on my face.

She nodded and gave me a weak smile in return. The steady hands of her practice seemed to kick in on instinct as she pinched the butterfly needle. She braced one hand on my forearm and slipped the needle under my skin, hitting the vein on the first try.

I pursed my lips against the pain. I wouldn't give Gideon the satisfaction of seeing me flinch.

There was such still silence in the room as Karadin began the draw. My metallic blood looked stark against the sterile white of the clinic.

"Breathe, Lissa," Karadin murmured to me when we were about halfway through, and I exhaled the breath that had gotten trapped in my chest.

"Did you kill them?" I asked, bracing myself for the answer as I thought of Felina and Kenji and Phenola.

Gideon didn't bother to answer.

Maybe it should have been obvious. But I needed to hear him say it. I needed to know.

He said nothing.

"I deserve to know." My voice was pinched as I kept a rein on my silver. "And what about me? Will you keep me tied up as your personal blood bank, Gideon?"

His eyes flashed to me then, and for a moment, I saw the devastation on his face.

But it was gone.

And he was silent.

That storm was back in his gaze, the one that spelled trouble.

After the eighth vial, Karadin slipped the needle from my arm, pressing a tissue to the wound. It felt so utterly normal, that gesture against the backdrop of Gideon's glare and my silent tears. Never a bandage since she knew how quickly I would heal. Once she'd dabbed at the blood until it was nothing but a pinprick left behind, she straightened.

"She's done," Karadin said, dropping the used butterfly needle with a *plink* on the metal table.

Gideon's answering smile was an oncoming storm. "Oh, but she's not."

Karadin looked confused and turned her head, counting the vials on the table. "Eight vials," she confirmed.

"Yes." Gideon pressed up from the wall. "Now, get one from the cooler and inject her with a vial of silver from one of the other Queens."

"What?" Karadin's voice was small.

"You bastard!" I said, struggling against the binds again. My silver was noticeably diminished as it sparked weakly. My strength also waned quickly, and the room grew fuzzy at the edges.

He knew exactly what he was doing.

Injecting me with another's Silver would effectively nullify my blood, making me powerless and weak. He'd taken eight vials of my pure blood, which would no doubt get him through the week with a surplus all so he could inject me with another Silver's blood to ensure I wouldn't be able to use my silver.

"That will make her sick," Karadin dared.

"Go to the cooler," Gideon repeated. "And get the fucking blood, Karadin."

She jerked at his tone and hurried from the room.

"Gideon!" I said, still trying to pull at the restraints. "Don't—"

Even Laykin looked pale now from where he stood by the door.

"Please, Gideon!" I wasn't above begging. I'd never had another's Silver injected into my blood before, but I'd heard—all of the Silvers had heard. It was violently painful. It made you sick for days. And it nullified silver blood for a week, if not longer. The one time I'd tried to drink my own blood as a kid had been bad enough.

Gideon wasn't acknowledging my pleas at all.

Karadin returned to the room, clutching one of the vials tightly in her fist. "We don't know—"

Gideon stalked to her, grabbing it from her. "Get out," he said tersely.

"But you—"

"Get. Out."

Karadin gave me one final look, her eyes full of sorrow before she turned and left.

"You too, Laykin," Gideon said to him. "You're dismissed."

Laykin nodded and turned from the room like the good soldier. Honestly, he was probably relieved he didn't have to witness this.

Gideon turned back to the room and moved behind me to the counter so I couldn't see what he was doing.

Faint wisps of my silver trailed from my fingers, coming in sputtering bursts just like my panic.

"You know," Gideon said over my shoulder, his voice almost conversational. "I used to take vials like this out in the field with me. I liked using the needles instead of drinking the silver. It hits your blood more quickly that way. It's more potent. I became an expert at using needles."

"Gideon—" I felt like I had been locked in a room with a wild animal. He was completely unpredictable. "I'm sorry I left. Please, I'm sorry."

Gideon walked around beside me where Karadin had been standing only a few moments ago. He set the needle of silver he was holding on the side table and slowly, so slowly, he peeled off the gloves he was wearing.

"I thought we had an understanding, you and I. I allowed you to keep your kick because I like it, Lissa. I like that you fight me. I like when your eyes burn for me both in lust and in hate. Yes." He grinned, setting the gloves down. "Like that." He leaned over me in the chair I was strapped to, his hands braced on either side of my arms. "But you took my trust, and you stabbed me in the back, little Queen. So you've left me no choice for what comes next. I won't make the same mistake twice."

Angry tears fell from my eyes, and he cupped my face, brushing them away with a swipe of his thumb.

"God, I missed you," he murmured, hints of that blue flickering through his pupils. "And we'll have so much time to make up for your time away. I'm going to bend you and break you until you remember exactly where you belong, begging me to take your silver or your body or whatever else I decide to use you for."

"Gideon—" I choked again, making his name a plea on my lips.

"Shhh." The sound was a caress against my cheek. "Lesson one, Lissa, you are mine. No matter where you go, it doesn't change."

More tears leaked from my eyes as he recited the words I knew by heart.

"Lesson two." He pulled my chin closer to his until our breaths danced together, mine ragged and his so smooth. "Tell me lesson two, Lissa."

I sobbed instead, but he was patient.

"Tell me lesson two." His lips skated across mine, and then he licked along my cheek, cleaning up my tears until he reached my ear. "Lesson two, little Queen."

I shook my head. I wouldn't say it.

"Mmm," he groaned, leaning his cheek into mine as if he realized he would have to force me. One hand wrapped around my head, holding me against his body as he leaned into me. With his other hand, he grabbed the needle from the table. I couldn't see it, but I heard the clatter as he picked it up.

"No," I breathed as his hand trailed down the side of my face.

"What you want doesn't matter," Gideon said. And I could almost believe his words were sorrowful as he smoothly pressed the needle into the side of my neck, still holding me closely against his chest.

I jerked, but with his hand around the back of my head and my arms pinned beside me, there was nowhere to move.

Pain blossomed from the spot where he pressed the injection in deeply and then deeper still. I could feel the blood entering my body as if it were a dagger worming its way through my veins.

I cried out, and his grip around me tightened.

I could barely make out his words around the pain lighting through my body, but above the roar in my head, I heard him say, "I will remind you that you are so much more to me than your body or your silver blood. But not today, little Queen. For now, I'm using you as you've forced me to use you."

And then he released me, withdrawing the needle, and I turned my head just in time to vomit on the floor.

40

Lissa

Once I'd emptied the contents of my stomach, Gideon undid the latches around my wrists.

The thought of so much as trying to lift my arms didn't even filter into my agony-addled mind. It felt like someone was zapping me with my own silver from the inside out. The energy throbbed to the very center of my chest, where I thought my heart might rupture from the pull of pain.

It was an effort to remember to breathe. Each rattle of my chest was shallow and aching.

I wished I would just pass out, but my vision flickered in and out of blackness instead. Another wave of nausea wracked me, and I barely managed to roll over before I dry heaved over the side of the chair.

When I was done, Gideon seemed content that I'd emptied the contents of my stomach and scooped me into his arms. I whimpered in agony. My head fell against his exposed chest as he cradled me.

I managed a weak, "No," but was powerless to do anything but hang limply in his arms. My body didn't feel like my own.

He carried me from the room.

"It will need to be cleaned before your next appointment," Gideon said as he walked easily from the clinic. I assumed he was talking to Karadin but couldn't see her. "Come to my room tomorrow morning," he ordered without stopping.

He walked with me out onto the lawn, and I groaned against the light from the sun. It hit my skin like silver burning through me. The warmth from the rays was agony, and I struggled to get away from it and hide within Gideon's shadow.

Gideon pulled me in tighter against his chest as he said, "I know, little Queen."

Everything hurt.

My body felt as fragile as a newborn. My senses were overwhelmed with the sudden exposure of not having my silver as a shield to protect itself.

"Only a few more steps and then you can sleep," he murmured.

God, I wanted to sleep. I wanted the pain to pull me under. It wasn't just the pain of my body, but the pain of knowing that my actions had led to this. Tayna had told me leaving the community was too dangerous. He had tried to get me to stay. But I had insisted. I had insisted, and for what? At least I had gotten to see Madam Cartenoth one more time. At least I'd gotten to hold her hand and hear the words she seemed desperate to say. Hopefully, that brought her some peace in the end.

At least one of us would go in peace.

I was sure whatever Dia had done to Kenji had not been peaceful. Felina, hopefully, was caught by surprise and felt nothing. But Phenola. God, Phenola. What had happened to her? Had they left her body at Tea and Trinkets? I thought of her swollen belly as another wave of agony crashed into me, and I spasmed, unable to fight the cry that tore its way from my lips.

"Don't fight it," Gideon said. "It's easier if you just give in. It will hurt until it runs its way through your veins."

All of the foreign blood would mix with mine, slowly diluting and tamping down on the power that made me, me. It wasn't something my body would simply give in to, consciously or otherwise.

The excruciating pain radiated through my body, causing my muscles to spasm and contract. It was all I could do to groan as wave after wave chipped away at all of the pieces of my soul.

Gideon walked with me up the stairs and down the hallway into his corridor of the mansion. Guards were waiting outside of his door who must have opened the room for him because he breezed inside without stopping.

Everything was just as I remembered it—white and stark and devoid of anything that felt alive. I wanted to go to my room. I wondered if he had left it untouched. If he was as confident as he seemed that I belonged to him, then it made sense he would have left it.

"No," I groaned as Gideon set me on his bed, and I felt the plush mattress cocoon around my body, enveloping me like a cloud.

"Sleep, little Queen," Gideon said.

And I did.

It felt like falling, this sleep, falling and falling and falling. Until I swear I felt myself hit the bottom with a body-shattering crash.

41

Gideon

M y fingers traced the outline of the tattoo on her shoulder as she slept, deep and still. Her full lips were parted slightly against her small breaths. I wanted to capture them with my mouth and breathe her in, relearn the taste of her. Her blood wasn't enough. It was never enough of her.

Little silver.

Little Queen.

Little liar.

And I was the pawn she'd chosen to play.

She was smart. I'd never doubted my little Queen was smart. It was one of the things I loved most about her.

Love.

Just the word made my lip curl in disgust as the betrayal of her actions wound deep within my chest.

My father had warned me about emotions.

I'd thought he was a silly, jaded fool, scorned by his own love.

A man truly becomes a man when he fully realizes the wisdom in his father's words.

I turned from the room, barely making it into my office before picking up a black lamp from my desk and hurling it into one of the bookcases. It shattered into a thousand tiny fragments of glass, sparkling as they fell like Lissa's blood sparkled in the vials Karadin had drawn today.

I was the bastard, but she was the betrayer.

And it fell to me to pick up all of the tiny pieces left to hold this world I'd carefully crafted together even now.

I needed to release this rage. I needed an outlet for the fury coursing in my veins. And I knew the solution. It was one of the reasons I'd asked Dia to keep him alive.

There was wisdom in calculated mercy, too.

A strategic play in this ever-evolving game.

42

Lissa

The room was still when I woke.

The curtains were drawn, and I saw no hint of light.

I had no sense of how long I'd been asleep.

My limbs felt sluggish, but they felt like my own again. My fingers twitched with tired movement, and I slowly clenched and unclenched my fists, the muscles stiff.

I wanted to close my eyes again and allow myself to be dragged back under. For a few moments, I kept my eyes shut, willing darkness to pull me into its embrace.

Too much had happened. There was too much death and destruction to deal with in this hell of reality. My heart ached for Kenji and Phenola and Felina. As soon as they entered my mind, I had to push those thoughts away, push them down, and swallow back the grief. I couldn't start crying again, not so soon. If I started now, I wasn't sure I would ever stop.

And my heart ached for Tayna.

Did he know by now that I was gone?

He'd promised never to leave me again, and here I was, back in

Gideon's grasp. This reckoning wasn't something I was certain I could endure. Gideon's anger had been such a tangible force that I'd seen the darkness in his eyes.

He'd taken my silver so casually. It had been so clinical to him, so emotionless. He saw my power as a threat, so he'd removed that threat. It twisted my heart with more grief for the boy who'd chosen to follow in his father's footsteps.

I finally blinked my eyes open, giving in to the fact that there was no more sleep to be had.

My body felt empty. Where my silver usually flowed, I felt nothing alive beneath my skin. It was as if the color had leached from my body just as no color could be found in this room.

There was a slight throbbing at the base of my head, and the hollowness of hunger had settled deep within my belly. When was the last time I'd eaten anything?

I rolled over, pressing myself up to find the room empty—not just of color. I was alone.

The white linen dress I wore was splattered with vomit, and I cringed.

Tentatively, I swung my legs from the bed and onto the floor, bracing myself on the mattress and testing my weight on my feet.

I felt weak, but I managed to stand. My breath was heaving just from the effort of lifting myself.

The bathroom was the priority right now.

Not that there was any use attempting to escape out the door. Those guards I'd seen when we entered were definitely still standing outside.

There wasn't a lock on the bathroom door, but I closed it and peeled the smelly linen dress from my body, seeing to the needs of my bladder first.

The bathroom was as stark as the bedroom. White tile and black appliances were framed by a giant mirror that took up the entire wall above the sink. There was a spa-style tub, which was the size of a small pool. Another benefit the rich and plentiful of this city used to enjoy, no doubt.

While I ran a bath, I brushed my teeth with a toothbrush I found set out for me on the counter. I drank the water from the sink. It was the best I had currently, and my body needed the liquid. Hopefully, it wouldn't make me sick.

My face was pale. The skin under my eyes was bruised. My lips were nearly the same color as the skin of my cheeks. My dull hair hung around my slender shoulders.

As I sank into the tub, I let the water scald my skin, just to feel something aside from the aching emptiness in my bones. I submerged my head and exhaled the air from my lungs until I felt the burn in my chest.

Only then did I emerge, using whatever soap I could find to clean myself. The idea of smelling like Gideon, of him marking me in any other way made me hesitate. Hadn't he already stained my soul enough? But staying unwashed with the remnants of vomit on my skin was, at the moment, an even less favorable option.

I needed to figure out how to escape the compound.

That was my first priority.

Find Tayna.

I'd done it once before. I would do it again. Gideon couldn't keep me in this room forever. He was mad now, but he would trust me again. I would make sure he trusted me again. There was an ache, not just for Tayna and my friends, but for what Gideon and I could have had, too.

Things had changed in the weeks I'd been away from the compound.

I was not the same little mouse, the same little Queen.

But being back here was a stark reminder that it wasn't too long ago when I had almost given in to him. He'd chipped away at a piece of my heart. He'd broken it just enough to let me know that more than a piece had almost been his.

Almost.

As I rinsed the soap from my body, I traced the small scab on the inside of my arm from the blood draw yesterday. Not healed. That small mark made me feel raw and vulnerable. As if the overwhelming emotion I was fighting desperately to keep under my skin might just leak out from beneath at any moment.

But there was no buzz of silver in my veins.

Only the aching of my heart.

There was yelling outside on the lawn. Loud cries and cheers erupted.

I sat up abruptly, splashing water over the lip of the tub as the hollering continued.

It sounded like it was coming from a crowd of people. Men, to be exact.

Grabbing the towel hanging on the rack, I didn't even bother to dry as I padded out of the bathroom and to the window, leaving wet footprints that turned the white carpet gray.

I pulled open the blinds, blinking back against the light as the lawn below came into focus.

A group of Cards—at least fifty of them—had formed a circle around the lawn. They were whooping and cheering, calling out insults and jeering toward the center where two men were fighting.

Kenji.

It was Kenji. His head had been shaved, and his shirt was torn and dirty. I would hardly have recognized him without seeing the Jack of Hearts tattoo on his deep brown skin.

He was alive.

Kenji was alive.

But Gideon was grinning, his smile bloody in one corner. He'd removed his shirt entirely, his sculpted chest and arm of tattoos glistened with sweat in the midday sky. He stood tall and proud, beckoning Kenji forward.

I searched for a way to open the window so I could better hear or see what was happening, but the window was sealed.

Clinging to the windowpane, I pressed myself closer to the glass, refusing to move even as my weak legs began shaking with the effort of standing.

One of Kenji's eyes was swollen shut. He had a cut running along one of his cheeks. He was scrambling to keep himself upright.

There was a game here. Gideon was toying with him. If he had kept him alive, then he did it to make an example out of Kenji, and I knew this wasn't a fair fight. Dia had beaten Kenji bloody at Tea and Trinkets. He had pummeled him so badly that I thought he'd killed him. But I didn't see any bruises on his torso now, which meant they'd most likely given him silver and then thrown him in the ring to face off against Gideon.

It meant I'd been asleep for at least a day.

Kenji's chest heaved as he barreled into Gideon's midsection.

And Gideon laughed.

He laughed.

And threw an elbow down between Kenji's shoulder blades.

Kenji crumpled into the grass, his body folding in on itself.

Still, Kenji struggled into a stand, pressing himself up.

But it seemed Gideon was near the end of his fun. He kicked Kenji in the chest, sand and blood flying with the impact.

Kenji sprawled onto his back, his hands splayed wide, his head lolling.

"No!" I screamed, pounding my fists onto the window. "No!"

Gideon stalked toward Kenji like a beast, claiming his kill. He bent just low enough to pick up Kenji's wrist in his fist as he dragged him. He yanked Kenji's unconscious body across the lawn until he reached a flag post near the barracks at the back of the property.

He used the chains attached to string Kenji up until he was hanging by his arms, barely able to touch his toes to the dirt beneath him.

Kenji's head hung limply. Dirt and grime covered so much of his body that I couldn't tell where he was injured.

Gideon barked an order to the guards standing nearby as he stalked away from the yard and toward the house, looking up at the window where I stood as if he'd known I'd been watching the entire time.

43

Lissa

I scrambled to the closet, finding one of Gideon's shirts. It was long enough to wear as a dress, and I hastily put on a pair of ill-fitting boxers as well.

Fuck staying in this room. Silver or no, I wouldn't just watch from the window while he hurt my friend. I'd break the damn window if that's what it meant to get to Kenji.

There wasn't much in the room I could use. The door that connected the bedroom to the office was locked. But a ceramic vase sat on the side table, filled with white calla lilies. I dumped the flowers onto the floor and picked up the vase to use like a small baseball bat.

The door behind me swung open, and Gideon stalked into the room.

He'd come straight here from dealing with Kenji, which I hadn't anticipated.

Faster than I could react, he was across the room, picking me up by the waist and hauling me backward. "Don't you fucking dare, Lissa."

I screamed, kicking out from him.

He smelled like blood and sweat. His bare chest was grimy where our skin slid against one another as he held me.

"I hate you!" I raged, and he carried me to the bed and dumped me onto the mattress, wrenching the vase from my fingers. "I fucking hate you!"

He pinned my arms above my head, his mouth crashing down onto mine as I continued to scream obscenities at him. He pried open my mouth with his lips and plunged his tongue inside me. I bucked my hips as I tasted the salt from his body. He was high on adrenaline and silver from the fight with Kenji.

Managing to turn my head just enough, I bit his lip, blood coating my teeth.

He reared back, his smile feral, his chest heaving.

"Oh, little Queen," he said, his voice a low warning, the cut on his lip already sealing. "You're used to having your silver to protect you." He rubbed his nose over my cheek, inhaling. The stubble across his jaw was rough against my skin. "You're used to the marks I leave healing quickly."

My stomach dropped as his words settled over me, and I sucked in a sharp breath.

"But now." He pulled my wrists so he was holding both of my arms tightly in one hand. "Now, I can claim you with all the marks I want. If I remember right, your ass turned the prettiest shade of pink when I spanked you. How long do you think it'll stay that color now that your silver can't heal you?"

His free hand roamed over my body, running down my side and over my stomach before his hand cupped my backside and squeezed.

The faintest whimper escaped my lips.

Gideon held me in place as he lifted himself just enough to reach inside the dresser beside the bed, pulling out a long, thick rope from the bottom drawer.

"Don't—" My voice was a small and panicked plea.

But he didn't react to my words as he made quick work of wrapping the rope around my wrists and attaching the bindings to the headboard at the top of the bed.

"Can't have you trying to break windows again now, can we?" he said. "We have all afternoon to catch up." His eyes roved over my body. "But first, I need a shower."

He pressed smoothly from the bed, his arms flexing as he moved, and I pulled against the bindings, testing their strength. The ropes were so secure there wasn't any give, even as I attempted to wiggle my wrists.

"Gideon!" I thrashed on the bed, but it did no good as he walked into the bathroom, leaving the door open as he turned on the shower. The large mirror reflected his form to where I lay on the bed. I could see as he kicked off his pants and stood, revealing his nakedness, the full glory of his body on display. He was a predator, with his lethal strength and arrogant grace.

My pulse pounded in my throat at the sight of him. I wasn't sure anymore if I was watching him to track his movements or watching him because that magnetic give and take between us had somehow drawn me in.

He stepped into the stream of water, the glass pane of the shower giving me a full view of his backside as he tipped his head forward into the spray. He braced a hand on the wall as he squeezed some shower gel into his palm and began scrubbing his body with his hands, starting with his hair and working his way down. His hands glided over his chest to his abdominals and then to his erect cock.

He wouldn't. He...

He began pumping his length, his hips rocking in and out of his soap-covered fist as his other hand braced on the tile.

His head turned in the spray of water. His hair ran down into his forehead, and he opened his mouth, water spraying with his heavy breathing. His eyes connected with mine in the mirror.

I looked away, closing my eyes tightly against the image as my body betrayed me.

This man had just hurt my friend. He'd hurt so many people I loved and cared for, and now I was watching him jerk off in the shower.

I hated him.

But I also hated myself.

I felt sick. And this time it wasn't from the foreign silver in my blood.

It was because wetness pooled between my legs.

My body responded to him, even now.

This was the fucked-up game we played.

Because I wanted to hurt him. God, I knew in my very bones that if my hands were free, I would rage at him. If I had my silver, I would use it on him. He hurt me. He hurt people I loved. He took my silver. He forced me onto this compound and into his bed.

But I also wanted him.

That sick, chipped part of my heart had missed him and beat for him even now. My stomach coiled in anticipation, and goose bumps tracked over my skin as if seeking his touch.

I knew what would happen next when he emerged from that shower. My body was primed for it.

And I could tell myself I was helpless. I could pretend I didn't want to feel his body press into mine as his length entered the deepest part of me, but I knew myself well enough to feel the lie in those thoughts. And he knew me well enough that he would hear the lies on my lips and revel in them.

But what was wrong with me that I wanted two men? Two men who were positioned on either side of a war that I had somehow found my way into the center of. And what was wrong with me that after everything Gideon had done to me, I could hate him so fiercely but also want him so badly? If Tayna was the other half of my soul, Gideon was the darkness to my light, and I craved him even when I despised him.

My eyes flew open when I heard him step from the shower, and my core clenched. He grinned at me like he could see the thoughts playing out on my face. As if my desire was reflected in his own. He kept his gaze on me as he stood in his full, naked glory and used a towel only to quickly dry off his hair and skin.

"Look at you," he said, walking into the room, leaving the towel on the bathroom counter. "What has you so quiet and well-behaved?"

"Just waiting for the right opportunity." My voice was low but also heady with my desire. I licked my lips, realizing my mouth had gone dry at the sight of him.

"I'm sure you are." He leaned over me so his arms were caged on either side of me.

"Is Phenola alive, too?" The question was a whisper that filled the small space between our mouths. But I had to know. It was a desperate, hoping question. If they were alive, then there was still time to fix all of the fucked-up shit that had happened here.

His eyebrow ticked up, just a hint, as his gaze flicked between my eyes, debating how much to tell me. Finally, he settled on, "For now."

And I choked on a sob, nodding quickly, desperately relieved.

"Don't look at me like I'm not the monster you thought." He held my gaze. His was full of the midnight blue I'd wanted to see so badly yesterday. "I am."

"I know you are," I said and meant it. Yes, with his complicated morals and deep desire to maintain control over this city, this man was a monster. But he was also mine.

He nodded, his eyes sweeping over me as the heat returned to his gaze. "Good."

He kissed me deeply then, his tongue delving to explore mine once again. And then he kissed down my body. He sat back on the bed, picking up the collar of the shirt I wore with a finger. He shook his head.

And I heard the flick of a knife that he must have brought from the bathroom.

"Just as long as we're clear about the fact that you may see the monster in me, little Queen, but that doesn't stop you from wanting me."

My breath caught as he cut up the fabric and over the sleeves until it fell off me in ribbons. He pulled the fabric from my body, also taking the time to slide the boxers over my hips and down my legs before marveling at me the same way I'd watched him in the shower.

"Fuck you," I sneered, twisting in the bindings at my wrists but getting nowhere.

The chuckle radiated from deep within his chest as he surveyed my body, ignoring my insults. His dark gaze settled on my chest.

"I've fantasized about these breasts over and over again," he said, lifting his hands to cup both of them in his palms. He kneaded them, brushing his thumbs over my nipples until my head kicked back and my hips jerked.

He leaned his face down slowly between the peaks, keeping his hands squeezing and playing over my breasts while his mouth trailed down my stomach.

"Gideon, don't," I breathed as his mouth reached the apex of my thighs. He trailed his tongue through the wetness of my folds.

"Mmm," he said at the first taste of me.

I bit back a whimper.

"That's right." He ran a finger through the slickness he found waiting for him. "I heard you found yourself a lover." He licked me again, pinching my nipples at the same time his tongue ran across my clit.

I cried out then at the zing of pleasure that wound through me.

"Did he lick you like this?" Gideon asked, delving his tongue between my legs until I was choking on another sob.

It was all I could do to shake my head.

I didn't want to think about Tayna right now, not when I was so helpless to Gideon's touches and my needy body.

"Mmm." Gideon lapped at my clit as he continued twisting my nipples, the pain melding with the pleasure in a delicious sweep through my body. "Did he fuck you?" Gideon asked, pinching my nipples again at the same moment he lightly bit on my clit, and it was enough to have me screaming and thrashing before he soothed the areas with his tongue and his fingers. "Did he?"

I shook my head again.

"Say it, Lissa," Gideon ground out the command between my legs, his teeth scraping along my inner thigh in warning.

"No," I gasped, choking on the word because I had wanted Tayna so badly. That day in the rock pool, he had almost, *almost* taken me, and I desperately wished he had. "No, he didn't fuck me."

Gideon continued flicking his tongue across my clit. His hands worked my breasts for a few more breaths as he seemed to consider my words.

He moved one hand from my breast to between my legs, pressing two fingers inside me. "Good." My back bowed off the bed. "That's right," he said, working me with his fingers. "Mine."

He dipped his head again between my thighs, his tongue working my clit in time with his fingers.

God, I was going to come.

It made me want to scream. He had such control over my body.

Right before I fell over the edge, Gideon stopped, and I panted, looking up from the bed as best I could with his fingers stilled deep inside me.

"But he touched you?" Gideon's tone turned lethal, and I froze. His fingers were buried to the knuckle, his other hand twisting my nipple and his mouth hovering just above my clit.

"I—"

I opened my mouth to deny it, to find anything to say, but my vision was hazy.

"He touched you," Gideon repeated, pulling his fingers out and then slamming them inside me. "And you touched him."

He did it again.

Not a question.

"Yes," I gasped, knowing he already knew. Knowing the truth was my only option. Knowing I would be accepting whatever punishment he thought I deserved for allowing another man to touch me.

But his mouth was back on my clit.

And my head fell back onto the bed as the orgasm crashed into my body. The force of it had my body bowing to the point the ropes at my wrists strained, and I could feel them cutting into the skin. But I didn't care as I rode wave after wave of pleasure.

He continued driving his fingers inside me, his tongue frenzied as he sucked my clit.

Then he withdrew entirely from me, even as my body was still spasming with the aftereffects of the orgasm. I moaned at the loss of his fingers, clamping my legs together as the pleasure continued to wave through me.

I didn't resist as he rolled me onto my stomach, my wrists crossing above my head.

I didn't resist as he trailed kisses across my shoulders and back. The stubble from his face brushed along my skin.

I didn't resist as he rubbed his thick length between the seam of my legs, wetness coating my inner thighs.

But the fight took hold the second Gideon whispered in my ear, "I'm going to hunt him down, and I'm going to kill him. Slowly." And then pressed every inch of his cock deep inside me.

44

Lissa

Gideon kept me tied to his bed for three days just as he kept Kenji tied to the post outside.

Unlike Kenji, I was untied three times throughout the day to eat and attend to my needs in the restroom. Every time I was allowed to stand, I would look out the window to find him still hanging, his head limp and his body heavy, but his wounds had healed. They'd given him silver, meaning his skin burned from the sun, healed at night, and then burned again. It meant his throat was no doubt raw from dehydration, and his stomach twisted with hunger, but he would remain conscious. It meant he would feel every pinched nerve from the bindings on his wrists and the strain from his elbows where he hung, only to have his body keep him from breaking fully.

Kenji's punishment was in preventing his injuries.

Mine was in the making of them.

Gideon had used me so thoroughly that my core ached, and my lips felt swollen and rough. He'd marked my backside, too, just as he promised he would. His strikes had been so hard that welts appeared in the shape of his fingers. He'd smiled and rubbed his hands over them when he'd seen the raised skin.

"So fucking beautiful," he'd murmured in my ear before landing another blow.

The marks made everything uncomfortable. Even lying down was a constant and unpleasant reminder, and I walked stiffly when I was allowed to rise.

And still, each act against my body had been accompanied with unimaginable pleasure. He'd bring me to orgasm again and again and again until I was boneless and exhausted. My skin became so sensitive and hyperaware of his touch that even the stroke of his fingers along my body made me cry out and writhe on the bed.

Each day, whether it be sex or some kind of sexual torture, it was a reminder of his first lesson.

I was his.

I was *his*.

And my body responded accordingly, even if my mind screamed in protest. My brain demanded I fight, resist, do *something*. But no silver sparked at my fingertips. My blood was hollow and empty as it pumped through my veins. The marks on my body lingered, as red as the Queen tattoo on my shoulder.

And when he came into my room at night, after spending the day working, and played with my body until I begged him for release, well, then I felt the edges of my mind beginning to recede too.

It was easy to let go.

It was easy not to think.

It was easy to enjoy the pleasure he gave so expertly.

It was at the end of that third day, as he was still seated fully inside me, the two of us catching our breaths after a round of pleasure, when he whispered against my neck, "We're having a bonfire tomorrow night."

His words against my skin made me shiver, and a deeper part of me clenched around him.

He groaned.

"What's the occasion?" I asked, trying to focus on his words, even as I could feel him getting hard inside me once more.

"New recruits." He stroked light fingers up my torso until he traced the Queen tattoo on my shoulder. "Would you like to go?"

My head jerked to look at him, and he rolled his hips so my eyes fluttered.

"You want me..." Focusing on my words was difficult. "To come?"

He chuckled deeply, sliding his hips along mine again. "Oh, I know you'll come. Again. At least once more."

I didn't even have it in me to scoff at his words as he braced his arms on either side of my head and began slowly, so slowly, sliding in and out of my slick core.

"But yes." Gideon captured my mouth for a sweeping kiss before adding, "I want you to attend the bonfire as my date."

My brow furrowed as the pleasure kept me from thinking clearly. "Why?"

Out...

And in.

"I think it'll be a good chance to reintroduce you to the compound. As much as I'd like to keep you in this room forever." He pushed his hips forward until he was pressed to the hilt within me as if to prove the point. "It isn't realistic."

I moaned, my hips rolling with him now.

His eyes were dancing with the deepest blue. "But there will be rules."

I nodded, breathlessly, my lips brushing his.

He was going to untie me. He was going to let me out of this room. This could be my chance to run. It was a bonfire. People would be everywhere. He couldn't possibly plan to watch me all night.

He grabbed my chin, forcing my gaze to focus on him. "I can already see you plotting."

I groaned as he kissed me, his tongue delving as deeply as his length pumped into my core.

The pleasure in me was building. My hips moved on instinct in time with his.

He broke the kiss to say, "You'll stay with me the entire night."

I nodded.

"You won't attempt to talk to that traitor Jack."

My eyes flew open. His movements were growing faster. Harder.

After a gasping moment, I nodded.

"You won't talk to anyone unless I explicitly give you permission."

I thought of Enver. I'd been desperate to know if she knew I was back, desperate to know she was okay and talk to my friend.

But I nodded.

"And if you try anything..."

Gideon leaned over me until our chests were pressed together, his thigh pushing my knee wider. His hand reached down to grip my leg, pulling it to bend and allow him deeper access to the very center of me. He gripped my knee, tucking it into his side, the new position giving him the perfect angle to slide his pelvis across my clit each time he rolled into me.

I moaned, my head falling back.

"Look at me, little Queen," he demanded.

And I did. Too afraid he'd stop if I refused.

"If you try anything," he continued, "I'll push Kenji from the cliffs and keep you tied up for a month. If you think these three days have been rough, I'll show you just how much of your skin I've left unmarked. I'll fuck you and let the entire compound watch. I'll put you naked in the cells until you're begging me to tie you up in my room again."

His words each hit me like a slap, and I resisted the building orgasm.

He continued his punishing rhythm inside me, my breath catching in my throat as I fought the building pleasure.

I cried out against it, but he didn't stop, didn't slow, just grinned savagely.

"No, you fucking don't," he said, reaching a hand between our sweat-slicked bodies to pinch my clit.

And that was all it took to send me careening over the edge.

I was sobbing, my head thrown back against the mattress, yelling in pleasure but also in frustration at how thoroughly he owned me and how easily he could control me. Still, the orgasm crashed into me in wave after wave of dizzying pleasure as he found his release, too. I could feel his cum filling me as he roared his own pleasure, his hips jerking and then stilling.

He claimed my mouth as he pulled the final dregs of pleasure from my body.

My limbs shook. My arms were stiff and aching from being stretched overhead for so long.

"Good girl," Gideon said, slowly pulling himself from my body.

I didn't even have the energy to tell him I despised him.

I simply did my best to roll away from him and begged sleep to claim me as he pulled my back into his chest and wrapped an arm around me, keeping our bodies flush as our breathing stilled.

At that moment, I couldn't fight the thoughts of Tayna. I missed him. I missed talking with him and being with him. I couldn't stop the wave of wanting him that washed over me, nor could I stop the single tear that slipped down my cheek.

45

Lissa

A dress and sandals were brought upstairs the following afternoon, and Gideon unfastened the ropes around my wrists.

He wore a black Henley, and his hair was pushed back from his face in a long swoop that curved down to frame his ears. He quirked his brow in warning as I stood from the bed, but no hint of my silver sparked at my fingertips. There was no pulse of it under my skin.

Meanwhile, Gideon practically glowed with power and not just from my silver blood running through his veins. No, he was a commander in his element. And he'd won the game. I was back. I was *his*.

He gave me a few minutes alone in the bathroom to get ready—to wash my face and brush out my hair. I opted to tie it up in a high ponytail, braiding the long strands down my back, creating a severe look I'd seen Felina wear that made me feel more like a warrior instead of a captive.

"What about my cloak?" I asked, emerging from the restroom. The dress was a gauzy black material. It swooped low in the front with rope ties that twisted over the shoulder, dipping down to the small of my back. A long slit caressed up to my thigh as I slid on the sandals and fastened them.

No undergarments.

"Oh." Gideon eyed me. "Now you want your cloak back?"

"I just thought—"

"You haven't earned it," he said, pulling on a jacket with the Ace of Hearts embroidered on the shoulder. "A night outside, yes. But not your Queen's cloak."

It was warm enough outside now that I didn't need the cloak, but I wanted it like a security blanket.

He murmured next to my ear, "You wanted to be an outsider, and here you are."

But I didn't want the cloak so I could feel like a Card again. I wanted the cloak because if I found a chance to escape this compound, I would need something to help get me through the chilly nights along the coast. With its gauzy fabric and small straps over the shoulders, this dress wouldn't work. But of course Gideon knew that, and it was simply another way to keep me compliant.

I could already hear the bonfire beginning below us. The sun was barely dipping beneath the cliffs, but the music had started on the speakers, and I could see outside from the window as the cooks set up a long buffet table.

Kenji still hung in the distance, but I could see his form from the window. His head was downturned. He looked like a fallen hero framed against the final slivers of light. My friend. My protector. And here I was, completely useless to do anything but watch him endure his punishment.

Gideon saw me watching and turned my chin so my eyes met his.

"Red lips," he said, pulling a tube of lipstick from his pocket. "I want them as dark as blood. Well, mine," he considered, "not yours."

He pulled the cap off with his teeth.

"What will you do to him?" I asked as he began gently painting the color across my mouth.

"Mouth open," Gideon said instead, running a finger just below my bottom lip until I obeyed.

I waited, his brow furrowed as he took his time getting the lipstick just right across my mouth. His strokes were crude, but his hand was steady.

"Did you know women used to paint their lips like this every day?" he asked, turning my chin as he filled in the space at the cupid's bow of my mouth. "It must have been incredibly time-consuming." He ran a thumb across the corner of my lip with a final, "There."

"Gideon, please." I kept my eyes on him, sensing that this night was all somehow another game of power. He was toying with me by not answering my question about Kenji.

He gave me one more hardened look and finally said, "Remember the rules tonight. By my side. No talking without my approval. No alcohol. I've made myself clear on the consequences, haven't I?"

I nodded, my stomach twisting with the thought of him throwing Kenji from the cliffs.

"I'll behave," I said.

"I know you will, little Queen."

He gently kissed along the edge of my jaw, careful not to smudge any of the lipstick as he worked his way to my neck and then to the place right at the apex of my shoulder.

I didn't realize what he was doing until his teeth sank into my skin. Hard.

I cried out in shock and in pain, but he held fast, one of his arms coming up to brace against my back as I dug my nails into his shoulders and tried to push him away. My eyes flew wide as I struggled to dislodge him, instinct causing me to panic.

But then he was pulling away, laving at the bruised skin with his tongue, and I choked on a sob.

I felt him smile against my neck, his teeth grazing my skin again, and I braced myself for more pain. But instead, he murmured, "You are mine, little Queen. I want to make sure you and everyone else remember tonight."

With a final kiss to the spot, he straightened, and I glared up at him.

"You are insa—"

"I wouldn't," he said, cutting me off as he straightened out his jacket so casually. "Not unless you want me to bend you over the chair right now to further prove my point." His eyes flashed darkly. "I wouldn't mind missing the bonfire."

My jaw snapped shut, but my breathing was ragged as I seethed.

He ran a thumb over the wound from his bite, and I bit back on the gasp of pain. It was sharp and throbbing, and not getting any better, only settling into a dull and constant ache.

"God, I love being able to mark your skin. If I didn't need your blood, I think I'd always dilute your silver. It makes playing with you so much more fun."

Over these past few days, I'd learned what marks felt like for those who couldn't heal. For the first time in my life, I'd felt the pain of bruises, of forgetting them only to brush them across the bed and wince from the tenderness. I'd experienced the sting of reddened skin that took hours to dull. But he was careful not to break my skin, only pushing me far enough to cause discomfort.

Gideon offered me his arm, and I shoved him away.

All he had to do was raise an eyebrow for me to see the threat in his expression, and I gave in, looping my arm through his as we walked from the room.

I didn't do it because I particularly wanted to go to the bonfire. I didn't care to see anyone other than Enver. But this might be one of my only opportunities to escape. I didn't know the next time Gideon would let me out to wander the compound grounds. If I had the chance to run, I had to take it.

But then... would Gideon make good on his promise to kill Kenji? And what about Phenola? My stomach twisted at the thought of leaving them behind, at the thought of Phenola's swollen belly and her tear-streaked eyes when Dia had beaten Kenji. The thought had me stumbling in my dress. Gideon kept me upright, with a stiffening of his bicep beneath my hand to brace me.

Laykin waited for us outside the door along with another guard I recognized as Reggie, one of the Cards under Dia who the Whigs had attacked in those days before I left the compound.

He was an eight of Clubs, high enough to be deemed trustworthy but not particularly notable. If he'd been chosen for assignment guarding Gideon, the Cards must be getting more desperate for people. Had they lost so many?

I eyed Reggie as Gideon whisked me into the hallway and down the stairs.

I didn't look at Laykin. I couldn't bring myself to look at him, not after everything he knew and had seen. I was too afraid Gideon would see the secrets between us if I acknowledged him.

As we emerged from the house, all eyes seemed to be on Gideon and me.

The bonfires weren't lit yet, and the sun was low enough in the sky that the hundreds of figures who had gathered for the festivities were silhouettes against the setting sun. But I searched for Enver's face in the crowd. She was at the front of the line as if she had been waiting for me too, and her eyes looked watery and afraid as they met mine.

Her gaze flicked to my face and then to my neck and back to my face again, her brows creasing just slightly. It was a silent question that she'd answered on her own. No, everything was not okay.

I wondered how much Laykin had actually told her about what he'd seen on that hill and resisted the urge to touch the bruise I knew had blossomed on my neck in the shape of Gideon's mouth.

Not only was it a mark of Gideon's ownership, it was also a signal that he now fully controlled my silver. It had been four days since he'd injected me with another silver's blood, and there hadn't been a single sign of my abilities. No spark at my fingertips. No rush in my blood. No heat rising when I was angry or afraid. Only the hollow emptiness in the very core of my soul.

"What are we waiting for?" Gideon called, throwing his arms open to the gathered crowd and swaggering forward with me tucked in closely at his side. "Let's start this damn party."

Cheers and hollers erupted from the crowd, and Enver stepped forward. "Of course." She inclined her head. "Tonight, we've chosen Baxter to light the fires since he survived so bravely against—"

Gideon cut her off with the wave of his hand. "None of that tonight, Enver." Gideon laughed. "Let's make 'em burn! And someone get me a drink."

More cheers erupted, and Enver nodded demurely, shrinking into the crowd.

Moments later, the bonfires lit in quick succession, thanks to the Queens' silver. The heat from the flames was so strong, it licked across the side of my face as the fire shot skyward. Their brilliant silver flames cast a white light over the entire compound as the last of the sun slipped behind the ocean waves.

My gaze caught on Kenji's in the distance to find his head lifted and his eyes on me. I couldn't fully make out his face through the darkness, but it was the first time I'd seen him alert in days. His eyes caught the light of the bonfire as if he was trying to tell me something.

I shook my head mutely at him, a silent, pleading apology I hoped he understood. I swallowed down the bile rising in my throat. The urge to run to him was so strong that I was surprised silver wasn't sparking at my fingertips when I looked down.

Someone handed Gideon a drink, and he threw it back, returning the glass before he kissed along my shoulder, murmuring in my ear, "Dance with me."

His breath smelled sharp like vanilla and smoke from whatever drink he'd downed.

He pulled me to the center of the lawn, where the crowd swayed in time to the steady, deafening beat that had already begun to resemble some living, breathing creature. The mass undulated with the music, bodies rolling into one another.

Once we reached the center of the crowd, Gideon pulled me flush against him, one hand settling along my lower back, the other twining into my hair as his hips pressed against mine. It was a similar motion to our lovemaking, and my hips followed his like muscle memory. For a moment, I allowed myself to relish the feel of him pressed into me until it caused my heart to twist, and the ache in my chest returned.

"You look beautiful tonight," he growled low in my ear. "I can't keep my eyes off you, little Queen."

I rested my head against his chest as if I could hide from my shame, clinging to the edges of his shirt as we continued to move. The songs transitioned from one to the next, and I lost track of the moments.

It was all I could do to stay upright. I wanted to sob. I wanted to vomit. I wanted to go back to that room and allow him to tie me to the bed. At least then I could deny my body's reactions. At least then I could pretend his words and his compliments meant nothing to me.

Dancing like this, with him, made me think of what I'd seen in the club all those years ago. The women dancing for men, and Tayna promising I would never be one of them.

Shame and guilt washed through me at the part of myself that wanted to be one of them— had almost been Gideon's entirely.

I closed my eyes against the people around us. I didn't want to see their questioning glances pointed in my direction.

I was a traitor. But not a traitor to the Cards. Or the Whigs.

No, I was a traitor to myself.

I'd failed to protect my friends. I'd gotten people hurt and, worse, gotten people killed. Thanks to my reckless decisions, Kenji was tied to that post at the back of the lawn right now. Phenola was in the cells being held against her will. Felina was dead. And still, I stood here dancing hip to hip with the enemy. An enemy my body couldn't deny, didn't want to deny.

When my eyes fluttered open again, writhing forms flickered in every direction from the silver light from the bonfire. Heads were tilted back toward the sky as if in the throes of pleasure. Cards tattooed onto shoulders pulsed around me.

There was such a crush of people that I couldn't see the ocean beyond, only able to make out the tops of the bonfires as they continued to blaze into the sky.

And then my eyes connected with his.

Sudden gold stark in a night filled with silver flames, black ink, and red cards.

Tayna watched me, standing still in the mass of bodies.

I covered my mouth to bite back the sob that erupted from my throat, my chest still tucked against Gideon's as we danced.

Gideon moved us in a steady circle, and I lost sight of Tayna as Gideon's body blocked where he stood.

When we moved around again, I turned my head to the spot where I'd seen Tayna standing, only to find it empty.

Had I imagined him?

I shook my head.

Of course I'd imagined him.

Tayna couldn't possibly be at the compound.

"Lissa?" Gideon bent to catch my gaze, and I realized I'd stopped dancing, my body rigid among the sea of movement.

I swallowed and nodded, my gaze feeling unfocused and distant.

"Maybe I need to eat something," I muttered.

That was all Gideon needed to hear before he pulled me from the dancing and toward the food. He twined our fingers and used his body as a barrier as we navigated through the crowds of Cards. He walked just slightly in front of me, which gave me more time to scan the faces around me. I clocked each one.

None of them were tall and brown-haired with a golden gaze and a scar through one eye.

It was only my mind playing a cruel, cruel trick.

Gideon grabbed a plate for me and filled it with a burger, a helping of fries, and a handful of pickles.

"Pickles?" I asked him, eyeing the green slivers on my plate, afraid I might vomit into the grass right then and there.

"Millie told me you liked them." Gideon watched me carefully. "I had her make as many as she could for tonight."

I braced myself on the table before sinking onto a bench.

"Lissa." Gideon reached for me.

"I can't." I shook my head. "I can't."

His eyes narrowed at me, and then he grabbed my arm and pulled me to stand. "You can and you will." He glared at me, eyes flashing dark as he realized I was on the verge of a breakdown.

"Gideon—" My breathing was coming in shallow gasps.

He set down the plate of food and gripped my chin, his other hand snaking into my hair to hold me in place. "Look at me." My eyes flickered to his dark depths. "You can fight me. You can hate me. But you are not allowed to do this simpering bullshit. We're not done with our game, little Queen. We're just getting started. And you don't get to opt out. Do you understand?"

My eyes went wide at his words, at the insistence in them.

It was all I could do to stare and slowly nod.

"Good." He released my arms and straddled the bench. "Now sit down and eat. Then I have some business with the new recruits I need to attend to. After that, I can bury myself inside you before we get some sleep."

46

Lissa

Once I finished eating, Gideon pulled me from the bench.
A few of the Cards had tried to approach him while we'd shared our meal, but Laykin and Reggie had intercepted them all, leaving Gideon and me in peace.

That didn't keep the eyes from lingering, though. Or from pointedly looking away when I caught them staring. There were questions in those gazes and accusations. I wondered what they'd been told about my absence and return.

Gideon twined our fingers and walked us toward the main house, under the awning that made up the back patio. The outdoor furniture had been pushed to the sides, clearing space.

The gauzy cotton of my dress caught and swished around my legs, and I used a hand to hold it up.

Dia stood in front of a group of a few dozen Cards as we approached. They were under the covered portion of the home, the walls lined with colorful graffiti save for the windows. Under the bright spotlight that was pointed at the men, the images on the wall almost looked 3D, as if I could reach out and touch the edges of the cartoonish black letters scattered across the stucco.

A chair from the clinic was set up on a slight incline, and a diminutive man with glasses holding an ink gun sat in a swivel chair with supplies poised at the ready.

This was the inking ceremony, and these men were new recruits.

"You'll get your suit first," Dia told the men. "That's the only tattoo you'll receive today. Once we determine your worth on this compound, we'll add ink. The more ink you have, the more respect you've earned. 'Earned' being the operative word, here."

I couldn't help the curl of my lips as I watched Dia. If I had access to my silver, it would be sparking at my fingers. Looking at Dia only brought me back to that moment at Tea and Trinkets when he taunted me and beat Kenji mercilessly. His brutality and his love for blood made me want to rage.

"You've all been given a card from a deck," Dia continued. "As you approach, look at it, announce your suit, and get your ink."

As the first man approached, he flipped the card in his hands. "Spades!" he declared. He seemed pleased with the selection and handed over the card to Dia pinched between two smug fingers.

The tattooing itself only took a few minutes, though the black shading made the man's teeth clench and the veins in his neck strain.

Baby.

He was a big baby trying to act tough. I'd barely felt the ink when I'd received mine. Though, I supposed I'd been too stunned during those initial days here to feel much of anything. It had happened in the clinic, my silver sparking so erratically the nurse on duty at the time had threatened to sedate me. I couldn't stop crying in the beginning. And with my shattered heart aching so profusely, the pain as the man had tattooed my shoulder was almost a relief.

Once the first man had gotten his Spade, the next walked up to Dia and the artist.

Gideon and I stayed in the back, watching as each man approached, flipped his card, and received his ink.

My feet began to ache. After spending so much time on a bed, my muscles were straining. To suddenly be standing for hours was exhausting, and I cursed myself for the hard-earned strength I'd lost in so little time.

"What are we doing here?" I asked Gideon, who didn't so much as spare me a glance. He only wrapped a firm arm around my middle.

My eyes snagged on a taller head among the new recruits with artfully disheveled brown hair and a broad frame that formed a perfect v from his shoulders to his waist. His back was to me but... but...

My vision narrowed, blackness curling at the edges, and it felt like someone was pulling the silver from my veins all over again.

Tayna stepped forward, revealing his card.

A heart.

He was here, and he'd been given a heart.

It was an effort not to lunge for him as he lay down on the chair, his eyes meeting mine for only a flash before he closed them as the tattoo artist began sketching the lines into his shoulder.

The panic I felt rising in my chest was a living beast clawing at me from the inside. He couldn't be here. This couldn't be happening. The only thing that had given me any sort of comfort in the past four days was the thought that Tayna and the Whigs were safe at the farm. I would endure all of this if it meant they were safe.

But Tayna had come here.

And he hadn't just come to the compound to get me out. He'd submitted himself as a willing new recruit.

I'll never leave you again.

If Tayna was anything, he was a man of his word.

I realized I'd been digging my fingers into Gideon's thigh to brace myself and quickly pulled my hand away. He flashed me a lazy grin, giving me a slight shove forward as Tayna stood.

"I have a new recruit," he called, his hand braced firming on my back as he marched me forward. "A returning member who must prove herself, if you will."

"Gideon—" His name was a panicked plea on my lips.

The tattoo artist squinted up at Gideon through the crowd, and his eyes widened.

"Ace." He stood. "Of course, sir."

"Red ink," Gideon said. "Something a little different."

Gideon produced a piece of paper on which an image had been drawn. I couldn't see it as Gideon gripped my shoulder and pressed me to sit in the chair.

As soon as my backside hit the black leather, I moved to rise again.

"No, I—" My gaze flicked from Gideon to where Tayna now stood at the center of the crowd.

Could he see the desperation in my eyes? He needed to run. Now.

"Eyes on me," Gideon said, tilting my chin. "No one there is going to help you."

"Give me just a moment to sketch it out," the tattoo artist said over my shoulder. "If you could just sit still?"

But my breathing was too ragged to calm the shaking.

"Please don't, Gideon."

I tried to stand again, but Gideon braced a hand on my thigh as he leaned in and said, "Sit still, or I will strap you to this chair in front of these men and allow them to watch as you scream and squirm."

A shiver coursed over my spine. He would do it. I knew he would.

So I braced my hands on the chair and tried my best to relax as the tattoo artist began to sketch along my shoulder, just below the spot where my Queen's mark was already inked in red.

My lip trembled as I did everything in my power to avoid Tayna's hard gaze on me. I felt such wretched humiliation that he was seeing me like this. Gideon's Queen.

But the best thing I could do for both of us would be to make him leave.

If I had to endure this, then it was all only worth it if Tayna was safe. I could endure it all to keep him safe. So I kept my eyes firmly on Gideon as the needle began to work its way under my skin. It was rough like sandpaper scratched over the same spot again and again and again. But still, I watched Gideon.

My tears did not fall.

And I did not flinch.

Or make a sound.

I endured. I played the game.

But inside, my heart shattered into a million pieces just as a new one was sketched onto my arm. Because now that Tayna was here, I only had one option. If I was going to save Tayna, then I had to make him leave. And the only way I could make him leave was to make him think I had truly chosen Gideon over him. I had to make him firmly believe that I was in love with Gideon. That I only had eyes for Gideon. I had to reject Tayna so thoroughly that he wouldn't stay to save me because he would believe I was exactly where I wished to be.

It was the only way.

When the tattoo artist finished, I looked down dully at the new ink. It was an upside-down heart. But unlike the first I'd received under the Q of my Queen's mark, this one wasn't filled in. The outline was left with only a straight line through the center, and I realized why. It was both an upside-down heart and an A. Gideon had marked me with his card, inking a piece of himself onto my skin.

"Pretty cool, eh?" the tattoo artist asked.

I swallowed the bile down thickly as I said, "I love it," and hopped down from the chair.

"Wait," the guy called as I stalked away, "I need to bandage it."

Looking down again, a thin line of my dark silver blood welled at the red raised edges of the fresh ink. It wasn't healing.

Of course it wasn't healing.

Gideon had restricted my silver.

It was almost too much then.

My legs buckled.

Strong arms caught me, and I smelled grass and fresh soil and summer days, and I fell—just for a moment—into Tayna's embrace.

"I've got her," Gideon said, sweeping me into his arms.

"Of course, sir." Tayna nodded, but his fingers lingered on mine for a few beats longer as Gideon lifted me.

It crushed my soul to touch him and be so near to him.

"Ace," Gideon said over his shoulder as he walked with me cradled to his chest. The veins strained against his flexed biceps where he held me tightly. "Not sir. I'm the Ace here."

And with that, he carried me inside, my skin burning where Tayna had touched me and the new A/heart tattoo was inked on my shoulder.

47

Lissa

Gideon didn't tie me up when we returned to his room.
And I didn't have the energy to fight him. I slumped down on the bed and curled into a tight ball, not caring if the new tattoo bled onto his crisp white comforter. The stain would serve as a small retribution for all he'd done to me.

He left me there, going into the bathroom and emerging a few moments later in low-slung sweatpants and nothing else. My heart squeezed at the cut of his body, the v of his hips, and a small hint of dark hair along his sculpted chest. The gray-blue glistened in his eyes as he sat down next to me, clutching one of his oversized shirts.

"Come on," he said, gently lifting me by the shoulders and holding me so he could untie the straps of my dress.

I shook my head, clutching the fabric to keep it from falling down my shoulders.

"Lissa," he growled, "I'm not trying to fuck you. I just want you to be more comfortable."

Now that we were alone, the tears began to fall.

He pulled the oversized shirt over my head with the dress still half on me, and then delicately drew my arms through the baggy sleeves as if I were small and breakable. It felt like I was breaking.

Then he pulled me onto his lap, both lifting me to free the dress from my legs but also to cradle me against his chest. I fell into him, the sob pulling from my chest.

I heard something tear and realized he'd opened a large Band-Aid with one hand and his teeth. He spit the paper shreds of the packaging onto the floor and gently pressed the Band-Aid over my new tattoo.

"You need to keep it covered," he said into my hair.

I only sobbed harder.

"You did so good tonight, baby." He wiped my tears away with a thumb.

"I hate you," I managed to rasp but didn't move to pull away from him.

"I know," he said, cupping my head against his chest. "I know. But you are mine. No matter where you go or who else touches you. And I won't allow you to forget it again."

At some point, my tears dried on my cheeks, my breathing steadied, and in the silence between us, as my eyes grew steady with sleep, I murmured, "I hate you most because I almost loved you."

He didn't respond, at least not before I fell into a deep, dreamless sleep.

When I woke, it was morning, and I was alone in the room. The bite mark on my neck was still tender. The skin under the Band-Aid on my shoulder felt tight and hot like a bad sunburn, and I fought the urge to scratch at it.

How long had Gideon stayed? Had he returned to the bonfire after I'd fallen asleep?

A plate of pastries was on the table near the window, and a cup of orange juice braced a small note.

Outside, the mess from the bonfire had already been cleaned. There wasn't a hint of the raging festivities that had undoubtedly gone on well into the night.

I also noted that Kenji was no longer hanging from the post outside, and my heart lurched.

Tentatively, I picked up the note.

I thought you could use some company for lunch. Otherwise, the day is yours. There are books on the bedside table. Please do not use this plate for anything other than eating. As much as I liked the sight of you bound and naked in my bed, I'm hoping we can move past that chapter. For now.
—Ace

I flicked the note aside and picked up a pastry, moving back to the window as I forced myself to take a bite and surveyed the lawn. The buttery layers crumbled like dust in my mouth. I barely tasted the sweetness as I watched the men marching on their perimeter patrols and eyed the barracks for signs of movement.

But I saw nothing of Tayna and the new recruits.

There wasn't a trace of Kenji nor any hints from the Cards' movements about where they'd taken him.

The tattoo on my arm throbbed faintly. Still healing, which meant the foreign silver in my blood was still oppressing my abilities.

I assumed Gideon would wait for it to dissipate, take more of my clean silver, and then inject me all over again. But maybe I could convince him that it hadn't returned even when it had. My control had gotten so much stronger thanks to Alaric and my training with the Whigs. I made a fist and willed the silver into my fingers.

My veins seemed to strain hollowly in answer.

Nothing.

I finished the pastry and drank the orange juice. Eating was the last thing I wanted to do, my throat working rhythmically to swallow, but I needed to keep up my strength where I could get it. The healthier I was, the sooner my silver would return, and the better chance I had at hiding it from Gideon.

His note told me to expect someone for lunch.

Maybe he'd send the doctor to check the tattoo on my arm. Perhaps he'd send Laykin in to keep an eye on me and see if I would give up any information about the Whigs. Or maybe... I tried not to get my hopes up as I thought of Enver. He knew how close we'd become in the weeks before I left, and he did seem somewhat remorseful for his behavior last night. Maybe he would let me see her as an olive branch.

It was an effort to contain my excitement as I pulled one of the books from his bedside table.

I looked at the cover and groaned. It was Truman Capote's *In Cold Blood*. A classic, sure, but hardly the distraction I'd been hoping would get me through the morning. I sighed and let the book fall on the bed.

I stared up at the ceiling before giving in and reading the first few pages, but my thoughts kept drifting, so I put the book aside and went back to the window.

Then I tried the handle on the door connecting Gideon's bedroom to the office. It was still locked.

So I found myself in the closet, rummaging through the clothes, looking for any scraps of things I could use as a weapon. The space was massive, hung with row after row of clothing options. There were dark jeans and cargo pants and even a pair that looked like leather. All in black. He had T-shirts and jackets and button-downs and Henleys. And a small section had clearly been carved out for me — filled with the lightweight dresses of the coming summer, but no sign of my Queen's cloak.

I did want it back. The heavy weight of it made me feel more secure, more stable somehow.

There was even a nightdress made of cream silk. Interesting, then, that Gideon chose to give me one of his shirts last night instead. It hung loosely on my shoulders and reached down to my knees.

With each flick of the hanger, I dug into the pockets, only finding a spare copper coin and a piece of string.

The best thing I could have asked for would have been that knife he'd used the other night to cut my shirt. He must have taken it with him when he left the room. I knew it was wishful thinking. Gideon was meticulous and thoughtful in everything he did. He wouldn't be sloppy enough to leave me a knife to find.

When I heard the lock jiggle on the door, I slipped from the closet into the bathroom just as the bedroom door opened.

Enver stepped inside in a swoosh of her black Queen's cloak. But I stopped from running at her as her posture remained stiff. Her platinum-blond braid cascaded neatly over one shoulder.

"You can stand in the corner." She sighed, waving her hand behind her as a man entered the room.

A man.

No, not just a man. Tayna.

My heart seized as the door closed, and I stood frozen.

He wore the cargo pants and fitted black T-shirt of one of the new recruits. He'd most likely spent the morning training with Dia and the other newcomers.

"You can't be here," I breathed, keeping my voice low.

"It's okay." Enver grabbed my hand, dragging me into the room. "I told Dia I thought he was hot and wanted him as one of my guards. Laykin told me everything. I want to help."

She said it as if it were all some grand adventure and not all of us walking out on a tightrope that was sure to snap.

"No." I pulled my hand from hers, remaining still in the room. "You have to go."

My voice was hard. I knew it.

Tayna's posture remained stiff as he watched me warily. "Lissa—" His brow furrowed at my stone-faced expression.

I wanted nothing more than to run into Tayna's arms. I wanted his strong hands around my body. I wanted to feel his breath fanning across my hair. I wanted to bury my face into the crook of his shoulder and never let him go.

But not here.

I couldn't stand the idea that he had come to this compound, joined the Cards, and gotten the tattoo all for me. All for a girl who was well past saving.

It took everything in me to hold back the tears.

Tayna's eyes swept the room, to the ropes on the headboard and the rumpled sheets and the clear view of the shower from the bed.

My cheeks flamed hot with shame and guilt and embarrassment.

"You have to go," I hissed again.

"Lissa." Enver's eyes were pleading.

"You have to leave." I enunciated each word, a slight tremor hitching in my throat. "Now."

"I'll leave this room," Tayna said, "if that's what you want. But I'm not leaving this compound, Lissa, unless you're with me."

"I don't want you here," I snapped.

He remained, his golden eyes fixed on mine because he knew. He saw exactly what I was doing.

"I'm in love with him," I said.

A small smile pulled at the corner of his lip, the scar on his brow ticking up.

"I want to stay with him," I continued. "I don't want to go with you."

"Then we'll stay here," he said. "I'll become a loyal Card. I bet I could make Jack within the year."

Was that a joke?

I marched at him, grabbing his arm to spin him around while also very aware that my voice couldn't rise too high or the guards outside would know something was wrong. Laykin would let it slide but not Reggie.

"I don't want you here!"

He allowed me to turn him.

"I don't want you here!"

This time, I gave him a little shove, but he didn't even sway.

Enver shrank against the wall, watching my outburst and chewing at her bottom lip.

I pushed Tayna again. "Go! You have to go!"

"I told you I'd never leave you again," Tayna said over his shoulder, staring down at me.

"I don't want you here! I want—" I forced it out. "I want Gideon. I'm in love with Gideon."

Tayna turned then, gripping my shoulders, careful to avoid the new tattoo. His eyes fixed on mine, and I couldn't look away as he pressed into me. "That didn't scare me away before," he murmured. "You're not going to scare me away now. There's nothing you could do that would push me away, Lissa. I'll always come back for you." He considered, "Well, maybe if you honestly didn't want me around. But I'll be here as long as you're lying through your teeth like you are right now. I'm right here."

I realized I could fling every insult I knew at him, and he would still be standing here.

"I'm going to eat a pastry," Enver said, holding up a finger to point at the table near the windows and the scraps of my breakfast.

"He'll kill you," I finally breathed.

"Not if I kill him first," Tayna replied, stepping into me and cupping my face, the tension between us melting away as if it had never truly existed.

"You should hate me, too," I said as he ran his fingers over my cheeks and through the loose strands of my hair.

"Why?" Tayna snorted. "Because another man's touched you?"

I didn't answer.

"Oh, Lissa," he murmured, bringing his lips close to mine. "That's a non-issue. I plan on doing things to you that will make you forget another man's fingers ever existed, let alone touched you."

Enver choked on her croissant behind me and let out a dry cough.

Tayna chuckled darkly and grabbed my hand.

"Now," he said, "stop trying to shove me out the door. I did come here with things to tell you, and we don't have much time."

48

Lissa

"They've got Kenji, Phenola, and Felina locked in the cells," Tayna told me as soon as we were settled at the table. Enver had packed us a lunch from Millie in the kitchens and handed me a paper-wrapped sandwich as Tayna talked.

"They're all alive." The relief nearly made me dizzy, and I pressed the heel of my hands into my eyes as I processed the news.

"They're alive," Tayna confirmed. "But I can't get to them. If you think your rooms are guarded, they're being held in a fucking fortress. No one's allowed in or out except Gideon and Dia."

"They're in the cells. Laykin's been trying to get permission to see Kenji, but Dia's denied him every time," Enver said around a mouthful of sandwich. "And he can't keep asking without raising suspicions."

"And there's no way me, as a new recruit, can get anywhere close to them." Tayna shook his head.

"Gideon's trying to get them to confess about the location of the Whigs," Enver added. "So far, they've stayed quiet. But you know him,

Liss, he'll lose his patience with this game. And soon." She stared down at her sandwich like she might not be able to take another bite.

Mine was untouched.

"Gideon has to let me out of this room again eventually," I said, resisting the urge to glance at the ropes still hanging from the headboard.

Tayna's eyes flashed to the line of my T-shirt, and I knew his thoughts had drifted to the bite mark just underneath the thin fabric. Today, it was purplish, his teeth had blurred into a splotch of darkness on my pale skin.

"He will." Enver nodded encouragingly. "He already let you out for the bonfire. And he let me come here today."

"But the cells..." I shook my head.

My hands clenched into fists as, for the hundredth time in the past few days, I wished I had my silver. I'd spent so much of my life resenting the power that was in my veins. Now that it was gone, it felt like my bones had been hollowed out. He had clipped my wings, made me into the helpless little Queen I'd been before when I thought Tayna was dead. But now, now I wanted to fight. I wanted to rage. I wanted to show Gideon that I wasn't a pet he could simply keep.

"And what about Madam Cartenoth?" Tayna asked. "You haven't told me why she wanted you to go to her."

I winced as I thought of the reckless trip to Tea and Trinkets. But at least I'd been there to comfort Madam Cartenoth as she'd passed.

"It was mostly nonsense," I admitted. I'd considered the conversation a lot since arriving back at the compound. In the quiet moments Gideon had held me in this room, I'd had a lot of time to think. And while her words were riddled and garbled, there was truth in them. Truth that I finally felt ready to vocalize. "Well, except... she said my mother was a Queen. She called her 'the original.' She said my mother worked for Gideon's father." I shook my head. "And then she said something else about how a Queen trumps an Ace... and wheels turning."

"A Queen trumps an Ace..." Tayna raised his eyebrows at me.

"Yes, but then she said something about a King and a Queen making a princess. But Tayna, Alaric was Ishmael's King. Alaric was Ishmael's King, and if my mother was the Queen... Do you think that—"

"Enver!" There was a knock on the door as Laykin's voice called through the walls.

We all started. Tayna stood abruptly from the chair.

"Five minutes!" Laykin called in warning.

I folded up my uneaten sandwich. No more time for revelations from the past.

Tayna stood, grabbing my face in his hands like he might kiss me. He kept our mouths just parted as he said, "I'll come back as soon as I can."

"What free time do you have throughout the day?"

"Now that I'm watching after Enver, I'm lucky to have an hour for lunch."

"It's not too late for you to—"

"I'm not fucking leaving, Liss." Tayna's jaw was set.

Desperate emotion clogged my throat. "Tay," I breathed. "He took my silver. I can't protect us."

"We'll get out of here. I promise we'll find a way out of this, okay?"

It seemed like one-in-a-million odds, but I couldn't say that to Tayna. I couldn't tell him that we'd most likely all be killed before we could run to the gate of the compound.

So I reached up on my toes and bridged the space between our lips. His kiss was light at first, but then his grip on my face tightened.

I didn't want to let him go.

But I did. The taste of him was too brief.

I pressed away from him and hugged Enver, clinging to her in the way only friends can fall into one another as if coming home after a long day.

I hooked my arms over her shoulder blades, squeezing her back, and murmured, "Thank you."

"It was the right thing to do." She nodded against my neck. "Friends show up for each other."

"I think you're my best friend," I said.

"I'll challenge Kenji for the title once we get him out of this compound, too." Her words were forced optimism I wasn't sure I felt yet. And then to Tayna, she said, "All right lover boy, it's time to go."

Tayna planted another chaste kiss on my lips, his finger drifting down my arm to my wrist and along the sides of my hand.

Against my mouth, he murmured, "If he hurts you, Liss, I'll kill him."

I found myself reaching out to him as he brushed my fingertips, and then the air drifted between us.

Hugging myself around the middle, I resisted the urge to launch myself at him. He walked backward, watching me, and mouthed, "I'm not leaving," before he turned and held the door open for Enver.

Alone again in the room, I sank into the chair.

We hadn't finished our conversation before Laykin interrupted, and it was playing on repeat inside my mind.

A King and a Queen...

A King and a Queen...

Alaric was Ishmael's King or, one of them, at least. He'd left the Cards when... well, he didn't say when... but...

They made a princess.

And it settled over me in a sudden certainty that had been niggling at my mind since my conversation with Madam Cartenoth.

Alaric was my father.

Madam Cartenoth had been trying to tell me that.

But did he know? Had he always known he had a daughter? He hadn't seemed like he'd recognized me at all on that day when we'd first met. His hate and mistrust had been such a palpable thing. I'd thought it was because he was afraid of my presence at the compound, but what if it was deeper?

The possibility struck me hard in the chest.

A father?

I only hoped I got to see him again to ask.

49

Lissa

The next day, my silver returned.

I couldn't even hide it from Gideon. When I woke, it was crackling at my fingers like it had never left, and I felt like I'd gotten the best sleep of my life. My veins buzzed with the hum of energy and life. It was so relieving to feel it and see it that I felt tears prick at the back of my eyes.

But Gideon's gaze only narrowed as he stirred awake next to me.

Since there was no hope of hiding it from him, my mind went to the next option: I could use my silver against him.

"Try it, Lissa." His eyes flashed as he stretched next to me, revealing his bare torso. "Try it and see what happens."

The silver sputtered.

And then he was on me. He flipped me until my back was pinned to the mattress. His hips pinned against mine and his hands braced so his chest hovered over me. One hand slipped around my neck.

"Would you kill me?" he asked softly as if he were asking me if I would be his. "Would you run to your lover and leave me burning?"

I tried to turn my head, but his grip tightened.

"Do it, Lissa."

He almost seemed like he was genuinely asking, and for some reason, it made my heart ache.

But instead, I said, "Fuck you."

"Don't tempt me, little Queen." He rolled his hips into mine so I could feel his erection pressing into my stomach. He'd slept naked.

I thrashed but didn't let my silver burn.

If I killed him, could I make it back to the farm? Could I find Alaric and ask all the questions I had about him and my mother and a past that Madam Cartenoth had so cryptically hinted at repeating?

For a moment, I allowed it to play out. I could kill him, even with the silver in his veins making him stronger. I could probably make it out of this house. How many would I need to kill before I made it to the compound's gates? How many would have to burn for my escape? Enver and Laykin were in this house. What if they were caught in the crossfire? And what about Kenji and Phenola and Felina? I could probably get to Tayna, but what about the others? There wouldn't be time to break them from the cells.

No, Gideon had a hold on me with a tight leash that had nothing to do with the silver pumping in my veins. I wouldn't kill him because killing him would mean killing my friends.

A deeper part of me could also admit I didn't want to kill Gideon.

I wanted him to be the man who laughed on his office floor with me and fed me chocolate-covered coffee beans and talked with me about the world. That man was magnificent and complicated and stunningly dark. And had stolen a piece of my heart. Getting even small glimpses of that man felt as good as the silver returning to my veins.

He was a drug.

And I was his addict.

My body was pliant for him even as my mind resisted at every turn.

He seemed to understand the pivot my thoughts had taken. He kept his hand tight to my throat, bringing our foreheads together and groaning deeply in his chest.

"You look at me like that even when I'm about to hurt you," he said.

"It doesn't have to be like this." My voice was reedy. "You don't have to do any of this."

He kissed me. Gently. His lips brushed against mine almost as if he hadn't intended the contact, but then he did it again. The softness was a punishing assault to my already spinning mind. I tried to press up, to kiss him roughly. I wanted it rough. I knew where I stood when he was rough and pushed me to the edge. But he kept me pinned firmly beneath him, his lips skating just out of reach. Each of his breaths caressed over my mouth, across my cheeks, fanning to my jaw.

My chest ached at the tenderness this man rarely showed. His eyes blue, blue, blue as he studied my face.

And then he was pressing up from my body. The loss of contact made me feel empty, and I checked the silver at my fingertips to make sure it hadn't vanished. A spark crackled.

But why did my heart feel like it was breaking open?

"Gideon." His name was breathless on my lips as I rose from the bed to sit against the pillows.

He stood from the bed entirely and took a step back, his gray-blue eyes not meeting mine. His brow furrowed.

"Gideon," I said again but held myself back from reaching for him.

It felt like I was losing him, like a part of him had been so close to cracking in those moments our lips had brushed, and now he was spooling himself back.

"Get dressed," he said, turning from me. "We're going to see Karadin."

It was a gloomy day. The marine layer from the ocean had risen above the cliffs, hiding the sun behind a blanket of fog that was resisting the midmorning light.

Laykin brought me a pastry, which I dutifully ate as we walked to the clinic.

Gideon strode beside me, but he didn't touch me. His eyes were focused ahead, yet distant. He needed to shave. And his gaze was drawn. The corner of his Ace tattoo peeked from beneath the short-sleeved black shirt he'd pulled on along with dark jeans and black boots. He was like a pirate who'd swept in from the shores, bringing the blackness of the sea with him.

Karadin was already waiting for us when we walked into the lobby. Her hair was pulled up into a severe ponytail, and her coat was a cheery blue. A contrast to the day. Somehow, she'd known we were coming.

Her lips were tight. Her brow pinched.

"Her silver is back," Gideon said without introduction.

A muscle ticked in Karadin's neck. She hesitated. "Ace, I took an oath to do no harm—"

"Do it, Karadin!" Gideon's voice was so sharp that it made me jump, my breath hitching as tension settled over the room.

Karadin just nodded and spun on her heels.

We followed her into the clinic, where I settled into the examination chair.

"I'm guessing by the powdered sugar on your dress that you ate today?" Karadin eyed me.

I nodded.

"Good," she said.

"Eight vials first," Gideon said, leaning into the wall at the corner of the room, just like he had last time.

Karadin's jaw hardened, and she paused but then nodded and moved behind me to the counter, where she presumably began prepping her supplies.

As she came back around, she noticed the bandage on my shoulder.

"And what's that?" she asked, holding the still-sealed needle in her gloved hand.

My gaze flicked to Gideon, who just eyed me through his lowered dark gaze.

"A new tattoo," I said, forcing my voice to sound light. "I got it at the bonfire."

She sighed. "May I remove the bandage?" She wasn't asking me, but Gideon. "I'll need to make sure it isn't infected before we draw blood."

"Fine," Gideon said.

She was gentle as she peeled away the bandage. The red ink was healed thanks to my returned silver. The skin was flaky around the edges. It itched like crazy, but Gideon had given me some cream the previous night that had helped.

"Hmm," Karadin said, eyeing the upside-down heart. Her gaze flicked to Gideon in what I could have sworn was a derisive glare as if to say, *You marked her, you prick.* At least, that was what I hoped she was thinking. She said nothing but left the bandage off before straightening. "Okay. Blood first. Do you want to watch?"

I nodded and held out my arm, keeping my gaze on the blue vein as Karadin slipped the needle beneath my skin. My thoughts felt hollow and jumbled. There wasn't any pain as the blood welled into the first vial.

And then the second...

And the third...

Karadin's fingers moved deftly as she swapped out the vials.

The fog blanketed the compound beyond the window, and I could see the edge of the cliff that would lead down to the private beach. Tayna would be starting his day of training and watching over Enver. If I went to the kitchens after this, would I see him? Not that I could, even if Gideon would allow it.

I'd be too busy puking my guts up. Karadin would inject me with the foreign silver again, and I would spend the next day or two in bed.

I had to get out of here. I had to make Tayna leave. I had to somehow get to Kenji and Phenola and Felina in the cells.

Four vials...

Five vials...

My gaze turned then to the blood welling up inside the vial. Dark and metallic. My body began to feel hazy from the blood loss. Gideon had doubled the normal amount. Best to have a reserve stash when he was poisoning my blood, I supposed.

I nearly jumped when Laykin spoke, "Ace, something's happening in the yard."

My gaze flew back to the window. Someone was running toward the cliff.

Gideon pushed off the wall. As he moved with Laykin toward the door, he said to Karadin, "Wait to finish until I return."

They stalked out of the room as I lost sight of the person running to the edge.

It wasn't unusual for the men to get into scuffles or for some business or another to call Gideon's attention. But this—someone running—this was anything but typical. I prayed it was Tayna coming to his senses and bolting to the fence. I tried to catch a glimpse of something, anything from the window.

"Listen to me," Karadin said quickly, attaching another vial to the needle as the blood began to fill. "We don't have much time."

That got my attention.

My eyes connected with hers as deep as the gray ocean beyond the cliffs. There was a defiant purpose within them, a strength I'd always known she possessed. Now, it was alive just beneath her gaze.

"I'm going to take an extra vial. Just like old times." Her lips were thinned with her concentration as she continued, "You'll be tired. You'll need to rest. But I'm going to replace it with the silver and inject your silver back into your blood. You'll need to fake being sick."

"Wai—What?" My eyes tracked to the door, then back to her.

"I don't have time to explain it all," she said. "Laykin and Enver helped. We're going to get you out of here."

"I can't leave without the others," I said quickly. "Who knows what Gideon will do when I'm gone."

"Then use your silver," she snapped. "Goddammit, Lissa, fight, and we will fight with you. You are the only one who could possibly take a stand against him."

She was serious.

She pulled the vial from my arm and tucked it beneath her sleeve just as Gideon walked back into the room.

"Fucking recruits," he grumbled.

Laykin just nodded, resuming his stance near the door. "Dia will handle him. There's always one who gets it in their small head to run."

Gideon sighed, then cocked an eyebrow at seeing Karadin hunched over my chair.

"Everything alright?" he asked.

"Just feeling a little lightheaded," I said, forcing my tone to soften and my shoulders to relax.

"Only three more vials," Karadin said, picking up another empty one over my shoulder and attaching it to the needle. "But I recommend juice and rest today."

"I don't know if I'll be able to keep it down," I said, giving her a pointed look. If she wasn't going to inject me with someone else's silver but my own, I wouldn't vomit like last time. How the hell was I supposed to fake that?

"Your body will most likely respond more favorably to the silver this time," Karadin said. "It won't be such a shock for your system as last time. You'll still need rest, but my guess is you'll recover a lot faster."

Clever, clever doctor.

She pulled the sixth vial from the needle... then filled the seventh... and the eighth.

Once the draw was complete, she withdrew the needle from my arm, dabbing the small puncture wound with a cloth until it healed.

Then she said, "I'll get the silver."

But Gideon pushed from the wall. "Allow me."

"I don't mind," Karadin said smoothly, moving to the door.

But Gideon stopped her with a low, "Karadin."

She stopped with her hand on the door.

We were caught.

"I'll do the injection," Gideon said darkly.

"Of course." Karadin kept her voice even and professional. "I only think using silver from the same Queen as last time will result in a less painful experience, and I remember the exact vial used last week, so I'm happy to get it."

"Fine," Gideon said, settling back into the wall. "But then give it to me."

She nodded, leaving the room for only a quick moment.

My vision felt hazy at the edges as my blood spiked with nervous energy. Nine vials had left me feeling heavy. My limbs were like dead weight.

Karadin returned, offering the vial to Gideon, who took it between two fingers, spinning it as if he were studying it.

Finally, he said, "It's warm."

Karadin's neck flexed almost imperceptibly. "Of course," she said, "I held it for a few seconds between my palms. It's less painful for her if it's closer to room temperature."

"Right," Gideon said, walking behind me to pick up a needle from the counter.

He came to stand beside me, tearing it open with his teeth and screwing the cap onto the vial.

"The neck again, then?" he asked me, looking down at me as if this were a fun game we were playing.

"The arm will work just as well," Karadin said from behind him.

"You can leave," Gideon told her.

She cast me one final, long glance before she said, "I'll have juice waiting for you outside."

When it was just Gideon and me in the room, he sighed, running a hand through his hair.

He set the needle down on the tray and cursed.

"Gideon—"

I nearly reached for him, but he ran his hand across the counter, sending one of the trays flying. It clattered to the ground, ringing as it settled on the floor. He braced his hands on the counter, his back muscles flexing as he breathed heavily.

I sank as deeply into the chair as I possibly could, scared of this rage in him.

"I don't like this, little Queen." His voice was a low rumble.

"Don't li-like what?" I couldn't keep the slight tremor from my words.

"This," he snapped, whirling on me and grabbing the needle. "I want to trust you."

His gaze locked on mine as if searching for an answer in their silvery depths that I couldn't give to him, even if part of me wanted to. Because even if he owned a piece of my heart, he didn't have my trust, and I would never have his.

"I'm sorry." I shook my head. It was as close to an honest answer as I could give him.

He just nodded, hanging his head as he grabbed my arm, pinned my wrist, and pressed the needle into the vein at the base of my neck.

50

Lissa

It wasn't difficult to feign illness.

The room spun as I stood. I added in a gag or two for good measure, but it didn't seem to matter as Gideon caught me, holding me in his arms. He seemed to enjoy cradling me against his chest. And I sighed into his vanilla and leather scent despite my better judgment. But if all went to plan, this is the last time he would hold me like this. A part of me wanted to remember what it was like when it was good between us.

Karadin tried to hand over the cup of juice, but Gideon brushed past her.

"Got it, Ace," Laykin said. "I'll bring it to the room."

I didn't dare glance back at Karadin. We'd already been too close to getting caught. Gideon seemed suspicious in the clinic room. But maybe it was also simply that he was distracted by other things.

I want to trust you.

There was never a world where we could truly trust one another. He cared for me, yes, but he wanted to keep me like a pet and use my silver at his leisure. I wanted the freedom to make my own choices in this world. We were too at odds with one another to truly ever build trust.

The very idea of it was a fantasy.

I was leaving. For good.

But it was Gideon who left. He laid me gently on his bed when we returned to his room. He set the juice on the nightstand and pulled the down comforter over my body. He grabbed a washcloth from the bathroom and dampened it with cool water from the sink, pressing it to my forehead.

"Get some rest, Lissa," he murmured but didn't touch me again, not even a featherlight kiss before he was gone.

I didn't dare move from the bed until nightfall, not even when a tray of steaming chicken casserole was brought to the room by one of the guards.

It wasn't until well into the night that I realized Gideon wasn't returning to sleep.

But worry settled over me when he still hadn't returned the following morning. Was something wrong?

Finally, at midday, the door jiggled, and I sat up from where I'd been lounging on the bed after succumbing to boredom and *In Cold Blood*.

It wasn't Gideon at the door.

But Laykin.

"What are you doing in here?" I hissed, looking for Enver or someone else to be with him for a visit.

"I'm getting you out of this room," he snapped in his matter-of-fact tone. "Unless you'd like to continue as Gideon's captive for the foreseeable future."

"What?" I asked, getting up from the bed.

"You need to change your clothes and come with me," Laykin said. "I bought us about ten minutes before the guards return."

I threw the book aside and moved to the closet to change, my blood pounding with the hope of an escape. Silver pulsed at my fingertips.

"Gideon left yesterday on a scouting mission. He wouldn't have told you this, but the Whigs have been getting bolder. There have been two attacks on Cards in the city in the past week."

I knew it was Alaric. Alaric and the Whigs were fighting for us.

"He went to deal with them," Laykin continued, "which gives us a prime opportunity to get out."

"What about Kenji and Phenola and Felina?" I asked.

Laykin turned his back to me as I started changing into a pair of cargo pants and a long-sleeved T-shirt. The pants were loose, so I had to roll up the bottom, and the shirt was one of Gideon's that hung nearly to my knees. But I'd be damned if I was going to wear a dress on the run. Gideon hadn't left me my boots, but I found a pair of sandals that at least had a sturdier sole. They would have to do.

"There's something you should know, Lissa..."

"What is it?" I demanded, pulling on the shoes.

"Felina is the one who told the Cards you were at Tea and Trinkets that day."

I froze.

"No—" The objection died on my lips as I thought back to that day.

I hadn't even considered how the Cards had found us, how they'd known at that exact moment that we'd be at the shop. But Felina had offered to wait outside. She had volunteered to let us go in without her and then I hadn't seen her again. She hadn't alerted us to the Cards arrival. She hadn't fought them.

The truth of his words settled over me. The silver jolted along my hands.

"Gideon's still keeping her in one of the cells," Laykin explained. "He doesn't trust her fully, but he's considering allowing her to join the ranks. He and Dia have been discussing what to do with her for a week now. Same with Kenji and Phenola. Gideon's a monster, but he won't kill a pregnant woman. But Kenji... it's a small miracle Gideon hasn't killed him already. I think you're the only reason he's still alive. Gideon knows how much you care about him."

"So we get them out before we leave," I said as we made our way to the door.

"There's no way—"

My silver crackled. "I won't leave them, Laykin."

We hurried down the hallway and the double staircase, then out onto the lawn.

"We'll get them out," Laykin said, "but I need to get you and Tayna out of here first."

Laykin pushed me just slightly behind him as we broke out into the daylight. The fog had cleared, and the sun was warm on my skin.

"Tayna is meeting us below the cliffs on the beach," he murmured. "From there, you'll sneak around the back side of the compound. We'll have to climb over between the guard rotations and pray no one spots us."

"Seems like a half-baked plan..." I murmured.

"Do you have a better idea?" Laykin snapped.

"Maybe..."

Laykin nodded casually at a group of guards.

"What about you and Enver?" I asked.

"We're coming with you. We'll make sure you're out first, then will follow once things calm down."

I pursed my lips against the smile I felt at those words, and Laykin didn't glance over his shoulder. We were doing this. We were getting out of here.

Together.

I thought of the rock pools and the fields of crops and the cozy house where Grant and I had cooked breakfast together each morning. I finally allowed the longing to fill through me. We would be there soon.

As we climbed down the stairs of the cliffs, I didn't see anyone on the beach. The waves were melodic as they crashed in and out on the sand with the low tide.

But Tayna emerged from the shadows created by the overhangs, and this time, I didn't hold myself back from running into his arms.

He held me tightly.

"It's almost over," he whispered against my ear. "We're almost there."

My heart twisted at his words. We were almost to the life we had dreamed about as kids. I could feel it in my bones, that call to be with him.

Home.

And though it meant leaving Gideon behind, I knew this was right. I could build something at the farm and have some semblance of a life. Alaric and I could talk about my mother and all that had happened between them. Phenola and Kenji could have their baby and live in one of the little cottages on the land. And Tayna and I... well, we would figure it out.

There was peace in that dream. There was hope in a choice that was all my own.

I pulled back just enough to rest my palms on Tayna's cheeks. They'd cut his hair down once he'd arrived at the compound, but the wispy brown strands were already starting to grow. The scar over his eye crinkled as he grinned at me, his golden eyes bright.

"Let's go home," he said.

And I nodded. That was exactly what I felt like we were doing.

"But we need to get Kenji and Phenola first," I said.

"It's impossible." Laykin shook his head. "You'd have to give the guards all the silver in the stores to—"

His brows rose as I cut him off. "I have a plan."

51

Lissa

The cells were situated in the basement of the mansion. It meant there were always Cards around to see the comings and goings. But it mattered less that people saw us going in and more that we could get out.

Tayna stayed hidden near the clinic while Laykin and I slipped inside the mansion and to the stairs at the top of the cells, only to find ourselves face-to-face with two armed Cards standing just a few steps down.

Both were sixes, guys I didn't know well and didn't need to get acquainted with. They looked at Laykin and me as if we must have made some sort of mistake by opening the door.

Just beyond the bottom of the staircase, I could see a concrete floor but not much else. I'd never been down here before. I'd never had a reason to be down here.

The cells weren't large. The space was once a basement that Gideon's father had repurposed. Rarely did the Cards keep anyone prisoner. Gideon didn't normally keep people alive who had acted against the Cards. And if he did, they were banished from the compound quickly and without fanfare.

"Back up. And close the door," a meaty guy with tattoos up to his neck said, looking Laykin up and down. Clearly, he didn't give a shit that Laykin was a Jack.

The other guy, younger, with shaggy blond hair and a round stomach, seemed more apprehensive as he explained, "Gideon told us to shoot anyone who tried to come down here."

"Shut your trap, Mansfield," the meaty guy said.

"I need to speak to one of the prisoners," I said, my voice coming out clear with a confidence I didn't feel. But this plan had to work. If I was going to save Phenola and Kenji, this had to work.

"Not on my life." Meaty guy snorted.

Mansfield just looked down at his boots.

"I only need to see them for a minute," I pressed. "Gideon and Dia are gone. No one will ever know I was down here."

"We don't want trouble, but Gideon's not here to approve the request," Laykin added.

"No," Meaty guy spat.

"He's my old guard," I explained. "And when he abandoned the Cards, he stole my mother's ring. I want to know who he sold it to so I can get it back."

"You're that bitch who left, too, ain't ya?" Meaty guy spat.

"Nelson..." Mansfield muttered, but it was a weak protest.

Laykin, however, was not so calm. I put a hand on his wrist to keep him from throwing a punch.

"I was kidnapped," I said simply, knowing the narrative Gideon had spun. "And that traitor in there stole my ring."

"Wait till Gideon's back, then." Nelson shrugged.

"It could be sold by then!" I took a breath. "Look." I waited until he met my gaze with narrowed eyes. I let him see the silver raging in my pupils. "I can make a trade."

Keeping my smile tight, I saw the flicker of interest in the man's eyes as I produced the two small vials of silver Karadin had just given us from the clinic. She'd given me four in total, though I kept that to myself. I asked her to give me small amounts from vials she knew wouldn't be missed. Just enough to bargain.

"And this could only be the start of the deal." I made a point to gaze at his arm. "As a six, you must get, what? An eighth of a vial a week? If that? I'm Gideon's bitch, as you said. I have his ear. And I have silver. I could be a useful ally for you, Nelson."

Nelson chewed his lip with a dirty scowl, spittle flying from his mouth as he said, "No."

But Mansfield surprised me. "I'll take that trade."

"Boy," Nelson snapped, stringing out the word.

I smirked. Mansfield was more ambitious than I'd given him credit for, then.

Nelson eyed the silver again. Then looked at Mansfield. Then back at me.

"A vial like this every month," Nelson said. "For us both. And you talk to that sweet little Ace of yours while he's licking—"

"I wouldn't finish that sentence," I said.

He smartly shut his mouth.

"Good." I offered him the silver. "It's a deal."

"And only a minute," Nelson said, snatching the vial.

I gave the other to Mansfield. Hopefully they wouldn't get into too much trouble for this.

"Better drink up," I said, "I need to take the vials with me to ensure there isn't any evidence. Can't have word of silver distribution getting around the compound."

Both men uncapped the vials. Mansfield held his up to me in a silent cheers before tipping back the liquid. Nelson just tossed it back like a shot. Both made a face as if it didn't taste as bad as they'd expected. I'd never considered the taste, but well, it was blood.

Nelson handed me the vial and opened his arms, allowing me to pass.

And then his eyes rolled into the back of his head.

Laykin caught him by the shirt before he could tumble down the staircase, and Mansfield crumpled to the step as if he were a puppet whose strings were cut.

I knelt to rest his head gently against the wall as I said, "Well, Karadin wasn't joking about how quickly that would work. And from such a small vial, too?"

Obviously, the silver wasn't just for bargaining. She'd also added a sedative to the two I'd offered in trade.

"Remind me never to underestimate you again, Liss," Laykin said, stepping over Mansfield's limp body, giving him a small kick in the side as he did. It was a subtle enough gesture that it could have been an accident, but... well, he had called me a bitch. And Laykin *really* didn't like that word.

I reached into the men's pockets, searching for the key.

"A little help here, Layk?" I called.

He turned and looked at me blankly, then looked down at Nelson, who was already drooling. "I'm not touching that sniveling man," he said, wiping the chest of his shirt as if the mere thought of it was giving him wrinkles.

So I sighed and dug through Nelson's pockets too.

There was nothing but lint, a few stray coins, and a tin of tobacco.

"There isn't a key," I hissed.

"One of them has to have it," Laykin said.

I glared up at him, and then he did bend, running his hands over Mansfield's belt line.

I rechecked Nelson's pockets. And then even stuck my hand under his shirt to feel around his belt. His skin was sweaty and sticky, and it made me swallow a gag.

Nothing.

Laykin shook his head too.

"Fuck," I breathed.

Laykin scowled but didn't say anything. Apparently, that was an appropriate way to summarize the situation.

Silver sparked at my fingers. "Guess we're going with plan B then." I sighed, standing.

Once we reached the bottom of the stairs, the cells stretched out before us. Bars protruding from ceiling to floor made up small rooms that weren't even large enough to lie in unless the person was curled with their legs to their chest.

Kenji was pacing, his face and arms covered in barely healed scrapes and wounds. Phenola sat against the wall, her head tipped back. Felina, in the far cell, was throwing a rock against the wall and watching it bounce. The steady *click... click... click...* echoed around the room.

Kenji was the first to see us and froze.

As if sensing the shift in the air, Phenola cracked open an eye, and Felina turned.

I ran to the bars between Phenola and Kenji.

"Oh my god!" Phenola said, running to grab my hand through the small space that barely fit our wrists.

"Are you both okay?" I asked.

"We're alive," Phenola murmured, touching her belly gently.

"Queenie, you have no idea how happy I am to see your little button face," Kenji said, and I noted that one of his eyes was swollen shut.

"Lissa." Felina's voice was a soft shadow from the corner of the room. I knew she wouldn't beg me to let her out. She wasn't one to beg for anything, but her jaw was set as I glanced at her just long enough to glare.

I didn't acknowledge Felina. I was too angry to acknowledge her. Not yet.

"I brought you this," I said, taking out the third of the four small vials of silver I'd tucked into a separate pocket so I could distinguish between the drugged vials and the safe ones.

Kenji took the vial. "How did you—"

But I shook my head. "We'll have time to explain once we get you both out of here."

I made the "both" pointed.

"And you're in on this." Kenji's eyes tracked to Laykin.

Laykin deadpanned, "Please don't look so surprised, Kenji."

Kenji popped the lid off the vial, held up his hands to Laykin, and then downed the contents. The swelling on his face only took a few seconds to dissipate.

"Queenie, I have never been so grateful for your silver in my life." He sighed from the relief at his healing injuries.

"It's not mine." I shrugged. "Karadin gave it to me from her stores at the clinic. It's the best we could do."

"I'll take it. Thank you."

"Well..." I studied the bars. "Don't thank me just yet. Those Cards guarding you didn't have a key, so now it's up to my silver to break the locks on these doors."

I studied the lock for a while longer.

The doors were made of some sort of metal. Probably iron, I assumed, but I wasn't an expert at metals. They opened on a hinge, and the lock was made of three pieces: a latch that slid into a place behind another piece of metal soldered onto the cell. And a deadbolt-style lock secured the whole contraption into place. If I could break the lock, I could presumably slide the hinge out and open the door.

"Okay," I said more to myself than anyone else. "Okay."

"That doesn't sound particularly confident, Queenie," Kenji murmured.

"Kenji," Phenola snapped, "let the girl concentrate."

"No," I said, "I've got it. I got it. I've been training with Alaric. Maybe." I glanced up at both of them. "Maybe just take a few steps back."

"There aren't exactly a few to take in here, hun," Phenola said, but she backed against the wall.

"Right, okay." I studied the lock. It would require an intense jolt of silver directed at the exact right spot on the lock to melt it from the door. If I missed, it could hit the bars and zap this entire room.

I steadied my breathing as I spooled the silver into my fingers.

If I focused too heavily on getting this right, I knew I would lose my nerve. There was no turning back now.

So I shot my silver into the metal.

The piece of metal looped around the hinge melted away, and the lock fell to the ground with a thud.

"Ha!" I said, looking up in gleeful excitement at Phenola and Kenji. "It worked!"

But their expressions had gone pale and drawn.

Had I hurt someone?

A lump formed in my chest as I spun to Laykin.

He was alive and standing.

But Gideon and Dia stood next to him. Dia held a gun flush against the underside of his chin. Laykin's hands were raised in the air.

Gideon took a step toward me, clapping slowly.

Each hit of his hand together made me flinch.

"Bravo, little Queen," he said, looking up at me through hooded black eyes. His steps were lazy, and his smile was testing.

I took a step back.

"I wondered how far you'd take this game," Gideon said, his eyes blazing with his barely contained rage. His mouth was pressed into a thin line of disgust. "And you've come so far. It's been a pleasure watching you try so hard to run."

My back hit the bars as he struck, caging me in with his arms.

"But the game's over now. I've seen enough."

52

Lissa

Silver sparked at my fingers, but Gideon was faster. He must have amped himself up on it before coming to the cells. He stuck a needle into the side of my neck before I could even raise my hands. The silver that entered my veins burned.

I cried out, still trying to fight, but the silver sputtered at my fingertips. My arms were leaden at my sides.

Somewhere behind me, I thought I heard Kenji bellowing my name.

Gideon caught me by the shoulders, lowering me to the ground as he murmured in my ear, "Did you think I wouldn't know about you going behind my back, Lissa? I knew your lover would come for you. I knew that street rat would be back. The second I saw him touch you at the bonfire, I knew. And then I let you spin your little web, watching your lies and the traitors who helped you."

The bile rose in my throat, but I fought against the silver worming its way through my veins.

More Cards filed into the cells, their black outfits stark against the drab room. Two of them held Mansfield and Nelson, dragging them by the shoulders. They were awake now, blearing-eyed but panicking.

Mansfield was blubbering. "We didn't know! We didn't know!"

Nelson simply hung his head.

"Ace!" Mansfield pleaded, "We didn't know! We—"

Something splattered across my face, and I flinched only to see something growing on Mansfield's forehead.

Blood leaked from the center of his head. It didn't make any sense, but then Nelson slumped as well. Sticky dark liquid dripped from his hung head and onto the ground. It was red.

Red.

Looking back at Mansfield, I realized he'd been shot.

Shot. That was a bullet in his head.

Dia lowered the gun, unscrewing the silencer from the barrel and tucking it into his back pocket. He eyed the dead men with a disgusted curl of his lip.

Phenola screamed.

Kenji was yelling profanities.

I vomited onto the concrete.

"That will probably stain," Dia said, eyeing the blood.

More bile rose in my throat, and I spit it onto the concrete, fighting not to curl into the fetal position and let the darkness at the corner of my vision have me.

My hands shook violently, but I held myself up, fighting to stay conscious.

"Get them out of their cells and take them up to the lawn," Gideon said, grabbing my arms and looping a zip tie around my wrists, binding them tightly together. Then he hoisted me up smoothly into his arms.

The room spun, and there was a ringing in my ears. The foreign silver in my blood was traveling through my limbs, snuffing out the charge there like dousing a fire with water and leaving only a sodden mess of ashes in its wake.

The Cards left Nelson and Mansfield on the ground, blood pooling around their bodies. I thought of how the stains might haunt future prisoners held in those cells. I imagined them spending hours watching the dark spots, wondering if they would share the same fate. Just as I was sure the bullet holes in their heads would haunt me for as long as I had left in this miserable world.

I just hoped Gideon would kill me quickly.

"Now," Gideon said to me when we reached the lawn. "Where is your lover?" He didn't keep his voice quiet, just for me. Instead, he called it out, scanning the compound.

I shook my head, doing my best to press away from him, but he kept me tucked into his side.

There was a breeze today, and it kicked up around us, causing my hair to whip back from my face, and a chill washed over my exposed skin.

"Oh come on!" Gideon called as we walked nearer to the cliffs. The waves crashed below so fiercely that hints of spray peaked over the edge.

"Gideon—" I would beg. I would beg for the lives of my friends.

The Cards had Kenji, Phenola, Felina, and Laykin line up along the cliffs. Their hands were outstretched in front of them, bound like mine, their eyes straining with the same panic I felt.

Cards were coming out of the barracks, looking around in confusion at the commotion and then approaching to watch. Violence like this was common at the compound, and a lot of the men enjoyed the show.

Gideon set me down on the lawn but kept my weight supported with an arm around me.

"Come on, street rat!" he called. "It's done!"

Still, Tayna was nowhere, and I prayed that meant he'd already run. The best-case scenario was that he had taken off on his own when he'd seen Gideon was here.

Gideon pulled a gun from his back pocket and pointed it at Kenji's chest.

"I'll start shooting," he called.

A sizable crowd gathered around us now, but Gideon's eyes were still on the lawn beyond, in the space where someone could hide.

"He's gone," I rasped, shaking my head. "Please, Gideon. He's already gone!"

A commotion came from the mansion as two Cards dragged Enver from the thrown-open door. She was like a feral cat the way she was fighting them, screaming and slamming her elbow into them wherever she could get a hit in. Her chest heaved from her heavy breathing as she was hauled to the front of the watching onlookers but not dragged to the cliffs.

At the sight of Laykin, bound and standing near the cliffs, she froze.

Their eyes connected and held. Her silvery gaze turned watery, but she didn't speak.

"I'm here!" a voice called from behind the crowd.

A voice I knew.

It made my heart crack.

And the words, "No! Run!" broke from my lips before I had even thought them.

But he didn't run.

"I'm here," Tayna said again as he stepped from the crowd, hands raised. His eyes were so piercing as he looked at only me. "You don't need to hurt anyone."

Didn't he understand Gideon was going to kill us all? This was it. This was the end.

As if sensing my thoughts, he said, "I'll never leave you again, Liss. Even at the end." And I held those words between us, meant only for me.

Because this was the end.

Two Cards grabbed him, yanking him by his jacket collar toward us.

Tayna let them manhandle him as his sorry eyes stayed on me.

I imagined how pathetic I must look, hanging limply from

Gideon's arm, my hair flailing in the wind, blood smeared across my face, eyes hollow and bloodshot.

"Ah," Gideon said, "good. You're just in time for the show."

And then he jammed the gun into Kenji's stomach, firing as he pushed him backward until Kenji fell, toppling off the edge of the cliff.

53

Lissa

Maybe I blacked out for a moment.

Perhaps everything was happening too fast for my brain to catalog this reality.

Maybe this was my mind finally fracturing.

Because I saw Kenji fall.

And I knew he was dead.

I felt wild and out of control, struggling to get free of Gideon's grip, but his fingers only dug more deeply into my skin.

I needed to get to the cliffs. I needed to help him.

But my weak motions only served to fling my tears across my cheeks.

I couldn't breathe.

I couldn't make sense of this moment...

Kenji was my best friend, my guard, my protector. He couldn't be gone.

He couldn't be gone.

The waves crashed over the cliffs, the spray misting my face against the heat of the sun. Only waves. Not a hand, pulling itself up and back to safety. Not a yell or a cry for help. Just the ocean, crashing below, a stark reminder that the sea took no prisoners.

Gideon spoke again, but I couldn't hear him even though he held me up. My ears rang too loudly. My breaths were too hollow in my chest. My heart pounded too rapidly.

But then the ringing seemed to reach a crescendo, and everything from the moment came washing over me.

Phenola lay crumpled on the ground, her sobs wracking her body.

Felina screamed wildly, saying, "This wasn't a part of our deal! We had a fucking deal!"

Laykin's eyes seemed unfocused as he stood, straight-backed and staring blankly in front of him.

Tayna was raging. He'd already taken down one Card and was fighting the others who were struggling to keep a grip on his arms as they dragged him toward the cliffs.

And Gideon was grinning. As I looked at him, his face seemed to transform into a dark and twisted thing. His eyes gleamed like a cat's at night from the amount of silver he'd clearly taken. He was high from the rush of the kill.

And at that moment, I knew. I knew I would have to kill him if given the chance.

He'd let the monster out entirely, and the man I'd been so close to loving was no more.

More tears leaked from my eyes.

For him and for me and for the people we could have been if this had been a different life. Maybe if we didn't live in this city where silver meant power and gangs meant control, maybe then he and I would have built something together. Perhaps we would have made our own sort of empire where street rats had a way to become more than pawns in this world. It was a moment, a dream, when we would create opportunity instead of destruction.

But that dream between us was dead before it was ever even realized.

That was not the game we played.

The knowing certainty settled into a deep rage in my belly the second Gideon shot Kenji and pushed him from the cliffs.

Gideon seemed to see it as he looked at me, and he gave a small nod of his chin, the challenge and acceptance clear on his face.

"Now that you know I'm serious," Gideon said, his eyes leaving mine to travel around at the others. "Let's talk."

I didn't want to talk.

I wanted to burn.

But there wasn't any silver left in my veins. Gideon had stifled all of it with the foreign blood. It was a miracle I was still conscious.

"Where are the Whigs?" Gideon asked, looking at each of us in turn. "Who wants to talk to me?"

None of us answered. Laykin's eyes were on Enver, tears pooling down her face. Phenola continued to sob, her cries louder than the waves and the wind. Felina was quiet and swallowing back tears. Tayna's hard jaw was set.

I struggled not to lose the contents of my stomach again, choking on my gasping breaths. My throat burned, and my vision darkened. I had to stay conscious.

"Hmm," Gideon mused, looking at each of us in turn. "You're up, Layk," he said, taking a step toward him and dragging me by his side.

Gideon raised the gun. "Where are the Whigs?"

Laykin's eyes slowly turned to him. He was stoic as he shook his head, accepting his fate with as much dignity as he could. He didn't know where the farm was, but even if he did, I knew he wouldn't say.

"How about you, street rat?" Gideon turned the gun on Tayna then. "Where are your people?"

My breath hitched, and Gideon heard it.

"Oh, little Queen"—his attention turned to me—"don't be sad."

I struggled in his grip as he caressed my cheek with the barrel of the gun, smearing my tears.

"Shhhh." His breath skated over my skin, making me shiver. "You don't even know him."

Gideon tightened his grip on me as I tried harder to pull away.

"Please, Gideon." My voice shook, but I didn't care. "P-Please."

He wasn't done. "I know I'm a monster, but at least I've never lied to you. What does that make him?"

Gideon pointed the gun at Tayna again.

I couldn't speak through the terror in my chest that I was about to lose Tayna again, and it would again be entirely my fault.

But I also couldn't process the words he was saying.

What does that make him?

"You wanna tell her, street rat?" Gideon said it almost as if they shared an inside joke. "Or should I?"

"Lissa—" Tayna's voice was a low warning.

But the skin at the back of my neck prickled at Gideon's words.

"Okay"—Gideon chuckled—"I'll tell her. Your lover isn't a street rat at all, little Queen. He's been a prince all along. He's Olita's son. He grew up in a life of luxury. I mean, have you seen the Veiled's compound? If you think ours is nice, Olita is not messing around. Tayna had a house and servants and all the silver and possessions a boy could dream of having. It was his for the taking. And when he found you, he wasn't looking for a friend. He was looking for a silver—"

"Stop!" Tayna's voice was sharp, desperate.

Gideon's eyes narrowed at the interruption. He cocked the gun pointed at Tayna and continued, "He was looking for a silver who would grow to trust him so he could use them to avenge the death of his father and brother and start a war. With me. This is exactly what he's wanted this entire time—to create this divide between you and me, to start this fight."

I was shaking my head even though I knew deep down in my bones that the words were true. Silent tears fell from my face as I watched Tayna's expression and knew it was all true.

"I can explain—" Tayna said, his voice breaking.

"No need." Gideon cut him off. "But you can tell me the location of the Whigs so I can clean up the mess you've made of my city."

"I won't do that," Tayna said.

"Too bad." Gideon shrugged, then aimed the gun steadily at Tayna.

"Gideon, don't!" It was my voice. "Gideon, please!"

I took a breath. One breath.

I glanced behind me at Laykin and Phenola and Felina and Enver.

At the empty spot where Kenji stood only moments before.

When I brought my gaze back, it was to Gideon. And then to Tayna.

They had been telling me all along that I had to make a choice. I'd been on the board but never really playing the game. I'd only been a piece, a pawn for others to use and move and manipulate as they saw fit. I hadn't wanted to pick a side because picking a side meant hurting people. There was never a good choice.

But there was a good choice now.

The path in front of me had always been there. And I was ready to take it.

It was a desperate decision. Anything to distract Gideon long enough to keep him from hurting another one of my friends. From hurting Tayna, even as the truth of Gideon's words about Tayna's family settled deep in my bones.

"I'll take you!" I said. "I'll take you."

Gideon's eyes gleamed in his feral delight. "You know, little Queen, somehow I knew you would."

Madam Cartenoth's words came back to me as she pointed at my heart.

It's in here.

My brow furrowed at the words as if they were being whispered into my ear, her hand pressing into my chest.

It's in here.

I had the urge to scratch at my chest.

But no... no, my silver was gone. Gideon had taken it.

In most games, a Queen trumps an Ace.

It couldn't be...

"But I need you to remember, little Queen," Gideon said, drawing my attention back, "I keep my promises."

He fired the gun.

Tayna opened his mouth as if to speak as the bullet hit his stomach, blood spreading over his abdomen as he gasped, sinking to his knees.

And my silver erupted.

Not from my skin. Not from my veins. Not from my fingers.

From my heart.

Where it had always been waiting for me, buried so deeply within myself that I hadn't felt its presence until now.

And no Card could stop it. No copper could ground it. No silver could stifle it.

It was mine, *mine* to control.

And I was ready.

54

Lissa

Gideon was thrown, his body flying until he hit the edge of the cliff where he clawed his way in the dirt to avoid falling. The silver had burned his face and arms in patches that were healing as soon as he turned his dark gaze on mine, spittle flying from his mouth at his ragged breathing.

The zip ties melted from my wrists just as he launched himself at me, pinning me as we rolled in the dirt.

Chaos erupted around us.

Most of the Cards started running at the sight of my silver. A few stood to fight.

"Lissa!" Enver screamed somewhere over my shoulder as the dust flew around me, and Gideon rolled on top of me, pinning me to the earth.

I flung my hands up to hit him with my silver again, but he knocked them away. The silver in his blood protected him from the worst of the electricity at my fingertips.

"Enough, Lissa," he seethed down at me, his eyes dark and wild.

My every need screamed at me to get to Tayna. I wouldn't

abandon him again. Even after everything Gideon had just revealed, I wouldn't let Tayna die. This time, this time, I would give him the silver he needed. This time, I could save him.

But I couldn't see Tayna through the haze of people fighting and dust as I strained against Gideon's grasp.

"Let me go, Gideon! You have to let me go!"

He only held me tighter. His voice a dark shadow as he promised, "Never."

Clawing into the dirt, I grabbed a fistful of sand and threw it into Gideon's eyes.

He bellowed like a feral beast, but his hold loosened enough that I could scramble from his grip.

I saw Enver crouched in front of Phenola, working to free her from the zip ties around her wrists.

Laykin was fighting Dia. His eyes trained to the ground for just a moment before Dia whirled on him. The gun lay discarded on the ground near the edge of the cliff, only a few paces in front of where I crawled on my hands and knees in the dirt.

Scrambling to right myself, I ran for it.

Only for a body to collide with mine from behind. Gideon's hard chest pressed into me.

I pitched forward, barely catching myself. My cheek scraped across a rock in the sand, but the adrenaline kept me moving, kept me reaching, scrambling from his hold.

His hand wrapped around my arm, twisting it behind my back, and I turned, kicking out at him, landing a silver-fueled blow to the side of his shoulder that had him releasing me.

I made it a few more steps.

"Stop it, little Queen," Gideon said, his hand coming around my ankle in a viselike grip.

My fingers brushed the cool metal of the gun before I was roughly yanked back. I screamed, a battle cry as I unleashed the silver under my skin. Still he held me, crawling up my body until his hand was wrapped around my throat.

"You've exhausted yourself, Lissa," Gideon said, shaking his head as he loomed above me. "Your silver is getting weak. I can feel it."

His arms were burned, but the exposed muscle and ragged skin slowly knitted itself back together even as he held me down. He'd taken enough silver to withstand my burns.

"You are mine," Gideon said, pressing harder against my windpipe until I could barely suck in air.

My vision began to blur.

I fought him, my silver sputtering as I clawed at his arms, digging into the exposed flesh to make it hurt. My fingers came away slick with his blood, but still, he held.

"Enough, Lissa," he demanded. "Enough!"

My hands scrambled in the dirt, looking for a rock, anything I could use as a weapon.

The images in front of me swam, clouded with adrenaline and lack of oxygen.

He'd stolen my breath with his kisses so many times, and now he was stealing it one final time. Would Gideon kill me rather than let me go?

"Gideon—" His name was a wheeze.

My limbs grew heavy, and still, I struggled.

The flicker of light and dark passed as I blinked my eyes against the haze. Like the days spent between his office and his bedroom. Like the color of his eyes, ever-changing with his moods. Like the push and pull of our relationship, always a fight for us to find the light.

He was dark now.

So, so dark.

And he was going to drag me under with him.

And then I remembered the final vial of silver.

My fingers twisted into my pocket, searching... clawing. My nails brushed against the small container.

As the world darkened at the edges, I slipped it free and flicked the top open. A tear slipped from the corner of my eye, carving a path through the dirt and blood on my cheek.

"Lesson one, Gideon," I said, with the final wisps of air in my lungs. He had just enough sense that his eyes narrowed at my words. "I belong to myself."

And with all of the force I had left, I shoved the vial between his lips, clapping my hand over his mouth.

His head cocked in momentary confusion before his eyes went wide. He jerked back, his hold breaking from my neck as he spat the contents into the dirt.

But it didn't matter.

One small swallow of the foreign blood would be enough.

Spinning in the dirt, I crawled the last few feet to the gun, grabbed it, and turned it on him, both hands wrapped around the handle, my finger on the trigger.

I felt unsteady, my gaze hazy with tears and adrenaline, but Alaric had taught me to use one of these.

I cocked the pistol with shaking fingers, even as my gut twisted.

He was going to make me do this. He wasn't going to let me go. He would never let me go. This was my only way to truly escape him.

Gideon's gaze came back to me, and he slowly, cautiously raised his palms from the dirt into the air by his shoulders. I was shaking with my rage, shaking to breathe, shaking with the reality that I had a gun leveled at my lover's chest.

"Lissa—" he growled, his voice low.

"No." My voice resounded with a strength and certainty I did not feel. "No, Gideon. We're done." My words broke as I held in a sob. Dust clung to the tears on my face, but I didn't dare wipe them away.

I could see his jaw flexing as the silver began working its way into his veins. I knew from experience that it hurt like hell. His insides would feel like they were electrocuting him as the blood ran its course.

But he managed a weak smile, and my grip on the gun tightened. "You..." he breathed, strained and low. "Are still... everything."

We watched each other from where we both lay in the sand. There seemed to be puffs of it in the air as the fighting continued around us, but at that moment, it was just the two of us, accepting that everything had changed.

I had changed.

Or maybe it was simply that I had finally allowed myself to embrace what was always inside me. The silver crackled at my fingers as I held the gun, braced with both hands. My finger tightened on the trigger.

Gideon nodded, a small, resigned smile curving his full mouth. His eyes flashed blue for the briefest moment as he took me in.

And then, before I could track the movement, he stood, sprinting the few steps to the cliff, and flung himself, arms wide, over the edge.

I cried out, pitching forward as if I could reach him.

In that breath, the moment that passed as he opened his arms wide and accepted his fate below, I saw it.

I saw the future we could have had.

I saw a thriving city bathed in the afternoon glow of sunlight. I saw us walking through the streets hand in hand as his midnight-blue eyes smiled down at me. I saw children with full, chubby cheeks and women with book bags instead of high heels.

I saw him pulling me into his office after a long day of work, our sweat-slicked bodies aligning like a dance we'd both memorized. I saw him kissing my neck as I slid down his length, his body rising to embrace mine in a tight hold. I saw us laughing on his bed, sharing meals beneath the sheets.

Mine. That word from his lips echoed in my head.

It was hope and promise and safety.

It could have been.

Maybe, in another life, it could have been.

The waves crashed as I clawed my way forward, only to see the ocean's violent swells below. The waves were as midnight blue as his eyes had been in those final moments.

I choked as hot tears spilled down my cheeks.

"Gideon!" I screamed into the waves, my silver sparking as the sand and grief lodged in my throat.

My entire body ached.

I held my breath. Allowing a moment. A moment to see him rise from the waves.

The swell crashed, misting against my face as the sobs broke free from my chest. My silver sputtered at my fingers.

It felt like a dream.

All of it was a nightmare.

But I had to wake up. There wasn't time to process everything that had just happened. There wasn't time to process the fact that Gideon was gone. There wasn't time to allow the heartbreak to sink into the very depths of my bones.

Because then, maybe I would never move again.

And right now, I had to get to Tayna.

My chest cracked as I moved from the cliff, stumbling through the swirls of dust.

By the time I reached him, Phenola cradled his head in her lap, stroking his hair.

Laykin limped toward us, Enver supporting him under his arm.

Most of the Cards had scattered. The ones who had stayed, watching, seemed frozen in shock, unable to move within the chaos erupting around them.

I fell next to Tayna, my hands going to his ashen face.

Blood welled in a small pool within his stomach. It looked nearly black against the backdrop of the dust that swirled around us from the fighting.

"No, no, no." That word pounded through my head and was all that was coming from my lips.

Phenola was crying, rocking him. "They're gone," she said, shaking her head. "They're gone."

"No!" I said again, more forcefully this time. "Someone give me a knife!" I screamed.

No one moved.

"No," I said again, more firmly, searching for something to cut my skin. Desperate for the hint of silver I could offer Tayna.

But there was nothing but sand.

And so I did the only thing I could think to do: I bit the inside of my lip. Hard.

Adrenaline kept me from thinking about it too long. I simply reacted.

The blood welled, and I sealed my lips to Tayna's, kissing him. I kept our mouths pressed together, willing this to work.

This had to work.

His lips were still warm beneath mine, my breathing heavy, even as I kept our lips sealed.

When I pulled away, my dark silver blood coated his mouth.

"Come on," I breathed, my body shaking as the adrenaline subsided and reality settled in. "Come on, Tayna." My voice was a choking, cracking plea.

Phenola grabbed my hand, squeezing as I bent over Tayna's body, my forehead resting against his chest, and let my grief win.

I had failed him again.

I had failed them all. Kenji, Tayna, and, yes, even Gideon.

I had entered the game too late, and it cost me everything.

The sob that welled in my chest and spilled from my lips was devoid of any silver crackling at my fingertips. I was exhausted. The well within my veins had run dry. I had nothing left to give, no moves left on the board.

There was only utter and complete defeat.

And I surrendered to the pain as the magnitude of the death and the violence and the lies washed through me.

As my heart broke into a million pieces, I willed the pain to drag me under. It hurt too much. For a moment, I imagined following Gideon off the cliff. The rush of cool water would be a relief to my shattered soul. And I would do anything, anything to ease the agony consuming me alive.

But then Tayna's chest heaved as if a jolt of electric current had shot through his heart.

My head bounced on his chest as I gasped and pulled back.

It happened again.

And then he inhaled.

A large breath had me covering my mouth with both of my hands as my body jolted along with his in shock.

His eyes fluttered open, and he groaned.

"Tayna!" I threw myself on top of him, my relief stark and quick, sending icy adrenaline down my spine.

He grunted, but his hand reached up to brush through my hair.

He was grinning weakly as he murmured, "You kissed me."

But I froze in his arms.

The rush of whiplash emotions made my vision swim. My chest tightened. The relief had momentarily clouded the grief and the anger and the betrayal. But it was still there. And it was bubbling to the forefront now that he was alive.

He was alive.

But he had lied to me. About everything.

He was as much a player in this game as any of the Cards. He was Olita Ravidian's son, the only living heir to the Veiled empire. The only difference between him and Gideon was that Tayna had lied to me about who he was. At least Gideon had never pretended to be anything other than the Ace.

My nails dug into Tayna's shoulder as I pulled myself back from him stiffly, wiping at the blood on my lips. The grit of the dust was like sandpaper against my mouth.

"You lied to me." The words came on their own, my emotions as erratic as the silver sputtering at my fingers.

"Lissa—" His fingers brushed over mine, but I pulled back just as a jolt of silver had him wincing against the contact.

"You lied to me." This time, my words held more conviction.

My grief became the electric current that fueled the blood in my veins. The pain threatened to bow me over. Kenji and Gideon were dead.

And I'd saved Tayna.

This time, I'd saved him.

But he'd *lied* to me. My whole life up to this point had been filled with lies and betrayals. I'd thought Tayna was the one person I could trust. I thought he was the one person who truly saw me when everyone else only saw a Silver.

But that was a lie, too.

So I would trust myself.

I would find the truth about who I was. I would not accept this game of lies and secrets. I would find answers, and I would fight against anyone who tried to stop me.

I stood from the sand.

Tayna's eyes widened as he watched me rise, his head still resting in Phenola's lap. He tried to sit up but winced at his still healing stomach.

"Lissa—" My name was edged with panic as he tried to reach for me.

But I stood now, stepping back from the man who felt like a wolf in sheep's clothing.

"Lissa!" Tayna was more desperate this time. His voice turned raw with pain.

Enver and Laykin watched me silently from where they'd crouched next to Tayna. All of our faces were streaked with dirt and blood and tears.

My limbs ached, but I did not falter.

And as the dust settled around me on the cliffs, I turned and walked away.

END OF BOOK 1

ABOUT THE AUTHOR

Jess Stevens is a dark fantasy romance author living between Phoenix and Los Angeles.

Remnants is the first in a series of three and combines all of her favorite things: Women whose dreams shape the world. Men who would light the world on fire for said women. And fast-paced action that will keep you on your toes until the very end (toe-curling or otherwise).

When she's not writing, you can find Jess working in tech, getting out for a run, maybe crocheting a thing or two, and most definitely snuggling with her cocker spaniel pup.

For more, follow Jess on Tiktok or Instagram.

tiktok.com/@AuthorJessStevens

instagram.com/AuthorJessStevens

www.ingramcontent.com/pod-product-compliance
Lightning Source LLC
Chambersburg PA
CBHW020543120726
47903CB00001B/100